The
Light After
The Orange

Beverley J. Hall

The Light after the Orange

The Tundra Stone Series: Book 1

Beverley J. Hall

Leirsinn Publishing

First Published in 2022 by Leirsinn Publishing

Beverley J. Hall

483 Green Lanes, London, N13 4BS.

A CIP catalogue for this book is available from the British Library.

ISBN: 978-1-7396948-0-7

Cover Design © Angelee van Allman

For my mother, Elizabeth Haggerty,
for teaching me everything was possible.
It was.

***

For everybody that finds the beauty in an ugly world.

Prologue

Jennifer Somerville

"Do you still remember it?" asked the small voice, so full of wonder and curiosity, from such a wonderfully curious thing. A daughter. Something I had never wished for. Never dreamed of. Never dared imagine. My little princess.

"Remember what, sweetheart?" I said, pulling her closer. Her little fingers around my neck sent a warm wave of love through every fiber of my body, relaxing every muscle and creating a feeling of time standing still.

"Life before."

My heart ached. She was too small to remember life before but I did. "You mean before the day? Before the war?" As I ran my fingers through her wild red hair, tears welled up in my eyes. Not tears of sadness for what we had lost, rather for what we had gained. "Yes. I remember clearly."

"Was it wonderful back then? Danny says it was."

"Danny was a child. He saw it with a child's eyes." The words stuck in my throat. Was there anything better than a child's eyes? How wondrous the world seemed through them. Even now.

"I have a child's eyes. Is that bad?"

"Oh, no, sweetheart. That's not bad. It is beautiful. I wish I saw the world through your eyes. The world, the mortal world, was busy. There were so many people back then. So much of everything, except time."

"Did time change?" Her icy-blue eyes stared through me as though she was trying to see more than my shell. More than my body. How I wished I had seen the world as she did, before. I wished the world had been able to look at itself that way, before.

"No, the world did. Nobody ever had time. Until there was none." I knew she didn't understand what I meant. I hoped she would someday when I was a memory. "We were all so busy, we never saw each other. We never saw people the way you see people. We only saw bodies. Skin. Clothes. Age. Gender. Not like now."

"I'm glad I see more."

"Me too. Now, I need to sleep. I'm tired."

"Okay, Mom." The feel of her kiss on my cheek brought a happiness I never thought I'd feel. "Love you."

"And I love you. Every bit of you."

"I know. Pink."

How strange it seemed even now, to see love. Not in actions. In color. How much better the world would have been if we could have seen that before.

I wished I hadn't seen before. Sitting in the old chair, staring across what used to be a city, the springs poking through the patched-up fabric, I was too tired to care.

I wanted to explain to Alex, so innocent and unaware, what the world was before. How do you tell someone that your generation destroyed everything and left them nothing? Yet, her nothing was worth more than my everything. I rarely thought about the old world anymore. Did I still remember? Unfortunately.

I remember us laughing at the farce that was politics back then. He had been amusing at first. A man building a repertoire out of division and hatred. It had been funny until we realized he might do it! He might win!

As we watched the country rip itself apart, turning people against each other, we still believed it would sort itself. We let him do it. I let him do it. I watched as he started arguments and wars nobody could win. We watched. We moaned, but we watched. Until the Orange.

We watched as most of the world died. We were glad to be the five percent left alive. The human instinct to survive was never more amazing than when we had nothing left to lose, and we had nothing left to lose.

It had been a Monday. I remember being seated in a classroom with thirty children, sure we were about to die. We watched the news of the first blast of Orange (somewhere so far from us it wouldn't matter). Deep down, in the gnawing pit of our stomachs, we knew it would matter. I had seen this a million times before in the school playground. The I-can-hit-harder-than-you-can solution to every argument. This time, the playground was the world.

Of course, it had mattered. Most children had been collected by parents and family following the evacuation warnings. Most of them were never seen again, and I have lived my life fearing they never survived. I remained with those who were never collected, which probably proved my salvation.

By the end of that day, there was blackness. The Orange that had blasted around the world, as bomb after bomb exploded, disappeared. The Orange had left black. Ash, dust, and death. That video had been the last thing I saw before the blackness. No electricity. No telephones. No internet. No . . .

Yet, as we appeared from the black, we had something amazing. Something we didn't really appreciate at the time. A new start.

Strange—the way we all try, at some point in our lives, to figure out our purpose. I was a school teacher. Society never really perceived it as much of an aspiration. We didn't seek glory, or fame, or fortune, or even celebrity (all the things society held so highly, before). That's what I did before and that's what I did after. I found the children's strengths and helped them develop them.

I don't pretend to know why. I don't care why. Maybe it was because we stopped labeling and medicating the children. Maybe it was because we stopped trying to make them workers for tomorrow's society. I still don't know what tomorrow's society will be. What I do know is that, one by one, the children developed gifts. They saw the world differently. They felt the world. Perhaps we were already developing, before? Perhaps it was the Orange?

What they learned most of all was love. Hate died in the Orange. We had no room left for hate.

The small voice of my princess, Alex Chegasa, returned. "I've got you something, Mom . . . Mom . . . Is it beautiful where you are?"

PART ONE

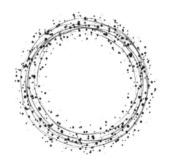

Surviving the Orange

ONE

ALEX

I stared at the dust covering my Converse sneakers, willing my feet to move. My eyes followed the shadows of the skeletal trees behind me. Their dead silhouettes, like fingers, pointed and directed me toward my past. My eyes rested on the debris filling the street, and I struggled to remember, even imagine, the houses, the homes, the families who lived here, before.

This was my world and my time, but the lone white house, hemmed in by what must once have been other homes, was a lie. With its paint peeling from the wooden boards, it stood as a memory of a world long gone. A time that was gone. A life that was gone. A life that was taken from me.

The silence filled me, allowed me freedom, but the house dragged me back to a time I didn't truly remember. How many of my earliest memories were real? Were they the result of stories told to me as a child?

Fear flooded through my veins, pulsing faster and faster, in time with my heart. Today I turned eighteen, I became an adult. I had been sure I would cross the road and step back in time, to my childhood.

I sighed, kicking the rubble and creating a dust storm. How should I spend my eighteenth birthday, if not remembering my mother? I reached to break off a blackened finger from a tree, and the pathetic click it made as I pulled it matched my mood. I held it tightly between my palms as it grew leaves and then small orange flowers.

A small smile curved my lips as I twisted my mass of orange curls and pushed the branch through them to hold them off my face. I picked up a ragged, clay-colored brick and threw it at the house. It bounced off, as I knew it would. The magic that protected it still stood guard. I knelt on the ground, stones poking through the holes in my jeans and scratching my legs, and drew in the dry mud covering the road. My fingers traced an M-O-M in the dirt, which the wind soon hid as it danced along the street.

Tomorrow.

Tomorrow, I would go in.

Tomorrow, I would forget I was all alone.

I stood, brushed hands over my clothes, and headed for home, knowing Danny and Calesta would be annoyed I'd sneaked out of the school, again. Faced with over an hour's walk back, I regretted my choice.

As I climbed over the debris and mud of what had once been streets, the sunlight fighting through the clouds tried to warm me. After the Orange, clouds of dust and darkness filled the sky for the winter that followed. The sun was making a comeback and those of us who survived were beginning to appear from our hidings.

The lines where roads would have been, now covered in debris and mud, were lined with the shadows of once-trees and barely-dressed homes. Gone were the roofs and windows, along with many walls, from when those that lived through the Orange found themselves perishing in the earthquakes and tsunamis that followed. The final roar of a devil.

After I crossed under the highway, I quickly turned up Nichols Street to use the once-trees as cover for my return. A house still standing and looking like a house peered out from between the trees. Houses in anything resembling one piece always attracted my attention. We went scavenging weekly, hunting for anything we might need, but today I looked for myself. I loved collecting the unclaimed memories of those long gone: photographs, jewelry, ornaments, clothes, relics of a life from when purpose could be beauty.

I clambered through an overgrown hedge, now brown and lifeless, its branches scratching at my skin and pulling me. I cursed as I scowled at the new holes in my woolen jumper, which would cause more moans when I got home. I ducked my head as I entered under the rotten wood of what must have been a front doorframe. Furniture scattered and piled in the hallway blocked my path. I stooped to squeeze through a small gap between two sofas, only just managing to pass through.

As I dragged myself out, I looked at the dirt now covering my clothes. I shrugged my shoulders, already imagining the faces of Danny and Calesta.

I had climbed out of the window as the sun reached the horizon, the glow illuminating the tops of the ruinous buildings and once-trees. They would have realized I was gone by breakfast, but I still harbored the hope they had left me to sleep late for my birthday.

I placed my feet on the stairs, holding my breath with each footstep as I waited for the crack of the rotten wood to give way. I reached the top and took long, deep breaths, one step closer to finding the trinkets I loved to collect. The floorboards of the landing creaked under my weight, but I carried on, staying close to the walls, curiosity driving me beyond the point of recklessness.

The first door I met was closed, sealed against the years that had ravaged the house. I pushed it open to reveal a small pink room, its curtains still pulled shut to hide the atrocities of the outside. I stared for a moment at the small bed with teddy bears and plush animals, knowing this belonged to a child, the bed made and pristine. Somebody made this bed, unaware nobody would sleep in it again. The toys sat waiting pointlessly for the child that never grew up.

I lifted a small grey bunny. Its floppy ears shed ashes and soot when I stroked it. Dust filled the air, creating a hazy halo around the toy. I was lucky to be eighteen. I had a bedroom like this once, in the white house I couldn't bring myself to enter. A bedroom I couldn't quite remember. I wondered if my mother placed a bunny like this on my bed, waiting for me. I closed the door gently before moving on to the next room.

The door lay ajar, allowing me to glimpse into somebody's past. I pushed the door and peered at the enormous bed, still made and covered in a dirty quilted bedspread. I walked in, suddenly aware of how scruffy I looked. I opened the wardrobe to stare at the rows of colorful garments and the countless boxes of shoes at the bottom. How different life must have been to need that many clothes.

I pulled them out and scattered them on the bed, hoping there would be something practical I could borrow. Not that I intended to return it but I rationalized it would be a birthday present to me. They were all too small. My frame was as tall as most men I had met, and the lady of the house had clearly been more feminine than me.

I moved to the opposite wall and opened the wardrobe doors, no longer faced with colors and femininity. I pulled out jeans and tried them on. Although perhaps a touch wide in the waist, their skinny fit allowed my hips to hold them up. I grabbed a t-shirt and sweatshirt, about to put them on when a noise stopped me. I squashed myself into the wardrobe. Closing the door, I listened for footsteps that never came.

The sound of my breathing filled the space as the air grew hotter. I edged the door open to look for any signs of life. The silence greeted me. I closed my eyes and breathed deeply in through my nose and out through my mouth. My heart rate calmed and I stretched out my aura to feel for life. I got no reply.

I squeezed out of the half-open door and rolled under the bed, still holding the stolen clothes. I crawled to the far side of the bed, sticking my head out when I heard the creak return. Again I reached out with my aura, probing for a response. It stopped as it bounced off another aura. An aura that didn't know it was an aura. Unguarded energy, full of happiness and kindness. I poked my head out farther to squint around the door when suddenly a wet, slobbering tongue washed my face.

I spluttered, rubbing my face with the t-shirt, looking at the owner of the aura and of the tongue. A large bundle of golden fur, remarkably clean and clearly well fed, looked back at me. Its dazzling blue eyes stared at me as it tilted its head, its pointed ears sticking up like antennae, waiting for me to speak.

Most dogs died during the Orange, or soon after. My mother had explained animals didn't understand that they couldn't drink the water and they slowly poisoned themselves. We had taken some in and tried to heal them, but none of them withstood the poisons of our bombs. I couldn't imagine how this dog survived, but her beautiful face caused me to squeal and roll around the floor, stroking and rubbing her fur.

I looked at her. Her eyes as blue as mine, as my mother's, stared back, and I knew she was a gift from beyond. My mother may be dead, but she wouldn't miss my eighteenth birthday. "You're called Jen now because my mother gave you to me."

I threw my ripped jumper on the floor, pulling on the borrowed clothes. All the while, she watched me, her eyes full of love. I placed my hand on her head to share my feeling of love, and she licked me.

"So, up for being my friend, Jen? Just a word of advice, though, people who I love tend to die. Just so you know." A dull ache squeezed at my heart as I spoke, knowing the truth of my words. Those of us who survived were lucky, but lucky meant lonely.

We exited the house and cut through the open land and once-trees, heading for North Street. Jen ran behind me, her tail wagging as we passed the remnants of the houses until we reached the Rocky Hill Conservation Area. I darted in among the once-trees and slowed down, hidden among their dark silhouettes.

Jen panted and I pulled my water bottle from my bag. I poured some into my palm and she lapped it up. I took a mouthful before pouring the rest into my cupped hand. She drank the water before licking me and barking her thank you. We walked through the trees toward the rear of the school. I looked at Jen and realized my plan to climb back in the window needed to change. I would have to walk through the doors.

I paused to look at the trees as I approached the school, noticing small green buds on them. Was the magic escaping from school, or was the world beginning to live again?

TWO

BILLEY

Loneliness ate me up from the inside, nibbling away at me and leaving an aching emptiness. I didn't know what I missed or who I missed but knew, deep in the part of my soul that holds my intuition, there was a person-size hole nobody could fix, except for the one.

The person we all hunt for but so rarely find.

The person we were made to fit with.

The one imperfect, perfect, mismatch our soul longs for.

The trees swayed in an elegant dance, keeping time with the breeze that, even on the calmest days, blew on top of the hill. I closed my eyes and lay back on the grass. The cold and damp of the earth chilled me.

My State-sponsored family had long since stopped worrying about where I was and if I would be alone. It was rare to meet anybody up here and it had unofficially become my place.

I hated living in the Rural but I loved this place. I found it soon after being placed here when I tried to run away. The trees called me, even now, when the strange and disjointed tune of the wind flitting through the branches sent the leaves bobbing frantically in the air. I imagined I could hear them.

Adults talked about me, not to me, and they rarely heard what I said. They discussed how my grief caused me to act out, how I needed to make friends, and how I would settle into school. I was one of the lucky ones, being schooled.

Nobody ever asked what I wanted.

I wanted to belong somewhere. To be a part of something. To feel like more than a weird burden.

The trees listened to me. They asked nothing of me and didn't care about my life, before. The death of my parents didn't matter to them, and they never demanded I behave, or be quiet, or tidy my room, or do my homework. They were content to share their time and space with me.

Out of the corner of my eye, a red streak attracted my attention and I leaned forward to see the source. A small man, no more than the height of a child, strode down the hill, oblivious to my presence. I peered through the long grass at the pointed red cap of the funny little man disappearing at the bottom.

So few people lived here, in this area of Bearaig. The cost of maintaining life so far from the capital of Nuadh Eidyn was too expensive unless there was a socially beneficial reason. I was here to be educated. My parental unit, Brigina and Gaevoin, were stationed here because they were the foremost botanists and were often credited with saving humanity after the environmental collapse. They denied this but I sensed there was some truth in it.

I couldn't stop staring at where the man and his red cap vanished. The sight of anybody wearing anything other than State Grey was almost unheard of. Red was a vulgar color, prevalent before the disaster. Now, equality was marked by uniform grey.

I jumped with a start when the man appeared from the long grass and glared at me for a few seconds, his stare piercing my soul as he penetrated beyond my eyes to something deeper. The evil painted in his old face, contorted with anger and hatred, was visible for the first time beneath his red cap.

Hidden behind the tree, my breathing dragged me into an unknown panic. I closed my eyes, his face etched into the darkness behind them.

When I opened my eyes and stared at the sky, the white clouds began to dissolve and hinted at the obscured blue. The sun battled through the cracks to create moments of light and shade, and my worries evaporated, soaked up by the trees. He was no longer visible. I shook my head and let out a small chuckle.

"You're losing it, Billey. Your imagination's getting the better of you." I wriggled to get comfortable and sat up, pulling my knees up to rest my head on them, and stretched my hands to untie my shoes. Dragging my heels along the grass, my shoes landed in a bundle on the ground. I wiggled the toes of my left foot in the damp grass and it tickled. I ran my hand down the cold wood of my right leg from the wood of my foot to the grass in one sweeping movement. Leaning back against the rough bark of the tree, I laced my fingers through the grass. The moisture clung to my skin and sent a chill through my hands. I dug my fingers deep into the soil.

I imagined roots spiraling away from my hands and feet, drawing deeper and deeper into the earth, growing closer to the core of the earth.

"Hello," I said, not expecting an answer but hoping the trees understood I was glad to see them again.

"Hello," came a small voice behind me and I turned to face it.

A beautiful young woman I guessed to be about the same age as myself stood leaning against a tree, her head tilted slightly. She scanned me from top to bottom with eyes that sparkled with a mischievous glint. I found a smile on my face.

"I'm Geilis," the beautiful young woman said, stepping forward and holding out a delicate hand.

I stared at her, a comfortable sense of recognition embracing me. "Sorry, do I know you?" I asked, reaching my hand out toward Geilis. "You look familiar and yet I don't remember you."

"I've seen you but I don't think we've met," she replied, taking my hand in hers. Her opalescent skin was so delicate I worried touching it might, somehow, damage it.

When I pulled my hand away, I took a step back and took a good look at Geilis. "It's nice to meet you. I'm Billey." My mouth, usually so articulate and full of opinions, froze, hunting for words. I stared at Geilis's long dark woven dress. Dresses and skirts, although regulation wear for breeders, were rarely worn, and something about the way it floated around her hips seemed so wasteful of fabric. Who would be allowed to be so extravagant with natural resources?

Without a word of explanation, Geilis sat cross-legged on the ground, tucking the billowing dress between her legs. Her eyes gazed up at mine as I sat to face her, mirroring her position. Geilis stared without making a sound, forcing me to fidget, the shape of the tree roots no longer fitting my body.

"How long have you lived in Bearaig?" I asked, my usually loud, brash voice sinking into silence. My eyes watched my index finger following the lines of my palm.

Geilis laughed a low, contented chuckle. "I was born here."

I wondered if I had ever felt the confidence and comfort of Geilis. The abandon and freedom of it tinged the edges of my discomfort. "I only arrived here a few harvests back. I was sent here to learn at the Institute. What's your assignment?" I asked, raising my eyes to look at Geilis, desperate to sound more like the girls who usually made fun of me. The girls who laughed at everything and always managed a smart reply to everything. For once in my life, I wished I could be like them, just once.

When I first arrived in the Rural four harvests ago, I had been unprepared for life outside of Nuadh Eidyn.

Since my parents died I'd been passed from home to home after the State took me into their care. I hated every family I had been housed with. I never quite fit in anywhere and gave up trying after a while.

My mass of curly hair and my funny accent all made me stand out. But, more than any of those, was the fact nobody knew where I came from. I didn't remember anything from before the accident that killed my parents. Everybody assumed the memories would return, but as time moved on and I still never regained any memories, everybody started to doubt me.

I saw the mistrust in their eyes when they looked at me, wondering what I was hiding.

I hadn't hidden anything. I never remembered anything. I wanted to belong, to be like everybody else.

With time, I stopped trying to blend in. I realized the futility of trying to belong. Every new home brought somewhere else to escape from. The ruinous ramshackle streets of Nuadh Eidyn provided many hiding places in the dark and deserted corners for somebody hoping to be invisible.

I hadn't been very good at being invisible.

By the time I was found, again, I had passed my thirteenth harvest, and this time I was sent to be assessed for use. It was decided I was to be sent to be a brain. My intellectual ability allowed me to avoid the breeding centers most of the other girls I saw went to, but it also saw me sent off to the Rural to be schooled.

When I arrived at my new home with Brigina and Gaevoin, a tiny part of my soul had sparked to life. I wanted to hate them but I couldn't. They may be part of the State but they seemed different.

They were different but then so was I.

The trees gathered around me, although I understood it was my imagination, and protected me from the breeze that grew and took on a new life. I rested against the rough bark of the largest tree, my rear now fitting into the roots that formed a seat in the ground. The tree, I almost believed, was shaped for me. Its branches wrapped around my tiny form as I snuggled among the roots. The wind grazed my cheek and I pulled my scarf around my face, desperate to stay here for every second possible.

The sound of the wind howling through the branches vibrated the leaves and created a voice I longed to understand. I closed my eyes, listening, imagining I could hear the voices of the trees. I felt my soul combine with the tree, and contentment that existed nowhere else in my life melted my anguish and pain.

My eyes shot open and I stared at where Geilis had been moments earlier.

Empty space filled my view.

I was, again, alone.

A hand stroked my head and I jumped with a start. My eyes darted around, taking in the empty scene. My hands fumbled on the ground, grasping for the books I had been reading, throwing them in my bag and tripping over the roots that, moments earlier, comforted and cradled me.

"My soul recognizes your soul," a voice said. Except the words weren't spoken. I heard them not with my ears but inside my head.

My leg ached with a burning I had never known by the time I caught sight of the dilapidated stone building of Brigina and Gaevoin's home, my home.

I threw my belongings over the wall that circled the house, or at one time had. Now it was a strange collection of stones piled on top of each other with a height that changed every meter or two and then vanished. I jumped the gate, unwilling to battle with the rusted relic today.

My breathing echoed in my ears, my heart threatened to pound through my rib cage, and my body screamed at the exertion. Landing in an unceremonious heap on the yellowed grass, I tried to calm my breathing and found a laugh filling me, starting from a place deep inside. I rolled over onto all fours, about to push myself up when Gaevoin appeared from around the corner of his workshop.

With no top on and a dirty old apron wrapped around his body to protect his regulation-grey trousers, his presence was so unlike anybody else

I knew. The State was clear on dress and presentation, but somehow Brigina and Gaevoin managed to get away with it.

"Hey Billey, what you doing down there and why are your books everywhere? Are you having a weird moment?" he said with a laugh, gesturing at the belongings I had thrown over the wall. He tilted his head, genuine concern sparking in his eyes. "Are you okay?" he asked, holding out his hand.

I placed my hand in his and he bent to grab my elbow with his other hand, pulling me to my feet in a swift movement. "Sorry. Yeah, just a weird moment, I guess." I forced a small smile in an effort to avoid telling anybody about the feeling of something or someone being with me at the trees. My head was swimming with insecurities about my mental state, and it was unwise to say it out loud, even to Brigina and Gaevoin.

"Ah well, the greatest minds among us are always a bit weird. Told you before, take it as a sign of greatness." He bent to pick up my books while I straightened myself. "You better hurry inside. Brigina has a guest she wants to introduce you to." His face took on a slight grimace, with the small creases around his eyes deepening to form cracks on his perfectly tanned face. He ran his fingers through his wild mass of long grey hair, twisting his fingers through it.

My shoulder sunk as I sighed. "They've sent another child for the Institute, haven't they?" My words merged with a sigh and formed a despondent answer to my own question.

He handed me the books and patted my shoulder. "Sorry, but it's only for a few days, supposedly. They say they don't want to interfere with our work but they can't find another home for him."

"Him? Oh, joy of joy. Just what I need." I took the books from him. Eyeing the top book, I said, "We were learning about you and Brigina today in botany."

He laughed. "And what nonsense were they telling you about us?" he asked, guiding me toward the house. His modesty prevented him from admitting what I already knew. After the environmental disaster that wiped out most of humanity and a huge chunk of life on Earth, they developed seeds and plants capable of self-fertilization and produced food for those still alive.

They probably saved those who had survived.

"Oh, you know. Just how the two of you helped save humanity from starvation." The way he would brush off the compliment, and the modesty of both Brigina and Gaevoin, were two of the reasons I had grown to love them despite my desire to hate them when the State housed me here. I also loved the fact they never considered me weird when my mind wandered in strange ways. They encouraged me to follow my brain's strange paths. They also taught me to avoid attracting attention from those who ruled Nuadh Caled.

"Nonsense, now let's get washed up before Brigina murders both of us for being late and dirty."

When we entered the kitchen, Brigina's soft, round face glowed in the way only she could. Even as a sullen teenager, when I first arrived so desperate to hate them both, Brigina's face always managed to make me feel like I was the best thing to happen, just by being there. Despite being so much shorter than Gaevoin, in fact than everybody, her massive presence filled the room in a way that made it impossible to ignore her.

Gaevoin walked to wrap his arms around her and a pang of something —longing, jealousy, or maybe teenage hormones—caught my breath. After all these years, they still looked at each other as though they were the most important thing in the world. In the years I had lived with them, I had come to realize they not only looked it, they felt it. It was inspirational and so in contrast to life for most people in our society.

They weren't hampered by being able to breed or not breed. Their use was academic and therefore the State ignored their nonconformity. I doubted I'd be so lucky.

The smell of food wafted toward me, tempting me from the bubbling pots on the old wood-burning stove, and reminded me how little I had eaten. I moved to wash my hands, knowing Brigina had been waiting for us. I was washing my hands when Brigina put her hand on my shoulder.

"Billey, this is Codrin. He'll be joining us for a few weeks while his familial unit is in the Capital."

I turned on my heels, taking in a deep breath as I prepared to be pleasant for Brigina and Gaevoin's sake. I took a quick inhale of breath when I saw Codrin. A small, skinny boy, barely old enough to study at the Institute, stood there. He stared at the floor. His gaze moved to the rip in my trousers, the wood of my leg showing through. He glanced up at me for no more than a second before his eyes returned to their downward glance. A momentary feeling of discomfort filled me.

I knew he was still staring at my leg. I couldn't see his eyes but I could feel them.

He nodded at me. "Hi," he said, ignoring my outstretched hand and heading to sit down at the table.

I glanced at Brigina and Gaevoin, confusion scrunching my face. Gaevoin placed his hand on my back, whispering in my ear, "I recall another young person that antisocial a few harvests ago."

I rolled my eyes. "Ha-ha," I muttered under my breath.

All memory of the hand that had touched me, or the voice that had spoken in my head, disappeared as I battled to make conversation with Codrin. Before long, I was drained from the energy wasted on the act of being sociable.

This was why I rarely bothered.

THREE

ALEX

Jen ran ahead as though she knew where we were headed. She stopped on the boundary between trees and the school that had been my home since the Orange. Her tail wagged, her head constantly turning to check I was still there, right behind her.

We were lucky to have this home. Before the Orange, my mother had been a teacher, and she explained the building had been protected by the same magic that had shielded the house I never entered. When the bombs landed, some of the children she taught were left in the school and, without parents, she became a surrogate parent to them. Her curriculum no longer one of academia, she set about teaching us all how to reach and use the magic that lay deep within the earth.

After she died and the children grew into adults, they moved on, searching for loved ones or a community to belong to.

Before long, only Danny, Calesta, and I remained. Although only ten years older than me, they had taken on the role of parents, teaching me the skills my mother had taught them and ensuring I knew how to use them to survive in our new world.

The modern glass and steel of the school's rear stood out, not only pristine and free from the damage inflicted on the rest of Danvers but also in contrast with the white-painted houses of the town. Now I needed to get to my room without being seen. Difficult to do on my own. Impossible with Jen.

I reached out to hold her and prevent any barking while I opened the door. "Not a sound now, okay?" I tickled the fur under her chin and she rubbed her head on my arm. "Seriously, I've only ever done this on my own. Having you has meant I've had to change my plans, so, a bit of respect, please." She licked my face and, for a moment, I convinced myself she nodded in agreement.

Holding my hand over the lock, I pushed my magic to open it. I inched it open, reaching my aura to sense Danny and Calesta. The empty harmony of my home was all that met me. I pulled off my shoes and padded toward my room, and Jen, following my cue, moved with stealthy steps, the marble-print flooring cushioning the sound of our feet. As we passed the central courtyard, now full of vegetables, fruit trees, and herbs, thanks to the magic of my mother, Jen wagged her tail. Her mouth opened, giving the appearance of a smile, and her tongue panted in time with her tail when her eyes fixed on the unique greenery.

I shook my head and whispered, "No, we need to get to my room without being seen. Shh!"

Her head lowered, her eyes registering she understood, and we climbed the stairs leading to my room. Reaching the top, we had turned toward my room when Danny's aura reached me. I sighed and looked at Jen. "We're busted." Her tail wagged, no idea what I said, happy to be the source of my attention.

I paused outside my room, probing to gauge Danny's emotions, immediately regretting it as he probed back. I hissed through my teeth and, with a deep breath, pulled my shoulders back and threw the door open. "Danny. How are you, and what are you doing in my room?"

He stared at me, his eyebrows creeping up his forehead. "Good morning to you as well. I came to say happy birthday, but you seemed to be missing . . . again."

"Yeah, I know. I got a birthday present from Mom. Look. Meet Jen," I said, stepping to the side as Jen ran in and jumped on Danny, licking him.

Danny's eyes dimmed as the argument in them escaped. "You know it isn't safe to go out alone. Not everybody out there is like us. Not everybody evolved the way we did." He perched himself on my bed and combed his hand through Jen's fur before his eyes glanced back at me. "So, did you go in?"

"You knew where I went?" I flung myself into the chair. Its springs poked in all the wrong directions. I pulled my knees under my chin, wrapped my arms around my legs, and sighed. "No . . . tomorrow."

He stood and placed his hand on my shoulder on his way to the doorway. "Calesta made breakfast and we've got you a present. When you're ready, maybe you could meet us in the cafeteria?" He turned to look at Jen. A small chuckle escaped his mouth and any chance he had of looking angry disappeared. "Don't be too long, we've already waited quite a while. I'll tell Calesta you were tired and slept in." He nodded at Jen. "And, you can explain that."

I pulled off my sweatshirt, throwing it on my bed before looking in the mirror. The dirt streaked my face and spoke of anything but a long peaceful sleep. I picked up a rag and soaked it in the bowl on top of the drawers to scrub away the telltale signs of my lie. My hair matted and twisted in all the wrong directions, and I sighed, looking at Jen. "You don't know how lucky you are to have fur. You should try having this," I said, pulling my fingers through my hair. "Never mind, c'mon, let's go and introduce you to Calesta. Best behavior, okay?"

Calesta's face smiled at me as I entered the cafeteria, her eyes moving past me to gape at Jen. "What is that?" Her mouth shrunk as it puckered. She glared at me. "Yours, I presume?"

I bent to stroke Jen and her tail wagged. I extended my aura, my being, toward her, sharing images of Calesta playing with her. She ran at Calesta, her tail and her tongue ready to play.

Calesta pretended to moan for two seconds before landing on the floor and rubbing Jen's stomach. Her eyes rose to look at me, a smile vanquishing the moan she was preparing for.

"You know dogs are a mistake. You can't leave them alone, but if you take them with you, they will give you away to attackers. Why would you want . . . this?" she said, turning back to Jen.

"Mom gave her to me for my birthday. Besides, If I can control a person's emotions, I think I can safely control a dog." I watched as sadness filled her eyes at the mention of my mother. She had been my mother, but she had also been a mother to countless others. "Anyway, happy birthday to me?"

"Sorry. Yeah. Happy birthday. That was a long sleep. Turning eighteen must be tiring work." She laughed, both of us knowing she knew better than to believe Danny's story. He had always been rubbish at shielding his emotions and thoughts. We could both read him too easily to fall for his lies. Calesta liked to allow him to believe she didn't read him, but we both knew.

I looked at the cake on the table.

Before the Orange, people made cakes with eggs, but I had never seen a hen outside of a book. Like most animals, they died from the poisoned aftereffects.

I understood how difficult it would have been to make (and how awful it would taste), and a warm glow burned my ribcage thinking of the effort they had gone to.

I sat on the black plastic chair, of which there were hundreds scattered around the building, a hangover from when it was a school. At least when I had been little, there had been lots of others, those whose parents never made it to collect them before the Orange happened. Now that most had moved on, the rows of tables and chairs accentuated how alone we were.

"Gosh, thank you. The best thing about birthdays is the cake. Thanks," I said, sticking my finger in and pulling a corner off.

Danny stared at Calesta, bouncing on the balls of his feet. She nodded, and he pulled a box from behind a column, one of many in the large, open void of the cafeteria. "We got you a present. We got them a few months ago but kept them for today. I can't believe we found them. Almost a miracle." He held the box in front of me. "Happy birthday, Alex."

I opened the lid, hoping to shield my emotions from them, not wanting to upset them if I seemed disappointed by it. It would matter to them and they had been so good to me. I peered inside and a lump caught my throat. A brand-new pair of Converse sneakers, identical to mine, only without the holes. I looked up at their faces, expectant and proud. "Wow, how did you . . ."

Danny spoke, bursting to explain how lucky they had been to find them. "We were scavenging out toward Marblehead. Pure fluke. We were looking for wood and fuel and they were just there, hanging on a tree. Never figured why you like them—a solid, hard-working boot would make so much more sense—but we knew you'd love them."

A tear rolled down my cheek and I didn't bother to wipe it. "I'm absolutely thrilled. They're . . . they're . . ." I jumped from my seat and hugged them both. I held them, resting my head on their shoulders to hide my face. We enjoyed the moment and I shared my joy with them. We could have stood there forever, but Jen barked and broke the silent harmony binding us.

We reminisced about my mother and the lessons she had taught, the people she had saved, and the fantastic stories she would tell. As a child, I cuddled up with her around a fire while she told me tales of other worlds she had seen, where she had visited with my father. After she had died, I clung to the dream of these worlds, basking in the possibility of the universe. I even clung to the idea my father would magically appear and sweep me away from this poisoned planet until I was old enough to take the stories for what they were—fantasy.

FOUR

ALEX

The barking and panting of Jen dragged me from my slumber as my muscles fought, but lost, to the noise of a desperate dog. The sun cut through the makeshift curtains, landing on the furry face licking my toes.

I stretched my hand from under the sheets to stroke her, making the catastrophic mistake of letting her know I was awake, and she abandoned my toes to sit staring at me. There could be no peace now. Throwing back the sheets, the chill of the morning jarred me, sending me scurrying for my jumper. Having wrapped my sheets around me and secured in place by the jumper stretching and struggling to contain the wad of fabric, I slipped my feet in my new shoes and headed downstairs toward the courtyard garden.

The door was barely open when Jen pushed past me to pee on the plants. I looked around to see if Calesta or Danny were in sight, shrinking at the moan I would get on Jen's behalf if they saw her. After holding my breath for several seconds, waiting for one or both of them to appear, I reasoned I was safe and picked a handful of raspberries.

I sat on the ground to watch Jen, but the cold biting through my sheets forced me to stand. She sniffed at everything and I wondered if her interest was the sight of living plants. I didn't remember the courtyard before it was a garden. One of my mother's first aims had been to contain enough magic in this area to allow plants to grow. She told stories of a garden my father had on a hidden-floor roof, self-sustaining through magic, and she set about making our food source healthy.

We scavenged for years and had all varieties of tinned food, more than enough for years, given there were only three of us now. However, our ability to grow fresh fruit and vegetables was, according to everything I'd been told, unique, and having seen the death painted in every landscape I had witnessed, I was inclined to imagine it was true.

I longed to see the world beyond my life, to meet other people. The cloaking spells on the school, although not making us invisible, managed to cause people to ignore us. We were unnoticed. On the rare occasion people passed—and it was rare—I found frustration building inside me. Why would we keep this to ourselves?

The teenagers I grew up with were all too much older than me. As the only child, I often lived a lonely life, especially after my mother died, but when I wasn't being taught the magic my mother had encouraged in the other students, I had relished my solitude in the library. It had been my window into a world I was too young to remember, a world I could only find in books.

My mind was wrapped in a blanket of cold and memories when I noticed Jen scratching at the tree that stood in the middle of the garden. My legs forgot their half-awake state and sprinted.

I yelled, "No," at Jen, her face gazing at me with her ears back as her sad face searched for what had caused my anxiety. I stroked her fur, lowering myself to look in her face. "That's my mom's tree, you can't touch that, please. There's a good dog."

My heart pounded as I watched the confusion in her eyes. One of my mother's many stories had been about something she called rejoining, where a body was buried with a tree to allow a person's consciousness to continue to exist as it became one with the universal connection. I might not believe it but accepting the lie made reality easier.

I always doubted the concept of continuing to exist after death. Though, I accepted the connection. I could feel it. It was the source of our magic.

I wrapped my arms around Jen's neck, rubbing my cheek in her fur, and she licked my ear. I extended my energy to encompass her, sharing my emotions, trying to make her understand the importance of the tree to me and the garden.

With the cold cutting through to my bones, I stood. "Come on, Jen, let's go. I need to put some clothes on."

Washed and dressed in several layers, I wandered along the empty corridors, passing the many deserted rooms. Jen ran back and forth, turning to keep an eye on me with every few bounds. Bounce, wag, bounce, wag, turn. The sound of her panting echoed in the desolate space, adding to the sense of isolation. Ghosts of the past filled the gaps, and I imagined the teenagers who once lived here. A gnawing ache attacked my chest, the barren hole that should be filled by family and friends. Were any young people left?

I walked into the cafeteria, still haunted by the images of other teenagers. I headed for the kitchen, and Jen's tail wagged so fast I feared it might fall off. Her intuition told her we were about to eat. Food, her basic primal need. I sifted through the tins lining the shelves, wondering what she would like. Dog food had never been a priority in our scavenging. I stood with a tinned ham in one hand and a bland tinned stew in the other. I looked at her face and decided to go with both.

Watching her devour the food off the plastic tray I had filled with the grey stodge declaring itself as a stew, I examined her. Her fur was healthy and clean, nothing about her looking starved or desperate. How had she survived? How had her parents survived in the aftermath of the Orange?

Grabbing a tin of fruit and a fork, I headed back into the cafeteria. Today was a scavenging day. Not that we had any particular shortage, but there was never any harm in looking. Besides, it was a good excuse to get out. My first outing with Jen, and I knew Danny and Calesta would disapprove despite the fact we rarely saw another soul.

Those who occasionally returned to the school told of people who had headed north to Canada, others told of communities that had flocked to islands like Martha's Vineyard or Nantucket. I hung on their every word as they spun tales of communities and groups of survivors, and the thought of going to find the others had been a constant one somewhere deep in my brain, but I lacked the motivation to move. The subconscious hope my father would come for me had wasted so many years.

Jen's ears went back and she dashed to the doors, a low groan emanating from her belly. I walked to pat her. "It's only Danny and Calesta. We're going out." The groan continued and I followed her gaze to see Danny and Calesta with two visitors: a tall, muscular, dark-skinned man and a thin, blonde woman. Their faces took me back to a time of childhood before I understood the depth of my sadness and existence. I didn't know their names but their faces teased a familiar longing for the teenagers they had once been.

"Oh wow, look at you. All grown up. I'd recognize that hair anywhere," the man said. His dark brown eyes, like deep chasms full of peace, pulled me in. His aura, a beautiful violet field of serenity, complimented his rich bronzed skin.

I stared, so unaccustomed to company, unable to combine the words swimming in my head. I fiddled with my curls, staring at Danny, my eyebrows creasing into a question. His mouth creased up at the corners. "You remember Roberto and Abi? They were your mother's students."

I leaned my head to the side as I shrugged my shoulders, Jen mimicking the tilt of my head. "Sorry. Honestly, not really. It's nice to meet you though."

"Why would you?" said Abi, placing her skinny arm around my shoulder. "It's great to see you, though. You look a lot like your mother, and, if Danny and Calesta are to be believed, you have a lot of her magic."

I bent to stroke Jen, dislodging the boney hand from my shoulder. "Thank you. Although, I'm fairly sure my looks are from my dad. My mother did, however, give me the hair, which I am eternally grateful for. As for the magic, well, none of us knows where that came from, and I'm fairly sure Danny and Calesta probably exaggerated."

I sighed inside. I enjoyed the rare moments of company yet struggled to be friendly. We sat in the comfortable chairs next to the wall of windows. Jen laid her head on my feet while Danny disappeared, returning soon after with a tray of water cups and a water bowl for Jen. He smiled at me and I smiled back, a corner of my heart soaring at the gesture that nobody else registered when he placed the water bowl on the floor.

They shared their stories about their travels. They had traveled to New York, hoping there would be a lot more survivors, but if there had been any, they had long since left. They found a group of survivors living on Long Island. Most of the houses and buildings had disappeared after the Orange, but a wave of refugees found each other and set about building a site. They had tried growing crops, which failed in the poisoned earth. They had survived for years scavenging, but when it became harder, the group started to disintegrate.

They had heard rumors of a community called Jericho in the rural landscape of Beverly. I stared at Danny and Calesta, both refusing to look back at me. I knew what they were thinking, and anger burned in my stomach, flaming a rage inside me. Could there be a community only a few miles away while we had hidden here in Danvers? Of course, they would insist we needed to stay clear. I didn't understand the people out there, and they wouldn't have our magic. Yet, how could we know? If we had found the connection after the Orange, wouldn't others?

I gazed out the windows, watching the plants dance in the breeze, calling on me to join them. Jen, sensing my thoughts, raised her head to stare outside. After a minute, I lost their conversation, now centering around scavenging and today's excursion, and I walked out to the gardens with Jen at my heels, without saying anything.

The wind flitted around me, and watching Jen bound through the greenery, my mind filled with questions and ideas. Jen's oblivion to the trials and challenges of our society began to infect me, and I found myself returning to my mundane existence. I was eighteen and many of the others who had lived here had left by my age, but my connection to my mother tied me.

When she died, I had hidden in a bubble of childish whim, waiting for my father to sweep in and rescue me. He never came and I outgrew my childish belief in my mother's fanciful stories. Now listening to the gentle patter of Jen's paws through the garden, accompanied by the whisper of the wind, my mind freed itself of the past. My future could not be tied solely to the past. The past made me, the future was whatever I made it. No more living in stories. Real life called me.

FIVE

BILLEY

My dreams had been fretful, and by the time I awoke to Brigina's yelling from downstairs, my head pounded to the beat of a dream that faded, leaving only pain in its place.

Thrashing around in the mess of sheets my overactive mind created, I came dangerously close to falling out of bed. Eventually managing to free my limbs, I placed my foot on the cold stone floor, winced, and pulled it up under my chin. Brigina's increasingly voluminous yells forced me to let out a frustrated moan that seemed to vibrate through my fingers as I ran them through my hair.

"I'm coming," I called, knowing nobody would hear me from downstairs. Only the sounds of me treading the creaky floorboards would stop Brigina's onslaught.

So, having splashed the cold water on my face in a hit-or-miss manner, I sat to pull on my regulation-grey trousers and top. As my hand ran down my wooden leg, my fingers hesitated, following the fluid lines of the carvings. I had been wearing it when I was found, and it brought me a sense of calm and peace.

Somewhere, at some point in my life, somebody loved me enough to create it for me. The part of me that hoped to remember that person grew smaller with every passing harvest. It was enough to know somebody had loved me, for now. I also loved the idea that a part of me was a part of a tree.

I ran down the stairs, jumping the last two and landing in a hopping movement, before grabbing a square bun filled with something yellow from a plate Brigina held out.

"Thanks," I called as I ran past her. "Sorry, can't stop. I'm going to be late."

Codrin stood shivering, staring at the horizon, and I wondered how long he'd been there waiting for the horse cart to collect him.

He glanced up, I thought. It was difficult to see his eyes through the mop of red curly hair. The small nod of his head as he registered me was, I decided, the most I was going to get, and I stood next to him. I pulled my scarf around me, trying to keep out the damp chill blowing across the land from Bearaig. The winds blew in from the sea and scattered its salty breath across the already dying corner of Nuadh Caled.

"My soul recognizes your soul," said the voice floating on the wind.

I turned to face Codrin. "What did you say?" My face grew dark, and although he barely lifted his eyes to look at me, he shuffled back a step.

"What? I didn't say anything." His words were muffled by the collar of his coat.

I rounded on him to stand in front of him. Glaring down, I could feel panic boiling in my chest. "Who else is here to speak? Eh?"

He looked up, staring into my face for the first time since we had met. "Everybody told me you were weird. They weren't wrong. You're hearing things, get out of my face."

He moved a few paces farther along the worn path, distancing himself from me. I was about to pursue him when I spotted the horses rumbling across the horizon. I crossed my arms across my body, pulling my coat tighter and cursing myself for sleeping in late this morning.

This was why I preferred to walk the forty minutes to the Institute.

I sat alone at the back of the cart, my legs dangling off the end. I watched the landscape disappear behind us, shrinking until it became unidentifiable. I knew how that felt. Shrinking.

An awkward presence crept up my spine, sending warning sparks flying. The voices I couldn't quite hear belonging to the other youngsters, including Codrin, shot invisible arrows at my back. The venom and hatred of their glances and whispers created a toxic veil threatening to suffocate me. I was grateful for the regular bumps that threatened to dislodge me from the cart. The focus of staying seated and inside worked to help me ignore the many insults I had heard a hundred times before.

Weird.

Ugly.

Boy or girl?

Her hair!

Too small.

Too skinny.

And on and on.

When the clattering of the wheels changed to a steady whir, I breathed a sigh. Turning my head, I stared over the heads of the others, who all looked away when I had turned to the sight of the monstrosity of a grey box that was the Institute of Learning. The hope for our future lay within these crumbling, decrepit walls. The greatest minds in Nuadh Caled were brought together here to find answers to the problems our forefathers created by their greed.

Leig an Seòrsa Buaidh (Let the Kind Prevail), the Institute's motto, carved into a marble slab set into the steps, caused me to let out a small 'hmmphhh' and contort my lips. The ironic pain of it.

When the cart came to a halt, while some of the others jumped over the side, I lowered my foot, stretching out for the ground. My toes touched concrete as my other leg, loosened by the bumps along the way, landed with a solid, resounding thump.

My heart, filled with lead, unable to resist gravity, pounded its dull, aching thud inside. My eyes refused to move from the sight of the leg.

I sensed the presence of others gathering and staring, a prickling sensation slithering up my back. The quiet sounds of them sucked the air from around me. With my hand balancing me, I bent to pick up the leg. My fingers shook as I grabbed for it. The outer, hard shell I wore like armor most days melted, revealing the little girl who didn't know who she was all those years ago. The pain of the years of bullying created a swell in my guts, and I fisted my hands to hold back the tears. Each breath I sucked through my nose fought to pull the tears away from my eyes and hide them from sight.

They failed and a single watery sign of my anguish slid down my cheek.

The voices of those I tried to ignore now filled my head.

"Freak."

"What the . . ."

"Seriously did you see that?"

A hand touched mine and I looked up to see the face of Codrin. His eyes, dark and heavy, held a pity I had no interest in seeing. A pain took hold of my throat as I acknowledged the disintegrating wall holding back my sadness. The tears blurred my view when they came and I wiped them with the back of my hand. "Thank you," I whispered as Codrin placed his hand under my arm, helping me up.

The leg had brought me joy hours earlier, imagining the love it took to carve, but now hurt my sweating hand as I sought to grasp it.

"Do you need a hand inside?" Codrin asked, his hand still supporting my elbow.

I hopped to the steps, deliberately sitting on the carved motto. "No, I got it," I said, pulling open the side seam using concealed fastenings Brigina had sewn in for me. I secured my leg, and Codrin sat in silence, watching me.

A comforting blanket of stillness wrapped me. The wind, the air itself, hushed, and those who watched me minutes earlier now disappeared into the building to head for their learning rooms.

I let out a sigh as I pushed myself up from the cold stone. "I guess we better get inside," I said. "Thank you. I know it isn't easy. You know, to put yourself in their line of vision. Thanks, though."

In the learning lecture, my brain battled to focus. A small part of me, the same part that causes goosebumps and chills, could not escape the recognition of so many eyes on me. The whispers bristled around the periphery of the lecture room as I listened to the dull, droning tones of Mr Robertson. He spoke with the conviction of a man who knew what he had to say and it was something you needed to pay attention to. He knew atmospheric science was a compulsory subject to all those in the room. He didn't need to make it interesting. They had to listen.

By the time the lecture ended, everybody, including me, who usually enjoyed science, found themselves one thought away from sleep. Stepping out of my seat, I picked up my bag and threw it over my shoulder, then I climbed the shallow steps leading to the exit.

What happened next took on the unreal feel of a moment slowed down and yet offered no chance to pause or think.

A student I had never spoken with but recognized pushed past me and knocked me off balance. The girl turned and, with a laugh creasing and contorting her perfectly symmetrical face, glared at me and said, "Careful, we don't want you losing your footing. Sorry, foot."

"What? Are you serious?" My voice poured from my mouth but I lost all power of thought. Like fire spewing from a dragon, my emotions formed a roar of anger.

When Miss Symmetrical turned and faced me, her eyes emotionless and her arms hanging limply at her sides, she picked at invisible fluff on her sleeve. Her absolute indifference broke something inside me, and I lashed out, wrapping my fingers in the perfect blonde hair and pulling it down until her perfect face met the floor.

Hands appeared from everywhere, dragging me back to my seat as Miss Symmetrical screamed. The slow burn of satisfaction filled me, creating warmth inside me, but brought with it numbing guilt. I knew I should feel guilty but it became about more than today. My hatred grew, and my anger for years of isolation and ridicule formed a heavy, nauseating lump in my stomach. It manifested into a rumbling bomb ticking and threatening to explode.

A scream filled my head. A sound alien to me, yet with a familiar knowledge to it. An angry melody that defied rhythm and reason, evidence of hatred and evil beyond anything I believed I knew.

My consciousness focused on the screaming, desperate to recall how I knew the sound. Why was it familiar and why was it in my head when it wasn't my scream?

Fear overtook me.

Out of the corner of my eye, a red flash I couldn't catch sight of drew my attention.

Beaten by the emotions ravaging my soul, my head fell into my hands and tears ran down my cheeks. "Please make it stop," my voice mumbled, barely audible.

I battled to stifle the sounds of the sobbing but knew it was pointless and gave in, drained of any resistance.

I lay on the bed only just large enough to fit even my tiny frame and pulled the soft white blanket over my head. I forced my eyes shut, trying to block out the sound of Brigina and Gaevoin downstairs.

Their voices drifted up the stairs and a blanket didn't stop them.

The house was a rare thing, a stone house predating the collapse. The solid structure afforded them a massive amount of space compared to the State Units most people lived in. It also meant they had a remarkable degree of privacy.

Their home unit was visible evidence of the importance of Brigina and Gaevoin to the State. Surrounding the house were swathes of land the Social Farming Committee would have loved to use. Instead, Brigina and Gaevoin carried on their work in isolation. A privilege rarely afforded anybody. It allowed them to grow their crops and re-create or engineer many extinct or previously imagined plants.

I knew they must have used their position to influence the Head of the Institute. Despite the solid-concrete walls that soundproofed the Institute since before the environment had collapsed, I heard Brigina and Gaevoin talking with the Head of the Institute. I couldn't identify what they were saying, but the emotion and volume said enough, and remorse stabbed at my chest. I had been so determined to hate them when I arrived, and yet they had persevered, convinced I was worth it. They were the only people in my life, or that I remembered, who had been there for me.

They weren't the type of parental figures to play games. So, when they said they would discuss it with me later after they calmed down, I knew better than to push them. The door handle clicked and I held my breath, a churning sensation in my stomach I didn't care to name. Anger? Frustration? Disappointment? Failure?

Gaevoin's face peered around the door. No sign of anger or annoyance was visible, but then, I couldn't remember ever seeing him annoyed. He pushed the door open to reveal Brigina and, wrapping his arm around her shoulder, pulled her into the room. Brigina smiled at me but it barely made it to her eyes. Her face creased in all the right places but carried a different emotion. Her smile lied.

I stood up from the bed but my feet refused to move toward them. My eyes stared at my feet, and my tongue pushed against the roof of my mouth, desperately hunting for the words.

"I'm sorry," I mumbled, my voice barely sufficient to carry across the room and certainly not indicative of the effort of speaking. "I am."

Brigina and Gaevoin both moved to stand on either side. They sandwiched me in a hug, a show of emotion that would usually make me uncomfortable.

"We love you. You know that, right?" Gaevoin said.

They had never said the words and I had never imagined hearing them. Suddenly, the years vanished and I felt every atom of me becoming the child with no memory whom nobody wanted.

His hand squeezed my shoulder, pulling me closer, and tears again flowed down my cheeks. This time I did not attempt to identify the emotions racking my body. Love, sorrow, confusion. It didn't matter. I knew the truth of the words. They mattered. I raised my eyes to meet Brigina's, scared to see the truth in hers.

Brigina moved closer, laying her hand over my heart. "You were the thing we never realized we wanted, but when we got you, we knew we needed you." She looked at the bed, indicating her need for them to sit.

I lowered myself until the bed made the familiar creaking sound, my eyes glancing from Brigina to Gaevoin. "Okay, how bad is it?" I asked.

Brigina spoke first, seating herself next to me. "Gaevoin has agreed to do some lecturing at the Institute, which will get us past this time. But, the girl's parents are insisting the incident is reported to Central. We'll do everything to make this go away, but . . ."—she glanced up at Gaevoin—"we can't make any promises."

"I know I was wrong but that girl just pushed me. They are so horrid. It doesn't seem right."

Gaevoin sat on the floor in front of me. "There's no point worrying about it. I think the fact your intelligence score is off the wall will work in your favor." He placed his hand on my knee. "Trust us. I know it's hard, but please."

I nodded, scared to speak. I hugged them both and closed the door behind them before daring to breathe.

I stared out of my bedroom window, not registering the view. The hours dragged and my brain flickered, desperate to spark and be used.

As I stood there, zoning out, the voice that had called me spoke up as though answering my loneliness.

"My soul recognizes your soul."

This time, rather than worrying about the irrationality of the voice, I replied. Unsure how one should reply to a voice in your head, I closed my eyes, calmed my breathing, and focused my attention on the voice. 'Thank you, for recognizing me. Can you help me recognize you?' I thought, hoping that was enough.

Laughter filled the room, the carefree laughter of one who knows when all is right with the world. A laugh I recognized but couldn't quite place.

I lay on the bed, allowing the laughter to swim around me. I relaxed, deciding that if I was losing my mind, at least I could enjoy myself. The laughter was joined by the sound of trees dancing in the wind. Seconds later, in my mind, I saw my trees, the small circle that called to me from on top of the hill.

My eyes flew open, and, for the first time in a long time, I knew I was not losing my mind. A part of me, long forgotten and buried, recognized the call of the trees.

I had always recognized it.

Six

BILLEY

My heart pounded against my ribcage. The pace with which I found myself moving created an agonizing pain in my chest. I assumed it was my speed, although as my stomach lurched and fluttered, the confusion of emotions brewing inside me flitted between speeding me up and slowing me down. The closer I came to my trees, the more fear wrapped me, trying to bind my legs and prevent me from discovering whatever it was, or whoever it was, I needed to remember.

The trees, their branches waving and beckoning me in the dying light, soothed my soul. My anchor over the past years, they were the place I knew I was my true self. This time, apprehension sent small surges chasing through my limbs. Their energy forced its way out through my fingers and toes. The voice, now quietened, still loomed in my thoughts.

Taking the last few steps through the overgrown grass covering the slope, my pace slowed. My feet struggled against gravity. My breathing echoed in my head and the hairs on my arms bristled as I stood in the center of the trees I had sought refuge in many times before.

The wind, which restricted itself to the treetops, whipped the leaves in a manic, swaying motion that made them feel closer, more claustrophobic.

"My soul recognizes your soul" came the voice, and I spun around on the spot to face Geilis, her beautiful angular cheekbones accentuating the smile that consumed and lit her face. Her eyes danced, the light flitting through the leaves sparkling in them. She stepped forward in a slow and almost imperceptible movement.

Yet, I felt the move even if I couldn't see it. Awareness Geilis had entered my personal space was as real as if we had bumped into each other. Her physical presence sent a rush of sparks through me. "Geilis. I don't understand. What is going on? How? Why? I mean . . ." My voice disappeared as my brain misfired, unsure what I wanted to know. What could explain this?

Geilis held her hand out to me and I stared at it, questioning if I could touch her. An irrational fear took hold of my muscles. As if remembering a loss, I found I was unable to move my hand.

I knew she might not be real.

She might vanish.

Geilis rocked on her heels in desperation at something I couldn't give.

"Do you really not remember me? Don't you feel anything?" Geilis stepped forward, grasping my hand, holding it between hers. "Is there nothing? I was sure you would feel something." She threw her arms around me. "I don't care. We can start again."

I wanted to recoil, to remove myself from the physical touch, and yet I found the familiar glow from the first time we met. I relaxed into more contact than I could ever remember. My heart melted, the cold, hard edges of my icy core disintegrating. "I have so many questions, I don't even know where to start. Who are you?"

Geilis stepped back only far enough to allow her to look into my face. She held my hands in hers, her thumbs rubbing my palms. "I was so sure, when you asked the other day about me being familiar, that it would come back." She pulled me toward a large Rowan tree and sat down, patting the ground next to her. "Please just sit for a while and I'll try to explain."

We faced each other, our eyes looking for different things but both searching for something. Geilis's shoulders slumped and her eyes moved to gaze at her fingers as they fiddled with the buttons on her boot. She pulled her skirt up over her knees to reveal the dark, polished-wooden hues of her legs. They matched mine. The detailed carvings were different but just as intricate and done with as much love as mine.

My eyes froze, unable to look away from the leg so much like my own. Geilis cupped my chin, pulling it up until we were looking in each other's eyes.

"You carved them for me," she said, holding my chin as she waited for the reaction.

"I. You. Sorry, I mean . . . I did that? So, who?" I pulled open the fastening on my trousers to reveal my carved wooden leg. Her fingers followed the carved lines before she stopped, and her eyes examined my face.

She reached out to touch mine. "I did that. That's what you want to know."

Tears filled my eyes and I swallowed, battling the lump forming in my throat, restricting my breathing. My mouth opened but no words came. A groan, sounding more like a wild animal than a human, flew free from me, from deep in my soul.

Rasping screams replied. The screams from my head broke free and fear filled my body. The trees moved to surround us, forming a solid barrier around us, and I stared at Geilis, needing answers to questions I didn't yet know or understand.

"What is that noise? Who?" The question hung in the air. Recognition sent a coldness racing through me. I stood, holding my hand out for Geilis. "The Banshee. I know the sound. I remember it." I turned to look at her, my eyes pleading. "Am I one of them? Why do I understand their pain? Why do they respond to my pain?"

She held out her hand to touch the tree, her other hand gripping mine. "You can hear and feel all things. You have always been destined for great things. You are the connection, the link between the human world and your world, Solas."

I grabbed my head, red searing pain shooting through it. "Red." The word filled the air. "I feel red." I landed on the ground. My knee buckled under me, and I curled up against the agony inside me.

Geilis knelt in front of me. "The Redcaps. They were the first to cross when the barrier started to fade. You can feel them, which means they are close. I think the trees knew. They are shielding us, but we are only safe in Solas. Please, trust me. I once trusted you and now I need you to trust me. Please."

I sat up straight, shook my head, and dug my fingers into the soil. "I always recognized this. The trees are my friends, and you . . . you . . . I know you. They wanted to burn you. The humans." My eyes took in the smile spreading across Geilis's face.

"Yes, you saved me, but you had to cross the barrier between our worlds and it left a tear. You saved me at such a high price." Geilis brushed away the tears rolling down my face.

"My soul recognized your soul. Even across worlds." I placed my hand on top of Geilis's, pushing it hard against her face. "I know you, Geilis Duncan. I love you. I know that now."

"Trust me, Billey. I love you, Billey Moaraigh NicNevin."

Without thought and in complete faith, I nodded. I couldn't put all the pieces of the jigsaw together, yet. But, I knew I wanted to. Geilis grabbed both my hands and stared into my eyes. "Close your eyes and feel me. Feel my soul. Focus on the light inside you and Solas will come for you. Solas is you and you are Solas."

Light filled me. I saw it. I felt it. I became it.

I realized at that moment that belonging isn't about a place. Belonging is in your soul.

"My soul recognizes your soul."

Seven

Alex

A strange sensation flowed through my body as I stood waiting by the cars. Jen's wagging tail beat in time with my heart, with the pulse pushing me forward. I could no longer live in the shadow of my mother. Could no longer hide my magic. It must have a purpose. We all have a purpose.

My body, oblivious to the chill, floated inside my skin by the time the others arrived. "Where are we going then? Can't imagine there is anywhere we haven't scavenged bare," I asked, a part of me excited by having somebody, even if it was a dog, to do it with.

Danny laughed, the mocking and affectionate shake of his head making me realize they had told me when I wasn't listening. "Roberto and Abi said earlier about some intact houses over in Salem. Near the top of a hill. Must have been lucky enough to escape the worst of it. Worth a shot? Besides, I know how you love a good rummage around in the past."

"I'm not feeling the past at the moment. More into the future, but I get to drive," I said, walking to stand next to the driver's door. "It's my turn to drive. So who's in my car?"

They exchanged glances, an agreement passing between them. Calesta threw a key to me. "Fine, you can take Roberto and Abi. We'll meet you there, but drive carefully. Stick to the roads we know are clear. Don't get reckless. Okay?"

"Okay," I said, leaning against the car, twisting my head to face Roberto and Abi. "Excellent, you can give me directions."

Abi stopped to touch the hood of the car. "I can't believe this is still working. I haven't seen a car running in years. Once the gas ran out, we were all forced back onto our feet. We were so lucky somebody knew how to plug them up to those solar panels, but I never imagined them still going ten years later."

Roberto climbed into the front seat, laughing. "Tesla's sustainable future. Ha. Bet they never imagined this."

Abi clambered in the back next to Jen. I smiled. I loved the feel of driving. Although, I guessed it couldn't have been so exciting when there were other cars on the road. I sat in the driver's seat, waiting for the gentle hissing sound of the engine. Silence filled the car and my shoulders sunk, the weight of defeat threatening to pull my joy off track.

Roberto turned to face Abi and we watched Danny and Calesta speed off, leaving us behind. I placed my hand on either side of the steering wheel as though to strangle it in my frustration. I stretched my energy, willing it to spark into life. It spluttered and wheezed before finally starting to hiss.

"Bravo" came Abi's voice from the back seat as we pulled out. My foot hit the floor to catch up with the others.

Avoiding the inaccessible streets, we took longer than I hoped, and Danny and Calesta were already leaning against their car when we arrived in the parking lot. Their faces, smirking and joking, said what didn't need to be said. I parked next to them. "The car wouldn't start. Needed a magical touch. Don't make out like you've been waiting long."

Calesta laughed first. "No, we just got here, and I see what you meant about its condition. Almost looks like before the Orange, only shabbier. So, who's going where?"

We all looked at each other. With no particular aim or objective, it didn't matter. "Well, I'm going into them," I said, pointing up the hill to three white houses still in one piece, paint flaking and peeling off their weatherboard exteriors. "Somebody ought to go in there," I said, looking at a brick-built box with red remnants of what would have been a name. "Just in case there's anything we could use. Although, it's highly unlikely there's anything left. If there ever was anything."

Danny and Calesta walked toward the brick box. "We'll take the smelly box. Roberto and Abi, watch her. She loves to rummage."

I walked up the hill, Roberto and Abi falling behind as I sped up to keep up with Jen. I stopped outside the first house, a house similar to my old home. The house I stood outside yesterday. The house that haunted and taunted me. This house was somebody else's home. I hoped, whoever they were, they weren't home. I had seen many corpses in various states of shriveling and rotting, but it never got easier.

"I'm going in here. I'll meet you back there," I said, pointing to a small paved area next to it. My attention lingered on the space. A small green tree stood defiantly in the middle. "Wow, how did that survive?" I asked, taking a few steps farther up the hill to stare at it.

"Maybe there's a witch buried there," Abi said. "It is Salem."

My mother told me stories of witches, who were magical healers and helpers left behind by my father's ancestors, and how her ancestors killed them. "Oh, haha. I've heard all those stories too. Look, I'll meet you back here."

Abi's casual laughter carried with me, and I walked toward the front door, its blue paint peeling. I pushed it to find it locked. I thought about using magic to open it, but kicking it was so much more satisfying. The door gave way with no argument. Jen sniffed in disdain when a stale smell greeted us. We stepped carefully, unsure what would greet us. This floor had been washed by the waves that followed the Orange. Little remained other than broken furniture and dirt.

Shattered glass from the windows lay scattered on the floor, like the lost hopes of life. I walked up the stairs, brushing the glass aside, scared Jen would cut her paws on it. They creaked but stood solid. The upstairs was exactly as it would have been. I sat on a sofa, a faded floral pattern that matched the curtains, my eyes fixed on the faces of a family smiling back. A small empty part of my heart filled with their smiles, the hope they felt at that moment. A hope I had never experienced.

I walked into another room, stark and white, with posters of long-forgotten heroes, knowing this had been somebody like me. A teenager. A girl. I wondered what her hopes had been. I sat at a dressing table, looking at my reflection in the mirror; my skin, darker than Roberto's, glowed, and memories flooded back. Lectures and stories about how people had judged others by their skin, before. I wondered how I would have fit in their society, with my incongruous mixture of blue eyes, red hair, and dark skin.

It didn't matter now. It seemed difficult to imagine why it mattered then, but now we were all too busy surviving to care.

I pulled the drawers open, rummaging through their contents. I grabbed a few hair clips, not that they'd do much for my hair. I lifted out a small box and opened the lid. A small figure spun and danced as sounds of music flooded the room, its melody washing away the years and releasing the child hidden deep inside me. I emptied the box on the top of the dressing table to look at the necklaces, rings, and earrings of the missing girl.

Barking dragged me back to the present, and I glanced around, looking for Jen. She wasn't here and the hairs on my arms stood to attention. My instinct told me to call for her, to run to her, but my intuition and years of boring lectures told me to be more careful. She was barking at something or somebody outside.

I crept down the stairs, my heart wrestling my lungs to escape my chest. My deep breathing caused me to swallow the putrid smell of decay and death captured in the house, and my stomach joined the skirmish. I peered out the door, preparing to retreat or run, using my energy to search for life close by. My aura reached to Jen, her fear and confusion blending with mine as I sent positive emotions of calm and peace, hoping to sense what upset her.

Feeling no other life, I moved cautiously to see her barking at the leafless once-trees behind the small paved area where I agreed to meet Roberto and Abi. I bent down to stroke her, my eyes staring into the trees, preparing for anything. She looked up at me, licked me, and ran up the hill into the once-trees behind the houses. I moaned inside, fighting a scream, before chasing after her. Reaching the top, I saw her sitting and glaring at nothing, panting and tail wagging.

"What's wrong?"

She gazed up at me as I laid my hand on her head, sensing her happiness. Her happiness is what confused me. Was she playing a game? Had the barking and attention-seeking that caused my panic been nothing more than a game?

I sat on the ground, sticks, branches, and dead bark creating an uncomfortable cushion. She rolled over for me to tickle her and play with her. In silence, we enjoyed the moment, free from the strains of isolation and survival. Her contentment and peace in the world infected me as the colors of our auras combined. I wrapped my arms around her neck, kissing her head.

"Time to go, before the others start to worry."

I stood, brushing the dead tree bark off my jeans, and headed down the hill. No more than two steps later, on the ledge, my eyes were drawn to the green shoots and new life budding from the death of Mother Earth. Bending to touch them, to feel the energy of their new life, a sensation overcame me. I found myself curled up on the ground, a wave of orange sparks and glow sweeping over me while I fought to breathe. I breathed deeply, searching for the connection, struggling to reach it. A new feeling greeted me. A new connection to a deeper life, a deeper magic.

The orange wave, threatening to drown me, swirled around me, engulfing me in color and a scent I didn't recognize. The sweet smell spoke of peace and tranquility. I acclimatized and it ceased, disappearing into the air. The wave that had flowed over and around me left me, now sucked up by the earth, and I stared at my hands. The magic rushed through me, and I turned to Jen, who was still staring at me with her tail wagging.

"Was this what you wanted me to see? Do you know what it was?" She padded over to sit next to me, resting her head against my arm, tilting her head up to lick my face. "Good girl."

My legs wobbled as I stood, and I paused for a few seconds to breathe. Heading down the hill, Jen raced ahead, leaving me in my confusion. My steps, slow and controlled, edged back down the hill, toward the voices of Roberto and Abi.

On seeing me, they both stopped talking, their stares going through me. Abi's gaunt face froze in a frown as her icy-blue eyes darkened. "What's wrong," she asked, her eyes fixed on me.

"Nothing. Honestly. I was just playing with Jen and slipped. Gave myself a bit of a scare. Silly, really." I gave a small laugh, brushing off whatever it was they saw in me, unsure I should share. I sensed that whatever it was, was for me. "Find anything?"

"Nah, nothing interesting. A few tins and a new comforter," said Roberto, glancing at the ground where his scavenging lay. "Let's go and see if the others had any more luck."

We all headed, without any discussion, down the hill to the brick box. Danny and Calesta's car, now full of bags, bottles, and boxes, told us they had been luckier than us. Roberto put his new belongings into the car while Abi and I walked to the open door. She reached for the handle when an energy touched me.

"Stop," I yelled louder than I meant to. I placed my hand on top of hers. "Do you feel that? There's somebody else in there."

Her eyebrows creased into a V-shape and her brow furrowed as she shook her head. "I don't feel anything."

"A desperation. A negative energy. That's not Danny and Calesta; there's definitely somebody else." We both looked back at Roberto, his eyes filled with confusion. He shrugged his shoulders, questioning what he had missed. I placed my fingers over my lips, pointing inside the box with my head.

For such a large man, he moved with remarkable speed and stealth to stand next to us.

"There's somebody in there," whispered Abi.

He nodded, pushing past us to enter first. I turned to stare at Jen, commanding her to stay, and she lowered her head and lay on the floor. Abi and I followed Roberto. I stretched out my energy, searching for Danny and Calesta, finding no reply. Only hatred and desperation replied, getting closer. I pulled Roberto's sleeve, pointing toward the back of the building. He nodded and we changed direction, moving toward the strangers.

Voices drifted through the air, surfing on the negative energy. "Search their pockets. There are two cars out there so there must be a second set of keys."

"Maybe there are others. Maybe there's more o' them."

"Jessie, Brandon, head to the door an' keep an eye out for others."

Roberto backed us between two rows of tins, and we knelt, hidden from sight as two younger men walked right past us toward the door. He held up his finger to his lip to silence us. My stomach churned and fought its way into my throat as I suppressed a scream. I placed my hands on my knees, trying to stop them from shaking. We sat, watching in silence, as they disappeared down the aisle.

Roberto and Abi stood, pulling knives from their waistbands. I had nothing but followed, still searching for Danny and Calesta. At the end of the aisle, Roberto knelt to look around the corner, then recoiled, the horror of whatever he saw painted in his eyes as they blackened. The feeling of death emanated from him as he held his head in his hands. I knew, without him saying, what he had seen. Danny and Calesta gave no reply to my probing.

I knew.

I retched, unable to sit still. Anger pulsed through my body, empowering me, blinding me. The tears rolling down my cheeks burned my skin. I stood with no idea what I intended to do, knowing I needed to do something. Roberto grabbed for my leg as I walked past him to face the three men. My eyes fixed on Danny and Calesta, lying on the floor, surrounded by a pool of blood. Its red shimmer caught the light from the small windows high up on the wall.

I screamed, "What did you do?"

The men turned to face me, guns in their hands. I had never seen one in real life. My mother told me about their destruction and man's addiction to them. Danny and Calesta told me they were rare now that bullets had begun to run out. But, in the early stages of life after the Orange, people turned on each other. So few survived, yet, despite the rarity of people, they still killed each other, desperate to survive at the expense of their humanity.

The tallest and skinniest of the three stepped forward. "What we got here? Eh?" He laughed, turning to face the two men behind him.

I stared past them at the bodies of the only two people I had left in the world. I could hear Roberto sigh as he stood next to me, his calm energy merging with mine as he touched my shoulder. I breathed to calm my energy.

"Why? Why would you do it? What danger would they have been to you? Why?" I screamed, running at the man.

He raised his gun, pointing it at me, as a voice behind him spoke. "She's little more than a kid, Charlie, seriously."

The man didn't flinch, his eyes boring through me, the hatred flickering in them matching the anger in mine. Life slowed as I stepped off the path I had followed my entire life. The love and compassion my mother taught disappeared, replaced by frustration and anger for Danny and Calesta, for my life, and for the world the man's generation stole from me. I watched as his finger squeezed the trigger, as the bullet flew with a grace that belied its purpose toward me.

The anger burning deep in my soul overtook my aura and I raised my hands, sending a wave of energy toward him, toward them all. The bullet floated for a few seconds, its energy and mine meeting in a battle of wills. It landed on the floor with an insignificant tinkling sound, and the energy continued to move, throwing the men flying to land next to Danny and Calesta.

My brain sparked and stuttered, the moment requiring knowledge I refused to accept. Time moved around me, but I stood frozen. My muscles lost contact with my brain and neither fight nor flight came. Roberto plunged his knife into the chest of the man moaning and coated in the blood of Danny and Calesta. Abi took the guns from the other two and their lives ceased.

At what point my feet moved I still don't know, but I found myself staring at the bloodstains on my birthday shoes. The blood pooled and moved as Roberto and Abi moved. My eighteenth birthday present. Happy birthday to me. I knelt, or my legs gave way, and I landed next to Danny and Calesta's bodies. I placed my hands on them. Their energy had gone. I stared for what seemed to be hours at the blood on my hands, wiping it on my jeans, watching my tears create small, circular patterns as they merged with the blood on the floor.

"Alex. We need to move. There're still two of them outside. Alex. Come on." Abi's voice reverberated around my skull. How many times she called me, I don't know, but her fingers dug into my arm as she tried to pull me.

I looked up to see Roberto. He bent, placing his arms under my arms and pulling me up in one rapid movement. I felt his muscular arms wrap around me, and I fought back, kicking and screaming. He pulled me in tighter, wrapping his arm around my arms, his other hand on my forehead.

"Calm. Breathe, Alex, breathe. You need to center yourself. We aren't done yet." I looked in his eyes, at the reflection of my grief mirrored in the deep black of them.

"I'm coming," I muttered, rubbing my arms across my face to wipe the tears. I realized I was just smearing the tears and blood and didn't care. "Let's go." I looked one last time at Danny and Calesta, knowing the gaping hole inside would never go away.

I followed Roberto and Abi down the aisle toward the door we entered through moments earlier, before my life had altered irrevocably. My brain suddenly sparked, all the gears hitting the right cogs, and my thoughts flowed with a forgotten fluency.

"Jen," I yelled, racing ahead.

I heard the footsteps of the others behind me when I reached the doorway. I burst through to see Jen sitting, her tail wagging at me. My eyes squinted, hunting for the other men. I saw them standing next to the cars. Their eyes fixed on me, and I realized what a terrifying image I must make in my clothing painted with death. They both stared, their hands moving up until they held them in the air.

"Move away from my car," I screamed, barely able to control my voice. I breathed, struggling to calm my heart rate. "Your friends aren't coming out. I'm sorry if they were family or friends, but believe me, I had no choice. You have a choice. Two choices. We fight it out here and now, and some of us die. Those men inside are what destroyed our world. Don't let them destroy our future. This is our world and we need to decide what kind of world we make it. This brings me to choice number two: you run that way as fast as you can, and if we ever meet again, it will be our first meeting. This will be a forgotten hiccup on our journey of survival. So which is it?"

They exchanged confused glances, looking back at me. They hesitated, their feet desperate to flee, while their brains battled their instinct. I prayed they would trust me. My heart weighed too much without any more death to carry.

They fled, disappearing around the corner before I landed on the ground, rubbing my hand through Jen's fur. I looked at the red streaks my fingers left. I leaned my head on her and cried. Roberto and Abi knelt beside me.

"What was that?" asked Roberto.

"Which bit?" I said, turning my head to gaze at his face.

"What did you do in there? What was that?"

"Honestly, I have no idea. It just came out of me. I doubt I could do it again."

Abi placed her hand on top of mine. "We need to go now, you know that."

"But Danny and Calesta. We need to do something. We can't just leave them there." One last tear slithered down my cheek.

"Honey, there's nothing we can do for them now. Their energy, their soul, is gone. You know that."

Roberto stood. "We can't stay here. There may be more of them. You need to go home. Danny and Calesta would want that. They'd want you safe. Are you okay to go alone? Do you need Abi to come with you?"

I shook my head and Jen followed me to the car. I sat in it and turned on the ignition and my body filled with numbness. Driving away, I wondered why I was going home. What was home with nobody to share it with? It wasn't home anymore. It was just a building.

EIGHT

ALEX

The school dominated my view, its size and scale larger than I had ever given any thought to. Its looming presence was no longer one of a home. I sat in the car, my hands gripping the steering wheel as I drove somewhere else in my head. I now had two homes I couldn't bring myself to walk into.

A whining sound, a cross between a yawn and a moan, came from the backseat, and I released the steering wheel. A sigh escaped the empty chasm in my chest, and I rested my forehead on the steering wheel instead. I needed to go in, knowing I would need to say goodbye. The only home I truly remembered was now just a deserted school.

My body ached to cry, yet no tears came, and I opened the car door, then placed my feet on the ground. As I stood up, leaving the car behind, Jen jumped out to stand next to me. I left the door ajar and turned my back on the school, walking away. I had to move on and I couldn't until I had faced the past.

I knew where I needed to be and it wasn't here. My feet gathered speed as my walk became a run and Jen followed. I ran without any awareness of the trees, or houses, or roads I passed. I had to finally go home, to face the ghosts of the past. I found myself, again, facing the perfect white house I had stared at many times but never dared to enter.

I now knew why.

I had hung onto the past, my safety net. It had been my childish dream of family and home. A dream where my mother was still alive, or my father hadn't deserted me, or he swept in and rescued me. I had to rescue myself. I had to move on.

My old home managed to stand intact, debris surrounding it from what should have been the neighboring houses. My mother would have declared it divine intervention, but I knew better. No god would have allowed this. Magic was the answer, not a false god, but was God the connection? I felt many things: devastated, robbed, angry, sad. I never felt lucky. I never felt somebody was watching over me, yet I had survived against all odds.

Having stood staring until the sun moved to the horizon, I found the courage to enter. I pushed open the front door, oblivious to the ash showering me, and held my breath, waiting for my mother to shout from the kitchen. Instead, the silence deafened me. My footprints, followed by the padding of Jen's paws, left an eerie trail as though we disturbed something that should be left buried.

A wave of sadness flooded my senses as I stood in the doorway of the familiar yet long-forgotten living room. Emotions, long buried in the rubble of the war, raged through my muscles.

Despite the layer of ash and dust showered on the furniture in the room, my heart pulled me to the small wooden box with the tarnished brass plaque. The unremarkable box sat among the many knickknacks on the fireplace. My heart pounded. The cushions still stood to attention on the ash-covered white sofa, and my mother's voice echoed through my head: 'Mess is the enemy of calm. Cluttered environment. Cluttered mind.'

Then, a voice came from the box. Calling me. Pulling me. The memories of the mother I loved. The mother who always wore the Firestone around her neck. At some point, tears started to roll down my cheeks. My mother left me the Firestone here, knowing I would have to face the past before I could step into the future. My legacy, but I couldn't bring myself to wear it. In the little wooden box, like so many I rummaged through, I found trinkets and jewelry, but this one held the next step in my destiny, my existence, my life alone.

Jen whined, and a voice in my head started to scream at me as I pried the lid off the box.

"Your legacy!

"Your legacy!

"Your legacy!

"Your legacy!"

As I lifted the necklace from the box and watched my tears turn the ashes dark, I heard a noise. The sound of voices not attempting to conceal themselves, confident in their right to be there. Not in my head. In the hallway. Somebody else was here. Somebody followed me.

"I believe that's mine!" came the gruff and angry voice as I turned to see the two men from earlier, staring not at me but transfixed by the Firestone.

I froze for a second as I attempted to figure out what to do. How had they been able to follow me? The Firestone belonged to me and my fingers tightened around the stone.

Almost as if to answer, the Firestone exploded, sending flames shooting across the room, licking the walls and blanketing both men. I stared in confusion, my heart pounding and my head telling me to run. My feet itched to run and never stop. To run as far as my legs would take me, never looking back.

The heat from the flames repelled me, forcing me backwards, but Jen never left my side. Yet, the dancing and laughing of the fire's tongues called to me to join them.

As everything transformed into the barren husks I saw before me, I knew I should be sad, angry . . . something.

A deep, thunderous laugh rumbled its way up my body as I stared at my previous life burning. Since the end of the war, I held on so tightly to the memories of a better time, it had become an unconscious obsession. The time before.

Now, I found myself laughing and joyous as I allowed the therapeutic wave of release to wash away my past. None of it mattered. The flames swallowed my life with increasing greed and forced me to accept something I should have known. That was my past. It was gone.

I looked at the pyre of my past, grieving and then basking in the freedom of the present. There was a safety in the fire, but beyond it, the darkness loomed. The possibilities of the darkness enticed me. Yet as my heart pounded, I found my hands still ready to defend.

The screams of my two unknown assailants disappeared into the burning mass, but I was unable to look away. This was what life brought in a world after the Orange. Death. Too soon. Too brutal. Too much to risk.

I forced myself to turn and walk away and leave it all behind. I closed my eyes and relaxed my breathing, increasing my personal auric field and hoping I would at least get a few seconds of awareness, should anyone choose to attack. However, the pulsing of the few trees still struggling to grow in the rubble sent off an immense amount of energy, which I hadn't noticed earlier.

It was unlike anything I had encountered before. The strange, dark pulse of the trees, slow and unintentional, as they probed back. Trees were my grounded connection to the energy of the earth, but the trees now felt more. There was an awareness that caused me to reel backwards, my foot catching in the undergrowth and forcing me onto my side as I fell.

The Firestone dropped from my hand and the fire disappeared, leaving nothing standing in its wake. Bending to pick it up, I walked away, taking in one last look at the blackened shell of my life. The empty space inside me filled with something new. Something I couldn't name, but it was empowering. Whether it was leaving the past behind me or the power I had found within myself, I knew life was about to move forward, and I had no idea what that would mean or where it would take me.

Part Two

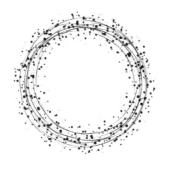

Journey to Jericho

Nine

Iggy

The dying embers of the fire sizzled as Emmy threw water on them. The darkness was beginning to creep in and we couldn't risk being spotted, no matter how much the cold gnawed at us. Besides, we needed to leave soon to meet Roberto and Abi.

Watching his delicate hands move soil to cover the spot our fire had been, I wandered to thoughts of the small boy I had been when he and his husband, David, had found me.

"Okay, will we go? We'll be early but better than late, eh? Grab them, will you?" he said, his hands waving a grand gesture at the two bags on the ground, as though they were something so much more magnificent than two grubby and shabby old rucksacks.

I paused for a moment, remembering the times he carried me when I was too small and too tired.

"Hello? Iggy? Are you with us?" he said, his hands resting on his hips in mock frustration. The warmth of his gentle smile told the truth of his meaning. "Are you okay?"

I laughed. "Yeah, sorry. Just thinking."

"A dangerous habit. And, what were you thinking?"

"I was, well—Do you ever feel like we're climbing an uphill battle that never gets us anywhere? How do you manage to always be so confident and positive?" I bent to pick up the bags, sliding my arms into the first one, placing it on my back, and throwing the second one over my shoulder. "I was thinking about the first time I saw you. We've come so far but . . . have we really?"

He walked to stand in front of me, reaching up to place his hand on my shoulder. "The universe brought us together for a reason. Of that, I have no doubt. That sad, hungry little boy I met all those years ago is the best thing that ever happened to me. We survived. That's a major accomplishment. Don't underestimate it."

He paused and I knew his thoughts had flitted back to memories of David. He didn't speak of him, but I knew his death had ripped a hole in Emmy. He had become quieter, more delicate, since David. I nodded and pulled him in for a hug. "You're my savior."

"Oh, don't be silly. Look at you now. My own personal bodyguard." He laughed. "Who knew you'd be so big and so hungry?"

He glanced over at the dirt where the fire had been, checking we had hidden any traces we had been here. He might not be tall, strong, or have any magic, but he had a strength inside that kept him positive. It infected me when I was at my lowest.

His strength hid deep in his chest, in the huge heart that always saw the best in everything.

He headed off toward the road. "Come on, we don't want to keep Roberto and Abi waiting. Besides, I'm curious to see this school they grew up in," he said, turning his head to look at me. "Tell me you aren't?"

I followed behind him, catching up in a couple of strides to walk next to him. "Honestly, I can't imagine growing up in one place. I can't imagine having a home. Even less, I can't imagine leaving it. Why would they?"

"Ah, the great mystery of human nature," he said with a sigh. "We are all hardwired to want to belong, to hunt for a community we can call our own."

"Mm."

We walked in silence, watching the sun as it sunk lower until it hid beneath the scorched world we live in. The silence of the unspoken words flowed between us. After years of searching for somewhere to belong, a community to call our own, Emmy still found a way to believe. To hope.

TEN

BILLEY

Leaning on the sink, my brain scrambled to make sense of the night before. I knew Geilis. At least, a version of me did. She loved me and I loved her. That, I didn't doubt. I knew that with certainty. However, I had a night of tossing and turning, her pleas for me to come with her rattling around my head.

She talked of places I didn't know as though I should. Talked of home and, yet, this was the only home I knew. Here, with Gaevoin and Brigina, was the only place I had ever belonged.

I looked around at the room I called mine. There were no personal items, no clue I lived here. A bed, piles of books scattered around the desk, and a few pieces of clothing hanging on wall hooks—but they could belong to anybody. Who was I?

Sounds of life drifted up the stairs as I brushed my hair back, pinning it at the back of my head. It was easier than trying to make sense of the frizz and mess of it. A small part of me that was easily quashed wished I had to go to the Institute today. Any distraction from the thoughts muddling my head would have been welcome, and I let out a loud sigh as I pulled a grey pinafore over my head.

My feet slowed as I walked down the stairs, and I secured my invisible mask of confidence in place before facing anybody. Brigina's voice reached me as I neared the end. Turning the corner to enter the kitchen, I found Brigina at the table with Codrin, discussing a book on the table. Gaevoin was the first to notice me.

"Good morning, lazybones. Sleep well?" he asked without looking away from whatever he was cooking. My stomach sank. Brigina was such a wonderful cook.

I forced my face to form a smile. "Good morning. Yes, thank you," I lied. A lump formed in my throat, blocking the truth of my night despite my need to discuss Geilis.

Again, I found myself wondering if my head was playing tricks on me. If it was, what would happen if I agreed to go to Solas?

A scream filled my head and I placed my hands on my head without realizing it.

"Are you feeling alright?" asked Brigina.

I turned to look at her; the warmth of her smile reminded me why I couldn't leave. Codrin continued to stare at his book and all I could see was a mass of hair. "I'm fine, thanks. Good morning, you two." The screaming in my head subsided, and I moved to sit at the table.

"Do you want some breakfast?" asked Gaevoin, walking toward the table with a bowl of some sort of sludge.

His face, full of pride at whatever it was, fractured a corner of my heart and, despite the rebellious churning of my stomach, I smiled. "Thanks. That'd be lovely. Erm, what is it?"

"Taste it and tell me it isn't glorious."

Codrin let out a small moan and I knew all eyes were now on me.

I stared at the plate in front of me, running my spoon in circles, watching the steam rise from it. I looked up at his face and took a spoonful. "Oh, that is glorious," I blurted out.

"Thanks for the vote of confidence. Clearly, you weren't expecting it to be."

"No, it . . . Well, it doesn't look great but it tastes lovely. What is it?"

Brigina answered for him. "We've been working with some people from Central who have been trying to replicate the genetic makeup of bees to allow pollination. We've been breeding the products of that research in one of the fields. That is what honey tastes like."

"Oh, wow. I read lots about bees and honey and stuff, but to taste it. That's something else."

They smiled at each other, and for a few moments, all worries about Geilis, my mental health, and my past vanished.

"So, what are your plans for the day?" asked Brigina.

"Nothing much. I'll just go for a walk, read a book. Unless you want me to do anything around the house?" I held my breath, a part of me hoping they needed me. My heart ached. My mind raced with thoughts of going back to the trees, but I knew it wasn't to read. My breathing became shorter as I thought about seeing her again.

"No, we're going to take a lazy day too. You feel free to go for a walk," said Brigina, standing up and patting my hand as she took the empty plate in front of me.

The sweetness of the strange honey-and-oats concoction began to lie on my stomach, but I had cleared the plate to the delighted smiles of Brigina and Gaevoin.

I looked at Codrin. "What are you up to today?"

"Nothing. Schoolwork." He did look up before staring back at his book.

I looked up at Brigina. She shrugged her shoulders. I sighed and leaned back in my chair. "Do you need any help?"

He looked up. "No." For the first time, he made eye contact. "Thank you, though."

"No worries. Well if nobody needs me, I'm going for a walk, then."

The cold wind, crossing the open lands, bit into me and my skin burned. I pulled my scarf tighter, beginning to regret wearing a dress. I began to remember how much they annoyed me. The sight of the trees on the horizon moving closer warmed my soul. Each step up the hill made my leg ache more, but the gentle wind rustled the leaves, creating a quiet calm.

Reaching the top, I took off the grey bag slung across my body, threw it on the ground, and sat down, tucking my skirt up so I could cross my legs. I leaned against my favorite Rowan tree, fidgeting until I was comfortable. I rummaged in my bag, pulling out a sandwich. I held it to my nose and realized it was honey. A smile crept across my face and warmth filled me. I had never known this type of belonging. I never belonged before. Not that I remembered.

Reading proved more difficult than usual, as my mind wandered and my brain moved into overthinking.

Instead, I relaxed back against the tree, closing my eyes and breathing in the smells of the damp grass and leaves. The smells of nature calmed me and the worries of Geilis, voices, and Solas vanished in the breeze. I placed the book on the ground and enjoyed the peace of my trees. My muscles eased and I realized how much I had been tensing.

"You've always had a beautiful smile," said the voice I now recognized as Geilis's.

When I opened my eyes, I saw her looking down at me, her mouth creasing in a smile that caused dimples in her cheeks. My heart made a weird skip. I hadn't understood how much I wanted to see her until that moment.

My face reddened and I blustered, "Nobody's ever said I looked beautiful. It's not a word that matches with this." I waved my hand up and down my body.

She sat down so close her arm brushed mine. "Oh, that's not true. I've said it many times. I remember the first time I saw you. You were like an angel sent to me." She picked up my hand, placing it in hers, laying her other hand on top of it. "I was prepared to die and then you appeared. You were the most beautiful sight. And, you look even cuter when you blush," she said, elbowing me.

I laughed again. "I wish I could remember this stuff. I find it difficult . . . No, impossible to imagine me saving anybody."

She shuffled to sit in front of me, leaning forward to place her hands on my knees, and let out a sigh. "You have no idea how much I want to tell you it all, but I promised you that I'd give you a chance to remember first. I wouldn't be here yet, if we weren't running out of time." She shuffled farther until our knees touched. Her face was so close I could feel her breath. "You do need to remember, though. You need to trust me you did this for a good reason and, now, it's time to move."

My hands twitched, my fingers desperate to touch her face. "That's what doesn't make sense. How can any of this be true? I remember everything since I was twelve. I have a blank before that but I couldn't have done these things as a child. Besides, why would I leave you if I loved you? All I've ever wanted was to fit in, to belong. So, why would I do that?"

My body moved to drag itself backwards, away from her. Instead, I banged my head on the tree. I had nowhere to go. I opened my mouth to speak, but I couldn't find the words. "Is this some sort of joke? Are you trying to fool me? You're pretty and think that makes it alright? Either you're playing a joke or I'm going mad. I can't see the third option," I yelled, twisting my body to the side, away from her.

Her arm reached for me but I pulled away, grabbing my bag and pushing myself up. She stood to match me. But being taller than me, she looked down on me. I wanted to believe her but this didn't make sense.

I watched as a tear rolled down her cheek. "I know none of this makes sense. I, of all people, get how impossible the truth will be."

I walked in the opposite direction, my breathing struggling as I fought back an anxiety attack. I bounced between wanting to cry, curl up, and run away.

"Please," she yelled after me.

A scream filled my head, sending me spilling to the ground, grasping my head.

Her hand stroked my head. "Please. You always said I was your calm. Let me help you." She knelt next to me, placing her other arm over me. "Please, trust me." Moving to sit in front of me, she cupped my face and the screaming began to fade.

A memory flooded my senses as though watching somebody else yet knowing it was somehow me. A vision of me, another version of me, crying about the death of my father and Geilis comforting me. I looked up at her. "How were you there after my father's death? I don't even remember him. How would I forget somebody I loved?"

She let out a sigh, throwing herself backwards to lie on the grass. "A memory, I take it? What do you remember? Tell me and I'll try to make sense of it for you." She hugged her knees and looked into my face. "I'm sorry I'm not able to do what you asked before, but I didn't realize you'd forget everything. It never occurred to me you'd forget me."

"No, that's the thing: somehow, I do remember you. I remember you comforting me after my father died. Well, me but not me. It looked like me but I was older. But. But, it looked like me." Finally, the tears flooded out. "I am going mad, aren't I?"

I sat there rocking backwards and forwards, tears blurring my vision and fear blurring my head. I didn't belong anywhere. I didn't belong here, or with Geilis; I didn't belong in any world. I was losing my mind and loneliness took on a new meaning. My heart pounded faster and faster, battering a rhythm against my ribs that I couldn't keep up with. Rubbing my sweaty palms up and down my now muddy pinafore dress, I fought to regain control of my breathing, forcing myself to breathe in time to the rocking of my body.

With the cold of the wind blowing around me, my flushing skin stung as it hit me. The sweat on my face formed pin prickles of icy chills where the breeze touched it.

Geilis grabbed my hands, placing them on the ground. Her hands lay on top of them, her thumbs stroking their backs. "Breathe. Feel the connection, Billey."

I looked up into her eyes, staring into them. Sprinkled in the pale blue of them, small golden flecks seemed to reflect the light, creating a warmth that pulled me in. I gazed into them, my breathing becoming secondary to the warmth in them. They are where I belong.

When I closed my eyes and my body relaxed, my heart stilled to something close to a normal rhythm. A memory filled my vision. I stared at the fragments of memories scattered like pieces of a broken mirror. Each reflection showed some event I knew as a memory and, yet, I didn't recognize them.

ELEVEN

ALEX

By the time I returned to face the overshadowing presence of the school, Roberto and Abi were back. Their car and mine were charging as they should be. I looked to see what was different and realized it still looked the same; I had never seen it for what it was. Empty.

The echo of my footsteps performed a sad tune, clashing with the speedy clip-clop of Jen's paws. I headed straight for the kitchen, not because I wanted to eat but because I wanted water. I needed to wash away the day. I saw Roberto and Abi in the garden but tried to sneak past them, hoping to be left alone. Abi spotted me and ran to me.

"What happened to you? Where did you go? Is that soot? Are you alright?" She stood between me and the kitchen, a deliberate barrier between me and my goal.

"I'm fine. I had to do something." My eyes couldn't meet hers, my desperation to be alone too obvious in the pain etched in my eyes. I took a step back. "I need to clean up now."

She held out her hand to touch me but I pulled back. "If you're sure. We're here when you're done. Roberto has unpacked the food. We'll see you soon for something to eat." Her voice, more of a command than a request, caused me to sigh.

"I want to be alone for a bit."

"You need to eat even if you don't feel like it. You need to talk. Please." The ice that usually filled her eyes had melted, and I fought the urge to grab her and hug her.

"Okay."

I walked around her, aware of her eyes following me. I grabbed two large bottles of water and headed past them to my room. My sanctuary.

My room felt empty. I dumped the bottles on the floor and threw myself on the bed. I cuddled my comforter, burying my face in it. I sank into my own bubble, the depth of my despair threatening to suffocate me. Jen lay next to me, her paws touching my arm, and I rubbed my hand in her thick fur, allowing her heat to warm my hand.

"Is this why the universe sent you to me? So I wouldn't be alone?" She licked my face and tears came once more. I stared at her face, noticing the blood and soot from my hands on it. "Think we both need a clean?"

I threw off my blood-stained clothes till I stood in my underwear. My reflection appalled me and I looked away. My entire body was smeared with the red paint of death. I stripped and grabbed a rag, wiping from the top down, starting with my hair, which I had to soak several times, the red highlights refusing to budge.

The puddle forming around my feet, pink and swirling as it tried to fill the room, proved to entertain Jen. She jumped up and down in it, splashing me with the blood I had just washed away. By the time I was brave enough to look back at my reflection, all visible stain of today was gone, but I knew the stains inside would never be washed away. They had scarred me and shaped me into somebody I hoped I would not grow to hate.

I cleaned Jen before dressing myself, which seemed to be less fun than playing in the water. I chased her around, soaking the room until I gave up. Time for Future Alex to get dressed, and I gazed at the Converse sneakers Danny and Calesta had given me yesterday. How could I have outgrown them already? The colorful shoes were too juvenile and pointless now.

I pulled clothes from my wardrobe, discarding everything that wasn't black until my room was a mass of color. I gripped my mother's Firestone, wondering what magic it held to allow me to burn an entire house yet walk away unburned. Perhaps some of my mother's stories weren't so ridiculous.

I placed it under layers of tight black clothing suited to the next step on my newfound path. My path was outside of here, and I pulled on the knee-length black boots Calesta had tried to get me to wear many times. I rummaged through my bag, pulled out the hair clips I had borrowed in Salem, and scraped my hair off my face.

It was time to say my goodbyes to Danny and Calesta, and the walk back to the garden seemed to be everlasting. My breathing became heavy, and I stopped several times to center myself before I stood in front of the wall of windows leading to the courtyard. Roberto and Abi were nowhere to be seen, and I presumed they had gone to clean up.

I opened the door and hovered on the precipice, my foot hanging in the air as if an invisible force barred its way. My shoulders dropped and my resolve vanished. I looked at Jen, who was panting and begging to be allowed out. I stepped back to make room for her and said, "Go on." She didn't hesitate, running through the door and rolling around in the plants, the dirt sticking to her wet fur.

I walked through the doorway, joining her. I breathed in the smells of the plants and herbs that would always remind me of my mother. Their scents wrapped me and filled me, and I closed my eyes, standing in the moment, creating a memory. I tried to make the moment a celebration, the wonder of the life I had been afforded, and my senses responded.

I raised my head to the sky, the light of the sun warming my skin, while at the same time, the biting chill of the breeze reminded me I was alive. I sat on the ground, its cold dampness meeting my jeans. I ran my fingers through the leaves of the greenery, sending the smells floating into the air, allowing it to swirl around me. The soft, fluffy surface of one leaf would change to a rough leathery leaf as my hands swept back and forth, and I reached my energy down into the earth, joining my energy with it, feeling it consume yet complement mine.

I was lucky to not only have survived but to have flourished in our world after the Orange. My mother's words bounced around the cushioning of my brain, 'You will be the Light in the Orange; your generation has been given things we couldn't even dream of. You have a blank canvas and a unique set of gifts. Use them wisely.'

I had no idea how many of my mother's children still survived out there, but I knew I had to push my mother's destiny to the next step, and I couldn't do it here. I opened my eyes and placed the palms of my hands on the tree that stood green and central to our garden. Life could survive. If one tree could survive, so could many.

Life never ended, it changed. It was my job to make sure it changed for the better. Only I could direct my life, and now that I had nobody to rely on, I could, should, and would take steps, both bold and baby sized, toward it.

My energy met Abi and Roberto's, and I realized they had joined me. I turned, smiling.

"Hello, welcome to the future. Time for me to move on."

They rushed toward me and we hugged, lost in the depth and warmth of needing each other, leaning on each other, knowing if one of us moved, the other two would fall. When we let go, our sadness had transformed us, increased us into being something more, in a way only true loss can. We had lost something that forced us, forced me, to be all I was destined to be and had hidden.

Roberto breathed, hesitation hanging in his words. "I'm sorry, but we had made plans to meet up with two friends before we set out for Jericho. We don't want to leave you but we need to meet them." He looked at Abi, who nodded an unspoken agreement.

"Honey, we can't leave you here alone when we leave—"

"I'm not staying here. It's time for the next step, and Jericho seems like a good place to start." My words got muffled and echoed against her shoulder as she grabbed me.

"Do you want to come with us to meet Iggy and Emmy? We'll bring them back here. I know we've never allowed any strangers into what your mother's magic protected, but it's a bit of a moot point now. Abi says she'll stay with you if you don't think you're up to it, and I can go and collect them. It's completely up to you," Roberto said, staring at my face, trying to judge my reaction.

"I'd like to come, and I think it's time others saw what my mother made for us. She protected and taught us—no, she helped us find our inner magic so we could share it. I'm ready to meet your friends. Honestly." My words seemed to have come from a thought I hadn't been aware of having, yet I knew they were what I needed. We had one last hug before setting off.

It took an hour to arrive at the deserted mall where they had arranged to meet, moving through heavily housed streets. None of us were comfortable at being so open and visible. We had discussed taking the cars, but driving at night drew too much attention. We had left Jen behind. I was scared I would lose her in the dark.

Standing in front of the curved entrance that had once been glass, I stared at the tree sign hanging precariously from what once had been an archway. I'm not sure whether it was a result of my mother's stories or the constant sight of once-trees, but I had always been attracted to them. I dreamed of trees, connected to them, and felt a bond with them. Perhaps it was loneliness.

I was in the middle of pondering this and fiddling with my hair, which was fighting to be released from the confines of the hair clips, when an energy touched mine. I spun around, trying to see the source of it. I pushed back, probing to find out about the person, or persons, that were nearing. An inner jolt when my probe was repelled and a probe returned. I had never met anybody who could better my magic.

"Do you feel that?" I whispered.

Roberto chuckled, a small, quiet sound. "That'll be Iggy. He likes being felt before he's seen. Never understood why."

A voice behind me made me spin, nearly falling over as my hand instinctively raised.

"Yo. Hope you haven't been here long. Emmy, over here, was busy napping. And who are you?" He stepped out of the shadows to stare at me. "Love the hair . . . Fiery." His stature was a tool he used well. Taller than me and twice as broad, his muscular frame spoke of latent power and a man who hadn't suffered from the starvation many had lived through. His dark, deep-set eyes created a menacing look. His long hair and scruffy beard contradicted his smooth skin and made it difficult to age him.

Behind him, a short, thin man smiled. His dirty blond hair clung to his face, making it seem more pinched.

"Can we just go? I don't like being out after dark." He looked at me. "I'm Emmy," he said, reaching his hand out to me.

I placed my hand around his cold and delicate fingers. "I'm Alex. Nice to meet you." I turned to face Iggy. "Nice to meet you too."

He smirked, a dangerous taunt dancing in his eyes. "I think we already met. Next time, ask before you try to get in my head."

I blushed, turning my face and hoping the moonlight was soft enough to hide my embarrassment. "Can't promise that. Don't sneak up behind me and I won't have to."

I could hear Abi make a snorting noise behind me but carried on walking. Roberto sped up to stand next to me as we walked, the moon lighting our way. "He's a good guy. When I met him, he was younger than you," he whispered. "Give him a chance. He didn't have your mother but still found his magic. You might learn something from him."

The clouds covered the moon and we cast the world into darkness. Grateful for my hidden blush, I replied, "I will. I'm not good with strangers. I'll talk to him, though. I promise."

By the time we had returned to the school, fatigue ached every bone of my body, like a leaden weight filling me. I wanted to sleep. Jen stood at the door barking and panting when we walked through. She licked my face and ran in circles, showing her happiness after being left alone. I bent to stroke her until she darted past me to lick Iggy, and a pain stabbed in my chest. I could feel the muscles of my face stiffen, and I turned away to hide my annoyance.

"I'm off to bed. Today has been a nightmare and tomorrow's a new day."

TWELVE

IGGY

Life had always been about survival. The life my generation had been left offered no hope beyond existing.

Emmy and I had arrived at what had once been a shopping mall. Although the concept was one my generation never experienced, I did understand the excesses of the generations before me.

The giant tree sign had weathered in the years since the Orange, and we knew we were in the place Roberto and Abi had told us about.

Emmy sat down with a thud on the remnants of a wall. The exhaustion of the walk painted shadows on his face. The past few months had seemed to take a toll on him. He had always been the bouncing light of positivity. Even after David had died, he had hidden his pain. I worried if we didn't find a community soon I would lose him too.

I had been no more than three when I first saw him. I have little more than fragments of my father's stories, of sitting on his lap, and of the buzz of the many people who lived on our reservation. My life began on the day Emmy found me, crying, alone, and hungry.

He had been the face of a savior.

As the sun sunk below the horizon, we hid behind a collection of rubble around the side of the building. Emmy closed his eyes and I extended my aura, feeling for an early warning of anybody coming.

Telling stories of the school they had been raised in, Roberto and Abi had touched my heart. They spoke of a place filled with hope, with somebody to love them and guide their magical discovery.

A part of me ached, burning with jealousy. I had been saved by Emmy and David, but making sense of my magic had been trial and error.

When, at seven years old, I discovered that I knew the thoughts of people around me, neither Emmy nor David had any answers for me. David had taught me to read, and whenever I came across another book, I devoured it. The child in me had been sure that one of the books would hold an answer.

I never found the answer.

Perhaps the Orange had done it.

Perhaps the powers in the sky my father had talked of had given us the gifts to make up for what had been stolen from us.

Perhaps, as my father had said, my tribe had been gifted this to help them. I would never know.

Emmy made burbling sounds next to me by the time I sensed life coming our way. I soon recognized the auras of Roberto and Abi, but then somebody probed back. They had found me before I had found them. I closed my eyes, pushing their magic back toward them.

I had never anticipated magic more in tune, more powerful, than mine. Anger, tinged with amazement, tingled around my muscles.

I nudged Emmy, disturbing his slumber. He grunted, yawned, and looked up at me, his eyes widening with fear. It was a sad testament to our life that fear was always our first waking thought.

"It's them. They're here," I said, pulling him up by his arm. "And, they're not alone."

His eyebrows furrowed to create a deep crease on his forehead. He tilted his head to the side. "Are they with somebody or is somebody else, besides them, here?"

"It's a she and she feels safe. I'm guessing she's safe."

"You're guessing?"

"Her magic is stronger than mine. When I reached for her, she probed me. But, I'm sure she's safe."

He stared at me for a moment, contemplating his next words. "Okay, let's go and meet them, then."

As we edged around the corner, leaving the safety of our hiding space, we saw the outlines of three people, their silhouettes illuminated by the moonlight. Roberto and Abi I recognized, but my attention was drawn to the third silhouette, tall, thin, and framed by a mass of curls.

As they moved closer, I found my mouth getting dry as nervousness constricted my throat. As they wandered, unable to see us hidden in the shadows, I took a moment to feel the aura of the new person. The more I probed, the more she probed back. I sensed, for the first time, her magic would exceed mine with ease.

We watched as they passed us, checking they weren't being followed, before stepping out of the shadows.

"Yo. Hope you haven't been here long. Emmy, over here, was busy napping."

They spun around to face our direction. The moonlight, now shining on their faces, showed the smiles of Roberto and Abi, but my attention was fixed on the red-haired female trailing behind. Her face, beneath the perfect features, spoke of the pain we all knew, and I wondered who she had lost.

"And who are you?" I walked to stand in front of her. "Love the hair . . . Fiery," I added, as though finding an excuse for my inability to move my eyes from her face.

We stood there, wrapped in the silence of the night, both of us hunting for words.

It was Emmy, moving from behind me to walk toward Roberto and Abi, who broke the moment. "Can we just go? I don't like being out after dark." He looked at the redhead. "I'm Emmy," he said, reaching his hand out to her.

My hand fidgeted, eager to reach out and touch her. I watched as Emmy shook her hand.

They exchanged pleasantries as I stood mute until I realized she was talking to me. "Nice to meet you too," she said, and I reached out my hand.

My head scrambled for the words I wanted to say. Instead, I blurted out, "I think we already met. Next time, ask before you try to get in my head." My insides twisted. My default defense mechanism of wit seemed so inappropriate. I pulled back my hand, stuffing them both in my pockets, grateful the moonlight behind me hid my annoyance with myself.

She blushed, and a wave of guilt overtook me until I watched her posture straighten and she replied, "Can't promise that. Don't sneak up behind me and I won't have to."

My mouth closed and I followed the four of them, watching Emmy catch up with Roberto and Abi. The redhead distanced herself from the group, isolating herself in a way I recognized as a behavior I was guilty of.

Every muscle in my body screamed to follow her and chat, but the sadness surrounding her warned me off and I held back.

I realized I had paid no attention to the route we had traveled when the others led the way into a large, modern building, and I was aware I hadn't noticed it. When we entered it, the magic contained within it hit me unlike anything I had felt before. A sense of calm, life, and connection to something greater, wrapped its way around me.

Finding myself next to the redhead, I took a deep breath and turned to talk to her. At the same moment she announced she was heading to bed. A part of my heart sunk, filling with a disappointment that surprised me. As an introvert, I always hid on the periphery of any group, watching. Emmy had told me many times, my size, coupled with my constant glare and silence, made me seem intimidating to others. It was who I was, but, for no reason I could explain, I wanted to talk with her.

"Good night, Alex," called Roberto and Abi as she vanished up the stairs to my right.

"So, who is Alex? And where is everybody else?" I asked, moving to catch up to the others as they walked along the length of the long corridor.

I stopped, spotting a garden behind the glass wall of the corridor. "How? What?" I mumbled to myself. I had never seen so much life. Plants, trees, and vegetables grew with an abundant disinterest in the devastation of life outside.

Laying my hands on the glass, I closed my eyes, breathing in the life of the school. The latent magic was so embodied in every strand of the building. I wondered at the sensation of being surrounded by magic. Was it the containment that caused the buildup, was it the people, or was it just years of magic happening in one place?

Whatever the reason, the garden was the most beautiful thing I had ever seen. Never had I seen so much plant life unhindered by the Orange. The garden was a vision of hope.

It was Abi's voice that broke the spell. "It's amazing, isn't it. Jennifer planted it shortly after the Orange. Initially, it was full of vegetables so we wouldn't starve. But, as time went on and our numbers dwindled and we built up our stores from scavenging, we planted flowers and plants, just because they were beautiful. She said there is always room for more beauty in an ugly world."

"Wise words." I stepped back, looking along the length of the corridor, realizing Roberto and Emmy had disappeared.

"They went to grab something to eat and to map out our plans for tomorrow. Today has been an eventful day for us. Well, mostly for Alex, and we aren't sure whether we can come." She placed her hand on my arm. "We didn't realize there were only Alex, Danny, and Calesta left here. The others had all gone to see the outside world. But, when we were scavenging, Danny and Calesta were killed. It's a lot for Alex and we can't go and leave her."

I reflected on the sadness I had seen in Alex's eyes. "Of course. We can hang back a few days if you want. If you decide not to come with us, we'll understand."

Matching Abi's steps, I followed her into the depths of the school that had been her childhood home. "I don't get why you all left. This place is . . . Well, it seems so safe."

"I can see that. I can't explain it." She paused for a bit, deep in thought. "I don't think Jennifer expected us to stay. She was preparing us for out there. She taught us the skills to survive. Magic being one of those."

She spun around to face me. "But, this is the only world Alex has ever known. Jennifer was her mother. She has ties to this place that go beyond ours."

"There are a lot worse places to spend a few days than here," I said, not entirely sure I had said the words out loud.

Before long, the wall of glass vanished and we found ourselves in a vast, open room with functional tables and chairs. Emmy and Roberto sat against one wall, plates of food laid out on the table. I tried to imagine the room full of young people, all surviving the Orange. Then, I thought about my life, constantly moving, looking for somewhere, following along behind Emmy and David, never knowing safety.

THIRTEEN

BILLEY

I watched the sunset from my window. Its dim glow added warmth to the barren landscape. My mind was still full of thoughts about Geilis, about the fantastical stories she told.

The fragments of memories, if indeed they were memories, matched with the tales she told. Yet, it was incomprehensible to believe I was hundreds of years old. Although, I did not know my history. My life was a blank and she offered the possibility of filling it in.

The smells floating up from downstairs pulled me from my thoughts, my stomach grumbled, and, for once, I longed to be lost in a conversation about others. To sit around the table thinking about their lives rather than mine.

Codrin and Gaevoin sat at the table. They looked up, both nodding in acknowledgment of my arrival, and then continued their discussion.

"Do you need a hand?" I asked Brigina before sitting at the table, knowing full well she was almost done and it was a safe question.

"No, no," she said, waving me to sit. "It's all ready. Eat and enjoy."

The evening vanished in familiar conversations about work, studies, and general nothingness. I did belong here. Despite my best efforts, Gaevoin and Brigina had become my family.

Codrin rose from the table first to head to bed. I was about to follow when I noticed Brigina's face. Her usual happy face was frowning, the corners of her lips forming small wrinkles as she failed to force a smile. I sat without a word, waiting.

Her eyes darted to Gaevoin and back at me, pleading with him to speak. Eventually, he spoke and shattered my world.

"We had a communication from Central today. They are coming in the morning to meet with us about your future. They're, well, they think, maybe . . ." His words trailed off into silence.

"What he means to say is," Brigina interrupted, "they think maybe this isn't the right setting for you. They want to chat with us, and the Institute, and about, perhaps, sending you to the other Institute."

I found myself standing, my chair clattering to the floor behind me. "No. They can't do that. I won't be locked up, forced to learn. I enjoy knowledge. This isn't fair." My voice began to crack and I sucked in air, swallowing to fight back the tears I feared were on their way. I looked from one to the other, their faces echoing my feelings.

Gaevoin rose and wrapped his arms around me. "We hold a lot of sway and our opinion is that you are where you belong. Have faith in us. We won't let them."

I pulled away, backing toward the stairs to my room. "But, you can't stop them if they decide I need to go, can you?"

Their mouths opened to argue but no words came. I knew the answer.

Running into my room, I slammed the door and leaned against it, sliding my back down it. Tears flooded, leaving dark spots on the grey of my pinafore dress, and I rubbed my face with my sleeve. The tears began to dry and I found myself thumping the floor.

I had one world I couldn't remember but left for a reason, and one world that no longer wanted me.

Eventually, the fatigue from crying, anger, and the vast mixing bowl of emotions raging through me took hold, and my body gave up the battle. Fully dressed, soaked in tears, and with every muscle tensing in response, my sleep was more of a half-slumber. My mind still raced after my body had given up. Some hours later, screaming filled my head, and I woke to find the house silent, and darkness coated everything.

At some point, my overthinking brain had come to the conclusion that I had to understand why I had left Solas. Why would I have put myself through this?

Geilis's voice reminding me that, if ever I needed her, she would be there for me, echoed around in my head. The memory managed to compete with the Banshee noises clouding my head.

I pulled the curtains open, staring at the vast expanse of black where the view of Bearaig should be. My eyes fixed on the place where the hill with my trees should be. I imagined I saw them. In my head, they stood, a sanctuary from the screams, the fears, and the emotions racking my body.

I grabbed the old grey blanket from my bed and wrapped it around me. Glancing around the room, I worried what Gaevoin and Brigina would think if they woke and I wasn't here. I scribbled a note, telling them I had gone for a walk and I would be back soon. I placed it on my pillow and paused for a moment. I rummaged through the piles of books on my desk for the solar torch I used for reading in bed on the many nights I couldn't sleep. I found it and held it, staring at it. I had no idea how much light was left in it. With a deep sigh that filled the stillness of the night, I squeezed it into my pocket and headed down the stairs, avoiding the ones I knew squeaked.

With my hand brushing the handle to my door, a sound echoed through the peace of the night. The screaming in my head returned. This time, though, I spun my head, searching my room, expecting to see the source standing next to me. My head, the room, the house filled with screams, and I could no longer tell what was in my head and what was real.

Holding my head, a pain unlike anything I knew sliced at my body and mind, and I landed on the floor. I gasped for air. I battled to hear through the fog of the screams. I fought for clarity. My brain sought to hear the sound with logic, separating the pain from the sound in my head and the sounds in the house. With my breathing slowing, I opened my eyes.

Every second brought me one step closer to an uncomfortable calm. Calm should never belong in the midst of this, should it? The more I focused on each breath, the more the screams in my head subsided.

Managing to push myself up on the bed, I listened. A newfound fear manacled my limbs. I began to struggle to breathe again. My throat constricted and panic blocked my airways.

The screams were real.

Screaming filled the house, painting the night bright red.

Tears rolled down my cheeks. I gasped for air. I knew the owners of the screams.

Brigina and Gaevoin screamed. Gurgling, pain-filled screams. Anguish in every millisecond of them.

I ran through the corridors of the house with a strange, eerie energy, oblivious to the danger I would find when I found the source.

My feet stumbled when I passed the door to Codrin's room. The door lay open. Inside, lying in a halo of red, almost black in the pale light of the moon, was the body of Codrin. His hand stretched for something he never reached. His body, twisted in an unnatural pose, forced me to stop. I stared. My eyes sought to make sense of the scene.

My feet stumbled backwards, and, as my back hit the wall, I stood, unable to look away. His hair glinted as the moonlight streaming through his open window bounced off it. It took me a few seconds to realize the blood created the reflected light.

I edged forward, stopping in the doorway. I crouched down and reached out my hand. I hesitated to touch him but knew I needed to know he was dead.

"Codrin," I whispered. My voice cracked and, when I leaned in, I fell. My hands slid in the warm slick of his blood, and, in a bid to right myself, I pushed my weight backwards.

My back crashed against the doorframe.

Shaking the blood on my hands, a gurgled sound broke free from my throat. It took with it the fear. I had seen death, I had touched death, I was alive. I had no place in my head for it. I was too busy trying to put together the fragments of understanding I had.

The screaming in my head dragged me back to full attention. This time, I could no longer hear Brigina and Gaevoin, only the screams that had been partying in my head since I met Geilis.

Was Geilis responsible for them?

I squirmed onto my hands and knees, edging toward Codrin until I lay my hand on his lifeless body. The warmth of my tears was the only movement or sign of life in the room. I scrambled to my feet, refusing to look at him. My hands reached for the doorframe, my fingers oblivious to the rough wooden splinters where it must have been forced open. I labored to place one foot in front of the other. They took unsteady and uneven steps in the direction of Brigina and Gaevoin's room.

Since I had first come to live here, little more than an angry child, there had been no more than a handful of occasions when I set foot inside their room.

They had given me a space of my own and they rarely entered it. I, in return, allowed them their one place of peace. A strange sensation, an amalgamation of conflicting emotions, caused my fingers to hover on the door handle. The silence now filling the house created a lump in my throat, threatening to make me vomit everywhere.

Was it fear at what I might find?

Was it the knowledge that silence was worse?

Was it my head refusing to acknowledge what my heart already knew?

As I pushed the door open enough to peer around the edge, I held my breath.

The room was cloaked in darkness. Everything was as it should be. I saw Brigina sleeping in the bed, her clothes folded in a bundle on her bedside table, and the tiniest sliver of moonlight creeping under the curtains.

With a creak that filled the night, I nudged the door farther. My hands flew to cover my mouth as my stomach flipped in revolt at the vision before me.

The dim light provided more than I would wish for. Gaevoin's body lay half slumped against the bed, his arm twisted around the bedpost in an unnatural position. His face, misshapen and bloated, looked so little like the man who had guided me over the years. His kind smile, replaced with swelling, bruising, and cuts, had become difficult to recognize. His clothing, full of rips and slashes, told a story of resistance and defense. His side of the room created a different picture from Brigina's side. The bedside table and cozy chair he liked to read in were both broken and scattered across the floor. Brigina may have had little warning of what was happening, but Gaevoin had fought back.

Whether I stood there for a minute or an hour, I still don't know. I am also unsure how I came to be lying on the floor, my ugly, pain-filled sobs mixing with the death and destruction of the room.

Why had I been left? How had I survived?

My body gasped for air as the realization dawned on me. Everybody would assume I had done this. Had I?

As I stepped out of the house, the cold night bit at my skin. I paused, questioning my choice. I pulled the blanket tighter and stared into the darkness, squinting to adjust to the black of the night. The moon, too small to be of much use, was hidden behind clouds, or what I presumed were clouds. It hid behind the dark sky, refusing to even give me silhouettes.

The loud clicking of the torch as I pushed the switch to turn it on magnified in the quiet of the night. I pointed the light into the night and it created a glow around me, failing to show much ahead of me. I moved it to shine on the ground. The best I could hope for was seeing my next step. I had to rely on my mind to remember the route without any ability to see it. I let out a moaning sigh from deep inside me. The volume of it surprised me. I took one step and then another, concentrating on nothing more than the next step.

A calm settled over me as my focus narrowed to the next step, not caring about the second or the third step.

The smattering of bushes and trees told me I was near the hill. A thudding sound broke the stillness of the air. A thundering, uniformed sound made the ground vibrate.

My feet froze to the spot and my heart pounded with so much volume it was impossible to believe only I could hear it.

The thudding grew louder and I realized it was moving toward me. Whatever the source of the banging, it wasn't my heart any longer, and it was headed in my direction. The closer it came, the more I understood it had a rhythm. A rhythm somewhere at the back of my mind I recognized.

A blue-grey tail whooshed past me, sending me spilling onto the cold, hard ground. I stared after it. A horse? Horses were used for transport but I had never seen one wild.

I stared at the blackness of the space it had vanished into. Its hooves faded, and I crawled to recover my torch, glowing in the long grass around me. I waved it to illuminate the area around me. As if understanding my frustration, the clouds moved enough to allow the moon to cast a faint glow over my surroundings, casting dark shadows.

Ahead of me, the fuzzy-headed shape of my trees loomed. They called me. This time, not in my head. Not in my heart. But, they called with a need. A familiar sense of belonging they had always held for me.

Getting closer to the top of the hill, the trees towering over me, the torch sputtered. It flickered on and off, on and off, and died.

I stood in the middle of the trees. Only thin strands of moonlight flitting through the leaves broke the gloom.

I reached my hands out in front of me to feel for my large, comfortable tree. When my hand touched the rough bark, I lowered myself. My fingers ran along the lines and crevices of its trunk until they found roots and then grass. I twisted to wriggle into a comfy position and leaned against it.

Again, I realized how deafening the silence was. I sat wondering what I had hoped to gain from being here.

Life had decided I wasn't allowed to belong here with Gaevoin and Brigina. But, here, with my trees, I knew belonging. I had recognized it the first time I found this place.

The dampness of the ground soaked through my blanket, chilling me, then warmed, and I settled into a relaxed state. My muscles and limbs loosened, my head grew lighter, and I embraced the peace of this moment.

This time, I heard Geilis coming. The crunching of leaves and a small crack as she stood on a twig told me she was here.

"I wasn't sure you'd come," I said.

"I told you I would" came the reply from the darkness.

"How did you know? How did you know I'd be here?" I asked as she appeared, the moonlight casting her shadow on my legs.

"We are both connected to the Crann. You share with it and it shares with me. I know what you know. You know what I know. We are its guardians."

I curled my hands into my palms, determined not to reach out to touch her, to make sure she was real. "But, I don't know what you know." My words hung in the air as we looked at each other. Our eyes locked, both of us refusing to look away.

She touched my hands, curling her fingers around mine, and, with the slow patience of one who knew she could move slowly or not at all, intertwined them with mine.

"Do you remember when I first told you about Solas? The light you saw. That was the connection. You just have to allow the Crann to share it all with you." She moved closer, pulling my hand to her heart. "Can you just trust me?"

Her words seemed to fill the air while, at the same time, they sucked the air from the space. Could I trust somebody I still struggled to believe was real? Somebody who, despite the feeling of familiarity, was a stranger. Yet, the stories she told of strange and far-off places resonated with me.

Was the connection we shared enough when we were so far apart in experiences? So far apart in every way?

I looked in her eyes, the moonlight catching enough to show me the golden specks sparkling in the blue depth. I wanted to believe. My body ached to respond to the love, warmth, and security I found when she was near.

"I want to," I replied, meaning the words, yet unable to break the barrier, shielding my heart and my head. I grasped her hands, and she responded by squeezing mine.

"I do want to believe, but . . ." My voice trailed off, vanishing in the black expanse of the night. My eyes fell to ponder the spots of blood on my trousers I hadn't managed to clean away.

Her eyes tracked my line of vision to see what I saw. "Are you hurt? Is that blood?" Her hand brushed my face, her eyes searching for the answer my mouth refused to give.

I shook my head. "It . . . isn't . . . mine," I said through silent sobs.

"Who? What?" Her beautiful face scrunched up, confusion twisting it.

I gazed at the two creases forming between her eyebrows. A part of me wanted to stroke them, to banish them from the perfection of her face. "I don't know. They're . . ." I stared into her eyes, the blue almost icy in the moonlight. I straightened my shoulders and took a deep breath before carrying on. "They're dead. Somebody killed them all. Gaevoin, Brigina, Codrin. There was this dreadful screaming and then they were . . . they were . . . They're all dead." My shoulders slumped and my body sobbed but no tears came. The tears that had sought to clear the bloodstains of Brigina and Gaevoin's bedroom had run out. I was now empty in so many ways.

Geilis leaned back, lowering her face till our eyes met. "Do you believe I would hurt you or harm you? Do you feel, really feel, deep in your soul, that I would hurt you or risk you in any way?" Her eyes widened, pleading with me to trust her.

"I . . . I do trust you. It's just . . ." Again my voice vanished, the rest of the words jumbling in my head. I breathed in the cold air, again and again, and again. "I do trust you." A part of me, hidden deep inside, that I knew was there yet didn't recognize, screamed at me. "I do trust," I said again, louder.

Then, as though a dam holding back the vastness of emotions had broken, the tears returned.

She tilted her head forward and lowered her lips to brush mine. My throat made a sharp intake, creating a sound I had never heard myself make before.

Panic, trust, and hope warmed me down to my soul, and I leaned into her lips.

Her warmth, her love, her calm anchored me in the moment as though time had stood still.

My heart pounded and my body, cold against the night mere minutes earlier, filled with the glow of her. I could see and feel her, her aura, her very essence. Without thinking or knowing what I was doing, my body moved without moving to feel her. Every inch of me wanted to feel her and her calm.

Her.

A sensation took my fear and despair and replaced it with her peace. I opened my eyes, pulling back just a fraction to stare in her face. To believe she was real. To be with her.

Her face, somehow glowing with cheer, changed. Her smile reached her eyes and they sparkled in the reflected glow of the moon. But, they sparkled with something I could only describe as love. Her whole face lifted, accentuating her cheekbones, and I watched as her aura melded with mine. A rainbow of colors surrounded us.

Then I saw it. I saw the Crann.

I knew it was the Crann.

I recognized and remembered it.

The pages of my mind filled with memories as though written by a newly sharpened pencil that glided across the paper.

FOURTEEN

IGGY

Magic oozed from every pore of the school, creating a suffocating atmosphere. Roberto and Abi had been oblivious to it. Having grown up and developed their gifts in the school, they accepted this was how the building always was. The prevailing air of magic trapped inside whatever shielded the building from the outside, the aftereffects of the Orange, and the ravages of time, made my control of my own magic painful. Emmy, with no access to magic, enjoyed the calm and safety of the building.

I had tossed around the bed for most of the night. The functional room, with nothing more than an old metal bed and a battered chest of drawers, brought no peace. Yet, the pristine room gave no indication of the chaos outside the walls of the school. My mind wandered back through time, dredging up snippets of my early life. Moments forgotten, long ago.

I thought of my mother. I thought of my childhood bedroom. My stomach churned as I fought to remember her face. Instead, her smell and warmth filled my dreams.

Drifting between past and present, jealousy knotting my guts, I contemplated the world Alex grew up in. Her magic had been nurtured in this safe space. She had been robbed of her mother when she was young but not as young as me. Her mother saw the Orange, guided the children to a new future. They lived with a sense of security and safety in this place. I had memories filled with fear and death. My earliest memories were of watching my father wither and die in the aftermath of the Orange.

The sense of knowing I was alone, uncared for, and facing death stayed with me. Emmy provided me with somebody to guide me and care for me. But, magic and the confusion of navigating my way through had fallen to me.

Early memories, few and far between, of my father sitting with me, telling me stories of my ancestors, had been my first thoughts when I began to discover the connection to magic. I battled in my childish mind to make sense of them, assuming it was something I was blessed with due to my ancestors. With time, I met others who found a connection to the magic. We talked and I absorbed every thought they provided me with. I mashed all the weird and wonderful ideas into one self-made theory about magic. I hid it. I feared it. I was scared to be a freak. Yet, here everybody had been raised to embrace it, grab it, and nurture it. They didn't understand their good fortune being raised in such a safe space.

My head knew they struggled and lost, as I had. Yet, they knew safety. I wondered if I had ever lived at any moment knowing the warmth and security they had.

Eventually, I pulled on my clothes, dressing as always to flee at any given second. Plodding through the school, basking in the dim morning light filling the outside world, my feet echoed around me, accentuating the silence and isolation.

Before long, I took one turn too many and found myself in a part of the school nobody had used in many years.

Pushing a set of double doors that swung open to reveal shelves full of books, I stood there wondering at the knowledge crammed into these shelves. If not for the Orange, I would have gone to a school like this. I would have learned how to read the books filling this room. Instead, I stared, wondering at its magnificence.

I stepped as though scared to awaken the knowledge hidden in here. Some of the tables were covered in books, scattered with abandon, many of them open, and I wondered who read these. Who used this space and what were they searching for?

I ran my fingertips over the books, reaching my magic to sense them. The secret desire to absorb their information as I absorbed their magic sent a sadness through me, weighing me down. I allowed myself to ponder on the maybe of this place. Who would I be if I had been here instead of out there with Emmy?

Hunger dragged my attention back to the present, and I allowed a small sigh to fill the space before turning and closing the doors behind me. I pulled the doors, and a pang of guilt for disturbing the room caused me to pause as the doors gave up a click as they closed.

I moved with a new determination. Life handed me survival. I was grateful for it, but, was it enough?

My feet led me to the cafeteria I sat in last night listening to Roberto and Abi recounting the tale of Danny and Calesta, of their fears for Alex, and of their memories of growing up in this place. I had left them, not because I was tired, but because I couldn't understand why they chose the world outside when they had this.

Looking at the empty space and rows of tables and chairs, long unused, my mind scrambled to recall how I arrived here. My feet knew the way when my brain hadn't.

Rummaging through the shelves of scavenged food, I found myself overwhelmed with the choices. Never had I seen so much food in one place. Then, I spotted baskets brimming with vegetables and fruit from the garden I had seen through the glass wall last night.

I had seen many attempts to grow crops as we moved from one struggling community to another, but this was something I had never seen. I wiggled my hand into the middle of a basket. I let go of my magic, allowing it to feel the connection of the life in the food. Even now, no longer growing in the garden, it had traces of the magic it had used to grow.

My fingers wrapped around a carrot and pulled it out, causing the vegetables around it to collapse into the space it had been. I held it to my nose, smelling the newness of it. A new smell.

How had Alex's mother done it? How had they managed to keep it going?

The jealous sensation I had hidden from in my restless sleep last night wrenched at my insides again. They had used magic to bring life.

Biting down on the carrot, the crunch of it breaking between my teeth sent ripples of sound around the room. I closed my eyes, concentrating on the taste. A watery sweetness filled my mouth. I struggled to compare it to anything I had tasted before. I placed it on the worktop, grabbed for an apple, and bit into it. A spark of memory sent a warmth through my body as it recalled long-forgotten memories of life before the Orange. A joyous sadness ached at my heart.

I picked up an apple in each hand, the breaking sunlight reflecting off them, and wandered toward the garden. Since last night, when I first saw the greenery and vibrancy of the life and the school that had managed to defeat the death that ate up everywhere else, the pull of the garden's magic had stayed with me. The nagging guilt created by a sense of intrusion returned and made me pause. Pushing the glass doors open, the magic trapped among the trees, bushes, and plants called to me. A tickle brushed my arms and the hairs on them bristled. My feet still teetered in the doorway.

Everybody was still asleep and I was in no danger of seeing them soon. Yet, I doubted they would object. My guilt wasn't for them. It was for the person who created the magic. The person who trapped the magic in there. The person who had enough respect for life, even while others were scrambling to survive the Orange.

My first step caused me to close my eyes, breathing in the life held in the space. The scents of plants and flowers mixed to create something that forced me back to my childhood memories. I could, with my eyes closed, imagine I was four years old again in our family garden. My mother sat under the gnarled old oak reading a book. As she looked up at me, I remembered the feeling of love, the knowledge, and the security of being with her.

Then, as my nose grew used to the garden, something else attracted my attention and my eyes flew open. The magic of the space flowed through me unlike any I had known before. It didn't ask anything of me. It didn't want my magic. It wanted to meet and feel mine. Like a stream gently undulating on its path, it met me and pushed through me and around me as though I stood in its way. I wandered, each step an adventure, through the garden. My hands brushed through leaves, the life in them caressing my skin until I made it to the far corner, where the light struggled to reach. I sat down among the plants.

Her magic brushed against mine, although I couldn't see her. Her aura glowed as she stepped through the garden, a cacophony of color glowing in the most beautiful shades of purple and indigo complementing the greenery surrounding her. Her hair, blazing like a fire, merged with her aura, and I found myself holding my breath. She belonged here. She was one with the space.

I watched, hidden from sight by the bushes growing around me, as she knelt on the ground in front of the largest tree in the garden. Although its trunk, broad and dark, was no more than two meters tall, the green reaching out in all directions created an umbrella-like mass at least six meters high. My mind scrambled with questions about whether a tree so large could have grown after the Orange, or did it predate the end?

She shifted until she sat cross-legged with her hands lost in the grass. No matter how I tried, the nagging guilt of intruding eating at my insides, I couldn't look away. I stood slowly and, with each step closer, I found the image more entrancing. She had the look of somebody not of this world. She didn't belong in the world I knew. The death, despair, and ugliness of my world were not hers, and I regretted my blundering attempts at being funny last night. I now knew the toll the previous day must have taken on her, and my stomach cringed at the memory of our first meeting.

Taking a deep breath, I walked over toward her. Even with my guarded aura, I expected her to sense me, but by the time I stood behind her, she still hadn't noticed me and I began to fidget. Should I interrupt? Should I leave and pretend I didn't see her?

Standing there, my mouth opened and moved but nothing came out. My brain misfired and no questions, greetings, or words came forth.

As I towered over her, she looked up at me. Still, my mouth flapped in silence until I blurted out apologies and random nonsense. She smiled, somehow either too polite to comment or too oblivious to notice. I began to relax. Although not until after I'd made stupid small talk about her aura, breakfast, and nonsensical memories about fire-haired maidens from my childhood.

My insides shriveled and cringed the more I blustered and fought to sound in control of my own brain.

After a few moments too many of my awkwardness, she patted the ground next to her, asking me to sit with her. This close, I couldn't help but stare at her eyes. Last night with the darkness, I hadn't been able to see the amazing blueness of them, yet I could see the golden streaks glittering in there. The light in her eyes seemed so in contrast to the tale of Danny and Calesta I was told after she went to bed.

I found myself relaxing, and, before long, we were discussing her mother and her life here. I could see her shift and stiffen, and, despite the strange desire I had for her to come with us to Jericho, I shuffled back. I continued to chat, watching as her movements softened when I moved from her. The farther I went, the more her aura expanded, and I realized she held it back from mine. The rainbow colors of her aura danced around her.

The sudden weight of Jen as she laid herself across our laps, the heat of her body, and her panting as she glanced from Alex to me and back again could no longer be ignored. As Alex fussed with her fur, Jen's tail wagged with such force I held up my hand to avoid being slapped in the face. Watching Jen and Alex cheering each other, I found irrational jealousy sneaking into me.

Over the years since the Orange, Emmy and I traveled across much of North America, and this was the first dog I had ever seen that survived. She not just survived but she thrived. Her golden fur shone in the sunlight, now rising into the sky.

Yet, Alex seemed to accept the appearance of a dog without question.

Leaning back on my hands, I pushed my body backwards, slow enough so Jen wouldn't land in a furry ball on the grass, and stood up. I brushed down my clothes and held out my hand for Alex.

I turned enough to be able to see the doors back into the corridor, aware she was still holding my hand and staring at my face, an unasked question painting her eyes with quizzical creases.

"What is Iggy short for?" she asked.

The air trapped in my chest battled to compel my lungs to breathe. The heat of my face, with the return of my awkward discomfort around her, caused me to bumble again. "Oh, trust me, you don't want to know."

Tilting her head at me, her nose scrunched up and she stared at me. A smile, hidden from sight, caused the corners of her lips to crease.

"Oh, but I do, really," she said, her shoulders shuddering in a silent chuckle.

"Ignatius Dragonrider."

"Wow, that's quite a name. I know surnames kind of disappeared with the Orange, but Dragonrider seems a very unusual surname."

"Oh, no. My surname was Thrumblar. Dragonrider is like a middle name. In my tribe, being given a name to match your spirit animal was quite common."

"Your tribe?"

"Yes. I lived on a reservation in Canada, before. We were First Nation. It's a bit redundant to worry who was here first now. The question is who'll be here last." I could sense my body stiffen. Whether it was due to talking about the old world or because I told her more than anybody, except Emmy, I wasn't sure.

Holding out her hand, she smiled up at me and I again relaxed. "Well, it's a pleasure to properly meet you, Ignatius Dragonrider Thrumblar. I am Alex Chegasa."

An awkward laugh escaped from my lips before I could stop it. "It's nice to meet you, Alex Chegasa."

I strode toward the cafeteria, Jen plodding along beside me, glad my embarrassed face was hidden from Alex, who walked behind me.

FIFTEEN

ALEX

Sleep had been elusive, and despite the tiredness massaging every muscle in my body, by early morning I saw no point in the pretense of sleep anymore. The dreams, a reliving and reimagining of events I couldn't control and knew I had to just accept, caused me to wake in a sweat too many times.

The sun, hovering like a teasing promise on the horizon, told me my new life was about to begin, and I took the opportunity to say goodbye to the school before Roberto and Abi awoke. Jen lay across the foot of my bed and jumped up the second I sat up, her expectant eyes ready for a new day without question or expectation. Today was a blessing, an extra day that almost hadn't happened.

My clothes from last night sat in a black bundle, strewn across the old wooden chair next to my bed, and with the cold battling to reach my bones, I dressed quickly.

As Jen and I padded through the corridors, it was easy to believe we were alone, their empty anticipation suffocating me.

In the kitchen I pulled open the beat-up, old tin holding the remnants of my birthday cake and cut a slice, watching it collapse into bite-size crumbs. I placed it on a plate, putting it on the floor for Jen before having a second try with a sharper knife. The battered slice looked more appetizing and I munched with a hunger that surprised me. Jen looked up at me and at my cake, having demolished hers in the time it took me to cut the piece for myself.

I poured some water into a bowl, placing it on the floor while I poured a glass for myself. Watered and fed, I held the tin one last time, holding onto it as my vision blurred and I knew I would cry again. Taking a deep breath I tried to straighten my stooped shoulders, and a coldness froze the gaping chasm in my chest.

"Come on, let's get some fresh air," I said to Jen, who ran straight to the glass doors, her tongue hanging out and her whole body appearing to wag.

Walking into the garden, my eyes were drawn to my mother's tree and my arms hung at my sides. I rubbed the space between my ribs and the Firestone vibrated in response. Pulling my jumper's sleeves over my hands, I patted my eyes and dragged my feet to sit on the ground between the plants. I closed my eyes, controlling my breath, meditating.

My soul reached down into the earth, centering myself, and my energy charged. A sense of connection passed through my body as a floating sensation replaced the burden of guilt and sadness that hung deep inside. I sat like that for a while, enjoying the present.

An energy I knew could only be Iggy brushed against mine. I had never met anybody whose soul held as much magic and strength as mine. I turned to see his face staring down at me. Gazing up, the angle of the view made him seem even larger than the night before. How did anybody in this world get so large and so broad? His half-dressed presence caused me to hold my breath and avert my eyes.

"I'm sorry, I didn't mean to interrupt you. I didn't expect anybody else to be up, and when I spotted you, I . . . I . . . Well, your aura was amazing to look at. It was quite mesmerizing." His voice, soft, seemed at odds with the arrogant man I had met last night. He stood, his lips parted, words hanging silently from them. "I'll leave you alone. Do you want anything from the kitchen?" His eyes lingered as he slowly moved away, staring at my face, following the curls of my hair. "Your hair is amazing. My people have a prophecy about a fire-haired maiden. They would have seen you as a god." His cheeks reddened as he held his breath, and I smiled, knowing he had spoken an internal thought.

"Thank you, and I'm sorry we didn't get off to the best start last night. It wasn't a good day." My smile softened and warmed my face.

"Roberto and Abi told me about yesterday after you'd gone. I'm truly sorry about it. I'm also sorry I was a bit of an arrogant arse. I just never met anybody who could penetrate my energy and it took me by surprise." He looked away and his feet shuffled. I had perhaps misjudged him.

"Please, I wasn't exactly pleasant. It doesn't matter. Join me if you want." My eyes burned with the tears I wouldn't allow myself to cry. I looked away.

He sat next to me, so close his energy bristled with mine, and I flinched. "You're not good with people being close, are you? Can't blame you." He shuffled back a few steps before he continued. "I understand the wonders your mother did here. Roberto and Abi explained how she helped them, and many others, discover their inner magic. It's impressive, but growing up here, all alone . . . It must have been hard." His energy reached into the soil, and I could feel it connect with mine and I fidgeted. "There's a whole, great, big world out there. It isn't beautiful and not everybody is as good as you, but it's a shame to not have experienced it."

Silence fell and I pondered his words, listening to his slow breathing. I tilted my head slightly to the side to squint at his aura and wasn't disappointed. The indigo glow surrounding him glistened with strands of pink and green. As it grew, I found myself squirming to move. His connection was bright and bold to those of us who could see it. Nobody with such a beautiful aura could be the person I had imagined last night, and a pang of guilt shuddered through me.

We sat there for a while until Jen decided she was bored and laid her body across our laps. Iggy looked at me and spoke in a soft, warm tone. "I think somebody is bored. Do you wonder why the universe sent you a dog?"

His question threw me and my brain scrambled for an answer. "I thought my mother sent her to keep me company."

"That's a lovely thought. It's certainly a long time since I saw a dog. I wonder if it wasn't to take you out of your shell. To force you to walk, to discover new things. Dogs are such curious animals." He shrugged, not expecting an answer, as he pushed himself up and reached a hand down to me.

I hesitated for a second, rubbing my sweaty hands on my jeans, before placing my hand in his and allowing him to pull me up. I stared at his face.

"What is Iggy short for?" I asked, unconsciously wrinkling my nose.

He laughed. "Oh, trust me, you don't want to know."

"Oh, but I do, really."

He looked at me, his face flushing as he chewed on his bottom lip. "Ignatius Dragonrider."

"Wow, that's quite a name. I know surnames kind of disappeared with the Orange, but Dragonrider seems a very unusual surname."

"Oh, no. My surname was Thrumblar. Dragonrider is like a middle name. In my tribe, being given a name to match your spirit animal was quite common."

"Your tribe?"

"Yes. I lived on a reservation in Canada, before. We were First Nation. It's a bit redundant to worry who was here first now. The question is who'll be here last." A small grimace tightened the muscles in his face.

I held out my hand. "Well it's a pleasure to properly meet you, Ignatius Dragonrider Thrumblar. I'm Alex Chegasa."

He let out a small burbling laugh. "It's nice to meet you, Alex Chegasa," he said, turning to walk to the cafeteria. I watched Jen follow him. I trailed behind them, shoving my hands in my pockets, questioning my initial thoughts about this man.

We sat making small talk and learning about each other for hours until the others arrived. Roberto's eyes studied me, looking for signs of yesterday's toll. I eventually leaned in to whisper in his ear, "I'm fine. I will survive. You don't need to keep worrying about me."

He smiled and patted my knee. "I know."

Sixteen

ALEX

Hours later, I sat back in the cafeteria waiting for the others to arrive. We had all parted company to prepare for our journey to find Jericho. I had little to pack. My mother's pendant, a comforter, a book, a change of clothes, a bowl for Jen, and whatever food and water I could easily carry. Little else mattered. They were just belongings. Things.

Emmy was first to arrive, his blond hair no longer sticking to his face. He had clearly made use of the clean water to wash and change clothes. We had said very little to each other and an awkward tension filled the space between us. I gave an internal sigh when Roberto and Abi arrived. Iggy arrived last, now clean-shaven. His now-gone beard had taken the years with it, and his angular face smiled as he entered the room. "Okay, ready to go, people?"

We discussed using the car, but, given it would need to be deserted, it seemed unfair to anybody who needed the school after us. Previous students often visited, using it as a safe haven they could rely on. I didn't want to disrespect my mother's memory by taking the car. Besides, it wasn't lunchtime yet, and it should only take three hours to walk there. Although none of us knew how we would find it once we got there.

Despite the cold, I soon found myself baking hot under the many layers of black and wrapped my coat and jumper around my waist. The water, which hadn't seemed heavy when we left, now dug into my shoulders and my arms moaned in response. I moved it from shoulder to shoulder, falling farther behind each time, until Emmy eventually called the others to a stop.

"Come on, she's clearly struggling under the weight of the water. Iggy, give her a hand, eh?" he said, bending to pick up my rucksack that held my comforter and clothing.

Iggy turned to look at me, pinching his lips together as he clenched his jaw, and gave a heavy sigh. "Fine, but she needs to be able to carry her own if she intends to survive out here," he said, and I realized he was everything I had imagined him to be last night. This morning had been a temporary illusion.

I wanted to argue, feeling my hands clench and my face redden, but knew there was little point. I did need his help and I wasn't going to be stupid enough to allow my pride to drag me down.

"Thank you," I mumbled as he sauntered off ahead, giving no reply.

Abi fell back to stand next to me, and with her on one side and Emmy on the other, we continued. My eyes took in everything, trying to make sure I could find my way home if necessary, but the increasingly green undergrowth caught my eye. Life was returning—even if it was slowly—to our world.

I turned to Emmy to make conversation and satisfy my curiosity. "So, where did you meet Iggy?"

"Oh, we met years ago on the road from Canada. He was so young and yet so feisty. I was with my husband and some friends. Over the years, they all died and now there's only the two of us. He makes out like he's all hard and grown up, but he isn't really. He's only a few years older than you."

A barking laugh caught in my throat. The hypocrisy of him. He carried himself like he was much older, and yet, until I joined, he would have been the baby of the group. Calming my breath and waiting for the flush of my cheeks to lessen, I answered, "I thought he was much older than me. How old are you, if you don't mind me asking?"

He laughed. "I've kinda lost track. Maybe thirty-eight or thirty-nine. Gave up counting after the war."

"I was only three, so I don't remember much about before. I guess this is the only world I know, but I don't know it at all. I spent my whole life hiding in the school. I probably should have been better prepared." I lowered my head to stare at my feet as we plodded on.

"From what Roberto and Abi have told me, you've learned a lot and are well prepared for the dangers of our world," he said, placing his hand on my back. "You'll be fine, trust me."

I wondered what bit of my life so far made him believe I was prepared to meet the world. Before long Abi stopped and said she was hungry, and a flood of relief washed over me. We left the road to hide behind some almost-trees to eat and drink. Jen was the first one to get frustrated and wandered farther off into the trees, and I followed to bring her back.

I found her in the middle of a clearing, sniffing at the green undergrowth. I called her back, but she lay down and rolled over, so I walked toward her. I knelt to stroke her stomach and her tail wagged. I placed my other hand on the ground, the damp coating on the top of the plants chilling my hand. I reached to feel the energy of the earth. I closed my eyes and breathed until small flowers grew up, filling the small clearing.

"Pretty, eh, Jen." She rolled over and licked my face. "C'mon, let's go."

A voice behind me caused me to stumble. "That's a clever trick. How'd you do that?"

I spun around to stare into the eyes of Iggy. "Do what?"

"The flowers." His forehead frowned while he stared, with a shaking of his head, at the flowers carpeting the ground. "You know what I meant."

As the words jumbled in my mouth, I spluttered, "I just did."

"Well, it's a neat trick. Anyway, the others sent me to find you. We need to head out," he replied, crossing his arms and tapping his foot.

I stood up to follow him, my hands stuffed in my pockets while my shoulders stooped. I had only taken a few steps when an energy met mine. There were other people near us. "Wait, do you feel that."

"Yes. Somebody's following us. Quick, we need to get the others." He grabbed my arm, almost dragging me, when a group of six people appeared from between the trees.

"What have we here then?" said the grey-haired man clearly in charge of the group.

My leg muscles tightened while I tried to decide whether we needed to fight or flee. My eyes darted around at the faces, ending on Iggy's. His jaw hardened and his wide-legged stance told me he wasn't for running.

Iggy opened his mouth to speak and I prepared for the backlash. "We don't want any trouble. We're just passing through so we'll leave you alone."

"You'll leave when we say. Let's not get ahead of ourselves." The man leered through his narrow eyes, his twisted smile saying what his words didn't. He walked toward me, and Iggy moved to stand beside me, his fingers gripping my wrist. The man began to shout, spitting his words. "Separate them," he screamed, waving his hands at the others who stood behind him.

I knew we couldn't hope to fight six of them and looked up at Iggy's eyes, cold and hard, fixed on the group. Out of nowhere, Jen ran and jumped at the man, clamping her jaws on the man's arm. The others momentarily lost control, and we ran for it, Iggy dragging me.

"No. I'm not leaving Jen behind." I fought back against his grip, struggling to break free. A yelp came from Jen, and I broke free, running toward her.

Facing the group, I glared. "Let her go. Jen, come here." She sat beside me and we were back at a stalemate. A burning in my chest caused me to place my hand on it, feeling the pulsing and burning of my mother's Firestone. I grabbed it, as I had yesterday. Could I control the fire, or risk burning my friends with it? I turned to Iggy, "Run."

Within a second the flames appeared in my hand, and with a wave of the other hand, the beautiful blue flowers caught fire and engulfed the others. Their screams filled the air as they stumbled for us, landing in burning blobs on the ground. I stood, frozen to the spot, until Iggy grabbed my wrist, pulling me away. I lost my footing and fell on the ground behind him, unable to take my eyes off the flaming masses writhing on the ground.

The screams drew the others, and when I spotted Roberto and Abi, I ran to them. Their faces looked beyond us to take in the sight. The screams stopped and the burning masses became still. I released the Firestone, letting the chain fall back around my neck, and the fire disappeared. The smell of burning and death drifted through the air.

Silence filled the space and Iggy strode toward me and grabbed my wrist. "What the hell was that?" he asked, his voice gruff and menacing. "Who can control fire, seriously?"

I stared at him, unable to find the words. I doubled over, my stomach retched, and my lunch landed on the ground. Abi rubbed my back and, at the same time, Emmy moved to stand in front of Iggy.

"She just saved your life, probably all our lives. A thank you wouldn't hurt."

Iggy strode off and I watched his back as he disappeared between the trees. I stumbled a few steps to follow him. Roberto slipped his arms under mine, lifting me and holding me. "It's alright. You're safe."

I wrapped my arms around him and allowed him to hold my weight. I was clearly not ready for this world. I couldn't tell who to trust. Why did Iggy hate me so much?

The sun began to set and afternoon became evening. We passed through Beverly, arriving in Beverly Farms. My legs screamed to stop and my heart long since turned to stone as my eyes battled to focus on the road ahead.

Roberto stopped, still holding my hand, and the others followed his example. "We need to be realistic; we can't find it. We need to camp for the night before it's too dark. We can start again tomorrow."

Emmy sat on the ground, his head between his knees. "They said it was on Hale Street though. It could be the next house."

Abi sat next to him. "Or the next one, or the next one. We need to stop for the night. I agree, we should start again tomorrow."

Iggy stood ahead of us, as he had since we started. I could see his shoulders droop as his eyes took in the houses. He turned to face us, the anger I saw earlier gone. He pointed to a house to his right. Although most of the windows had gone and the wood was rotten, it looked sturdy and it had an almost-roof.

We all agreed and lifted our belongings, walking in the direction of the house with slow, heavy steps. We had passed through the gates when Jen decided she had other plans and darted up the street. I shouted after her, knowing my legs didn't have the energy to chase her.

I sighed, dropped my bags, and looked at the others. "I'll get her," I said, darting after her. I could feel my eyes watering and running down my cheeks, the cold wind freezing it to my face as I tried to catch up. She stopped and looked at me, her tail wagging. "I'm not playing Jen, come here," I shouted. My voice wavered while tiredness, exasperation, and tear-filled sadness cut at my vocal cords.

I rested my hands on my knees, straining to control my breathing, when Iggy ran past me, grabbing Jen. I watched as he knelt to talk to her. Even without hearing his words, I knew he stopped mid-sentence as he stared open-mouthed at a spot farther up the street, a smile slowly spreading across his face.

"Quickly. Come here," he yelled, waving his arms at us. I glanced over my shoulder to see the others pick up the bags and trudge up the street, the tiredness etching shadows around their eyes.

We all stood, only a few minutes later, wordless and gaping. The driveway before us to what we presumed was a house—we hoped was a house—was lined with green trees and grass. An Eden in Massachusetts. The life and greenery of the property stood out, even if we couldn't feel the energy and magic sprouting from it. Our eyes fixed on the flowers, the bushes, and the plants waving at us from inside the walls.

We all wanted to enter but the vision caused us to hesitate. Faced with the future, with our dream, it became difficult to force the first step, knowing life would never be the same. Somehow, no matter how terrible life was, it was safe because we understood it. This was unknown and we dug deep into our souls to find the energy to take the step. We stared at gardens unlike anything I had seen in my life. A small unified gasp was followed by a slow, infectious smile. We found it. We found Jericho. It was real. Abi placed her hand in mine and I placed mine in Emmy's, reaching for something to prove it wasn't a dream.

We stood there gazing in disbelief. Roberto was the first to speak. "You do all see that, don't you? It isn't just me?"

Emmy began to laugh, an uncontrolled sound that said as much about his fear as his joy. His body, as stiff as his laugh, relaxed, and his eyes glassed over, filling with tears. We looked at each other, none of us sure we could take the step across the invisible boundary between the dead and the living. A sudden, floating sensation vanquished the fatigue that slowed my body, and I stepped forward, gently placing my feet on the path. My thoughts jumbled and my words refused to leave my mouth. Actions, not words, would lead us.

When I stepped forward, the others followed, and we walked with uncertain, questioning steps. The farther we stepped, the faster our steps became until we all ran, oblivious to the tiredness that plagued us only moments earlier. The beauty of perfection lured us farther and farther.

Our feet again froze, this time in amazement, as we turned a corner and were faced with a house. The house, even before the Orange, must have been spectacular. Rows of windows, all decorated with window boxes of flowers, adorned the expansive, painted façade. The front doors, lined with etched glass depicting flowers, called to us, but we stared at each other, trying to decide who would be brave enough to knock. Deep inside, fear lingered, hoping to destroy the belief in perfection.

I stretched my energy to its limit, to encompass the house, feeling Iggy's join mine. There was life in the house and we both felt it. Our eyes met and we shared a nod of agreement before we stepped forward. The others shuffled behind us until we all stood in front of the doors. Iggy reached for the door, knocking with the heel of his fist.

The resounding bang caused me to step back, unsure of what to expect. When two armed men answered the door, we all turned in unison to the click of guns behind us. In eighteen years of life, I had never seen guns and now they seemed to be everywhere. My mind swam with thoughts of Danny and Calesta's warnings about the world outside of the school.

There was no opportunity to retreat or change our minds.

The men who stood in the doorway smiled. "Welcome to Jericho. You're late."

We gazed at each other. Confusion wrinkled our faces and twisted our mouths. "Late for what?" asked Iggy.

"The boat. You'll need to wait here till morning. Any guns or weapons must be left here. Jericho allows no weapons on the island."

"Isn't this Jericho?" asked Roberto and he stepped forward to stand in line with Iggy.

The men laughed a gentle, happy laugh. "No, this is the departure point. Jericho is an island. Come in. Leave your weapons at the door and we'll get you settled. I'm sure you have lots of questions."

Walking through the doorway, I found I held my breath, and I gasped for air when I saw the inside of the house. It was like the books I read in the school library. The marble floor squeaked under my feet, and I stopped, gazing around to take in the perfection of the furnishings. There were no signs of the Orange.

"If you don't mind, we need to pat you down for weapons. We can't have any on Jericho." The man not much older than Roberto and Abi held his hands out, waiting for us to comply.

Abi stepped forward first, holding up her arms and spreading her legs. "We don't have any guns and we left our knives at the door. Feel free."

He searched us quickly and then turned to walk ahead. "If you follow me, I'll give you the tour, and then we'll show you to your rooms."

We followed in silence as he showed us around, moving through the kitchen, several living rooms, a game room, a glass room he called a conservatory, and a library. My heart leaped as my eyes swept the rows of books. My fingers moved over the spines, lovingly caressing them."

A younger man, no older than me, stood next to me. "Do you read?"

I nodded, a smile relaxing my face.

"So does Jericho; he'll enjoy having somebody to talk to. He tends to lose a lot of us when he talks about them. Lots of us can read, but equally, lots of us can't, and even fewer bother."

I stared at him, rubbing the back of my neck. Brushing my hair off my face, my eyebrows crinkled. "I'm sorry. I'm confused. Is Jericho a place or a person?"

"Both," he replied, sitting in a large wood-and-fabric chair. The immaculate white of its cloth accentuated the deep, dark color of his skin. I momentarily wondered how the chairs could be so white before my thoughts returned to Jericho.

I mumbled into my hand. "I thought it was a place. I didn't realize it was a person."

"The island was called Misery Island before the war, and it didn't seem an appropriate name for our future, so people started calling it Jericho's Island. We all call it Jericho now, but he is a person. You can meet him tomorrow when you go to the island."

I became aware of Iggy standing next to me. I stretched my hand out to the man. "I'm Alex and this is Iggy."

His smile warmed the room. "I'm Prince. I don't often get to be in the Big House. I'm pleased I got to meet you both."

Iggy shuffled next to me, shaking Prince's hand. "Why aren't you usually here?"

"We take turns to wait here for any new arrivals. It's usually boring. We can go for weeks with nobody arriving. I got roped in to come tonight. The bloke who was supposed to be on tonight's shift wasn't well. I'm really glad I did, though," he said, looking into my eyes, and I found myself looking away.

"Can I borrow one?" I asked, looking at the books.

"Help yourself. Most people don't care about them. Really, other than Jericho, nobody else bothers."

The others turned to leave and I grabbed a book, dragging Iggy to catch up.

When we returned to the entrance hall we had first stood in, the two men who had opened the door were talking to Roberto and Abi. I tried to hear their conversation, realizing they were discussing bedrooms. I normally loved my own space, but tonight the thought of sleeping alone, in a strange place, sent an icy shiver ravaging through me.

Roberto turned to look at us, his eyes holding my gaze. "Who wants a room of their own? There are apparently lots of bedrooms, so show of hands: who wants to sleep alone?"

Iggy and Emmy both raised their hands, looking around at the others. My heart sunk and my eyes gazed at the lines of the marble floor. I sighed, raising my hand.

The older man led the way up the sweeping staircase. "Okay, four bedrooms it is." I noticed Roberto whisper to him and he nodded in response. I was curious about what they had discussed, but the fear chipping away at the bravado of this morning was causing me to shrink. I had spent my whole life as a moody introvert, yet now I was afraid to be alone.

The weight of the past few days caused my legs to struggle on the stairs as they shuffled up. Reaching the top, a long corridor went in both directions. The man turned to face us.

"Me and my men use those rooms, and you'll have free choice in that direction," he said, pointing along the corridor to his left. Roberto shook his hand and we walked away from the stairs.

Roberto stopped outside the first door. "This'll be our room," he said, wrapping his arm around Abi, "and the room next door will be yours, Alex." I wondered how he knew which room was which. "Emmy and Iggy, I think it's best if you two take the rooms opposite. I don't want us too spread out. Safer to be close."

I watched as they disappeared through their doors and turned to face Roberto and Abi, clearly waiting for me to go into my room before they settled in for the night.

I pushed my door, forcing a smile. "Night," I said, looking at them.

The room was beautiful. The bed was huge, covered in mountains of cushions, all in a shiny silk fabric. Next to the bed sat crystal candle holders, and I dug around in my bag for a lighter, dumping my clothes and comforter on the floor. As the candles caught the flame, the room filled with dancing colors. A knot caught in my throat and I swallowed as relief, fear, and joy combined. I breathed, refusing to cry again.

I sat on the bed watching the lights sparkle on the walls and ceiling when a knock came from a door next to the wardrobe, and I jumped up. Abi stuck her head around the door, and I knew why they had chosen the rooms and the conversation they had with the older man. Our rooms were linked. A rush of relief washed over me.

"We're next door if you need us. Are you okay?" she asked.

Roberto's head appeared behind her. "Hey, how are you coping?"

I shrugged. "Don't know, but I do know I'll be fine. Honestly. Thank you."

Abi rushed over, giving me a big hug, before returning to stand in the doorway. They both smiled and waved. "Night," they said as they disappeared, and I was left alone, again.

I kicked off my shoes before lying back on the bed and sleep consumed me.

Danny and Calesta haunted my dreams and I awoke in a sweat. The candles, still burning, cast their magical-flickering colors around the room. I sat up, kicking the sheets off my body, embracing the chill that wrapped around me. Jen, who was lying on the floor next to me, raised her sleepy face to gaze at me.

"It's okay, go back to sleep, Jen," I said and she obliged. She rubbed her head on the soft pile of the carpet before closing her eyes and returning to her sleeping world. I watched as her chest rose and fell, envying the contentment of her dreams.

I lifted the book lying on the floor near Jen and tried to focus on the words. My eyes refused to focus and the words jumped around the page. I sighed and lowered my feet out of the opposite side of the bed, trying not to wake Jen. I tiptoed to the door, stopped as I reached it, and listened to Jen's breathing. Confident I hadn't disturbed her, I coaxed the door open and dashed through, closing it quietly behind me.

My bare feet padded on the carpet as I walked back to the staircase. I had expected to hear the voices of the men when I reached the entrance hall. Instead, the silence of the house greeted me with indifference. I walked toward the kitchen. The cold of the marble floor made me wish I had put my boots on.

I grabbed a glass of water before walking into the conservatory. The candlelight from the kitchen left it in near-darkness. I stared out at the blackness of the world outside, wondering what I would see in daylight. The stars glistened, flickering happily in space, and I watched them, mesmerized by their happiness, slowly drifting back to sleep curled up on a wicker chair.

At some point later I awoke with a start when I felt hands on me. My eyes flew open, battling the darkness to see the face of Iggy staring down.

"Sorry, I didn't mean to wake you, but you looked cold and I thought a blanket might help." He smiled down at me and I patted his hand.

"It's okay. I wasn't sleeping very well and thought I'd take a walk, but there didn't seem to be anybody around, so I just sat here watching the stars."

He sat on the chair opposite, his face barely visible in the darkness. "I couldn't sleep either. Been a weird day. How you coping?" His voice echoed.

"Been better, but I'm coping, thanks."

We sat in silence and again sleep swept over me, dragging me deep into the depth of my nightmares. Visions of Danny and Calesta loomed in the darkness, and I awoke screaming, aware of tears chilling my cheeks. It took a minute to remember my surroundings, and I became aware of a hand holding mine.

"It's okay, Alex. You're safe. It was just a dream."

I focused on the voice and stared into Iggy's face.

"Are you okay now?"

I nodded, swallowing the lump of tears in my throat. "I'm sorry, did I wake you?"

"No, it's fine. I'm not a great sleeper anyway." He released my hand, sitting back in the chair opposite me, his eyes never leaving my face. I struggled to reconcile the Iggy who sat here patiently with the Iggy who had refused to look at me earlier after the fire incident. He made no sense, but I knew he didn't care, not really.

"I think I should go to bed and leave you in peace," I said, standing on my unwilling legs.

"Are you sure? Maybe you should just lie on the sofa there," he said, pointing into the darkness. "I'll stay with you if you want."

He made no sense, his feelings confused me, and I wanted to read him but knew he would know, would repel my energy. I also knew I didn't want to be alone. "Thank you," I said, allowing him to lead me to the sofa, and he then sat in the chair next to it. He draped the blanket over me and held my hand.

I awoke again with the sun lighting the watery horizon, and I looked at Iggy's sleeping body in the chair next to me, still holding my hand. I eased my hand free, standing to stretch my legs. He shuffled, twisting his position but slept on. I moved to the glass doors I hadn't noticed in the darkness last night that led out into the garden. They were locked and I looked around for a key. It was nowhere to be found so I walked back into the kitchen.

Prince and another man of similar age stood at the sink. "Morning, Alex. I take it you two couldn't sleep. You both looked so far gone, we left you. This is Adam. Adam meet Alex," said Prince.

The other man smiled, his blue eyes sparkling, and I stared. How had I not noticed him last night? He held out his hand, and I wiped my hands on my jeans. "Nice to meet you. Would you and your boyfriend like something to eat?"

I stared at him, my furrowed brow speaking my confusion. I turned to follow their eyeline to the conservatory and knew they were referring to Iggy, his sleeping body out of sight, sprawled in the chair. "Oh, he's not my boyfriend."

Prince and Adam looked at each other. Prince looked at me. "Well the daggers in his eyes yesterday when I met you . . . I presumed it was because he was jealous?"

I laughed. "No, sometimes he gets a bit grumpy, but it's just his way."

"If you're sure," he said, handing me a plate of fruit. "We grow that on the island; it's yummy."

I took it and sat on a tall chair to eat from the kitchen worktop. "Wow, this is lovely. How do you grow it? I thought that was impossible?" I asked, my mind returning home to my mother's garden with its flourishing plants.

Adam smiled, glancing from Prince to me, his smile accentuating his cheekbones, angular and yet smooth. "All things are possible on Jericho. You'll see soon. The boat should be here in a few hours, and you and your friends can go and meet the rest of the community."

I handed them my plate, my stomach fluttering with nerves at the prospect of more new people. "I'll wake Iggy and we'll go and get everybody ready."

They smiled back and Adam said, "No problem. It's been nice meeting you, Alex."

I was aware of them watching me when I walked back into the conservatory.

SEVENTEEN

BILLEY

The cold of the night comforted me. The chill biting through my blanket reminded me I was in Nuadh Caled. Only Bearaig could be this cold. The sharp pinpricks of the night air became a thankful anchor on reality.

My brain burned. Memories, some painful, some joyous, many insignificant, blazed through it with willful abandon. One or two, though, found their way to the forefront of my mind. I clenched my fists and banged them against the sides of my head without realizing.

"Billey."

The warmth of my tears rolling down my cheeks burned against the freezing chill of my skin.

"Billey. Stop."

A shrieking noise filled the trees. I only vaguely registered it came from me.

"Billey. Stop. Billey, focus on me." On the periphery of the thoughts filling my head, drowning me in memories, Geilis reached out to me. Her fingers stroked my cheeks, placing them between my hands and my skull. "Billey." Her hands stiffened, clasping my face and forcing me to stare at her. "Billey. It's alright. I'm here. It's a lot to handle. Please. Talk to me."

Suddenly, cold air filled my lungs and I questioned when I had last breathed. "My father . . . she . . . killed him. Why would I go back there?"

I scrambled backwards, putting distance between myself and Geilis. I hunted through the volumes of new memories to find her. There she was. The sad resignation in her face when I crossed over the first time, hundreds of years ago. "They were going to kill you because you were a witch." My words hung in the air, news only to me. "But, I felt you across worlds. How?"

She shrugged her shoulders. "Who knows? We've wondered that a hundred times. The Crann? Fate? Destiny? My personal favorite, though, is love." In the dark of the trees and the night, I watched her lips curve. Her smile was like the ripples on a loch spreading out across her face. "I know there's a lot of pain in those memories. But, I hope there's a lot of love and laughter too?"

"Yes." I reached my hand out to grab hers. "There is. But, she wants me dead. My mother. She killed my father. And let's not forget she'll stop at nothing to prevent the one thing the Crann says I must do." I sat back, tilting my head, my eyes squinting to study Geilis's face in the pale moonlight. "The Crann is a tree? Sorry. My brain is still putting all those bits together. Making them make sense."

She laughed. "Yes. The Crann is a tree. You have been here too long." She crawled forward a few steps, and then, turning to sit on her rear, she threw herself on the ground. "THE tree. That's a good place to start. It was my biggest question all those years ago when we first crossed. When I first saw Solas."

I sat upright, leaning away from the tree, only just aware of Geilis resting her head in my lap. My brain clicked and whirred, putting together the puzzle pieces of my memories. "My father, he was the Guardian of the Crann. So, now that he's dead, I am the Guardian of the Crann." My fingers tightened their grip on Geilis's hand. A grip I had been oblivious to until she squeezed back. "My father was killed . . . by my mother?"

"Mm-hmm."

I knew I wasn't speaking to her. I was making sense of the incomprehensible. "The Crann is the connection between all life and all magic. Wow!" I leaned back against the trunk of the tree again before sitting up instantly. "We. You. Me. Dad. The Druids. We're the First People. It's our duty to protect the Crann."

Sitting there, my hands covering my mouth, I knew the truth of so many things. I knew I had to return. I also knew I had no life here. Despite my best efforts, I loved Gaevoin and Brigina. They had been family. But I now understood things that were mere moments ago impossible. "I'm so confused. I'm torn. I don't belong here. But, I do belong there. Except I left it. That bit is still hazy. Why would I do that?"

Geilis turned her face upward to stare at my face. "You have always known that the human who would link the two worlds was coming. The Crann told you hundreds of years ago. But the closer we came to the time, the more the Fae grew to hate the idea. Queen NicNevin, your 'beloved' mother, and the Fae have hidden Solas from danger for years. The rest of Spirismus has forgotten we exist. We have become the stuff of stories. We only exist in the world of fiction."

I closed my eyes, hunting for the missing pieces of my memory, grasping at the space where a memory should be. The frustration of knowing and yet not knowing caused my muscles to clench and ache as my body stiffened.

"Aaaargh!" I screamed, thumping my fists against the ground. "There are still gaps, bits that don't make sense. Why did we hide? Why do we hide? Why are we a secret?"

"I can only tell you what you told me. The whole thing was before me. There were six Crann, all connected and uniting the planets they stood on. So, the people of these worlds began to splinter off, and, with time, they began to doubt the importance of the Crann. Because most of them couldn't connect as we can, they thought we were saying all this to be in control. They thought it was a power-play."

"What happened to the other Crann? Are they still alive?"

Geilis looked at me, her eyes pulling me in. A sadness spoiled the perfect features of her face, her eyes growing darker and her mouth twisting and contorting. "I don't know. I'm not sure they are still there. Or, at least, I don't think they're connected. Only you would know the answer. You're the Crann's gatekeeper."

"I'm what?"

She shook her head. "It doesn't matter. What do you want to do?" She pulled away, backing up to sit too far away to touch, and my body ached. "Your problem is you've always been an overthinker. You once said you were the perfect person if I wanted a decision right now, but the wrong person if I needed a decision next week, or next month. So, I want a decision right now."

A chill raced through my body like a snake slithering around with no aim other than to create fear. "Okay," I said.

Her eyes stared into mine, a smile changing her face. Even in the darkness, her face brightened. "Trust me." She reached for my hand, placing it between hers. "Close your eyes, trust me, and open your heart. Solas is within you. All you need to do is believe."

An odd calmness spread over me. She was right about me. I hated making decisions but once the choice was made, I went with it.

I stared into her face, hunting for something, not sure what, but knowing there was more than she would share. "You're hiding something. Why? I mean, we can agree I'll figure it out. Yes?"

"I'm not. Well, not really. Okay, maybe a wee bit." She sat upright and her fingers laced with the fabric of her dress, forming pointless seams and folds. "I just think it might be easier if you came and connected with the Crann. Then, you'll have access to all your answers. Answers to questions I can't even begin to hope to answer."

"But . . . why . . . I mean . . . why did I leave if I'm supposed to be guarding it? Why am I here?"

I held my breath, sucking in the cold, damp air of the night as I watched Geilis curl her fingers into fists. Her eyes became smaller, her eyelids struggled to stay open, and her jaw tightened.

"Look," she said, her voice louder and faster than was comfortable in the silence of the night. "I am here because I said I would be here for you. I'm here because I love you. I'm here because I want to do whatever it takes to get you back. So. Yes. Why are you here? That's a damn good question. Why did you leave me? Why was some stranger you've never met more important than me? Why would our love call across worlds, and yet, when push came to shove, you abandoned it to go and hide from your mother? That's why you're here. You're hiding. You refused to face her and just left."

I could have tried to reply but knew that there wasn't a valid response even if I had all my memories.

"I'm sorry. I am. I don't know why I would have left you. It doesn't make any sense to me either." I stood up, my leg stiffened from the awkward positions I had ended up in, squashed in the crook of the trunk. "All I know is, right now, I don't feel like I belong here. But, I don't feel I can leave. Brigina and Gaevoin . . . Everybody will think I did it. I mean, I don't belong in your world anymore. Did I ever?"

I leaned forward, gripping her hands in mine. With a strength that surprised me, I pulled her to face me. Her hand brushed my face, the cold of her skin sending a shiver through me. For the first time, I had no doubts about the truth of Geilis's weird and wonderful stories. I no longer worried about my sanity. Yet, it didn't help me. I'm a fugitive Fae princess, entrusted with guarding the Crann, now living and hiding in another world. That was such an improvement on me worrying I was going mad.

Before knowing the words were coming, I had already spoken. "Of course I'll come. The Crann has my answers."

I closed my eyes and tilted my head until my forehead rested on Geilis.

Standing there, our auras danced together, and in the silence of the darkness, I pretended there was nobody else who mattered that I could remember, or wish for, at this moment. This feeling. This was home. Not a place. Home was Geilis.

Why would I have left her? It made no sense.

Why would I cross worlds, spend hundreds of years with her, then leave?

What was I missing?

A gentle and almost invisible breeze, like the breath of a false god sighing his relief, brushed my face.

I extended my aura, searching for Solas, for a place I knew, but didn't. I knew Geilis and knew the Crann. I visualized the Crann, the trunk so broad it would have taken multiple versions of me to have any chance of wrapping my arms around it. I imagined—no, recalled—the feel of my fingers running down the lines of the bark. The smell of the heavy green leaves formed a canopy of life, casting its shadow as far as the eye could see.

I remembered the calm of it.

I yearned for its peace.

The constant of Geilis, her body pressing against mine, anchored me as my body began to bob and ebb like a buoy floating in an endless sea. The direction of the tide dragged me and I was powerless to argue with the might of nature. The light I had known when I first kissed Geilis, the light of home, of Solas, wrapped us in its warmth.

Nausea churned and threatened to burst forth, clawing at my guts. My stomach simmered and swirled, but my heart grew in its size and happiness.

Then, darkness swallowed me. A distant voice called me. "Billey. Billey, wake up. We're here."

The voice echoed through the darkness. The more I concentrated, the closer it became.

Geilis.

I forced my eyes open, a burning dryness scratching at them. I rubbed my eyes, still listening to the voice calling me.

"I'm coming," I mumbled.

EIGHTEEN

BILLEY

My eyes flickered, adjusting to the bright sunlight streaming through the gaps in the ancient trees, tall and magnificent, that surrounded us. My hands moved instinctively to my stomach to ease the turmoil inside me. I fought the need to retch all over the lush green of the ground.

My insides calmed to a mild revolt and, at last, I focused on my surroundings. The sheer scale of the trees was a sight I'd never expected. The trunks climbed up toward the sun, glowing with an indigo warmth. As it shone, its long slender beams of light took on an image of jewelry, like droplets of crystal glass.

I pushed myself up, my body consumed with excitement at all the new sights, sounds, and smells. I smelled the trees, the grass, the life of the land itself. I stopped as I saw Geilis standing between two equally broad trees, her gaze patiently waiting for me to catch up. Life in Nuadh Caled never prepared me for this.

"Wow. It's . . . it's, I don't know. But, the feeling, the life, I want to cry from the vibrations." I swallowed, fighting back a lump of emotions forcing its way up my throat. Any nausea the jump from Nuadh Caled to Solas had created was overpowered by sadness.

"Are one of these the Crann," I asked, spinning around, trying to decide which of these trees looked most important or oldest, which one called to me.

A small stifled laugh filled the air. Geilis took a step toward me. "Oh, no. These are not the Crann. The Crann is in Solas. We've landed in the

Darklands just outside Solas. It was safer. The second we cross into Solas, your mother will know."

A sharp, stabbing pain ripped at my chest. Grief consumed me. Memories of my father dragged me down, and I found myself on all fours on the ground, the dampness of the grass and foliage chilling me. An old memory, its freshness in my heart, cut me. I gasped, trying to breathe, desperate for air. Without hearing Geilis move, I sensed her next to me. She didn't touch me; instead, her aura wrapped around mine.

"I'm sorry. I know how much you loved him." She reached her hand out to stroke my hand, pulling it back at the last second.

"My mother killed him."

"We have no proof. Even the Crann couldn't or wouldn't tell us. All we know was that he was going to reach out to the people of Spirismus to reintroduce us. He felt we had hidden for too long. Without the Crann, the universe had allowed people to move too far from the path. They had begun to lose their empathy, their compassion."

"My mother didn't agree. She was convinced the outsiders would be jealous of us. They would want what we have. They wouldn't be able to settle for a single lifetime when they could have immortality like us. No. Not immortality. We live as long as we are connected to the Crann."

My head filled with questions, answers, fears, and heartache. I wanted to know more but I could take no more. Instead, I allowed my head and my heart to have their own conversation while I sat in silence.

Nineteen

Alex

The sea swayed and moved with the flow of an energy we were unaware of. The gentle lapping sound when it met the land had a calming inevitability about it, or perhaps that was in my head. I was about to take a step I hadn't planned for and wasn't ready for, but it was unavoidable the second I had entered the garden filled with life and energy.

I stared at the mist rising from the sea, imagining I could see the island. We always stayed away from the Earth's water, from the poison that lingered diluted in the water. Now, waiting to climb aboard a boat, to be surrounded by water, my muscles froze in unison. I tried to ignore the fact I couldn't swim. I stared, unable to move, as the boat rowed into sight, my terror consuming any confidence I had. I sensed the shared emotions of the others, except for Jen, who saw nothing but adventure. She jumped and wagged her tail, bouncing up and down.

Emmy asked, "Can any of you swim," and I took the grunting silence of the others' replies to mean they couldn't.

Prince, Adam, and the other men pulled the boat in and another group of people clambered out. We were unable to hear their conversations but watched them gape at us. The sight of the boat banished any other thoughts; my mouth was so dry I struggled to swallow.

Adam climbed the boulders that separated the sea from the gardens, waving at us. "Are you ready to go?"

None of us spoke; we merely followed him. My hands wrapped around my bag as though holding onto it was imperative to my survival. It helped to disguise the shaking of my hands, although we all had fear on our faces.

Roberto and Abi climbed in front. Their painted smiles, aimed to reassure me, did little to calm my nerves. I knew it would be a short journey and I had prepared for it. I sat at the back of the boat with Emmy and Iggy on either side of me and Jen resting happily on my feet. I lowered my heart rate as I focused on my breath, reaching for the magic of the earth. Only I couldn't feel it. The water blocked it, and I could feel my breathing quicken.

I looked at Iggy, his ashen color telling me I wasn't alone in my panic. I turned to look at Emmy, who tried to smile at me, only managing to contort his face and look more than scared. The bitter smell of the sea forced its way up my nose and a flood of nausea overtook me. The deeper I breathed, the more the smell found its way into my body, and I found myself stuck in a vicious cycle. The more nauseous I felt, the deeper I breathed to keep it at bay, then the worse I felt.

The island appeared in the distance, and I stared at it, watching it grow as we neared it, grateful for whatever it brought. The green of the land soon became evident, and the quiet gasps coming from my friends assured me they were watching it too. I could see small, random buildings scattered around and a wooden structure towering over the entire island.

When at last we reached land and the men at the front jumped out to pull the boat ashore, I found the fear subsiding, replaced by excitement. My stomach fluttered and I could feel the heat of my face.

Stepping out of the boat after Emmy, the magic of the land swept over and through me, causing me to stand still, steadying myself. I turned to look at Iggy in time to watch him stumble out of the boat as Jen decided it was her turn. I wanted to ignore it and pretend to not notice, but Emmy laughed and I couldn't hold it in.

I bent to offer him my hand. His eyes avoided my gaze and he straightened himself, rubbing his clothes as though removing creases or dirt. I stood back, knowing his pride was hurt, pulling a grim stare at Emmy. He apologized, helping Iggy up, and I walked to join Roberto and Abi, who were in the midst of a full-blown conversation with the older man who had first met us last night. I looked at his waistband, noticed the gun he had tucked into it, and wondered how much hypocrisy the island held at its root.

Abi wrapped her arm around my shoulder. "We made it. We're here.

Luther here says Prince and Adam will show you around while we go to meet Jericho. You can meet him when you get back, by which time we will have a feel of the place. Pay attention, I'll need you to give me the tour once we're finished." She pulled back and stared into my eyes, her hands squeezing both shoulders. You sure you're alright?"

I nodded. "Just getting my bearings, I've never been on the water and hope I won't need to again soon." I smiled as I wandered off to share the news with Iggy and Emmy.

Iggy frowned at the idea of not being in the initial meeting but agreed to accompany me on my tour. Prince and Adam both grinned, their eagerness making their speech speed up as they fidgeted. Iggy bent his head to whisper in my ear. "Whatever you do, don't flaunt your magic. You never know how people will react. For your safety, keep your cards close to your chest."

I crossed my arms over my body, sucking in my cheeks. "I wasn't raised to be a pretty little wallflower and I will never be embarrassed by my gifts. I am who I am, and I don't care who doesn't like it."

"You were also raised to stay alive. You are a survivor, so stop being a petulant child," he snapped through his teeth, and my face flushed as I walked behind him to meet up with Adam and Prince.

Having heaved myself up the rocks and boulders separating the sea from the land, I gazed at the life-filled green of the island. Jen, having found an easier route, stood waiting for me. My inner dreamer gasped, faced with a lush landscape covered in trees, plants, and people. My heart heaved. Was this what the world was like before the Orange? Children ran around a flat, grassy area, the sounds of their laughter and fun alien to me. This was what childhood should be, not the isolated, protected life I had led.

My eye was drawn to a tall wooden tower, its wood mismatched and rather hobbled together. I followed the line of its shape to the top, where I instinctively recoiled at the sight of men and women with guns. My instinct told me they were protecting the people and the way of life, but the idea of maintaining peace by violent threats seemed incongruous.

I spotted Prince walking toward me, effortlessly interacting and chatting to everybody he passed. Would I ever find social interaction easy? Looking far more relaxed, no longer dressed in black or carrying a gun, he looked more like the teenager he was. Like the many teenagers who once lived in my school.

Adam yelled from the distance for him to wait and he laughed.

"It's not my fault you're so slow."

I envied them. A vice gripped my heart, squeezing the blood from it, and my body threatened to crumble. The familiarity and casual confidence they shared made me smile. Iggy must have understood and he turned to smile at me. The smile I returned felt weak and pathetic, my lips barely curving.

"Hey, you guys, welcome to Jericho. We're going to give you the tour. Any questions, please ask. I know it's a lot to take in, so yell out if I lose you," said Prince.

Emmy turned around, and for the first time since we arrived, I could see his face. Suddenly seeming younger than I had seen him look, his face relaxed and the lines that aged him disappeared. "It's bigger than I realized. I wasn't expecting this. This is . . ." His voice trailed off and I nodded, smiling at him, knowing his meaning without the need for words.

Adam, having reached us, answered him. "It's eighty-seven acres, so it's the size of a small village. We have all the usual stuff: a dining hall, a school, a doctor, and a lot of homes. The school is over there," he said, pointing to a large stone building. It looked old, but the roof looked new, and although the windows had no glass, they were all decorated by wooden shutters.

"How many children are here," I asked, my eyes fixed on the building.

"About twenty are under sixteen, and Jericho insists every child learns to read and write." Adam's voice, now right next to me, made me jump and I laughed as I faced him.

"Sorry, my mind wandered there. My mother was a teacher. That's how I know Roberto and Abi. After the Orange, she taught those who were left behind in the school, but she's dead now."

He looked at me with an understanding, soothing look and placed his hand on mine. "Few of us have anybody left. We make our own family here." I wanted to pull my hand away, but equally, a small part of me wanted to leave it, to enjoy human contact, so I smiled in response and we walked on.

Walking past the school, we found ourselves in the middle of a group of trees. The sight of the leaves hanging from the branches and the new buds sprouting from them pulled at my hand like a magnet. It reached for a tree, connecting with its energy, and Iggy glared at me. Remembering his words about shielding my magic, I dragged my hand away and stuck them both in my pockets.

"Sorry. It's been such a long time since I saw a living tree. Not the blackened, dead silhouette of once-trees." I followed the rest of the group with Jen never leaving my side, either protecting me or because she was as petrified as I was.

Looking past Emmy, I saw a man and woman like those in the tower, carrying guns, patroling, and guarding the community.

"And this is where Adam and I stay," said Prince, waving his hand at two long wooden buildings. This is where most single people end up, so you'll probably be in here. And just around this bump is where couples and families stay."

We walked around the bump to be faced with a mismatch of yurts, huts, and tents scattered in no apparent order. People wandered between them, carrying on with life in the most normal of manner. This in itself was the most abnormal thing I had seen in my life.

We stood, hypnotized by the surreal nature of the normality. Emmy, next to me, draped his arm around my shoulder. "I never thought I would see anything like this. It is the stuff of childish daydreams. I keep waiting for somebody to wake me up."

I looked at him and smiled. "Me neither. Amazing isn't it?" I stretched out my foot to nudge Iggy. "You've been unusually quiet. You're usually full of opinions."

He twisted his head to look over his shoulder. His smile said what his silence didn't. Even he couldn't find fault with this.

Prince cleared his throat. "Anyway, I'll take you to your friends and you can meet Jericho. Then we'll find you somewhere to stay." He smiled at us and walked on.

I was two steps forward when I remembered the fruit he gave me for breakfast. "No. Wait. You said you grow fruit and vegetables. Can I see where?"

Prince looked at Adam, who said, "Sorry, we should have done that on the way. We'll need to go back that way." He held up his hand, pointing back toward the long wooden buildings we had passed, and we all turned to follow.

The smell of fruit and herbs wafted through the air soon after we set out. We could have followed our noses, using the sweet smells that transported me somewhere else. Passing some shrubs and bushes, their hotchpotch layout indicating something naturally occurring rather than an intentional man-made plan, we saw them. The uniform rows of planting, the trees hanging with fruit, and the flourish of life.

I looked at Adam and Prince. "Can I go in?" I asked.

"Don't see why not. If you want to, but perhaps I ought to keep the dog," Prince replied.

Iggy, Emmy, and I looked at each other. "I'm not coming. I have zero interest in the growing of food," Emmy said, taking a step back. "You two can feel free."

Iggy waved his hand, "After you."

The soil squished under my feet, and I fought the urge to bury my hand in it. I silently stood, extending my energy to meet it, and the collective consciousness that joins all things answered. The calm serenity of being connected relaxed me, easily transforming my nervousness into a blissful feeling of belonging.

Iggy spoke gently in my ear. "I get it, but you need to be aware of who might be watching. Your aura is dancing, and somebody with even half of your magic could see it. I know you want this to be the answer. So do I, but please hide your magic until we're sure."

"Okay, I promise . . . really."

We walked, our heads digesting the information and processing new questions, to meet Jericho. Curiosity niggled at me and I wished I hadn't promised Iggy I wouldn't use my magic. It would save so much time if I just read him.

We found ourselves outside a small house built of boulders surrounded by flowers of all colors. Two men stood on either side of the door, and I wondered if they held the guns Jericho 'didn't like on the island.' I was fairly sure I would. Adam and Prince looked at us, looked at me.

"There's so much more to the island when you have time to wander. There are beaches and open fields. If you want I could show you sometime? We could show you," Adam said. He flushed and lowered his eyes and Prince smirked at him.

"See you all soon," said Prince, walking away with Adam. I turned to watch them leave as Adam turned to look back.

"Come on in" came the voice I recognized as Roberto's. Iggy entered first, bending down to avoid bumping his head. Jericho must be short, I thought. My wild curls, left on their own for a few days, brushed the doorframe as I walked in.

My eyes swept the room, taking in as much detail as possible. The light in the room was gentle, the small windows affording little natural light. The fire burning in a fireplace against the far wall sent shadows flickering around the room. The room looked a little larger on the inside, but still far from majestic. A single metal bed pushed into the far corner of the room lay unmade, a man-sized potted plant sitting next to it. The flooring, covered with an old rug that turned up slightly at the corners, was made of reclaimed wood, none of it seeming to match.

Most of the room was taken up by two battered, old sofas, many of the buttons missing, and two multicolored reading chairs. In one sat a man not much older than me, his piercing eyes heightened by the shock of jet-black hair that framed his face. Was this Jericho?

My face must have asked the question as he rose to shake my hand. "Welcome. You must be Alex; I'm Jericho. Not quite what you were expecting?"

"No . . . I . . . I'm pleased to meet you." My words burbled, making no pretense at disguising my surprise. How could this man be the leader? He would have been little more than a child when the Orange happened.

He moved along our line, meeting Emmy, Iggy, and finally Jen, and I fought the urge to probe his energy, to discover this man who fell so far from what I expected. We sat and I squashed between Iggy and Emmy on the sofa. I hated being so encroached by others, my personal space being a fiercely guarded part of me, but on this occasion, it was a comfort and security. I allowed my mind to wander and found my eyes fixed on the long slender fingers of Jericho, perfect and manicured.

He told us of his dream for an ever-growing community living in peace, and the prospect made my soul sing. Initially, there had been only a few, and he had been little more than a child, but once the island regained its life, the potential to cater for more grew. There were now hundreds living on the island and nobody had ever chosen to leave; they were all happy.

I imagined the possibilities of a peaceful future for the first time in my short life. Could we leave the hatred and anger of the past behind us? A sudden but slow probing of energy invaded me, and my instinct to repel it, to reply to magic with magic, ceased as Iggy squeezed my knee. His warning about hiding my magic overtook me and I allowed it. My soul squirmed with hatred at the invasion, but I allowed it, allowed Jericho, into my most inner emotions.

The Firestone vibrated and I clenched my hands to avoid the temptation to touch it.

I looked in his face, into his eyes, hoping for a sign of what he hoped to find in me, to be faced with a false smile. The hidden truth of Jericho was deep inside, screened from view by his savior skin. What difference did it make? We had found safety and a world I could, at last, be safe in, and I relaxed, allowing him to search me, search my soul.

I lowered my eyes and watched as Iggy's fingers fidgeted with hatred for the invasion. I stared as his skin pulsed, the veins rebelling, and I knew the struggle he was going through. My thoughts went back to our first meeting when I had probed and he had pushed back. I knew the battle taking place inside him as he allowed Jericho in.

Why did I need to hide my magic, when Jericho flaunted his?

TWENTY

IGGY

Jericho's hand reached for mine and I could see no reason to not shake it. Staring at it for a moment, I wondered how anybody could have such perfect hands. The nails, perfectly even and rounded, were evidence this man had nothing to do with manual labor. Yet, he was our savior, after all? Although, how that was possible when he was only a little older than I remained a mystery for another time.

In the years since Emmy first found me, we found many new homes. Many dreams, new futures, and hopes for the elusive community we all sought had been found and lost.

I had shaken many hands with those who had been the promise of something more. They never had been and, usually, I didn't mind. It was a feeling, a disappointment, I was used to.

This time, I bubbled with simmering anger. I watched as Jericho's aura, so blatant, full, and without a care in the world, flitted around him. The dark colors and stillness of his aura froze my brain for a second. The moment I sensed it probe Alex, my hands became fists. I struggled to control my breathing. She had so much hope, and, for her, I wished Jericho could have been the savior she wanted.

The naivety of her years hidden like the princess in the tower ill-prepared her for the lies and deception of the real world. I sensed him probe her and then me, with no words exchanged, no permission sought, no acknowledgment that we could have magic too.

His superiority, born of a different isolation from Alex's, was no less dangerous. He had been afforded the opportunity to lord it over people, happy to ignore the possibilities of life and exchange it for weak security. A lie. A false promise.

Having seen Alex in action, killing and burning the men who had stood between her and her dog, I had no doubt she could repel Jericho if she wanted to with ease. A part of me sighed with relief she had listened to me, and, yet, a larger part of me shriveled and died watching her submit to something, somebody, beneath her, beneath her magic.

She was more than this.

She was more than Jericho.

In the moments since we arrived on the island, I had watched people living the most normal of lives, milling around me. The presence of magic and connection was, however, present. This sanctuary was built on magic. I needed to find the acknowledgment of it.

Who had held the magic? Who controlled it? Was magic encouraged?

Deep down, I knew the answer.

Any person who would, without consent, probe the aura of another so deeply, not to determine risk but to satisfy their vanity, had proven themselves not worthy of my respect. Not just because I had a strange need to protect her, but because such a personal and intimate intrusion was unforgivable.

My mind flitted back to the night Alex and I had met. So much had happened in a short time. I watched her fall apart, put herself back together, and fight on when most would have surrendered and shrunk. I couldn't deny I admired her strength. She possessed a positivity I lost many years ago, stolen by the bullies, the thugs, those who would kill indiscriminately, with no appreciation for the value of life.

Even now, with most of the world dead and rotting, there needed to be hope.

If Jericho acknowledged magic and its place on the island, I would have understood the probing, but, unlike Alex when we first met, he wasn't trying to judge character. He wasn't worried for his safety. He wanted to judge the danger of the threat somebody's magic might pose to his little world.

Watching a single yet almost invisible tear escape from Alex's eye, I saw her aura shrink. The vibrant colors and power I admired yesterday morning in her mother's garden withered. I told her to hide her magic but hated myself for it.

My wish to keep her safe, to shield her from those who hated magic, those who couldn't trust what they didn't understand, caused her to shrink. I watched her become less.

Guilt merged with my anger, and by the time Jericho probed my mind, searching for magic, I found myself struggling to take my advice. Fury raged through my veins, pounding its own rhythm. It formed a beat I doubted I would be able to get rid of. It caused me to shrivel inside, and by the time I relaxed my hands, I saw the blood where my fingernails dug into my palms.

I wanted to reach out and touch Alex, but to reassure her she had done the right thing seemed impossible. My head began to pound.

Yesterday, I had watched the many faces of Alex. The strong woman preparing to leave behind everything she knew in search of something better. In search of belonging.

I saw the defender she was of those she loved when she released the fire that burned the men. I saw a level of magic and power that would scare most. I knew in that second how most would view her, not because of her character, not because of how beautiful her heart was, or how easygoing and caring her soul was. She would be judged by many as a threat who would need to be controlled or destroyed.

Yet, last night in the darkness, curled up in a blanket, I watched the innocent optimism of nervous little Alex. The child she had been when her mother had died still held her greatest truth. She had no idea who she was or how powerful she was.

My head rattled with the words I wanted to say but knew, too well, I couldn't. By the time we were leaving, the weight of the unspoken words made me long for my own company to unburden myself.

Emmy stood next to me when he exited the room. "Are you okay? You're unnaturally quiet. I expected opinions by now," he said, an obvious attempt to make light of the worry etched on my face.

"Yeah. I'm alright. Honestly. Kinda feeling weird. We've done this more than a few times. The searching for a home. I wish, for once, I could enjoy it." I felt his hand squeeze mine, and I turned my face to look at him. Maybe this time will be the one, eh?"

"Yeah, Maybe." The smile he forced on his face failed to convince me he believed his own words. He turned his face quickly to look at the others. "Come on," he said, pulling his hand away.

Two men we had first seen at the boat as we were landing on Jericho's Island walked toward us, their smiling faces and outstretched arms a clear indication we were expected to go with them.

The blonder and older of the two spoke first.

"Hi, I'm Sean and this is James. Nice to meet you," he said, looking around to check we didn't have any belongings.

"No bags. Just us," said Emmy, falling in step behind them.

I followed his lead, stifling a sigh, as I watched the others head off in different directions.

Just as we approached a long wooden barn-type of building that appeared to have no windows, we turned right, weaving between a small gathering of green bushes. This was more life than I had seen in a single place in my lifetime. My thoughts flitted back to the flowers Alex had created in the meadow when we ate lunch. I glanced back to where she had been moments earlier, but she was gone. Her back vanished between the wooden barns we had just left.

Emmy ran his fingers through his hair and pretended he didn't notice me looking back. "Well, you can't deny, the company this time is much prettier than on previous visits."

I turned my face to look at Sean and James and didn't comment.

James turned toward us and Sean pulled open a door to the largest of the wooden structures.

"Most people are housed by job, etc. but, until we get you guys sorted, you're going to have to stay in the security annex. It's starting to get quite full. I think there's talk of makin' more accommodation soon."

We followed them into the building and were faced with rows of beds, all different sizes and heights, each with a different color of bedding. The mismatch of scavenged furnishings against the peeling paint of the wooden walls added a warmth to the very functional space.

"There are curtains between the bunks, so you can get some sort of privacy, but most people tend to be outside. It's a nice place," Sean said, glancing at James. "We're at the end of the building, the one with the green curtain," he said, pointing at a lurid leaf-print curtain. If you need anything, you just ask anybody. But, y'all know where we are."

James patted two empty beds, unmade but with bundles of bedding on the foot of both of them. "These two will be for you guys. Spend the first few days getting to know the place and the people. Do y'all want us to give you a tour or would you rather go and investigate yourselves?"

Emmy threw himself onto the bed. He ran his hand over the bundle of bedding. "I'd appreciate a tour, thanks. Iggy already had a guided tour."

He stared at me, no expression or emotion visible. "Do you want to come?" He had become good at leaving me to my own choices, and over the past year or two, he had been making a real effort to not influence them. It was obvious and I couldn't help but appreciate it.

"I think I'll just settle here for a bit. I'll go wandering and get lost later. You go ahead, though."

Alone on my bed, I watched Emmy chatter away, a smile on his face as he followed Sean and James back outside. I never ceased to be impressed by the resiliency of Emmy. He always managed to be full of hope and belief, no matter how many times life had gone wrong for us. He still believed this time would be the time.

This would be home.

This time would be the last.

We would finally belong.

I was, honestly, a bit jealous. Cynicism had become my default. Deep down inside, I wanted to believe it was because Emmy was old enough to remember before. He could remember life when it had been happy. When people had families and homes.

I, on the other hand, was part of the generation that only knew life after the Orange.

Then we met Alex. She was the same as me. She had no memory of life before but she still believed she could find a home, a community, somewhere to belong. She had spoiled my excuse for my cynical nature.

Maybe I'd just need to learn to be more positive?

Twenty-One

Billey

A strange calmness flooded over me. Despite the horrendous events of the day and the upheaval of my life, the scale of the forest we now stood in held a beauty.

Geilis told me we were in the Darklands but, deep in my soul, a familiarity of belonging comforted me. Happy memories of playing with family and friends, running through these trees, the buzz of life and vibrancy of this place, filled me.

The trees loomed, more magnificent than anything I had ever seen, or rather anything I had seen in my life in Nuadh Caled.

Here, I was old. I had enjoyed hundreds of winters. I had shared memories with people I loved and people who loved me.

Seeping into me were a collection of mismatched fragments of my life. Jigsaw pieces floating in the subconscious areas of my mind I had forgotten. They bashed against each other, colliding as they tried to connect.

While I stood still, soaking up the sounds of life that vibrated under the surface here, some pieces of the puzzle connected and memories became real.

"Oh, wow!" I laughed, stopping midthought to stare at Geilis. "You have a tattoo and I have a matching one. I'd forgotten I had it. Nobody has been near it for years and I couldn't see it."

A strange, fun-filled warmth swept over me and my face began to burn. The memory of us using magic to draw on each other. Minuscule but personal images, hidden in private places, hidden by magic.

Watching me blush and fumble with the memory, Geilis couldn't contain her laughter and she released a low and naughty chuckle. "I'm so sorry. I shouldn't laugh. But, you have to admit, given the number of memories you have to piece together, it is rather funny you came up with that one." She winked at me, pulling up her dress to hang seductively around the top of her legs. "Do you want to see it? It's been a while."

I laughed and tucked my hands in my pockets. Then, in an instant, my body changed. "I . . . How long . . . how long have I been gone." I moved to stand in front of Geilis. I remember leaving. I knew, we knew, we had no way to guess how time would travel on the other side of the portal. Even the Crann couldn't know. The more disconnected it was, the more time became free to go at its own pace.

She reached her hand up, weaving it through my hair, her fingertips rubbing away the headache she recognized. "I've lived over forty winters at my end. Less than ten at yours, as far as I can tell. You have missed a lot."

"Sweet Mother Universe, how much I have missed! Just as well we don't age."

My eyes darted around my surroundings, inspecting the trees, the leaves, the bushes, the grass, and the foliage covering the ground. Apart from the contrast with the struggling life of Nuadh Caled, I sought some clue time had changed since I left. That the two Darklands were indeed different places.

Then and now.

I pointed my face to the sky, a strand of sunlight warming it. I closed my eyes and stood there. I listened, I smelled, I connected with the energy of Spirismus.

"Spirismus. We are back," I whispered to myself.

"Where is everybody? I've never known it so quiet," I asked, opening my eyes to look at Geilis, unsure how I knew.

I tilted my head to hear the sounds of human life. All I heard was the silence and peace of a deserted forest.

"Oh, hardly any people live in the Darklands nowadays. The current king, King Arthanius Chegasa, invited everybody back to Spirismus. Hybrids no longer hide. Other than a few of the older souls who couldn't bear to leave, those hiding out for a nefarious reason, and those who have a calling to be here, nobody tends to venture into the Darklands anymore." Geilis paused for a second, inspecting my face for a reaction. "People like Durai are still here. I spend a lot of time with him. We both found ourselves alone and he never asks questions. He's always been good that way."

Deep in my chest, clattering behind my ribcage, my heart did a flip. "Oh, oh, oh, Kluzahr." My hands waved and flapped around me in excitement. "Is she still in the Darklands or did she go to Chegasa like she said she would? Actually"—I hesitated for a moment—"she must be getting old by now. The fun we had running riot in the Darklands, beyond mother's control, out of sight of my father. We did run wild, didn't we?" I stared into her eyes, no longer looking at mine. Whatever the reaction she had been looking for, she had found.

She bowed her head, her shoulders slumped. No words were needed. Without moving her mouth, she told me everything I needed to know.

"She's dead. Isn't she?" A sadness, cold and detached somehow, painted my skin bit by bit, soaking in to merge with my soul.

Geilis nodded, her hand reaching for mine. My hand rested on hers. Her thumb rubbed back and forth across the top of my hand. "She did what she said she would. She did what the Crann asked."

"She died for a Chegasa?" I said. I knew, given how honorable Kluzahr was, she would have made her life's mission about somebody else without question.

When we were younger and freer, we had called ourselves the Terrible Three. We hadn't been terrible, just lively. The possibilities of life seemed so grand back then.

"She became a tutor to the young princes after you left. She grew to love them. Their mother died and their father, King Aelfraed, had become distant. He hid away from the world, including his sons. Kluzahr thought of them as family. She loved that boy with every ounce of her being."

"Sorry, boy or boys? You said there were two."

Geilis draped her arm around my shoulder and pulled me to her. "Come on, it's a long story, and you've been through an awful lot today. Let's go and meet Durai. We can have a rest and plan our next step while I catch you up on a few things."

A smile spread across my face, and, without realizing it, I wrapped my hand around her waist, and we strode off in the direction I somehow understood was Durai's home.

The damp warmth of the forest and the jewel-like indigo lighting from the sun managing to break through the canopy of greenery created a safety, a home I only now remembered.

"How could I have forgotten this? It seems so weird. Anyway, let's go. I'd be lying if I said I wasn't tired and hungry."

TWENTY-TWO

GEILIS

A breeze fluttered through the trees, calling to us like a favorite pet pleased to see us home. The majestic trees barely moved, but, after hundreds of winters here, the changes resonated with me. I had lived with the trees, the life, the energy of the Darklands and Solas. My aura, or my soul, the part of me that connected to this place, filled with joy. The land had become like an extra limb, so integral and vital, I only noticed when it left me.

Visiting Nuadh Caled to see Billey had brought a new appreciation for it. Every time I had left, my soul yearned for home.

I walked a step or two ahead of Billey, her hand in mine, scared she would vanish if I stopped touching her.

Her breathing became shallow and her aura bristled as it registered the sensations of home. I glance over my shoulder, wondering if she remembered it.

"I feel so carefree here. It's . . . it's like . . . I don't know how to explain it. But, it feels wonderful."

I smiled and she returned it.

"It feels like home?"

She nodded.

The trees began to thin and the sun warmed the air. I missed this most of all when I had traveled to Nuadh Caled. The cold of it had added to the harsh inhospitality of that land. Here, warmth wrapped you like a blanket. They gave way to an open space, circular and yet not quite. A boundary of small wooden dwellings stood only just above the ground level.

A set of three or four steps led down to what I knew was a bed area.

When Billey had left, this place was full of people, all seeking sanctuary from the dangers of being a hybrid, their birth making them a criminal the second they had been born. How could they be responsible for being who the Universal Being had made them?

Now, silence covered the camp.

In the middle of the circle, tending to a large fire, stood a man. His wild head of shocking white hair aged him, even before the creases of living became visible. Standing two hands taller than either of us, he created a formidable person. His width almost matched his height.

Without turning to see us, he called out. "Hey, Geilis. I've missed you. Hardly seen you lately. I thought you'd deserted me."

His face brightened when he saw us, his inner warmth shining out from beneath the white halo of hair. "Billey! Well, I never. I was beginning to think I'd never see you again. How have you been?"

Billey froze for a second, her hand tightening in mine. Then, she let go.

"Rai," she screamed before running to hug him.

I had worried she would never remember home.

He wrapped his arms around her and lifted her off the ground, swinging her in circles.

"I'm an old man now. It's just as well there's still nothing of you."

A small sob vibrated up my throat before I could stifle it. I wiped the tears beginning to leak from my eyes and walked to join them.

"Told you she was coming home, didn't I?" I said, a smile filling my face. Every muscle in my face, in my body, relaxed. The years vanished and we were just us for a moment.

"So sit and tell me about your adventures. My calendar is quite empty today and I'd love to hear all about your missing time," he said with a deep, coarse chuckle. He knew he wouldn't get the truth. He had always accepted the secrets we hid from him.

"Oh, Rai, you know life without you was uneventful. Life wasn't worth the energy of explaining until today." Billey paused, steadying herself and taking a tiny step back to stare at his face.

"It's been a long time since anybody called me that," he said, a sadness aging his face. The shadows of pain etched in every wrinkle and crevice.

Billey's eyes flashed at me.

"I told her about Kluzahr. Well, only the brief details. It felt like it was your story to tell, not mine," I said, watching Durai's face tell the truth of the pain, even after all these winters.

Kluzahr, the only person to enter Solas in hundreds of winters, had been like our sister. But, in truth, she had been Durai's flesh and blood. She had been the last of his family. He had allowed us to share her, but he had loved her with an infinite passion.

"My niece made her own choices. You, more than almost anybody, know how headstrong she was. I know, if she had the chance, she would have made the same choices again." He shook his head even now thinking about it. With only half of the story, he had struggled to understand her choices.

He held out his hands and cupped Billey's face. "But, Sweet Mother Universe, it's great to see you."

He walked to sit on one of the logs lying around the giant stone fire circle. Billey moved to sit on the right side of him, and I hesitated, swallowing to break the lump forming in my throat before climbing over it to sit on his left. We sat there, huddled together, all leaning on each other as we shared our inner trauma. Not a word was spoken. Not a word needed to be said.

That had always been the way with Durai.

Time paused around us, or so it seemed. If not for the sun beginning to hide behind the treetops, I would believe we had just arrived.

In the Darklands, even in an open area such as the camp, the sunlight struggled to shine through the trees. The cracks in the canopy of leaves allowed for little more than thin, glowing strings of light.

"So, are you pair hungry?" asked Durai, breaking the silence none of us wanted to end.

My stomach woke up, letting out a low grumble. Durai laughed a deep belly-laugh.

"I guess that answers that," he joked, walking toward the largest of the wooden structures. That one we knew held food. He never shielded that knowledge. His food, like everything he had, was shared with anybody who needed it. His generosity was, without a doubt, one of his most defining characteristics.

When he stood up, Billey shuffled up to fill the space he had left.

She placed her hand on top of mine and we sat there, staring into the Darklands, our hands intertwined on my knee.

"I have so many questions still. I'm just too tired to know where to start," she said in a hushed voice.

A brief pause filled the air, one I knew wasn't meant to be filled. It was a thinking space. Over the many lifetimes we had spent together, I had become accustomed to Billey's pauses. Her brain worked with remarkable speed. Yet, she never spoke until she had worked through a thousand possible answers and scenarios.

"It's been a long day, or is it days? Time doesn't seem to match. We left Nuadh Caled in the middle of the night, and, yet, we arrived here in broad sunlight. I have no idea if I'm supposed to want breakfast, lunch, dinner, or bedtime." Her whole body sighed and her tiny frame shrunk more. "I don't know what time it is. I know I need to sleep and I feel safe here." She grabbed my face and kissed me. A long hungry kiss that reminded me of the life we had shared before her father's death. "I do know, though, I need to sleep."

I stood and led her to the wooden bedroom structure next to Durai's.

"Do you want to be left alone?"

She turned to me, her mouth moving as it sorted the words crowding it.

"Don't overthink, Billey. I know you too well to be upset or shocked by anything you say or do."

"Do you mind if I sleep alone? I just need time."

"Just knowing we're sleeping in the same universe is a huge improvement on the past forty winters. If you need anything, just yell. Okay?"

She kissed my hand and I held it to her cheek. "We'll be here when you wake." I stood, staring at the doorway she vanished through until Durai's voice broke the spell.

"Billey not hungry, then?" he said, his arms full of baskets and containers.

"No," I said, my voice vanishing. "I, on the other hand, am starving."

Durai and I sat in the comfort of the silence only true friends can know. The safety of being together without any pressure, or expectation.

When he dished the food, the smell of it filled me and yet my hunger vanished.

"We need to leave tomorrow. Billey needs to see her mother. The past needs to be dealt with. I think for just now, it is down to her to make right the mistakes of the past."

Durai sat, thinking, making no attempt to question the mysteries of our lives. "If any two people deserve to be happy, it's you two. For Kluzahr. For the pain of the past. For the pain you have both lived through. I may not know what it is, but you both wear it like armor. Except with each other. She'll need you but you'll know when."

"You know, Durai, I'd never really thought about it before, but you are the closest thing I have to family. You are the only person who would even notice if I ceased to be. You and Billey are the only two who would care or even notice."

He lifted his leg across the log to sit astride, facing me. "If you were in trouble you'd ask for help? Promise me? You are the closest thing I have to a daughter. The universe never blessed me with children. She sent me you instead." He held my hands in his. His huge fingers hid my hands from sight. "No questions. No recriminations. Just ask for anything you need."

We both leaned in and hugged.

By the time I let go of him, my body had lightened and my stillness held an acknowledgment of the love we shared.

"I need to sleep," I said. I looked down at him. "I promise. If I need help, I'll ask."

I walked toward my bed, now filled with Billey, and hesitated outside the door before walking past and climbing the steps down to the dwelling next to Billey's.

For the first time in forty winters, the emptiness of my bed ached my heart. It struggled to beat with the pain crushing and squeezing it. So close and yet still so far.

TWENTY-THREE

ALEX

The weeks turned to months, and as I lay in my bed listening to the chatter, laughter, and noise of the people I shared my new home with, an unease made my skin itch. A tingle of anxiety crept across my body, a sensation I'd become familiar with. I had assumed time would ease it, but I still found myself weighed with the burden of fear. Fear my safety would disappear, fear my life here would end, fear I would end up alone.

Working in the school helped me focus. Dealing with children all day made it impossible for the worries to find me. My thoughts were too busy keeping up with the children in my care. As one of the most educated, I helped out in the school, and it made me feel more connected to my mother. Besides, all the children loved Jen and she loved all the attention.

I was buried in my thoughts and doubts when Maria, who befriended me when I moved into the bed next to hers, stuck her head around the curtain.

"We're going to eat. Are you coming?" she asked, smiling as usual.

I forced myself to smile back. I enjoyed seeing everybody in the dining building. Families and those with children ate earlier, so I tended to go with the younger, single members of the community. I nodded and pulled back the curtain. I followed Maria as we shared stories of our day. The normality helped me to ignore the loneliness of being surrounded by so many people, to soak in at least a fleeting sense of belonging.

By the time we arrived in the dining hall, it was filled with a hundred others. Most sat at the long rows of tables, and we joined the end of the queue of ten or so people. I saw Iggy in the back, alongside those he worked with on guard duty. I hated seeing him with a gun. I hated the sight of the guns. He either didn't notice me or avoided looking at me, which he did a lot. We had spoken very few times since we had arrived.

Emmy, who I saw most days since he was assigned the job of working in the kitchens, sat at one of the tables near the front along with Roberto and Abi. They smiled at me. They had both been given work in the farming area, which I was a bit jealous of. I loved to feel the earth, the life, but knew deep down I was better suited to the school. Besides, it meant a much shorter day. By lunchtime, I would be done and left to read and wander on my own.

With our dinner, a vegetable casserole that tasted far better than it looked, we joined them at their table. We chatted about our differing lives on the island, all avoiding sharing feelings. When Adam and Prince walked in with other guards from the night shift, I expected them to sit at the back. Why do people gravitate to workgroups; was it a sense of familiarity? I supposed they had a common topic to discuss.

They waved at their workmates and came over to join us, to my surprise. Although, I also knew Prince had a soft spot for Maria, but neither of them would admit they liked each other. It was entertaining to watch them skirt around the issue. Adam sat opposite me and we chatted, leaving Prince and Maria to their peacocking.

I found the constant company draining sometimes, and when I said I wanted to go for a walk, Adam suggested we go together. I tried to suggest I should go alone. I offered an alternative: that tomorrow he could take me for a walk after the campfire, a monthly gathering filled with storytelling and company.

As I stood to leave, Jericho and Luther walked in. I saw little of Jericho since I arrived, which I didn't mind. I had relived the moment he had used his energy to probe mine, curious at what he hoped to find and more than a touch annoyed I allowed Iggy to convince me to hide my magic.

He smiled, though not at me, more of a general smile aimed at everybody. I was walking past him, trying to feel invisible, when he turned to me and said, "Hello Alex. How are you settling in? I hear you are working wonders with the children. They love you. Perhaps we could chat about it sometime."

I found myself a bumbling child, sounding like anything but an intelligent teacher. "I'm well, thanks; and, yes, that would be fine," I said, pausing for a second to speak, and rushed past him. I was aware I held my breath and my heart pounded, but I couldn't explain why. I tried to tell myself it was due to the lie I had told, by omission, when his energy connected with mine, but I didn't believe my own reasoning.

I stood outside the dining building stroking Jen, who had sat awaiting my return. I shivered, trying to remember why I wanted to go for a walk.

"You look cold. Here, borrow my coat."

I spun around to see Adam and tried to smile. "I hadn't realized how cold it was. I'll be fine, honestly."

"Don't be silly. I'm only going to bed. I'm going to have an early night and read a book." He placed the heavy woolen coat around my shoulders.

I laughed a small nervous laugh, fighting the urge to squirm at being so close. "You're reading? I thought you didn't like to read?"

"Well, you always seem to have your nose in a book, and I thought I'd try to figure out the attraction." He blushed and stepped back. "Look, I'm just trying to be nice. I'll get the coat back in the morning. You sure you want to go for a walk? It's dark and you don't want to get lost."

I struggled to smile, touched by the thought, and said, "Trust me, I'm only going for a little walk. I've been inside all day and I wanted a little air before bed. Besides I've got Jen. She's got a good sense of direction. Goodnight, Adam."

"If you're sure. See you in the morning," he said, turning and walking away. I watched as he disappeared behind the tents, and a regret sat on my stomach. I needed friends and enjoyed having them, but a part of me knew Adam wanted me to be more than a friend. I had spent time with him since my arrival, and he often visited me at school. I had grown accustomed to having him, Prince, and Maria around.

I pushed my arms through the coat, pulling it around me, and Jen and I walked in the opposite direction, away from people. The trees hid what little light the dying sun was managing to share, and the darkness caused a sense of loneliness to cover me. I was terrible at this. I wanted friends, but not too close.

I followed the sound of water, knowing if I stayed near it, the worst outcome would be that I walked in an uneven circle. The sound became louder, and although I couldn't see it, the crashing of the water hitting the island created a slow, peaceful tone that helped me clear my head, and my breathing slowed. After a few minutes, the sun created an ethereal glow as I came to a field and sat down to watch it set. The dying embers of its fire merged with the sky, causing ripples of orange and red to slide in between the thin clouds.

How long would it take until I accepted the island as home and allowed my worries to disappear? I wondered about too many things since I arrived, most of which made no real difference, such as where they found hundreds of plates, or how they got the wood, roofing, etc. from the mainland? It didn't matter, so why did I find myself fixating on irrelevant things?

Sitting here, I could free myself from the niggling fears and concerns that raced around my head too frequently. I placed my palms on the ground, oblivious to the cold tingling in my fingers. I picked a small daisy poking its head between the long grass, and a memory filled me. A memory of picking daisies in a garden with my mother. Was it my home? Was it a memory?

I stretched my hands and imagined a field full of daisies, willing the life to suck up the magic within it. I watched as small smiling daisies appeared, scattered around and dancing in the breeze. I picked one and then the sound of footsteps behind me caused me to jump up, to face the trees. Jen sat at my side, and if it had not been for her ears scanning backwards and forward, I would have doubted my hearing. When nobody appeared, I prepared to leave, but then Jericho strode from between the trees. Jen growled and I patted her.

His dark silhouette created an odd image disappearing and merging with the trees as he strode toward me. The white of his eyes floated in the darkness of the night. "I'm sorry, my dear. I didn't mean to make you jump. When you left the dining room, I realized how remiss I have been not chatting with you earlier."

I swallowed, trying to clear my throat. "I understand you are a busy man, and I'm settling in just fine. It'll take a bit to get used to, but I'm getting there." I could feel my hands beginning to shake and stuck them in the deep pockets of Adam's coat.

"I'm glad to hear it. I hear from Abi that your mother was a teacher after the war. Perhaps you have some ideas about what we could teach the children." He smiled at me and a cold shudder passed through my body.

"To be honest, I was only eight when my mother died, and I never had much in the way of teaching from her. I think Abi probably knows more about her lessons than I do. Most of what I know I learned from books."

He stared at me. "What a shame. From what I understand she was an inspirational teacher." I froze as I thought about what Roberto and Abi might have told him. If they had shared her teachings on magic and the universal connection, then he would guess my abilities. I had no idea whether they had followed Iggy's advice.

"But I'd be more than happy to visit you tomorrow if you'd like, seeing as there's no school." I tried to hide my panic but had little confidence in my acting skills.

"That would be lovely. I wondered if anybody had talked to you about doing guard duty on the mainland. We all take it in turns, you see. I was curious if you felt up to joining the roster yet or not?" he asked, bending to pick a daisy. "Oh, I hadn't noticed these before. How wonderful." His eyes looked into mine and my heart bounced off the soles of my feet.

"Oh, that would be fine by me. We all need to do our bit," I said, trying to look anywhere but at the daisy.

"Excellent. I'll let Luther know. Are you walking back? I could walk with you."

I heard my breath, curious whether it sounded as loud to him as it did to me. "I was going to sit a little longer until the sun went down. I like watching the stars."

He patted me on the shoulder. "I understand. I'll try to catch up with you tomorrow. Night, Alex." He strode off and I collapsed on the ground, staring at the daisies. I threw myself backwards and gazed at the sky, now lit with the gentle glow of the moon.

I was pushing myself up when I spotted a figure from between the trees, and I found myself panicking. Had Jericho realized I had created the daisies? My eyes fixed on the shadow person striding toward me. They were too broad, too tall. It wasn't Jericho. Jen ran to meet the shadow, her tail wagging.

"Alex, are you alright?" I recognized Iggy's voice and shocked myself by the volume of the sigh I let out, unaware I had been holding my breath.

"Yes. I'm fine. What are you doing here?"

He came into view, and I could for the first time see him rather than his shadow. The light from the moon created dark shadows in his wrinkled brow and under his eyes. "I was worried about you. You'd been gone for a while and I thought maybe something happened."

"How did you know I'd been gone a while?" I asked, straightening my shoulders. "I don't need a bodyguard, you know." I regretted my harsh tone. I was pleased he had noticed, pleased he cared. "I'm sorry. I didn't mean it like that, but you barely speak to me. Even in the dining hall, you don't notice me. Honestly, you confuse me. Mind you, everything confuses me at the moment."

He sat and I sat next to him. "You've been making friends, so I left you to it. You need friends. That doesn't mean I don't see you or care." He looked at me and his face looked pained.

"I am sorry, but I thought maybe we were friends, and then you ignored me. I'm not having a go at you, just . . ." I gazed at my hands cupping my knees. "Are you settling in well? You made friends too."

"Mm. I guess so. Sort of," he said.

"Why am I finding it so hard. This is what I wanted. I should be happy. Shouldn't I? Is there something wrong with me?" I looked up to see his face, feeling his breath on my cheek. A silence cocooned us, and I realized this was what I should have felt when Adam had put his coat on me. Static electricity buzzed around me as my energy fizzled. Instead, I felt it for Iggy. Except I knew he didn't see me as anything but an annoying child.

He looked away and leaned his elbows on his knees. "I know what you mean and there is nothing wrong with you. I'm struggling a bit myself. I keep waiting for it to go wrong, like a premonition I know is just my fear."

I sighed, my heavy heart dragging me down until I stooped. "I don't think it helps that I don't like Jericho. Everybody else loves him. There must be something wrong with me."

"Well, you and me. I don't trust him. I can't explain what I don't like but there is something."

Jen, growing bored, stretched herself across us, demanding attention. I looked at Iggy. "Looks like it's time to go. Thanks for worrying about me. It's appreciated. Come on, let's go." I stood holding out my hand to help him as though I could pull him up. He looked at it and laughed.

We both laughed and our worries were forgotten, for a while.

Twenty-Four

Iggy

As a child, I grew to hate noise. Noise formed a prelude to violence.

Life moving from one place to another, hunting for somewhere to belong, became harder and, with time, we realized small groups were more successful.

The more people you contain in one space, the more the likelihood of personalities clashing. Yet, the silence of death and loneliness from my earliest memories added discomfort.

My earliest memory was of death.

I stood staring at a mound of dirt, being told it was my mother. It was always accompanied by an all-encompassing silence in my memories. I know, somewhere in the depths of my brain, my father stood next to me. Yet, I cannot see him. All I know is the void. I couldn't find words to explain the feelings crushing my insides. My father's hand, always so large and rugged in my memories, sat like a leaden weight on my shoulders. His hand stopped me from running. I recall the desire in my brain to run. I also relive the fear of my feet freezing to the ground.

My father formed a larger-than-life space in my memory. He always had some story or wisdom to impart, and life was never quiet with him. On that day, the silence took on such an unnatural feel, like a rough, scratchy blanket. It wrapped me and I couldn't escape.

However, the memory of silence is the only other time I recall him being quiet.

The day he died.

During the Orange, I can only imagine I was somehow shielded. My mind had either blanked the horrors or my father had protected me. I remember life before, and then as if one second later, the silence of life after. All the people who filled our house, seeking advice and guidance from my father, vanished.

After, life was stories and history my father shared, knowing he might not survive to tell any more. I now recognized his desperation to share while he could.

I spent hours confused by the loneliness while he scavenged and hunted for food. I played with toys, drew pictures, and obeyed his rules about never leaving the house. All the time I sat there, worrying about why I was alone, he ventured out into the aftermath of the Orange. He couldn't avoid the poisons of the world. He made sure I survived.

Then one morning, I woke up. Life back then was filled with darkness and it was difficult to know when morning became afternoon or night. In the world after, in our new life, I slept in the same bed as my father. So, on that morning when I awoke and he wasn't there, a new sensation overtook me. More than fear, less than panic. A knowing in my childish mind. For the first time, I understood alone, even before I found his body slumped on the living room floor, blood congealed around his mouth and nose.

It must have been days by the time Emmy and David heard my cries. My heart-wrenching sobs were small and pained long after I ran out of energy to cry. My mouth hurt from screaming for water. Even in death, I remembered his rule about only drinking water from bottles, and, after they were empty, I found myself afraid to break his rule.

Emmy tells the story of how skinny and hungry I was, yet all I remember is the combination of thirst and despair. I would drift off touching my father's cold, hard corpse, scared he would be taken from me.

The creaking and smashing of the front door were followed by a bright light. As my eyes adjusted, all I could see was Emmy. His blonde hair, with the glowing light surrounding him, played tricks on my child's mind.

I stopped crying, the sobs vanishing as this angel walked toward me. Once I was old enough to realize he wasn't an angel, I knew he was my angel.

On Jericho's Island, with the noise of being surrounded by people all day, the sounds played on a different set of memories. People living life formed a background hum. I tried to make an effort to connect with those I shared a space with but found myself struggling.

Upon arriving on Jericho's Island, we were all separated. I floundered, unused to being so alone. For such an antisocial person, or so Emmy told me, my life on Jericho's Island should have been blissful, at last having the opportunity to vanish into the background.

As a couple, Roberto and Abi were farther out in the grandest of the wooden barn-like structures we all slept in. They adjusted with ease to our new life. They were both assigned to the farming and agriculture area and adapted, forming solid-looking friendships with other couples and families. They never forgot to say hello when they passed me, though.

We all visited each other the day we arrived. Roberto and Abi had the only space with walls isolating their area of the barn. Thin wooden walls, crudely constructed but solid enough to provide privacy. Alex and Emmy had been placed in different buildings. Theirs, like mine, consisted of a bed with only a curtain to offer some separation.

Emmy flourished, believing he had found community. When he was assigned to the kitchens, he had a place. Dealing with everybody every day, he soon became a known figure, socializing and belonging with other residents. He would visit every day in the beginning, and with time, we only chatted in the dining room he worked in as I ate my food with the guards I'd been assigned with.

Yet, happy as I became to see Emmy find some peace, I couldn't find my place. The guards never felt like a group I could belong to. They consisted of people I would, instinctively, have sought to stay away from. They tended to be older and, in the absence of magic, relied on weapons to protect the island from the trouble that never happened.

My experience of living in other collectives taught me there would always be trouble among people. Jealousy, ignorance, intolerance all caused outbursts, given time. Yet, here, nothing ever happened. All the people managed to live in harmony or a version of it.

So, why I couldn't trust Jericho confused me. Why couldn't I find the bliss Emmy had?

Being a guard, though, allowed me to cover the whole island. It was much smaller than we thought at first. This constant walking, always moving and never having to stop and interact, suited me. I could mingle and wander without aim.

Alex, the person I saw most, was often alone. I recognized her loneliness, but also, despite my first impressions, she made friends in her own time.

She walked to teach in the school every morning, and I made it part of my duties to cover her route. Watching her, I saw her grow in confidence, but something stopped me from talking to her.

She moved on and tried to belong. I couldn't stand in the way. I couldn't be the person to remind her of the magic she couldn't use. Her hair had grown longer and hung about her shoulders. She'd begun to tie it back in a range of styles to match her new friend's. Having asked around, I found out her new friend was called Maria. She had lived on the island since almost the beginning. She and her family were one of the first people to live here. She carried herself with ease and confidence that spoke of a peaceful life. The pain of the world hadn't touched her. She hadn't been spoiled by the suffering outside.

In the months since we first landed on the island, we all assimilated to our new lives, and that night, like many others, I sat at the back of the dining hall at the long table used by the guards. Luther, who I discovered was second-in-command to Jericho and head of security, informed me this table had been assigned to us to allow us to keep track of the comings and goings of the members of our island.

Watching Alex, guilt knotted my stomach. The words I wanted to say sat on the tip of my tongue. Yet, the longer I avoided talking with her, the more I struggled to speak to her. Much as all I had was observing her from a distance, I worried watching her was, in itself, wrong. Was I spying on a friend?

Life would be so much easier if I just walked over and talked to her.

She was flanked by Prince and Adam, who we had met on our first night.

As I watched Alex, I also watched Adam watch her.

I zoned out the conversations happening around me until the man beside me elbowed me in the side. I looked at him and he nodded to the door. I followed the direction of his look and saw Jericho, who never ate with everybody else. His eyes scanned the room until he spotted Alex, and the hairs stood up on my arms.

Judging by the speed with which she ate and left, I knew she shared my uneasiness of Jericho's presence.

I pushed my plate into the middle of the table, a second of guilt tugging at me, aware Emmy would be the one expected to clear it and all the others left by the guards. I nodded at the guard opposite me in a manner I had developed to avoid having to talk to people. He smiled back, a slight upturn to the corners of his mouth the only indication he acknowledged my leaving the table.

I pushed my chair in, stopping to lean on it for a minute as I watched Alex return her plate to the kitchen and head for the door.

Adam followed behind her, shuffling in a haphazard manner, banging into people and apologizing to each person until he reached the doorway moments after Alex.

I moved between the tables and chairs. I couldn't move too quickly or I would be in danger of bumping into Alex. I didn't want to attract attention to myself. I had mastered the art of being almost invisible. As much as that was possible at my height.

Pausing to squeeze between two tables at right angles, my eye caught sight of Jericho. Despite arriving only a few minutes ago, he headed to the door and my aura flared.

Were we both following Alex?

He paused by the door, glancing around for something or somebody.

Now, I no longer wanted to follow Alex. If nothing else, Adam posed no risk. She would be in no danger from him. Jericho, however, posed a real risk.

My plans changed, and, hanging back a few meters, I followed the direction Jericho had headed. Perhaps he wasn't following Alex but my father always told me to trust my gut. It was rarely wrong. I had over the years grown to appreciate the instinct. It had saved me more than once.

We walked away from the building, moving through the trees. I tried to step in the grassy, muddy areas, cautious enough to avoid any patches of leaves or twigs.

My aura reached out, desperate to feel for him. My magic took on a personality of its own, keen to break my rules about staying hidden.

I understood the risk of using magic to follow Jericho, but the sunlight hiding on the horizon and the trees blocked most of it, creating more shadows than there was light. My movements slowed and I worried I had lost him until I heard voices ahead. Skulking through the last of the trees, I crept toward the sound of talking. I recognized the voices. I recognized her voice, and as I reached the last row of trees, I knelt on one knee and peered out through the bushes forming a hiding spot. This close, there would be no way he couldn't sense me if he used his magic. I had to rely on Alex being too much of a distraction.

In the open, flat grass, they stood less than a meter apart, and Alex fidgeted, pulling on her hair, fiddling with a necklace, and twiddling a flower between her fingers.

I gasped, realizing the meadow was full of small pale-colored flowers.

Without needing to be told, I knew she had used her magic. If I knew, he surely knew.

Cursing and mumbling under my breath, I moved to my right to get a view of both faces lit by the sunset in the distance.

No matter how I tried, I couldn't hear any words. Sounds, recognizable as the hum of talking, were the best I could make out.

I watched Alex's mouth twisting. She was chewing the inside of her cheek. I had in the past found this endearing, but, at this moment, I knew she didn't know what to say. Her body stiffened and, as though planning an escape, twisted to turn away from Jericho. Jen sat obediently at Alex's feet and never took her eyes off Jericho. I could see the fluffy golden fur on her neck catch the light as it rose.

Jen and I shared the same opinion, it appeared.

Leaning against the smooth bark of the young tree, I pushed my body up against it, never taking my eyes off them. Moving to take a step toward them, no longer able to stand back, I dove into the grass as Jericho turned and walked back toward me.

I held my breath until the sound of Jericho's footsteps vanished. I straightened and moved to walk in Alex's direction when she fell on the ground.

Panic pounded in my head until I saw Jen's tail wagging as she lay on top of Alex, licking her face. I slowed my pace, not wanting to scare her.

Jen saw me first, jumping to her feet and dashing to me.

I leaned down and ruffled her fur. She licked my hand in return, and as I looked back to Alex; she was standing, brushing the grass and weeds from her clothes. Coat.

I recognized the coat. It belonged to Adam, and a wave of unreasonable anger flushed my face. I was grateful for the dark and gave Jen one more stroke before she ran back to Alex.

"Are you alright?" I asked, regretting the words as soon as they left my mouth. Alex was, even without magic, an easy person to read. Her emotions were painted on her face, and her face was dark, not from the night but from worries. Worries masked her sparkle.

"I'm fine. Why are you here?"

I fumbled my words, desperate to find a reason for being here. We both knew it wasn't a coincidence but she didn't push me. We avoided having to admit the truth.

She relaxed and we sat, oblivious to the dampness of the grass, and watched the last dying glow of the sun as it vanished for the night.

Chatting with her, my body loosened, and, for the first time since we had arrived, I felt my heart lighten.

For somebody so easy to read, I couldn't decide how happy she was. However, it had been obvious she was making friends and adjusting. My heart pulled in every direction, creating a heaviness in my chest when she opened up and explained how unsettled she was. "You've been making friends, so I left you to it. You need friends. That doesn't mean I don't see you or care," I said, rubbing my hands on my knees. I stared at my knees, wanting to look anywhere but at her. The ache of avoiding her for months was now doubled as I recalled just how good I felt next to her.

She explained how unhappy she had become and how much she couldn't adjust, and I understood. Yet, I had been in this situation before. I had tried and failed many times.

I wanted her to make it work. The ugliness of the outside world would be part of me forever, but she had the privilege of living in her protected school, unaware of people and the truth of them. I couldn't see her broken by human nature. In that second, I knew I would have to leave.

Somewhere deep inside, I found comfort and discomfort that she would never and could never leave here on her own. She would fight on until she made it work. I would always be the mirror of her fears.

I had to leave the island.

I had to leave her.

With an immense, burning pain shredding my chest, we walked back toward the sleeping area. The trees grew thinner and the sounds of people began to break into our peace.

My body itched with a need to grab her, but instead, I ran my fingers through my hair, allowing it to fall over my face, and I looked at my feet, unable to look at her anymore. I put my hands in my pockets, scared they would betray me. Reaching the point where we needed to walk in different directions, my muscles ached from the effort it took to not hold her.

"Anyway, I'll let you get some sleep, and, maybe, we'll chat soon," I said, knowing I would be gone. I had to go soon. I couldn't stay here and risk her happiness.

She grabbed my hand and looked up at my face. "We better," she said. She held her hand up to my face, and I couldn't stop the smile that spread through every muscle.

"Good night, Alex," I said, turning away. Every step was an internal battle of wills. I wanted to turn and watch her go. I wanted to leave her to be happy.

TWENTY-FIVE

ALEX

A buzz of life, happiness, and excitement had crept across the island as the sun rose. Its rays shone a new day and a rare chance to socialize with everybody. I found myself with a day of nothing to do, and as I watched the others running around, chattering and laughing, their emotions infected me.

Jen lay across my feet, keen to avoid the feet running around. She tilted her head, her questioning face pulling at my one true connection with another living thing. With so many people and a large fire, I worried she would have an accident, or cause an accident, and a space in my heart ached.

I sat up and Jen jumped, alternating between panting and licking me, desperate to escape all the activity, and I empathized with her. We sneaked between the throngs of people busy building the campfire and headed for the peace of the empty fields.

We were moments from freedom, away from all the noise and people, when Jen growled. I looked around to see Jericho and Luther heading toward me and my excitement vanished, leaving an empty space inside.

Jericho waved at me and I tried to smile.

"Alex, hi. I was talking to Luther about putting you on the guard rota on the mainland."

I looked from Jericho to Luther. "Of course, I'm glad to do my bit."

"That's great because we're short for tonight's shift. I was hoping you and Iggy could do it. Jericho has explained you would be looking forward to the campfire tonight, and I'm sorry. I wouldn't ask if I didn't need to," said Luther.

I tried to hide my disappointment at missing tonight's event. Jen growled at them both and I flustered. "Sorry, she just needs her walk." I bent to stroke her, but she barely hid her hatred of them. Was she picking up on my negative emotions or did she hate them that much?

Anger filled Jericho's dark eyes as he glared at Jen. "Never mind, can't blame her. Just meet at the boat after dinner. See you there." They spun around and walked away.

Watching them stride through the mass of people, I tried to convince myself that it was probably for the best. I was never comfortable around too many people. The sun disappeared behind the clouds and a cold breeze sped through the trees, and even Jen didn't seem to care when we left them behind to stand in the calm of the open field. She didn't run around or play like usual. Instead, she lay at my feet and I sat next to her and we hugged, her fur tickling my cheek.

The sounds of frenzied anticipation flowed past me as I fiddled with my spoon. I swept the soup from side to side, watching it ripple on the sides of the bowl. I tried to convince myself it hadn't been deliberate, Luther and Jericho choosing tonight to send me on guard duty. Somebody had to do it, so why not me?

Maria and Prince sat babbling next to me, but my concentration was on the soup. My stomach grumbled for food yet recoiled when the soup hit it. I placed my spoon next to my bowl, resigned to the hunger in me. I preferred it to the nausea of forced food. Since I would have little else to do tonight other than eat, I reasoned it didn't matter.

I pushed my chair back and it scraped on the floor. Those at my table fell silent and all eyes turned to look at me, and I mumbled an apology before rushing out of the dining hall. At least I wouldn't have to leave Jen alone now. She could come with me to the mainland.

I was walking back to my bed to collect Jen and grab a jumper for guard duty when I became aware of Jericho walking next to me. I twisted my head to look at him and tried to squeeze a smile out, but my cheeks refused to move.

"I was hoping to catch you before you left. I'm sorry about tonight, but I thought you might like to take this," he said, holding out an old book with no cover. I reached for it and examined the spine. *Native American Legends & Myths,* it said. My eyebrows knotted and I looked up into his eyes.

"Thank you."

"The story I am opening tonight's campfire with is from that book. I just thought you might like to read it. I've turned the corner down at the right place."

"That's thoughtful, thanks," I said, continuing toward Jen. I stopped for a second to say goodbye, but he had gone already. I looked at the book, turning it in my hands and flicking through the pages. I placed it in my bag, along with the food for Jen.

She ran to me and jumped up, sensing my sadness, trying to cheer me up. We walked to the beach in silence, and she never strayed from my heel even when we passed the campfire, now burning, sending flickers of fiery ash floating into the air. My eyes followed them as they found freedom from the fire. I had found freedom, hadn't I? Why did I feel so trapped then?

The boat was empty and the jetty creaked in the silence of the waves. We sat leaning against some large boulders to wait for everybody else to turn up. I flicked open the book to read, quickly becoming engrossed and distracted.

I read the story of a Fire Flier who had come to lead a tribe to safety, to a new land. By the time I reached the end, where they foretold of the final Fire Flier who would appear in the glows of fire to lead them home to their world by opening mystical portals, I found my imagination transporting me to new worlds and new possibilities.

A voice forced me from my imaginary worlds and I jumped up, spinning to face Luther and an older woman I didn't know.

"Alex, this is Betty. She'll be joining us on tonight's duty."

I breathed to calm my nerves, looking up at her smiling face. The cragged lines crinkling her eyes almost hid the warm golden-brown.

"Nice to meet you," she said, holding out her hand to shake mine. I placed my hand in her soft, warm one, shaking it. My eyes were drawn to her waistband and the gun sticking out from it. My eyes froze, unable to look away.

"You'll need a gun," said Luther, holding out a small silver gun. "This revolver should suit you. Have you ever used a gun?" I dragged my eyes from Betty's gun to stare at Luther. My mouth hung open but refused to allow words to escape.

"I . . . I . . . don't want a gun. I couldn't," I burbled incoherently as my eyes darted from the gun to his face.

"You don't get a choice," he barked, and I could hear the anger barely hidden in his tone. "It is our job to stop anybody who might risk the safety of the community."

I stared, unable to find a reason that would justify my reticence.

"Give her an empty gun. She'll probably be too dangerous with a loaded one anyway if she's never held one." I twisted my head, tearing my eyes from the gun to see Iggy. He walked to stand next to me, placing his hand between my shoulder blades. "I'll pair with her and I have held and used a gun."

Luther nodded in agreement, emptying the bullets into his hand and handing it to me. Iggy picked it out of my hand, hiding it in his back pocket, and directed me toward the boat. I looked up at him. "Thank you." He nodded and looked away, as keen to move on as I was.

When Adam and Prince arrived, we all bundled into the boat, allowing the wind to push toward our destination. I sat watching the patched-up sail puff and push us, clutching the book in my fingers, my white knuckles saying more than I could. Jen lay in the bottom of the boat, her head resting on Iggy's feet.

My stomach moved with the boat, and I was glad I hadn't eaten the soup. My stomach rose to meet my throat with every wave we bounced over, and I dropped my book. Bending to pick it up, my stomach finally gave its final act of rebellion as I retched.

Iggy rubbed my back. "Are you okay?"

I gave a feeble nod in response.

Adam and Prince had offered to work the first shift, and Iggy and I lounged on the sofas in the largest living room. The fire burned, lighting the room with a warm glow and casting shadows around. I reread the story of the Fire Flier aloud while Iggy feigned interest and Jen snored on the rug.

"Do you think there's any truth in the old stories?" I asked, not expecting an answer.

Iggy turned to face me, moving his body to lie on his side. "When we first met I told you about that story. Those Native Americans your book talks about are my ancestors. Of course, I believe them. There will come the one who can walk through the fire of the portal, leading us to the promised land. To our homeland. Have you never thought about why some of us are different since the Orange?"

"You mean the magic?"

"Yeah. I mean, in the old days the idea of somebody who could summon fire and not burn seemed ridiculous, but you're proof that's not true anymore. We both have gifts our ancestors didn't. I don't think you realize how special you are. Although it doesn't matter anyway. My people moved so many places and so far from the portals or gates, we'd have no idea where to find them anymore." He sighed and closed his eyes.

I wanted to let him sleep, but my curiosity forced the words to spurt out of my mouth. "Why wouldn't people have seen them before? I mean, surely it would be easy to see, even if you couldn't use it?"

He slowly opened his eyes to gaze at me. "It wouldn't be a physical thing. It would be a place with a strange vibration. Only those who could feel it would know. It would react to a Fire Flier. You know, dance, glow, consume them in its energy."

I sat upright, staring at him, my mind racing back to that fateful day in Salem. The day my life had changed irrevocably. The glow that had consumed me, causing me to feel dizzy. The connection it had offered had felt different from any place I knew of. I had been planning to ask Danny and Calesta about it, but then life had forced me in a different direction.

My face must have shown something of my thoughts because Iggy sat up, staring at my face. "What? You're thinking something. What is it?"

"It's going to sound silly, just childish fantasy, but I was in Salem before I met you and the strangest thing happened. An energy smothered me, covering me in an orange glow, and I felt a connection. A weird connection, like connecting to somewhere else. It's just stupid though." I looked into his eyes. "Isn't it?"

Betty ran into the room, gasping for air. "Come quick. There are people outside," she yelled, running back out without waiting for a response.

Iggy and I stood, and he passed me the revolver I had avoided thinking about all night. My head pounded, a throbbing inside my skull that I was trying to ignore. We exited through the conservatory, doubling back to get behind the intruders.

I thought back to the night we had wandered into the world of Jericho and hoped the intruders were simply seeking safety and community. Iggy pulled me behind some bushes and we peered through at the group of three people. In the darkness, I could see little other than their outlines. The third person had a smaller and slimmer silhouette, and I wondered if it was a child.

As they approached the front of the house, we stepped out behind them. Iggy raised his gun and I followed his example. Our footsteps behind them were slow and silent, waiting for their actions to cause us to break cover. Realizing Jen was at my heel, I reached my hand to touch her, sharing my energy and controlling her emotions. She sat shielded by the bushes as Luther and Betty opened the door to face them.

I heard Luther ask them to lower their weapons and an argument ensued. Both sides stood with their guns pointing at each other, and I looked over to check that Adam and Prince were in position on the opposite side of the gardens. They nodded and all four of us crept forward until we stood directly behind them.

A scream rang out as the tallest of the silhouetted intruders fired a shot at Luther. I watched in horror as the body collapsed on the ground. The smallest shadow, the one I had presumed was a child, backed up until the barrel of my gun poked into their back. With my eyes fixed on this child-sized shadow, I missed the argument between Luther and the remaining adult until further bullets screamed through the air, and I looked to see their body fall next to the first.

The shadow squirming against the barrel of my gun turned his face to look into my eyes. The face of a child, his eyes pleading with me. "Just put your hands up and get down on your knees," I said, begging him to cooperate. "Nobody else needs to be hurt, please."

He turned to face Luther, now staring directly at both of us. I looked into his eyes, the darkness making them look black, and I realized Luther was pulling the trigger. Shooting at him, shooting at me. My Firestone vibrated, and I dropped the gun and waved my hand, sending a wave of energy to the bullet. I watched as it changed direction, heading into the shadows.

"Stop," I yelled, "he's a child and he isn't armed." His eyes locked with mine, appearing to darken, the shadows filling them. The muscles in his face hardened and it was as though I could feel the veins in his neck pumping.

The child darted from my grip, heading for the bushes and the darkness. My feet stuttered. I glared at Luther, my eyes moving from his eyes to the gun still pointing at me.

"For fuck's sake, Luther. What is wrong with you?" I screamed, holding both arms out and sending him flying backwards before taking off into the shadows to find the child.

Darting about in the bushes, no longer hiding my magic, I probed the space to find the child. His heartbeat, pounding and full of fear, was easy to find, and I placed my arms around him. I ran my fingers through his hair, sharing my calming aura with him.

"It's okay. I've got you. You're safe," I whispered, bending to meet his face. I listened to the others moving through the bushes, hunting for us. "It's okay, I've got him," I yelled, standing up and guiding him toward the house.

We stepped from the darkness to see Luther, his eyes still locked on mine as though neither of us had moved. My eyes drifted to his hands, frozen to the gun that still pointed at us. In his hands, he held life and death, but it didn't provide him with the bravery he believed he held.

My mother had told me that magic could fool us into false bravery; the power would make us believe nothing could touch us and make us overconfident. Watching the tense muscles in Luther's arms, I understood guns do the same thing, but with the swipe of a hand, I had shown him my power. I lifted the sobbing child and took a step toward him.

"Luther, put the gun down, it's all over now."

His eyes darted from his gun to me and I could see thoughts flitting through his brain. He lowered the gun to point at my feet. Soft fur brushed against my legs and I knew Jen was with me, no longer hidden. At the same second Luther's eyes picked up Jen.

A grin, a mask of evil, hatred, and amusement took over his face as he moved the gun to point at Jen.

My arms, holding the child, took too long to move as I saw his fingers squeeze the trigger. A pained bark filled the darkness, and a cold horror stole my heart, replacing it with a stone weight. Jen. I fell to the ground next to her. I wrapped my arms around her, lifting her head to me. My hands stuck to the warm blood oozing from her side. I looked up at Iggy, who stood looking down at me. He darted to me and knelt next to me as I looked at Jen, feeling the energy drain from her.

I sat, rocking her deadweight as I sobbed. My brain misted and I could no longer seem to create a sentence. My thoughts bounced around in the fog. I looked at Iggy. "He shot at me. He was aiming for me."

Iggy placed his hands on mine, pulling them away from Jen.

"Come on. Come inside. You've had a shock." He wrapped his arms around me, pulling me to my feet, and my knees buckled under me. He looked over my shoulder at Adam and Prince. "Bury Jen."

I spun around, "No, she's . . ." I had no words for the pain that was chewing at my innermost feelings, ripping and shredding me from the inside. I collapsed, only vaguely aware of Iggy's arms scooping me up.

Jen was dead. Jen was dead. My only living connection to my old life, gone. Dead.

The soft stroking of my hand, a gentle-caressing movement, woke me. I opened my eyes to look around me. A dull glow where the sun had forced its way through the cracks in the curtains caused them to strain. I struggled to focus and remember where I was.

I was on a sofa, a comfortable, squishy sofa, with my head propped up slightly on a cushion, and as I became accustomed to light, my eyelids flickered. My brain stuttered, processing the fireplace roaring in the corner of the room and the paintings hung on the walls, large gilt-framed memories of a world that no longer existed.

I looked at my hand, watching the hand stroke it, and followed the hand to the arm attached to it. I looked up to stare into Adam's eyes, their usual sparkling blue dulled by the lack of light and sadness.

"Good morning. How are you?" he asked, letting go of my hand to move stray curls and tuck them behind my ear.

"I'm fine. Sorry, did I fall asleep?" I replied.

His eyes looked up to stare past me, and I followed his gaze to see Iggy and Prince behind me. I sat up, stretching and rubbing my neck, stiffened from sleep. Neither of them spoke, their eyes waiting for a reaction, or a word, or something from me.

Then a gushing memory, like the moment a dam bursts and you find yourself suddenly drowning where you had stood safely moments earlier, swallowed me. Jen.

I sat staring at the floor, following the colors on the rug Jen had laid on. "She's dead, isn't she?" I asked as I stood up and looked at Iggy. I could see the battle inside him as he fought the urge to look away. "Where is she?"

He nodded. "Yes."

I thought, fighting through a fog in my brain, revisiting the events of last night in my head. "Where is she?"

Adam, who I had forgotten was next to me as my attention focused on Iggy, said, "We can take you. Show you."

I stared at him, aware my confused movements were not normal to those in the room but unable to adjust to the situation. "Iggy. I want Iggy to show me."

Adam looked at Iggy, who walked around the sofa to hold my hand. "Come on, I'll show you. I've got you."

We walked in silence out of the room, leaving Adam and Prince behind, and then through the kitchen and conservatory to stand in the back garden, its flowers and plants no longer endowed with the beauty I had seen on my first day here. Now they looked artificial, like stage props designed to distract me from the emotions that were threatening to drown me.

I saw Luther and Betty in the distance and knew they saw me, but they both looked away, busying themselves with packing the boat. I looked up at Iggy.

"He shot at me last night. I'm not being paranoid or fogged by grief. I'm telling you, he aimed for me last night. He wanted me to die. That bullet was meant for me."

He pulled me in closer but said nothing, leading me to a hidden spot among some trees at the side of the house. "I knew how you'd feel about her being buried with trees, so I had her buried here." There was a pause, a moment where I could tell his brain was whirring behind his eyes. "I do believe you, but we may have a bigger problem. You unleashed enough energy last night to send Luther and Betty flying across the garden. There's no hiding your magic now. Jericho will know and he'll want to try to control you."

I stared at him. "I don't understand. Why do you fear our magic so much? Why do we need to hide it when it's a blessing?"

I knelt on the ground and closed my eyes, apologizing to Jen. She had been sent to me, I would never doubt that, and I was responsible for her death. The memory was blurred but I knew.

Everything I loved died.

I loved Jen.

Jen was dead.

Unlike the men who had killed Danny and Calesta, or the men I had set on fire when they attacked us, this death was not in defense. She had died because she loved me.

He sat next to me, resting his hand on mine. "You don't understand. Jericho has created a world that has to be built on magic, but have you ever seen him share it? Has he ever sought to teach the children? No. He wants to be special, and you may well have more magic than he does. Do you think that isn't going to worry him?"

"But magic isn't the problem. Angry old men are. People like Luther. Angry old men desperately holding onto power when they didn't deserve it caused the Orange, and those still left are paying the price. The Orange allowed us to become more than we were. We can't hide that."

He sighed. "That's a lovely sentiment, but not realistic. Jericho holds power, not Luther. Look, are you sure you want to go back? We could leg it right now. Just run and never look back."

I grabbed his hands, staring into his eyes, and I could feel him squirm as he fought his instinct to pull away. "Even if you are right, we can't just leave all those people. We need to stand up and show them the possibilities of the future. The connection isn't just for us. It's for everybody. You can go if you want, but I'm not. What about Roberto, or Abi, or Emmy? Are you prepared to desert them?"

He stood up, brushing the dirt from his trousers, and looked at the boat. "It's time to go. I wouldn't go without you."

I stood up and hugged him. "I don't get you sometimes, but thank you."

"You're welcome. Come on then. Before we get left behind." He walked off, and I followed, for the first time truly accepting that the island may not be the wonder I had hoped.

Approaching the boat, a sadness darker and greater than my own reached me. I stopped, frozen to the ground as I registered its source. I raised my eyes to gaze into the sunlight and saw him. The child I had held last night when Jen died. He had lost everything and everyone.

Darkness filled me, and I wasn't sure it was just grief for Jen. Fear filled me. I just didn't know what it was, yet.

TWENTY-SIX

ALEX

A sad silence hung over the island when we returned. We walked past the blackened mass of last night's campfire, and the story Jericho gave to me played over in my head. Had it been a coincidence? My mother told me there was no such thing as coincidence, but messages we weren't listening to. My father had told her this and she used it as a mantra to justify all sorts of things in life.

I knew I would have to face Jericho soon. He was bound to talk to me about the events that led to Jen's death. I found my body screaming to be alone, to sleep and never wake. The sounds of life when I crawled into my bed grated on my ears, and I curled up, my hands covering them to fight a losing battle.

The story of the Fire Flier battering around in my head permeated into my dreams. The stories my mother told of my father, strange worlds, magic, portals, all mangled as my brain sought to put them in order, and I found myself screaming for my mother. The scream echoed through every muscle of my body, vibrating the air I breathed.

A noise woke me and I stared at the faces of Maria, Prince, and Adam staring down at me. "Was that out loud? I thought I was screaming in my dream."

Maria rushed to sit on the edge of my bed. "I heard about Jen. I'm so sorry," she said and threw herself on top of me, hugging me.

I sat up in my bed, dislodging her arms. "It's fine. I'll get over it. We've all lost people. Not that she was a person, but you know what I mean." The bed seemed so empty without Jen trying to lie across my legs, and I pulled them up, placing my knees under my chin. "People have been killing since the beginning of time. It's just a fact of life." My mind floated in a fog of thoughts. Was it just something we had to accept?

"Do you need anything? Have you eaten?" Adam asked.

"No. Honestly I'll be fine. You all can stop worrying now."

"We're going to grab some lunch. Are you sure you don't want to come, or we could bring you something back?" he asked, and I was touched by his persistence but wanted to be alone.

When they left I pulled on my boots, deciding a walk was my only chance of solitude. I walked past the dining building, shrinking myself, hoping for invisibility. By the time I saw the trees that formed a natural boundary between the camp and the open spaces beyond, my muscles ached from tensing. I dragged myself as far as my tired body would take me but knew no distance would be enough. I needed to be somewhere other than Jericho's Island.

When I reached the field filled with daisies I often walked Jen in, I lay on the ground, watching the clouds drift by. Their gentle flow had a meditative effect and I found my soul calming. I relived the moment Luther fired the gun on a loop in my head, his face ingrained in my brain. Why had he shot at us? The boy in front of me posed no risk and was unarmed. I tried to convince myself he hadn't aimed at me, yet his eyes were fixed on me. It wasn't grief or some weird warping of the event. I saw his eyes and knew he aimed for me.

I replayed all the things I could have done. How I shouldn't have brought Jen with me, left her on the island. No matter how many times I replayed the events in my head, I saw Luther's eyes fixed on me.

I sat up, staring at the sun now visible above the tops of the trees. I stuck my hands in my coat pockets and set off. The walk back to the camp was cold, and the wind shook the trees, the sun flitting between the leaves, creating a frantic dance of light. Soon, I moved against the flow of everybody heading for dinner, and I realized how long I must have been gone.

The deafening silence of the emptiness in the bedroom buildings sucked what little life I had, and I threw myself on my bed, burying my face in the pillow. I teetered on the precipice of sleep, my memories dragging me back every time my brain sought the peace of slumber. Visions of Jen, Danny, Calesta, my mother, all engulfed in flames, haunted my near-sleep, and I strained under the fatigue of my grief.

The energy in the room changed, static negativity filling the space, and I knew Jericho was near before I could see him. I sat upright, crossing my legs, mentally preparing to face him.

"Alex, how are you? I heard about the terrible incident on the mainland. You must be devastated. I know how much you loved that dog." He looked at me, his eyes showing his sorrow, a hollow emotion his energy didn't hold. What a wonderful liar he was. What a pity he hadn't bothered to learn her name.

"I'm alright. Thank you for looking in on me."

"Nonsense. I care about everybody here. I feel so bad for you. If there is anything I can do to help, please ask."

I became aware of his energy pushing and probing, trying to break through mine. I thought of my conversations with Iggy and knew I should allow him to, but I no longer hid my magic and pushed back. I sought to feel his intentions.

I watched his eyes the second he realized I knew what he was doing. A smirk curled his mouth and his eyes widened to stare at me. Curiosity got the better of me, and knowing I could ill-afford to alienate Jericho, I allowed him to breach my aura and enter my mind.

The horrors of his mind merged with mine and I understood him. Truly understood him. I knew what he was doing, something I had done many times with Jen to make her behave. He was planting a false memory in my brain. I had practiced this with Danny and Calesta and knew I would be able to understand it as a false memory, so I allowed him.

He overestimated his ability, and while he rummaged around in my head, seeking a hiding spot for the lie he wanted to install, I rummaged around his. I found what I wanted to know and fought to not recoil. He didn't want to share the magic; he used it to control. He wanted to be a god-like figure. My stomach churned and I let go.

I battled to follow his magic, desperate to find the false memory I knew was there. I found it just as he pulled back. A memory I knew didn't belong. A memory of him saving my life. Hidden deep in my brain, such that I wouldn't recall the details, but I would know I owed him my life. Had he done this to others?

He sat next to me. "I wondered if I could ask you a favor?" he said, his hand tracing the length of my leg, and I twisted away.

I faced him, plastering a smile, struggling to match my energy with it. He would need to know he placed the memory or he wouldn't leave me.

"Of course I will. I owe you everything. What can I do for you?" My heart pounded an erratic beat in my ears and I struggled to calm my breathing.

"I thought, maybe you could grow some flowers for me."

I stared at him. The daisy field now haunted me. Did he know or not? "I will certainly try if you want. I've never grown anything before, but if you tell me how I'll give it a go," I said, trying to force my mouth to smile, unsure what my face did.

He patted my knee and stood up. "No, don't worry. It doesn't matter. Hadn't you better get some dinner?"

I stood up and faced him, my cheeks aching from the continued strain of coaxing a smile. "Yes, are you coming?"

"No, thank you. I already ate. Off you go now. See you soon, Alex," he said with a tone that caused a chill to freeze my skin. I watched as he disappeared in the distance before I could move. My muscles ached as my legs relaxed and regained their power.

The sounds of life taunted me, floating in the wind without a care in the world. With each step torturous, my body became more desperate to run and run forever. To run away. Why hadn't I run with Iggy when he suggested it? I thought of the friends I had made and knew why. Could I help them? Life was easier alone.

I found myself outside the dining hall. With its mismatch of wooden boards and peeling pale-blue paint, I wondered if it had been a barn before the Orange or if it was just built to look that way. I stood staring through the broken glass in the door, contemplating turning around and just hiding in my bed. Although, a bedroom with twenty other women made that impossible. I had nowhere to go. I was trapped on the island. I had walked straight into the trap.

The door swung open and I stepped aside, watching as a group of young people bundled past me, their laughter and chatter lightening the panic burning inside me. Everybody here was safe and part of a community. Did any of us have the right to ask for more? They didn't register I was there. I was such a small cog in a large machine. Did it matter what I felt?

The room was filled with noise and life, and as I walked in, scanning the room, I watched the vision of survival. We were proof survival was possible. Did it matter Jericho was maintaining it through false memories and rhetoric? He was abusing the gift the Orange had given him. Given us all. We had to be better than those who had ruled the world before the Orange.

Nobody turned to stare at me despite the conspicuousness covering my skin. I gazed around at the many faces, some I recognized and many I didn't. I wondered how many of them would stand up for me. How many knew I existed.

I walked toward the back of the barn-like room, toward the kitchen area. I picked up a small flowery plate and was relieved to see Emmy serving. His face was fuller and the gaunt expression of his icy-blue eyes no longer pierced through me. His blonde hair, now short and smart, made him look younger.

"Hey, Alex. I heard about Jen and I'm sorry," he said, his eyes lowering to gaze at the casserole on my plate. He raised his eyes and I knew he understood my sadness. "If there's anything you need, you know where I am."

I placed my hand on top of his, biting my lips and trying not to cry again. "Thanks." I turned and walked toward Roberto and Abi, who sat on the far edge of the room. Squeezing between the rows of tables, apologizing to everybody I bumped on the way, I spotted Iggy at the back of the room with the other guards. He looked up and smiled. I nodded in reply and faced Roberto and Abi.

I placed my plate on the table with a clatter as I almost fell over somebody's foot.

"Could you have chosen a table that was harder to get to?"

Roberto and Abi both laughed. "That was the intention," said Abi. "Gosh, not you though. It's still taking some getting used to, being surrounded by so many people."

"I know what you mean," I said, squirming to fit into the chair without thumping into the person behind me.

Roberto leaned across the table to squeeze my hand. "We heard about Jen and we're sorry. We know how much you loved her."

I stared at my dinner plate, not yet ready to talk about it. "Thanks. Who told you?"

They glanced at each other, and Abi said, "I think Iggy told Emmy, and then Emmy told us. We're all just worried about you." Her face squinted and she looked at Roberto. "Actually, we've got some news. It doesn't seem like the best time to tell you, but we wanted you to be first to know."

Roberto placed his arm around Abi, pulling her close. "We got married.

I know it's a bit outdated nowadays, but we wanted to. Jericho married us this morning."

"Wow. That's great. I'm pleased for you both. What brought that about?" For the first time in my life, I felt genuine hope. Life could be normal, have a purpose. They shared an aura and their happiness danced around them. I became aware I was basking in their happiness. My body relaxed, fed by a new hope.

"Well, if you promise not to tell anyone yet, we're having a baby. We want to keep it a secret for now. We went to Jericho about getting a family dwelling and he suggested getting married. We are so lucky to be here. I can't imagine what would have happened, with my being pregnant and all, if Jericho hadn't saved us."

I choked on my dinner as though somebody had punched me in the stomach. "What do you mean, saved you?" I held my breath, fear creeping through me. Thoughts of Jericho's attempt to plant a false memory in my brain screamed through me.

Abi smiled at me. "Well, after we arrived, we were both so ill. I doubt we'd have survived without his healing. We owe him so much."

I had expected Emmy would have been easy to implant with a false memory, given his lack of magic, but not Roberto and Abi. How could they not realize? I focused on a rip in the curtain behind them, staring at the frayed edges of the sun-bleached fabric. I pondered whether it had once been brightly colored. I needed to keep my calm and say nothing. Did everybody think Jericho was their savior?

No matter how I tried to focus on something mundane and safe, my heart thumped against my ribcage, and I battled to keep my breathing steady. I grasped the chair, desperate for something to ground myself.

"Wow. That's great. I'm happy for you. I've never seen a baby, except in pictures and stuff." I smiled, or tried to, unsure whether my face moved. The fear of the possibilities of Jericho's power turned my body to stone.

I stared at my plate, forcing food into my mouth. I don't know if the food was tasteless, which was a real possibility, or if my fear was numbing me to the taste of food. I knew I had to finish, had to leave, to get away.

Pushing my plate to the side, I stood up, grateful the person behind me had left. I leaned over. "I love you two. Congrats, but I think I need to be alone."

Abi's hand grabbed my arm as I turned to leave. "We're here for you if you need us."

I patted her hand. "I know. Thanks."

As I moved toward the exit, I realized the dining hall had half emptied while I ate. I had been oblivious to their leaving but grateful to be able to walk without bumping everybody in my path.

I pushed the door open and the cold air chilled me, reminding me I was alive. I walked with the sole purpose of being alone, the desperation to remove myself from the thing I had sought.

My desire to be with others, to be part of something greater, deserted me. The world I had once hoped I would find when I stepped outside of my school, my home, my haven, was now sullied and spoiled.

My mother had always talked of the opportunities the Orange had brought us. The potential to start again and make something better had rotted away, with Jericho at its core.

A silence hung over the camp, with nothing more than the whispering of the wind to keep me company. The connection I felt with the trees, with the plants, and with the earth itself, tried to bolster me. This was one thing I could rely on, pure, without demand or expectation.

I climbed into my bed, pulling the sheets and blankets to cover my face, and allowed sorrow to fill me. Every atom of my being suffocated in it.

The hope I had been raised to believe in, from my mother, from Danny and Calesta, from the inner spark I had faithfully believed in, began to dull as the child in me died.

Humanity had been offered a new start and new possibilities, and now they had been corrupted. Jericho was no better than those who had destroyed the world. History would repeat itself and I wondered what my place was to be in this new world.

I woke early and sat up in my bed to look at the peaceful sleeping bodies of those around me. The bed gave a gentle creek as I crossed my legs and placed my hands on the sheets.

The faint streaks of daylight flitting through the room brought no new hope. I always had hope. My mother had given it to me. My head rested in my hands and I battled to keep myself from breaking the silence that hung in the room, enabling the others to slumber in peace.

I wondered what they dreamed of. I had dreamed of the wonderful new world my mother had talked of when I was small. A world where people would realize we were all connected and all equal. Instead, I was now awake in a world where one man had spoiled the dream. The magic that should have been our future was now being used to control others.

I swung my legs out of bed, careful not to awaken the sleeping bodies that surrounded me, grateful I still wore the clothes I had worn yesterday. For once my laziness, if not my despondency, had stopped me from undressing last night. I picked up my shoes from the floor and crept to the door.

The rising sun sprinkled light on the island, creating halos around the rickety wooden buildings before disappearing into the trees. I thought of Jen and an emptiness overtook me. I had set off to find something better; the connection I had imagined would come from being part of something bigger.

My attention focused on the squelching sound of my feet as I padded through the grass, the dew sticking to my shoes and coating them in glittering sparkles. The wind that had whistled through the trees last night now slept alongside the rest of my community.

I was alone. It was a familiar feeling. I had grown accustomed to it. Yet, I had hoped for so much more. I had imagined something else. Something more connected, more awake. More. I knew at that moment I wasn't where I was supposed to be. I was where I thought I was supposed to be, and now that I was here, I realized it wasn't what I had hoped for.

Society isn't just a group of people living in the same place. It should have been a collection of connected people, all fighting for something greater. Better than before.

TWENTY-SEVEN

ALEX

Without any destination, I enjoyed the peace of a stroll around the island. Everybody slept and, for a short while, I could be alone. I breathed in the cold air that chilled my lungs, reminding me I was alive. The sharpness of the icy breeze blew through my hair and stung my face, but I embraced the feeling. I was alive and there was always hope. There was always an answer to every problem. I just hadn't found it yet.

I ended my stroll down by the boat, staring at the mainland, imagining how different life would be if I had stayed in the school. My bottom perched on a cragged grey boulder, its top worn and concaved. Clearly many people had sat here, and my mind wandered to the thoughts and emotions that weighed on them as my helplessness did on me.

I closed my eyes and thought of my mother, talking to spirits and angels and gods I knew nothing about. I wanted to ask somebody for help. I just didn't know who.

Listening to my breathing, I stretched my auric being down into the earth and asked the universe for guidance. The life force we all connect to if we want to, the only consistent thing in my life. In the absence of a person to ask for guidance, I called on the universal energy.

I found no answer but a calmness.

"Hello, what are you doing up so early? Are you coming scavenging with us?"

The voice broke the spell of the moment and I turned to face Emmy.

His smile made me laugh. "Sorry, you made me jump. No. I'm not going anywhere. What are you scavenging for?"

He perched on the edge of the rock, his bony hips digging into me, and wrapped his arm around my shoulder. "Apparently we need wood and building-type stuff. To be honest, it's nice to get a change of scenery. I was a bit dubious. I mean I'm not stupid; I know I'm lucky to have survived, and going back out there is a scary thought. I might have said no if Iggy hadn't agreed to come. I know I'm only alive today because of him. I took him in thinking I could protect him, but it was him who protected me."

I twisted to look at Emmy, releasing me from his arm. "What? Iggy's going with you? Where is he?" The mere mention of Iggy leaving the island caused a heaviness to land in my stomach. My calmness had disappeared. I was looking for a way to escape, to run away, and he hadn't even told me he was leaving. My mind wandered back to our conversations and a realization hit me. He was going to leave. He was leaving me.

Emmy stared at me, the confusion contorting his face. "He was getting dressed when I left. We're only going to be gone a day or so. I guess he didn't think it was a big deal." His hand reached for mine. "He'll be here soon. Talk to him then?"

Guilt racked me, but I stretched out my aura to probe Emmy. Content he had no idea what I feared Iggy was about to do, I hugged him. He was, as always, honest and upfront. He was settled here. He felt safe here. He was safer here.

I pulled back and said, "Ignore me. I'm being silly. I guess I'm feeling a bit lonely without Jen. I'll see you when you get back." I kissed him on the cheek.

I walked, my strides getting faster and longer. I knew I had made an unconscious choice, yet it didn't make sense that I was so angry. Iggy had asked me to run with him when Jen had died. I had said no. Why should he tell me?

As I neared the dormitories and other buildings that housed the growing community on the island, sounds of life were beginning to fill the air, and people were appearing from their sleeping stupor.

Some of the people were heading toward the dining hall, but it was the few who appeared to be moving toward the boats who caught my eye.

Prince and Luther walked toward me. Luther refused to make eye contact with me. We hadn't spoken to each other since he had shot Jen, and I was still sure he was aiming for me. I didn't know why. Prince stopped to say hello but Luther continued past me. He never paused or lost his stride.

It was as though I wasn't there or wasn't worth his time. My eyes followed him as he headed toward Emmy and the boats.

Prince, as always, smiled. "How are you?"

I knew he was talking about Jen but I didn't want to talk about it. "On your own? No Adam today?"

"No. Not today. He's on guard duty and I'm heading out to do some scavenging. I'll catch up with you soon, I don't want to get left behind." He looked so happy and I wondered for a moment, was this place so bad? People were safe and happy. Did they deserve more? I couldn't help thinking perhaps my mother had filled my head with nonsense. The Orange didn't give us a chance to build something better. At best it gave us a chance to survive.

Was survival enough?

Iggy was coming out of the dining hall stuffing food in his mouth when I spotted him. Now that I saw him, I didn't know what to say.

I marched up to him. He nodded hello and wiped the remnants of his breakfast from his mouth. "Sorry about that," he said. "I'm late and needed something to eat."

My anger overflowed. "You're fucking going and not saying a fucking word? Tell me I'm wrong," I shouted. My fingers stiffened, forming fists. "How could you? Just go and leave me here? Not even a word?" I took a step back, aware that if I spoke anymore I might cry. A lump moved from my chest to my throat and tried to force its way out of my eyes.

His mouth fell open. "I . . . I . . ." He stared at me. "Why are you angry? I asked you to come with me and you said no. You know I can't stay here. You want to stay here, don't you?" His forehead furrowed as he spoke, his usually icy eyes filling with questions and confusion.

"Why would I want to stay here? To stare at Luther, knowing he wanted to shoot me and instead killed Jen? So Jericho can keep trying to implant false memories? Why?" I shoved him, allowing the tears to spill from my eyes. "Why? Well? Why would I? You are a terrible friend."

He grabbed me and wrapped his arms around me. "I am your friend and I'm sorry. I thought Jericho had gotten to you. I'm sorry."

I pulled back. "Sorry for what? Not being a friend? Not trusting my ability?"

He lowered his eyes, focusing on his hands. "I was sorry for hugging you, but I am sorry for all those other things too."

"We survived an apocalypse. I think we deserve a hug and I think we both deserve a friend. Don't you? But what do I do now? I know you're going and I'm stuck here. You're the only person I can really talk to. You suck." I backed up, taking a step and then another until I fell backwards over a bump.

"Come with me. Let's both just go." He bent down, holding out his hand. "Are you okay?"

I grasped his hand, allowing him to pull me up. My voice quietened and my temper faded. "I can't. It's too late. Do you think Luther is just going to let me get on one of those boats?" As I spoke I watched his eyes. He knew the truth. It was too late.

He stood in silence for a few seconds, the thoughts flying around his head almost visible in his face. A smile crept across it, starting at his mouth and then animating his whole face. His eyes widened. "Not unless you offer them something they can't resist."

"What could I offer?" I tried to follow his thoughts. "NO. You mean my mom's school. I can't." I stared at him. He couldn't be serious. "I can't."

"Perhaps not quite, but the cars would be invaluable. Since the early days, when the fuel ran out, nobody has driven cars. Yours still work. I'm sure somebody could replicate the solar setup you've got going on. Even Luther and Jericho wouldn't be able to resist."

I knew he was right, yet it felt like I was betraying a trust. "Only if I don't have to let them in the school. Tell them we saw them on our travels, but not that I grew up there."

"Quickly, get dressed in everything you want to take and meet me at the boat. I'll sort it out. Be there in five minutes," he said as he darted off in the direction of Jericho's.

I watched him disappear behind the buildings before I ran to my bed. I pulled on my warmest clothes, tucking my mother's Firestone underneath the layers and hiding the one book my mother had given me in my waistband.

The universe had answered my plea for help.

I had no idea how we would get away from the others, but I was getting away from the island.

I ran through the people beginning their day, breathing so deeply that the icy air burned my chest. As I neared the crowd of men and women preparing to leave on the scavenge, I spotted Iggy, Luther, and Jericho. I could only hope he had managed to convince them I needed to go.

Iggy spotted me and waved. Luther and Jericho turned to look at me. Their faces gave no sign of what they were thinking. The smile on Iggy's face gave me hope.

As I neared them, I could hear Iggy saying, "She wasn't keen on leaving the island, but I explained she was the only person who could lead us there. I managed to convince her. She said she owes Jericho more than she can repay, and will do it if I promised to guard her."

Jericho stepped toward me. "Good morning, Alex. Iggy informs us you can lead him to an electric car that still works. Such a thing would be very useful to us and we appreciate your willingness to go, after everything that happened."

My mouth became dry and I struggled to form a sentence. "I didn't want to but . . . I understand it is for the good of the island and . . . it's okay."

Jericho patted Iggy on the shoulder. "Iggy has promised to stay close to you at all times. No harm will come to you. Be sure we all appreciate it. Thank you."

I forced a smile, unable to speak. Could it be this easy?

I could feel Iggy's hand on my back, guiding me toward the boat. "We need to hurry. We are already late. Come and sit down."

I nodded, grateful for the chance to look away from Luther's gaze.

The boat swayed with the waves, causing my stomach to meet my throat. I closed my eyes and concentrated on my breathing and thanked whoever had helped me escape.

I squeezed Iggy's hand, leaning into him, and whispered, "Thank you."

PART THREE

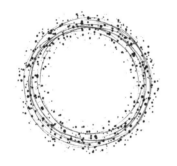

Home Sweet Home

TWENTY-EIGHT

GEILIS

My back ached, desperate for me to move. My heart refused to allow me. I knew, at least, some of the events of today before I had even managed to pull myself out of bed. Instead, the light crept through the joints in the wooden walls.

I turned onto my side to move my ear nearer to the doorway I had left open last night. Silence streamed in. Not the silence of peace but, rather, the silence of foreboding. It warned me to stay here, to hide from the coming day.

Despite the lack of sleep after a night filled with tossing and turning around the bed, I forced myself to sit on the edge of the bed frame. It gave a small creak, rebelling at any more movement. I bent over my knees, pulling my boots on. The effort of lifting my legs into them proved too much, and I sat there, doubled over. A tear rolled down my cheek. The cause of the tear was a mystery to me. A tear for the loneliness of Billey's absence, for the memories she would regain, plus the return and reunion of Billey and her mother, Queen NicNevin.

Since Billey had left, her mother and I had met only once. On the day following her departure, the queen noticed Billey's absence and sent her spies for me. I had gone; there was no point in refusing.

They had chosen a deliberate form, shifting into the face of my torturer all those years ago. As if my memory manifested into reality, I heard Billey yell from somewhere.

"Kelpies. Kelpies."

Her voice, filled with fear and anger, formed an ugly sound. The voice couldn't belong to the woman I loved, but it did. I stumbled out of the doorway, landing on the dry dirt ground, my head spinning as I battled to hear the sound of anybody other than us.

Running toward her bedroom, I threw myself through the doorway, barely registering she had left hers open as well.

My eyes scanned the space, looking for something, anything other than Billey. Instead, my eyes found Billey, with her knees pulled up under her chin, rocking back and forth as tears flooded everywhere.

"Billey. Talk to me. Where? Where are the Kelpies?"

She made a sobbing, guttural sound when she opened her mouth to speak. The effort to control her tears distorted her face and hid in her red eyes as she breathed.

"In Bearaig," she mumbled through the sobs. "They were there. I saw them. I didn't know what they were. I thought . . . I thought they were horses. I saw them."

She stared up at me, her eyes begging me to make sense of something I had no chance of sorting.

"When, Billey? It's important. When did you see them?" I knelt in front of her, my knees rubbing on the hard, bumpy floor. Placing my hands on her knees, I whispered, "When did you see them?"

She grabbed my hands, squeezing them with such force it hurt. "Last night, when Brigina and Gaevoin . . ." Her voice trailed off and I understood.

"Was this before or after?" This time my voice faded into the same unspoken void as hers. "Did you see them after they had . . ." She nodded her head and her tears began again.

"I had heard screaming in my head for days. The Banshees were warning me but I didn't understand. They died because of me, didn't they?" Her eyes lowered to focus on our hands. "If I had remembered them. If I had remembered Solas . . . and her." Her face hardened and her eyes grew dark at the mention of her mother. "My mother did this, didn't she? I just didn't remember."

I nodded. "Probably. If the Banshees were warning you and you saw Kelpies in Nuadh Caled, there could be only one reason."

As though somebody had wiped away her grief and guilt, she sat upright, straightening her shoulders. "She needs to pay. Her rule has become one of impunity and tyranny. The Seelie Court isn't what it is supposed to be. My father knew it and he . . ."

I knelt on the bed, my legs on either side of her, and they sunk to the mattress. I lowered my body until my face was in front of hers and wrapped my arms around her. Her body softened and the anger dissipated. She clung to me, pulling me in close. My shoulder chilled from the damp patch where her tears flooded. Her silent sobs created a rhythm as her head bounced on my shoulder.

"How could I have forgotten so much? My father died and yet I forgot. It's like I'm experiencing the grief for the first time. I forgot and now I have to relive it. Only"—she lifted her head to look in my face—"this time I managed to lose a second set of parents. Brigina and Gaevoin were like parents to me. It's my fault."

"No. Billey, it isn't your fault. It's hers. She is the one who made the choice. She is the only one to blame." My stomach burned with anger and my chest, a cruel combination of anger and despair, pounded. "None of this is your fault."

"What about Kluzahr? She was like my sister and I left her here. I knew she would age. She wasn't Seelie. She wasn't connected to the Crann. Her life would be short and yet I left her. Now she's dead too."

The space darkened and I turned to Durai, his bulk filling the doorway.

He opened his mouth to speak, pausing to judge his own words. "Sorry. I didn't mean to interrupt, but a friend is here for you both. She says you asked her to meet here," he said, looking at me. "Says her name's Storm Lightfall and you're expecting her."

I nodded at him and turned back to face Billey. Her face twisted, mimicking the tick-tock of her brain, putting one more piece into a puzzle. "Storm. I know Storm." Her nose scrunched, narrowing her eyes until her face formed a question.

"Yes, Billey. You've known her since you were both little. She's your oldest friend at the Seelie Court."

Her eyes widened. Her face froze. "My mother knows I'm here." She hung her head, covering it with her hands. "Of course she knows I'm here."

I placed my hands on hers, gently pulling them from her face until she looked at me. "Billey, stop worrying. I sent for Storm. She's a friend. She's here to help. Your mother didn't send her. I asked her to come."

Her eyes softened and glistened. "I remember Storm. We were friends when we were children. She always had this wonderful white hair I was jealous of." She jumped up and raced for the door, barely missing Durai, who moved at the last second.

I followed the route she had taken, stopping as I passed Durai. "Thank you."

"Does that mean you'll be leaving me, now? Now Billey is back."

I took a long, slow inhale of air and placed my hand on his, resting on the doorframe.

"No. Billey will need to go back to see her mother. My work is here. Others are coming to join us soon. They are coming for you. They are coming because of Kluzahr. They are the reason she left us."

"Friends of Kluzahr?"

"No. They never knew her. Sometimes those we help don't even know we exist. She made their existence possible. She was the reason Kluzahr left us to go to Peyton Palace."

"Alex. The one Kluzahr wrote the letters for?"

I nodded. "Yes, but, keep the letters secret a bit longer. Alex will have a lot to learn first. We need to finish what Kluzahr started."

He squeezed my hand. "For Kluzahr . . ." He studied my face, tilting his head. "For you."

He wrapped his arm around my shoulder and we walked toward the logs, his bulk dwarfing me.

We stopped as Billey and Storm cried, hugged, and yelled.

Through the weeping wails, the years vanished as Billey solved more of the puzzle of her past.

"So, you don't remember everything? You remember me, though. Right? Come on, Bluebills, you can't forget me?" Storm laughed, pulling Billey down to sit next to her on the largest of the old logs that surrounded the fire. Even next to Billey, Storm created a tiny image. Her hair was pulled low over her ears in a long white plait. Everything about her looked like a Seelie, even the ears she had so carefully hidden. Yet, the biggest bond between Billey and Storm was their hybrid history. Both of them were born Seelie-Druid. Billey had inherited her father's looks. She stood taller than most Seelie, and without ears that formed a point at the tops, she never looked Seelie.

"It's been a long time since anybody called me Bluebills. Not since my father . . ." In an instant, the joy of seeing Storm vanished in the pain of forgotten loss.

"I'm sorry about your father. He was a great man. I never had a chance to tell you how sad I was to hear about the accident before you vanished."

"Accident?" Billey jumped up, backing away from Storm until she stood on my feet and spun around to face me. "Accident? Is that what my mother told everybody? Does everyone think . . . Does nobody know the truth?"

Storm sat confused, her gaze wandering from Billey to me. "What am I missing?"

I grabbed Billey's arms. "Billey, we don't know the truth either. Yes, we have ideas but that's not the same as the truth. If you want that, you'll need to ask your mother." I glanced at Storm and back to Billey. "That's why I asked Storm to come here. You need to face her. You need to return to the Seelie Court. It's time."

Billey pulled away from me. She moved to sit opposite Storm, alone. She rubbed her leg, her fingers tracing the carving of the wood I knew hid beneath her trousers. Without thinking, my hand rubbed my leg. The bond we shared. All those years ago, against everybody's advice, Billey had taken me to the Crann and joined with me. The wooden leg we both have now was the price. All magic has a price.

Silence hung in the air; nobody wanting to be the first to break it.

Durai, always happy to feign a lack of understanding of our conversations, finally broke it. "So, who wants honey ti?" and that was all it took for the years to vanish.

We sat until the sun was high in the sky, listening to Storm regale us with stories of Gray chasing Amber and still, after all these years, failing to convince her he was a worthy suitor. The human in me, even now after hundreds of winters, found it difficult to understand the Seelie view on time. Gray had spent decades courting, or trying to court, Amber, and yet in human life that would have been a lifetime. I empathized with the ancestors of the Chegasa and how they must have grown frustrated with the Seelie. With a lifetime of less than a hundred winters, how could they ever view life the same as a Seelie? Only the Druids, living an eternal life connected to the Crann, could find a way to peacefully exist with them.

Twenty-Nine

Billey

Memories flowed in and out of my mind. Fragments were slotting together. Life, no matter how long, is never clear. Even with the recalled knowledge to paint the past, the gaps of blank canvas pulled on me more. Why was the unknown so much easier to pursue than the known?

As a member of the Druid Council, I was best placed to unite the Seelie Court and the Druids. Next in line for the Seelie Court throne by virtue of my mother, Queen NicNevin, I was unique. Never before had anybody been a controlling figure of both, and yet, my failing relationship with my mother left me floating in limbo.

How could I deal with her when I believed deep in the seat of my intuition she was the reason my father was dead?

Even from the Darklands, the strength and knowledge of the Crann reached me. It aided my understanding of the past, but, more important to the future of Spirismus, Solas, and Earth, it provided the guideposts to follow. I understood why I had hidden in Nuadh Caled. I followed the path it showed me.

Kluzahr, my sister in my heart if not in blood, had given her life for it. She had accepted her destiny and guided King Arthanius. She had sacrificed her life in the pursuit of an heir who would unite Spirismus and Solas.

As small children, we had stumbled into each other's lives. For hundreds of years Solas had been cut from Spirismus; nobody had entered unless Druid or Seelie blood flowed through their veins. The day Kluzahr wandered through the trees, an infant crying and wailing for the family she would never see again, my father had acted as though it was the most natural thing.

He lifted her, wrapped her in a hug, and calmed her with stories.

Torn by her tales of loss and the unforeseen ability to enter Solas, he carried her to the Crann.

What happened next was a tale she and my father told many times, each time growing grander and more magical.

The Crann spoke to her. It showed her a path without her parents. It revealed her ability to bring peace to our universe. She would help to unite the worlds.

No person from Spirismus had ever talked to the Crann. Her place became the stuff of myths. For years, as she grew, she would wander between her world in the Darklands and ours in Solas. She accessed an understanding of magic never shown to an outsider before.

Such is the Druid way. Nobody questions the wisdom of the Crann.

She became the little sister I wished for many times.

I abandoned her. I ran away. I hid in Nuadh Caled, waiting for the one who would arrive. A human from Earth, who carried the blood of Spirismus and Druid. Her ancestors had crossed the portal to Earth hundreds of years earlier. They had begun the path set by the Crann.

Now, it was my job to bring it to an end. I was supposed to unite our people. I had been gifted or cursed with the task of guiding Alex.

She was coming and I had unfinished business to sort before the time came.

The hum of the chatting around the honey ti became nothing more than a background annoyance.

The memory I sought to forget had returned. I hadn't run because of my father or my mother. I had run for Geilis and she didn't know. She couldn't know.

A deal made so long ago had come due. We all had our part to play. What would happen if I refused to play?

I stared at Geilis, her hair bouncing around her face as she talked. Her entire body talked. She never sat still. She never spoke with just her words. Her hands, her feet, her body moved in time. I watched and my heart crumbled all over again.

I remembered.

"Billey? Billey, are you listening?" Her face stared as her brows furrowed, creating the crease between them I found so endearing.

"Sorry? What? I wandered off for a sec." Storm nudged me in the ribs and I twisted my head to smile at her. "Oops. Sorry," I mumbled.

She laughed a carefree laugh I had always been jealous of. It wasn't the delicate body or the glorious hair I envied. The Crann had never called her. Her Druid blood had been ignored and she existed as oblivious as every other Seelie.

"I see you never lost that habit, then?" she said.

I tilted my head, my brain trying to put together the pieces and pretend I had listened to their conversation. I had, over the years, become masterful at pretending to listen when my mind had, in honest, wandered somewhere else.

"What habit?"

"Drifting off into your head, into imaginary worlds."

"Oh, yeah. Always have, always will." I made a small chuckling sound that failed to fool my breaking heart.

"I guess you missed the discussion?" said Geilis, looking at me. Her face squinted and I could tell she was trying to read the confusion of emotions painted on my face.

"Sorry."

"We were talking about your visit to Solas. You need to go home. You need to see your mother, and Storm is going to go with you."

My throat constricted and I found myself in danger of struggling to breathe. "I don't understand . . . Why aren't you? . . ." The words jumbled in my mouth and I struggled to put them into a sentence. "You're staying?" My eyes fixed on Geilis, watching her fidget, and I knew the answer. Looking at Storm, I knew this had been discussed and I was playing catch-up. She squinted her eyes, her knitted brows expressing her confusion.

Geilis moved to crouch in front of me. "I'm going to stay here. I need to wait for our friend Alex. She should be arriving soon. You know," she said. Her eyes widened as she begged me to understand without her needing to explain.

"I remember Alex" was all I said. I remembered how much we had all sacrificed to reach this point. Only I knew how much more we would need to give, the scale of it burning through me. Anger bubbled under my skin and threatened to spoil the moment.

I closed my eyes, breathed, and forced a smile.

Storm stood, oblivious to the tension building between Geilis and me. "So, where's your stuff," she asked. Her eyes gazed around at the circle of wooden dwellings.

I froze, never breaking my stare with Geilis. "I don't have anything. I'll get my stuff at the Seelie Palace, assuming my mother hasn't gotten rid of everything?"

"Oh, gosh, no. She's excited you're coming. She's planning a lavish dinner in honor of your return."

I shuddered and a chill raced down my spine. "I'm sure she is," I muttered quietly enough for Geilis alone to hear.

I scanned the campsite to look for Durai. He had, as he always had, left us to discuss things he didn't understand. He must know more than he said. After years of watching and listening, he must know a fair amount. I glanced at Geilis. "Give my love to Rai and thank him. I guess" —I took a step back and distanced myself from Geilis—"I guess I'll see you soon?"

She met my step, moving closer and wrapping her hand around my arm. "I promise. I will see you soon. As soon as I've seen Alex, I'll meet you at the Crann. We can plan."

My anger boiled up. She had known she wouldn't be visiting the Seelie Court with me. After vanishing for so long I had no right to complain. Yet, I wanted to. She brought me home and abandoned me at the point I needed her most?

I turned away and walked to wrap my arm around Storm. "So, let's go."

I pulled her in the direction I remembered led to Solas.

I glanced over my shoulder as we approached the thickening trees. Geilis stood there, still watching us until the trees shielded us, and her, from sight.

My anger vanished and my legs struggled to keep moving forward. I wanted to turn and run back to her.

The chill of the air, hidden from the sun once we entered the forest, added to my sadness, and my body ached from loneliness. I had thought myself lonely in Nuadh Caled. True loneliness was knowing who should be with you when they weren't.

I squeezed Storm's arm. "So, tell me, which beautiful young Seelie is keeping my mother entertained, now she's a widow?"

Her body stiffened. I could feel the tension in her arm. "Erm. She's— Promise you won't be annoyed?"

I moved to stand facing her. "Why would I be annoyed? She's single now. My father is dead. I don't expect her to pretend to mourn forever."

"She's with Laidir." She stared at my face, her eyes unblinking.

"My Laidir? The same Laidir she betrothed me to long ago? Seriously?"

I stood back in my place. I resumed my walking stance next to Storm and forced the first step and then a second.

She didn't reply. She squeezed my arm and walked faster.

"This is going to be an interesting visit after all."

THIRTY

ALEX

Iggy and I managed to distance ourselves from Luther during the journey back to the school. Neither of us knew how we were going to manage to ditch the group, but we had to.

"What about Emmy? He likes it on the island. Can we drag him from that?" I asked Iggy, trying to keep my voice low. Trailing behind the others was an easy place to fall. Most of them had already decided I was the weak link, barely capable of being any use to them.

Iggy paused, clearly deciding what to say. "I think he is safest with Jericho, weird as that sounds. He has no magic and he is no threat to anyone. I can't ask him to come. It wouldn't be fair." He sighed and I could tell the guilt of leaving Emmy was eating at his soul.

"How are we going to get away? I mean, I'll gladly show them the cars if that is the price I need to pay to be free of them, but it doesn't help us to leave them behind." I knew he didn't have an answer to my question, but I was curious what his thoughts were.

"I don't know. I guess our best chance is at night, but I don't know. Are we nearly there?" he said.

"Yeah. Once we cross under the old highway, it's a straight road. It's about twenty minutes from here. You know we can't let them into the school? They'll take one look at the plants and trees and know about the magic," I said.

"The thought had occurred to me too. That'll be impossible if Emmy puts his foot in it. Perhaps you should go up front and guide Luther. You could send Emmy back here so I could chat with him," he said, squeezing my hand.

My body stiffened. The prospect of having to talk to Luther made my stomach contract and my lungs struggle to work. I straightened my shoulders and marched past everybody else to walk next to Emmy, and, placing my arm through his, whispered in his ear, "I left Iggy at the back on his own. Maybe you could go and speak with him?"

He patted my hand. "No problem," he said and he fell back. I sped up to stand between Luther and Betty. For a moment, I thought about the fact they were together so often; perhaps they were a couple. I struggled to imagine Luther caring for anybody enough that he could be in a relationship. Although they were, on a despicable level, well matched.

"We're nearly there, do you want me to direct you?" I asked, holding my breath.

"Yes. Wait while I organize that lot," he said, stopping and turning to face everybody. "Prince, Jason, and Emmy, you three head in that direction. You know what we're looking for. Betty, you take Rick and Max. We'll meet back here in two hours. You all have a gun. Any sign of trouble, you fire it. Iggy, you and Alex are with me. Everybody be careful."

My heart sank. I hated the thought of being close to Luther, and the idea of him seeing my mother's school was worse. I closed my eyes and tried to focus. I could hear the pounding of my heart thumping against my ribs. I could do this. I had to do this.

I wanted to run and hug Emmy. I wanted to say goodbye, but I knew that after we had gone, Jericho would probably search around in his head. He had to know nothing. It would keep him safe.

Watching as they disappeared in different directions, my eyes refused to move. Emmy grew smaller and vanished. The familiar ache of guilt and sadness chilled me as I gazed at the empty horizon.

I still didn't know how I would get away from Luther. I knew he wouldn't hesitate for a second to shoot me. In truth, he would be likely to want to. My only comfort came from the fact I was sure he had no magic. Iggy and I could surely use magic against him?

We traveled in silence, Luther never more than a few steps behind us. I had walked these streets so many times, but now they felt so alien. I no longer belonged here. I had changed. I had been forced to. My mind raced with plans to get away from him. Yet, even as I reached the corner of Cabot Road and the school, I still had no plan.

Turning off Burley Street, I saw the school and for a moment a calmness centered me. This was my home, my mother's home. This was a sacred place. I also knew Luther wouldn't notice until I showed him. My mother's magic still protected it. Iggy, able to see past the magic, must have known what I was thinking because he grabbed my hand. I spotted the cars and looked at Luther, trying to decide if he had seen them, if he could see them.

"Keys," whispered Iggy.

I had been so focused on losing Luther I hadn't thought about the fact the key fobs for the cars were inside. "I need to go to the toilet," I said, knowing I had to get in without Luther. I walked a few steps toward the trees beyond the school, not waiting to give Luther a chance to argue.

Iggy moved to follow me. "I'll come to keep an eye on you," he said before correcting himself. "I mean, to protect you."

"You know how wrong that sounds, don't you?" I joked, struggling not to laugh at Iggy's embarrassment. "I think I can manage to go on my own. Just don't go anywhere. I'll freak if I come back and you two aren't here." His eyebrows frowned into a question and I smiled back. "Trust me. I'll be as quick as I can," I said.

He shrugged. "Fine. Be quick."

I looked at Luther, who seemed content that while Iggy was with him, I wouldn't disappear.

I dashed into the trees, pausing for a second to notice how many more of them were beginning to bud and flourish. In the space of a few months, the skeletal silhouettes were becoming green with life. Running as fast as my legs would allow, my gasping breaths caused my chest to scream in pain. I had to get inside and find the keys before Luther questioned how long I had been gone. I flung open the fire door and ran in.

My feet thudded on the solid floors, my breathing filling the space with sound as I dashed for the front doors and the keys I knew were hidden there. My feet jumped across the blue-and-white tiles, followed by my body, as I swerved to miss a pillar and landed on the ground. Pain shot up my side, robbing me of breath. My brain shut down and I felt the pain drag me down. With the keys my sole focus, I dragged myself to the desk I knew hid the keys. With the key fobs in my hand, I rested my head in my other hand. Only then did I feel the blood trickling down through my hair.

My return journey took longer as the pain began to stiffen my body and my lungs refused to cooperate. I knew I was taking too long but couldn't move any faster.

Rounding the corner of the building, I saw Luther and Iggy. They stood close enough to imagine they were sharing the air streaming from their angry mouths. I couldn't hear the words but their expressions told me everything I needed to know. I tried to move toward them but fell to the ground. My body would move no farther.

Iggy spotted me first. His mouth froze midword, and his broad shoulders and defensive stance shrunk before my eyes. He ran to where I lay and Luther followed quickly behind. "What happened?" he shouted.

I looked at his face and then at Luther's. In that second, I knew I could do this. I could escape without anybody being injured. I could only hope Iggy would figure out what I was about to do. "I was in the trees and I thought I heard a noise. I turned to come back here and something struck me. There was somebody there. They kicked me." I gathered up my top, revealing the red swelling along the lines of my ribs. "He was on me before I knew what was happening. I just ran."

I had evaluated Luther's reaction perfectly. Ever keen for an opportunity to exert his power and aggression, he grabbed his pistol from his waistband and pulled back the clip. Waving it toward the trees, he screamed at Iggy, "I'll go this way. You go that way and come from behind them. If you see them, shoot. Don't ask questions."

I stared at Iggy, hoping my face told him what I needed him to know. I placed a key fob in my palm and glanced at it. He nodded and ran around the corner as though to follow Luther's instructions. I watched them both recede into the trees, barely able to breathe.

Confident Luther was out of sight, I pushed myself up from the cold asphalt and hobbled toward the cars. I had no idea how long it would take him to realize there was nobody there. I was relying on his eagerness to shoot somebody. I was relying on Iggy understanding I had been lying.

I reached the car and looked around for Iggy. I wanted to sit in the car, check it to make sure it worked, but I knew, quiet though its engine was, I didn't want to start it. What if Luther returned and found me in the car with the engine running?

I paced despite the pain. I watched. Time stood still.

Iggy appeared around the corner, his eyes scanning for Luther. I waved my hands. "Come on. Quick," I yelled. As he reached me a smile creased his face, forcing my nerves to fade. "Do you want to drive?" I asked.

He stared at me. "I have never driven in my life. Perhaps today isn't the day to learn."

We bundled into the car, not a word more being said, both holding our breath until we were out of sight.

"How long do you think it'll take Luther to realize I spun a tale?" I looked at Iggy, allowing a smile to soften my face.

"I don't know but I'd love to see his face," he said, his laughter filling the car.

"So where to? We haven't actually talked about what we are going to do next," I asked. A calmness descended over me and the pain no longer mattered.

It didn't matter where we were going. My soul knew I was on the right path.

THIRTY-ONE

ALEX

"I'm starving," I said, slowing the car. I laughed. "We have no idea where we're going and we don't have food, water, or bedding." I braked, parking to look at Iggy.

If he had any worries about the state of our future, his face didn't show it. "Haven't you ever just trusted everything would work as it was meant to?" he asked, raising his eyebrows.

I stared at him. "Really? I asked for a way out of my life, a sign to follow so I could live the life I was meant to. I mean, life had to be more than being stuck in that school. The universe sent me you, Emmy, Roberto, and Abi. That worked out well. Mm?"

"Oh, come on. Nobody ever said the road would be straight from *A* to *B*. It has to have its uphill moments so you enjoy the downhill." He turned back to stare out of the window. "How long will this car keep going for? When do we need to get out and walk?"

"Honestly, I have no idea," I said, my heart pounding against my ribs. Did either of us have any sort of plan?

A comfortable silence joined us as I drove. The familiar ruins I had scavenged many times, the ruinous landscape of homes and families destroyed by the Orange, gave way to the new and unrecognizable.

Yet, neither the unknown destination nor the uncertainty of our future mattered.

We had taken the first step.

By the time night fell we had managed to rummage through some of the ruins. There had been a few houses still water-tight and reminiscent of their original form, but we had agreed we were safer heading for a rural setting.

The less pre-Orange life there was, the less chance there would be of having to risk a run-in with strangers.

Parked in the midst of what must have once been a state park, we snuggled under blankets we had scavenged, eating from tins Iggy had managed to open without a can opener. I watched Iggy's face, scarred by the moonlight flitting through the tree branches as he looked at me.

"Do you think Luther would have tried to follow us?" I asked, confident I knew the answer but unable to take my eyes off him, hoping for confirmation.

He let out a low, bellowing chortle that vibrated around the car. "Oh, I'm sure he wanted to but let's be honest. He had no idea which way we were going and we were in a car. Even if he was willing to walk three hours to reach us, he wouldn't stand a chance of finding us. He is if nothing else logical. It would cause more loss of face to hunt and not find us. I'm sure he came up with some convoluted story to explain our disappearance."

I rested my feet on the dashboard, tucking my blanket around my ankles, allowing the relief to relax my muscles. "Do you think Emmy will be alright? I feel so bad about leaving him," I asked, leaning my head on my knees.

Iggy turned to gaze out of the windscreen, his body shrinking into itself, and the moonlight accentuated the lines of his face. "Imagine how I feel. I was only a child when the Orange hit. Our reservation was decimated. At that moment I lost everything and everybody. I was so little, I sat there and cried. Eventually, after days, I was hungry, dehydrated, and prepared—or as prepared as a child can ever be—to meet my maker. I would have died a sobbing, starving wreck right there if Emmy and David, his husband, hadn't found me. I owe him more than I can ever repay, but someday I will."

Sadness chilled my body; I had been lucky enough to have my mother. I couldn't imagine what would have happened to me without her and the school. I reached over and held his hand. "Do you remember much about your parents?" I asked.

"Oh yes. My mother was a real force of nature. She was quite a short woman but nobody would have argued with her. My father was an amazing man. He tried so hard to keep the stories of my ancestors alive. He would tell me stories of them coming to this world to look after the earth."

I smiled in the darkness, thinking of my mother's tales. "Tell me one of them," I said, watching as his face relaxed and his mind returned to a happier time.

He sat back in the seat and said, "He used to tell me these tales . . . I sometimes wonder if he knew what was coming. He would tell me how our line would never die out because we were here to guide the Fire Flier back to some magical realm. We would someday help build the world as it should be, at one with the earth, the water, the trees, and each other."

"That's lovely. He wanted you to feel safe. I never knew my father. I don't think he knew I existed. My mother used to tell me the silliest stories about how he was a King Arthanius Chegasa from a magic universe, and someday he would sweep in and save us. I spent years waiting for him after she died."

"I guess we tell children what we need to make them happy, but we all need to grow up," he said.

"I think because my mom seemed to know so much about the magic that came after the Orange, I wanted to believe her. It sounds like our parents would have got on."

The silence that fell over the car took on a happier feel.

With the memories comforting and soothing away the pain of the day, we drifted off to sleep.

With the bruising from yesterday's fall now stiffening my right side, I couldn't sleep any longer. The sunlight on the horizon danced through the trees and tempted me to wake.

Unwrapping the blanket entwined around my legs, I let out a gasp as I winced in pain. I peered across at Iggy, trying to decide if I had woken him, but he was deep in his dreams and oblivious to me, so I pushed the car door open to leave him in peace.

I sat on the ground, the chill of it tempting me to lie on it to ease the pain. I increased my aura and connected with the earth and the trees. I concentrated on my breathing, willing my pain to disappear. It was easing when I heard a noise. I spun around to protect myself.

Iggy stood there, still wrapped in his blanket. "I woke up and you weren't there. I thought you'd gone."

"No chance. Can't get rid of me that easy," I tried to joke.

"Is it sore?" he asked, nodding toward where my bruising was.

"Yes. I'm not going to pretend to be brave, it hurts."

"Here, let me see," he said.

As he approached me, I found myself fidgeting with embarrassment. I didn't know why. He just wanted to check. I pulled up my shirt to reveal the bruises, now dark and turning a reddish-purple color.

"Wow, looks impressive. It must have been quite a fall," he said.

"More of a collision and then a fall," I replied, my voice wavering and cracking. I hoped he didn't notice.

"Wait here," he yelled as he ran off into the distance. I stood watching as he vanished with an "I'll be back soon." Confused, I sat back on the ground, allowing the silence to surround me. I took the time to thank the universe and whoever had aided my escape from the island, trying not to picture the reaction of those I left behind.

As time passed and Iggy still hadn't returned, I decided not to panic. He knew what he was doing. I wrapped myself in the embrace of nature returning to life despite what humanity had done to it. It had fought against the poison and was winning. I called on its strength to continue to fulfill my destiny when a sound fractured the silence.

A sound I recognized. A sound that didn't belong here. A whooshing of wings—but no birds had escaped the Orange. How was this possible? As it grew louder I found myself following it, oblivious to the pain in my side. The branches smacked me in the face and grabbed at my clothes, but curiosity pulled me farther and farther.

I lost track of time, my mind fixating on the sound pulling me until I reached the remnants of the road we had driven on yesterday. With nothing but the ruins of a few houses blocking my view, I scanned the horizon, sure I would see a majestic bird flying among the clouds. Nothing flew there. I was alone.

Had my mind been playing tricks?

I walked back through the trees, this time managing to avoid the branches and twigs trying to grab me, my mind whirring with the confusion of what had happened.

Unsure of my direction, having not paid attention when I had chased the sound, getting back to the car and Iggy took longer than I expected, and the pain began to cause me to doubt myself. It was Iggy calling my name that helped me find my way.

Thirty-Two

Iggy

The sun rose to meet my eyeline as I wandered through the trees. Their determination to fight back and find a way to live sparked a glow in my chest, a new sensation I couldn't place.

Hope.

The trees brought hope. Despite everything we did to the planet, life struggled on. Here, they were surviving against the odds. Perhaps the strength of having each other allowed them to return so soon.

Was community the answer for the trees? I stopped and spun around, stretching my aura to connect with the life in the trees.

For once, I spoke to them. "Do you speak to each other? Do you need each other?" I asked, knowing what I asked for was support from them.

Somewhere deep in the archived memories of my childhood, a memory of me crying with a grazed knee and my father comforting me called to me. I had been so small when the Orange happened, I had few memories of before. My father formed most of them. I closed my eyes, basking in the glow of remembering, love, and connection. My father explained to me how Mother Earth would provide the answer to all our questions, if only we knew how to ask.

As a child, I never tried to understand. Now, I pondered whether we had asked the wrong questions to end up here.

My father mixed a concoction of pine bark and herbs and smothered it over my knee. The child in me believed in magic when the mixture began to heal the pain.

The same desire my father had to heal me, I now had for Alex. I grabbed bark and a few dying leaves. I doubted it would help but I needed to try. The sight of her flinching in pain sent a shiver through my body. The pain she found herself living with was caused by our escape. She had pain because of me. I must help. My childhood memory was all I had to offer.

Pulling the battered water bottle from my back pocket, I flicked the lid open and poured a few drops of water into the can now holding the ingredients. As the mixture putrefied and created a beige sludge, a smell filled my nose, and I pulled back, taking a deep breath to avoid gagging. It might help but I doubted Alex would believe me.

I doubted myself. On so many levels, I doubted myself.

Alex's words from last night echoed around my head. 'I asked for a way out of my life. . . . The universe sent me you,' she'd said. Could I be the answer to anybody's problems when I couldn't sort my own?

How different our lives should have been. When we discussed our parents, they sounded so similar. What life would we have if the Orange hadn't stolen them?

Emmy always joked about me overthinking and, on this occasion, I knew how right his words were. My brain raced with too many thoughts.

Only one mattered.

Alex.

My step developed a bounce on the return journey to where I had left Alex until I neared the car.

"Wait till you see what I've got. You're going to hate it," I called out. My words vanished into the silence and my feet froze to the ground. "Alex?"

I forced my feet to move. My heart pounded so hard against my chest that it became impossible to believe I would hear anything, including her.

My eyes fixed on her blanket, still strewn on the ground, as I stood where she should have been.

My head and my body twisted and turned to look in every direction. "Alex," I called. Had Luther found us? Had Alex deserted me?

With no real knowledge of where to look, I flitted through the trees, reaching out with my magic, desperation fueling my hunt.

Branches ahead of me wavered, jiggling up and down, and I saw her. Her eyes, filled with a smile that brightened her face, and the unhidden sigh she gave when she spotted me banished the negative thoughts that had moments earlier consumed my mind.

"I thought you'd disappeared again. You need to stop doing that without telling me."

Without replying to the relief in my voice, she rambled on, telling a story of whooshing wings and the impossibility of a sound she had tried to follow. She raced her words in the way she did when she became excited, without worrying what anybody thought. She sounded as though she was losing her mind but I listened with natural curiosity. I knew better, by now, than to doubt the randomness of Alex. Although, I had to agree it was unlikely to have been a bird but could offer no alternative to madness as an explanation.

She looked at the can still in my hand, now filled with a beige-colored slop. "Please tell me you aren't going to eat that? What is it?" she asked, her nose crinkling in disgust.

I laughed. "No. It's pine bark, sap, and stuff. It's for your ribs. It will help, trust me."

She took a step back and I recognized the gagging I felt earlier at the smell of it. "I am not eating that."

"No. I'll rub it on. It'll help. Here, lift your top," I said, grabbing a handful of the concoction.

Her body recoiled but she pulled up her top, tying a knot under her breasts. As I rubbed the mixture on her ribs, my hands sent tingles through me and I blushed.

She pulled down her top and walked back to the car. When she sat in the car, she allowed her feet to skim the grass. "So a plan. Any ideas where you want to head? I'm guessing we're not going to stay here?" she asked, watching my mouth twist as I decided what to say. "Say it. Whatever you're thinking. You're doing that thing with your mouth you do when you're trying to decide how to say something."

My finger touched my mouth and my eyebrows furrowed into a question. "Wow, okay," I said, my face loosening. "I was wondering if we could visit the place you said had a strange energy. You said it had weird energy." In fact, I had been desperate to ask about it since she told me but couldn't bring myself to interrupt her grief for Jen.

"Did I tell you about that?" she asked. Her brain sent a range of twisting pained expressions across her face, changing every few seconds as her internal battle used her face as its canvas.

I regretted asking now.

"You know the memories that place holds?" she asked; her eyes, filled with sadness, broke me.

"No. Sorry. I didn't realize," I said, my words stumbling over themselves. "What happened there?" I took a step toward her. My arms fidgeted as I fought the desire to reach out to her, unsure what her response would be.

Her shoulders slumped and she leaned forward, resting her arms on her knees and staring at her hands. Whether due to the bark concoction or to the thoughts I could tell were ravaging through her brain, she no longer seemed aware of the pain in her side.

I watched her, knowing she had returned to a moment she'd prefer not to visit.

Her voice became tiny as she muttered, "Danny and Calesta. The day I met you. It was there. I . . ."

As her voice trailed off, I wiped tears from her cheeks. She looked up at me, and I knelt in front of her to look into her eyes. "It's fine. It doesn't matter. We don't have to do anything. Okay?" I wanted to rewind time and take back the idea.

"Okay," she said, surprising me.

I was aware of how close her face was to mine. I placed my hands on her cheeks and she leaned forward to kiss me, a kiss that lingered long after I had sat back on the ground.

I looked at her, trying to decide where it had come from. I had no answer. I leaned forward.

"Life is too short. Follow your heart and never regret, right?" she said. She waited for me to respond. I had no idea what I was supposed to say.

The silence of the forest was replaced with an uncomfortable one. Time slowed and I wanted to disappear.

Again, I wanted to rewind time. I wanted to be anywhere but there. I had imagined the moment a hundred different ways. In the end, she initiated it.

She pushed herself up, letting out a pain-filled groan. Desperation to leave forced her forward.

"I'm going to find some wood for a fire. If we're here for another night, I want to be warm," she said, striding toward the trees, keeping her focus on the horizon, refusing to look back at me.

Regret filled me. Regret filled the air and pulled me toward her.

"Wait," I said, now right behind her.

She stopped but still faced away from me, her eyes fixed on the silhouette of the trees. She had nothing more to say. Her actions had spoken more than any words either of us could muster, and my stomach contracted at the memory. We stood there for a few agonizing seconds. Painful, silent seconds.

She took a deep breath, spinning around to look in my face.

Anger at herself and her actions caused her to squirm and fidget. I wanted this moment to be so different but I couldn't be anything but ecstatic.

"Look, I get it, okay. I know you don't see me like that. It was a spontaneous thing and I'm sorry. Can we just let it go now?" she muttered, forcing herself to look into my eyes. "I'm going to get wood now."

"No," I said, grabbing her arm.

"What do you think you're doing? I kiss you once and suddenly you think you can tell me what to do?" she spat. "I can look after myself."

I sighed. The sound was more the result of my shrinking body as I pulled my arms back, curling them around my chest. I had gotten it wrong. I had sent the wrong message. I was so far outside my experience. "No, that's not what I meant. Please, stop. I know you can look after yourself. I've never doubted it. I . . . I . . ."

I wrapped my arm around the curve of her spine, pulled her toward me, and kissed her. All her anger vanished and her mouth responded.

"I've wanted to do that since I first saw you," I said, pulling back to look in her eyes.

Her mouth gaped open. "You have a funny way of showing it. You've been horrible on more than one occasion. You treated me like I was a silly little girl, you avoided me, and you had a go at me when I used magic."

"No. Well, yes, but that's not it. Look, sit down, please." I stepped back and sat on the ground. "Please. That was our first kiss and I don't want it to be this." My voice was softer and quieter than normal.

She took a deep breath and sat opposite me. I ran my fingers around the edge of her hair, pushing the curls away from her face. "The very first time we met, I remember thinking how beautiful you looked. Your eyes were puffy from crying and your lips were full and pouting. I wanted to grab you, wrap you up, and protect you."

Her body stiffened and recoiled. "I don't need protecting. I can take care of myself. That wasn't why I . . . why I . . . kissed you. I wasn't looking for a protector. I—"

My stomach lurched. I'd gotten it wrong, again. "That's not what I meant. I'm just trying to be honest about how I felt. How I feel." I reached for her hand. I stared at a scar on her hand, a scar I'd never noticed. "Then you went barging into my head, and I admit I was a bit miffed and a bit embarrassed. You don't understand magic out here in the real world."

"Oh, hang on a minute. I get magic. My mother made sure of that," she said, her voice getting louder.

"That's what I mean. Something changed after the Orange. Suddenly there were lots of young people developing gifts. They became more empathetic, more connected, some were even capable of things like healing a plant or merging auras, but you . . . I thought I was a bit special until I met you. Nobody ever got in my head and you did it so easily. You were barely trying."

"Okay, so I was good at getting into your head." Frustration and anger tinged her words. Her mood, my uselessness with words, and the newness of the situation were twisting things, but I couldn't control them.

"Yes, but then you grew a field of flowers, set a gang on fire—it just goes on. You don't get how special you are, and it makes me angry that you can't see how amazing you are. You just offer it up as though it's nothing special." My eyes moved from her face to her hands as I held them to my mouth and kissed them. "You've been brought to see magic as this wonderful thing that everybody has, but they don't all have what you have."

The fight against tears threatening to release her emotions down her face made my heart ache. I got this so wrong.

She straightened her shoulders and I could see the effort of self-control. "But that doesn't explain why you didn't bother talking to me once we got to Jericho's Island. You just dropped me instantly. It was like you didn't know me." She flung herself backwards to lie on the ground, dragging her hand from my grasp.

I lay down next to her, the heat from her body burning through my clothing, sending tingles over my skin. "I thought you might be happy there. You made friends and had plenty of admirers. I always saw you; I just didn't get it right and I'm sorry. I really am." I rolled onto my side and lay my arm over her, pulling her to meet me. I moved my face to look down at her. "I promise you that since the moment I met you I felt a connection. I don't know the words for it, but I knew then, and I know now, I want to be with you. When I'm with you it doesn't matter how messed up the world is."

My whole face smiled; I couldn't control it even if I wanted to. She reached up and kissed me. In a world full of wrongs, this was right. Even in the topsy-turviest of worlds, this would always feel right.

We lay there, oblivious to the cold earth and growing wind, until her stomach growled its discontent. She laughed a laugh that vibrated through her body. An infectious laugh. "Man cannot survive on love alone. I think my stomach needs something a bit more," she said, sitting up.

"Love?" I said, a chuckle making a bid for freedom as I spoke. I raised an eyebrow, knowing I'd sell my soul to hear those words again.

"You know what I mean."

I sat up, placing a gentle kiss on her cheek.

She looked into my eyes with a new seriousness. "Life is too short. Follow your heart and never regret, right?"

"Right. So, Salem, for food and weird energy?"

Thirty-Three

Alex

Iggy leaned on the car roof. "We need to go. We have no idea which roads are clear and whether we'll have to walk. Let's be honest, neither of us wants to be getting there in the dark."

I raced toward the trees. "I know, but look. Some of the trees are starting to bud. They're trying to live. If I can help just a few, leave this place a little better than I found it, it might be able to spark new life. What can be more important than that, eh?"

He sighed. "I thought you were hungry," he said, resting his chin on his hands, knowing there was no point in arguing.

I stood in the center of a group of once-trees, hoping that if I got them to spark back to life, it would create a ripple, spreading to the nearest trees that they could communicate with. I looked back in the direction I had left Iggy. "You could help, you know," I yelled, unsure whether he would be able to hear me.

I placed my hands on the tree, stretching my aura down into the earth to meet the tree's roots. Calling on the magic deep in the earth, I shared the energy with the tree, watching in delight as the branches began to bud, tiny leaves forcing their way out of the blackened bark.

"You know it'll take me ages, don't you? We aren't all as special as you," said Iggy, his voice reaching me before I could see him.

"Every bit helps. Besides,"—a smirk spread across my face—"I've been in your head, I know you have the magic." I fell to my knees and stretched out my hands on the ground, watching as the grass began to grow and small flowers spread between the trees.

He touched my shoulder. "It looks beautiful," he said, staring at the towering figure of the tree reaching for the skies.

I twisted my head to smile at him. "Isn't it? It must be so old," I said, hugging it. "You are a beautiful tree."

Looking around, my aura buzzed with the connection the trees shared with me. A warm sensation glowed in my chest; I didn't know whether it was pride, love, or their thanks, but I basked in the moment.

I looked at Iggy and placed my hand in his. "Maybe that's our purpose, our destiny, to bring new life? Maybe that's why we have these gifts?"

He pulled me close and kissed my forehead. "That would be a very worthy destiny."

The journey took longer than we had hoped as we were forced to turn into side streets and change direction, faced with roads blocked with debris and rubble. Neither of us wanted to admit we might have to walk.

Eventually, shortly after arriving in Salem, we admitted defeat after driving in a circle. We abandoned the car, wrapped our blankets around our shoulders, faced with the reality of not knowing where we might end up sleeping tonight.

Saying goodbye to the memories that haunted me of Danny and Calesta felt right. I was moving on, but I needed to honor the past one last time.

"I wonder if I would have gone with you if Danny and Calesta hadn't died that day?" I asked, giving voice to my need to find a purpose in the pain of losing them. "My mother used to say the universe will always find a way to force action, even if you try to ignore it. I had wanted to find more than my safe life in the school, but I don't know whether I would have if they hadn't died that day."

Iggy paused, missing a step. "We need to make our lives worth those who died to get us here. We will figure out how to do it, together."

We clambered over the debris of old Salem, Iggy never questioning my intuition about direction. Some of the streets held a familiarity, but I knew most streets looked the same around here. Now and then, I convinced myself I recognized a building or a house, but it wasn't until we reached the street with the brick-box building in which Danny and Calesta had died that I relaxed.

We had walked in silence, not the awkward silence of earlier, but the comfortable kind that only comes when you are at ease with somebody. The type that left us to walk in unison, content just to be together. The ease I had hoped Jericho's Island would bring but never did. It had taken a person, not a place.

My feet froze to the spot, unable to move, and I glared at the building. I became aware of the breeze in the air chilling my sweating body. I wiped my palms on my jeans, hoping to rid myself of the clammy sensation freezing my body and stiffening every muscle.

"Alex, what is it?"

My words stuck in my mouth, jumbling and creating a nauseous lump that blocked my throat. I gasped for air.

"Alex. Talk to me . . . Breathe." Iggy's voice echoed around me as my presence shrunk and hid.

Unable to answer, I raised my arm to point at the building, instantly pulling my arm back and folding both around my chest. I welcomed Iggy turning me around to face away from the memories that haunted the building and to look in my eyes.

"Look, we can go. You don't need to do this. We can just walk away and keep walking. We can do whatever we want."

I stared at him, processing his words while concentrating on my breathing. I pushed my shoulders up, straightening my body, and stuck my hands into my pockets. "No. Despite everything, there is a bit of me that knows I'm meant to do this." I looked into his eyes. "I have to."

I turned to walk toward the building, a mixture of fear and something I couldn't place pulsing through me. My steps became faster, their purpose more urgent with each stride until I began to run. I could hear Iggy's footsteps behind mine but never turned to look.

I stopped when I reached the parking lot. The ominous black door still lay open like a mouth readying itself to bite. I forced my feet, in a chorus of baby-sized steps, to push on with a new need. The physical exhaustion caused my feet to stick to the ground as my body grew heavy. I reached my aura out, remembering that day. The negative emotions that had greeted me. Today there was nothing but emptiness.

I stepped back from the door, sitting on the ground with my knees up under my chin. I needed to say goodbye to the memory, the guilt, and the pain that I had held on to. I didn't need to go inside. The problem was inside me, not inside the shop. I closed my eyes and whispered, "I'm sorry. I'm sorry I couldn't save you, I'm sorry I never told you how much you meant to me, and I'm sorry I never thanked you. Thank you."

Calmness and peace flowed over me, filling me and revitalizing me. The pain and fatigue were replaced by love. I didn't know whether it was from me, from the universe, or from something else. It didn't matter. Tears I hadn't realized I was crying dropped onto my jeans, creating small dark circles.

As I raised my head; three small tears had formed a tiny dark, love-heart shape. I didn't care if I was reading this as a sign. Sometimes all that mattered was whether the sign meant something to me. It did.

I couldn't tell how long I had sat there. I think time slowed for me, and therefore what had felt like forever was probably little more than a few minutes.

Iggy's pain drifted through the air and I stretched my aura to meet his, reaching inside his. He didn't try to repel me, allowing me to share in his emotions as I shared mine. The depth of his pain caught me off guard. He had never met Danny and Calesta, and I knew his pain was an empathetic response. My pain was his pain.

Hairline cracks exploded in my heart.

He positioned himself behind me, placing his arms under mine and pulling me to my feet. "Enough. You can't punish yourself for something that wasn't your fault." He lay his head on my shoulder, the warmth of his breath against my neck sending a tingle through me.

I twisted to face him. "I know. So, are you ready for strange?" I asked, placing my hand on his chest.

His eyes widened and his lips parted as though to speak words that never came. He leaned forward to kiss me. "With you, I'm always up for strange. I'd follow you to hell and back. Lead the way," he said, stepping back and waving his hand to motion for me to lead the way.

I grabbed his hand and pulled him up the hill, past the sad, white house I had scavenged in with Jen. Memories of the small pink bedroom flashed through my mind. I looked away, pulling harder on Iggy's hand as we neared the spot.

We stood at the foot of the slope, its deep life-filled green grass and trees looking like an oasis in a desert of despair.

"Ready?" I asked.

"You go, I go. Let's feel this weird then." His smile contrasted with the creasing and worry lines around his eyes. His jaw hardened and I knew he was putting on a brave face.

We made our way up the slope, my brain whirring, recalling the memory and my eyes taking in every section of the scene.

I felt it.

I also felt Iggy pull back, so slight as to be imperceptible.

We looked at each other and not a word was spoken. We had come all this way.

We stepped forward, allowing the energy to consume us. Waves of nausea filled me as the magic overwhelmed me. I fought to look beyond the colors, the energy of the magic. Like glimpses through the cracks in a fence, I saw fragments of a place, trees, darkness, but an all-consuming connection to something greater. Something calling me.

I was battling through the emotions and nausea, desperate to see the picture by putting the fragments together, when Iggy fell to his knees, the air escaping from his lungs as he retched.

Shifting my body away from the energy, I fell backwards, landing on top of him. "So?" I said, staring at him as I rolled to lie next to him.

He held up his hand and I gave him some time to gather himself. He stared at me, his eyes wide. "Wow. What was that? It was pushing me away. Whatever it was it didn't want me to be there."

I sat up straight. "Really? I felt it pulling me but there was something in the way, like a doorway that had been bricked up. But, I could see tiny slivers of the other side."

Moving onto his knees, he put his palms on the ground, breathing deep, gasping breaths. "It might have wanted you but it didn't want me. Do you want to try again if it was calling you?"

"Not if you don't want to," I said, not sure how I could walk away but knowing I couldn't and wouldn't leave Iggy.

"If you want to smash it open, do it. I'm with you. Just know that I'll probably throw up. Just lucky I'm hungry right now and my empty stomach isn't much use." He looked at me as he spoke, the determination to smile through nausea and fatigue cracking my heart further. I did not attempt to shield my emotions, sharing my aura with him.

"Together we can do it. We may never get another chance. There is life behind whatever that is. I can feel it." My mother's Firestone danced as I spoke, and I pulled it from under my sweatshirt, wrapping my hand around it.

He nodded at me and we stood, determination filling us, uniting us. We shuffled forward, his hand in mine and my Firestone in the other. I focused on the trees, the glimpses of somewhere, and we both pushed with our magic.

Just as I was sure I would collapse, energy flowed through me, through us, through the stone. Magic greater than anything I had ever imagined engulfed me, and I gasped for breath as a cacophony of colors and lights enveloped me, and I fell through the explosion. When I landed, and darkness wrapped me, suffocated me, I lost consciousness.

We had done something but it had taken everything we had

.

THIRTY-FOUR

ALEX

I reached for Iggy. My fingers touched the warmth of his skin, and I tried to push myself up, struggling to lift my head before falling back on the ground.

Iggy grunted next to me and rolled to lay his hand on my stomach.

"Are you alright?" he asked. His voice broke, expressing his pain. He moved onto his knees, moaning as he forced himself to stand.

My eyelids hurt along with every muscle in my body. I stared at Iggy, his face shadowed by the towering trees we found ourselves surrounded by.

The sun, now much lower in the sky than when we arrived in Salem, glinted through the gaps between the treetops, creating shadow and light painted across the lush green of the forest. I followed the line of the trees upward, trying to make sense of what I saw.

The sunlight was blue, casting a beautiful indigo glow on the world. Iggy stood, waiting for my reply.

"Sorry, I'm fine. It's just I . . . We . . . I mean. Oh, I don't know what I mean." I grasped Iggy's hand, allowing him to pull me to my feet. "Where are we?"

He held onto my hand. "I don't know, but I don't think we're in Salem anymore."

I moved closer as we wound our arms around each other. He leaned in to whisper in my ear. "Do you hear that? The silence isn't silent. That's life."

I closed my eyes, soaking up the sounds. Birds, insects, life. Sounds so soft and subtle, but to our ears, they were unique. Life. Opening my eyes, a smile spread across my face. I could feel it move up my face, reaching my hairline. "Do you feel that? Magic, connection, I don't even know the word. It's amazing."

He smiled. I moved from his hold to touch the trees. "Here, touch them, feel them. They respond, they feel me. Come on," I said, pulling his hand to connect it with the tree.

He let out a small laugh. "It's beautiful. I don't understand but, yes, it is truly amazing. Look," he yelled, pointing at a red-and-green bird resting on a branch above our heads. "I haven't seen a bird since the Orange. Look at it."

I held out my arm, extending my aura to connect with it. "Hello," I said, staring at it, "don't worry, I'm friendly. You are gorgeous." I gazed as it flew toward me. It was about to land on my arm when I heard a scream come from behind me.

"Don't touch it. You may be friendly, but it isn't." A woman, small and skinny with long blonde hair flowing around her face, leaped for me.

I saw Iggy jump for her, grabbing her by the arm, only to be thrown across the ground by this woman. He collided with a tree. I had raised my hands to attack her, to defend myself and Iggy, when her hands mirrored mine. "I am not here to fight you. I was watching you, but you obviously don't understand the Darklands. Not all things here are positive entities. Cruelty still exists here, and the bird would have pecked your eyes out before you knew what was happening." She took two steps back to distance herself from me before turning to offer Iggy her hand.

I shrugged. He ignored her hand and stood up. She looked from Iggy to me. "I'm Geilis."

We stared at each other until I held out my hand. "I'm Alex. Nice to meet you." She shook my hand, holding on for a few seconds longer than she needed to, and I knew she was sensing my magic. I looked past her to Iggy poised to pounce. "And this is Iggy."

She placed herself so she could see both of us. As she held out her hand to him, I could see the muscles in his face stiffen. He shook her hand, pulling his hand back and nodding at her.

I stepped closer. "You said you were watching us. How long were we lying there?"

"Not long. When I got here you were just lying there. At first, I thought you were dead but then you both moved," she said.

I glanced at Iggy and back at Geilis. "Why were you watching us?" I asked.

She shrugged her shoulders, beginning to walk farther into the trees. "Durai sent me to investigate the energy. I was expecting to see guards but I spotted you. I don't intend to hang about here till they show up. There aren't many left in the Darklands anymore. If you want, you can follow me and I'll introduce you to Durai."

We needed answers and perhaps Durai could give them to us. We walked behind Geilis, and I grabbed Iggy's hand, sensing the stiffness of his body. I stretched up to whisper in his ear. "We need answers. Trust me, it'll be fine." I could hear him sigh, although he didn't say a word.

We followed in silence. The farther we walked, the lower the sun moved and the denser the forest became. I tripped over rocks and tree roots, distracted by the amount of life visible in this forest. Flowers spread across the ground, linking the trees and winding up their trunks, forming intricate patterns against the gnarled, twisted form of them.

Geilis stepped with ease and familiarity, seeming to step over obstacles without looking. Our stumbling and sight-seeing slowed us, and we struggled to catch up, hunger and fatigue overriding any pain I had left.

I was preparing to give up and sit among the flowers when Geilis stopped. She leaned against a tree, moving her head to listen. She twisted her body to face us. "Wait here. I'll check there is nobody in the camp. Stay here until I come back for you." Without waiting for a response, she disappeared through the trees, her feet silently skimming the earth as she bounded between the roots and rocks.

Iggy and I stared at each other, a multitude of questions creasing our faces.

"Are you sure about this? I mean, we are following a stranger who threw me without touching me," he said.

"I know, but she possibly saved us, and wasn't it you that said sometimes we should just trust everything would work out?" I said, watching him smile and relax, knowing it would annoy him that I used his own words against him.

I landed on the ground, my legs grateful for the rest. He glared at me as he sat next to me, placing his hand in mine. "Fine, but it doesn't mean I have to be okay with it." We listened to the sounds of the forest, both trying to ignore the nagging doubt forming inside us. Fear of the unknown, of what we had done, of where the universe was dragging us, stabbed at my empty stomach.

Geilis moved with an unnatural silence, appearing in front of us without any sound of her footsteps. "It's all clear. Durai says you should join us for some food. This way," she said, waving her hand.

I gazed at Iggy, his face battling to form a smile that sat uncomfortably among the worry lines forming around the stiffening muscles of his face. I smiled back, or at least I tried to. I had no real idea of what my face did, but he stood and pulled me up.

A minute later, we arrived in a clearing. A circle of dirt with small humped dwellings formed a boundary. A fire burned at the heart of the circle surrounded by logs on which an old man with long white hair sat.

Geilis stood next to the man, who rose to face us, his face freezing into a fearful expression. His mouth moved to speak, yet his eyes spoke of something I didn't recognize. An uncomfortable silence grew to blanket us.

He finally stepped forward. "Sorry, excuse me, you reminded me of somebody just for a moment," he said, looking at me. "So you are the ones responsible for the energy burst, eh? I am Durai Sinjin. You have already met Geilis."

Iggy spoke first as a tingle spread up my spine. "I'm Iggy Thrumblar and this is Alex Chegasa." His words sparked me back to reality, the unfamiliarity of somebody speaking my surname. It had been so long since anybody had used my full name, and it held a strange tone coming from him.

He sat back on his log, Geilis now opposite him. "Please sit. This is a treat; we rarely meet somebody from Bassett. What brings you to the Darklands?" he said, now looking at Iggy.

Iggy and I gazed at each other, deciding whether to admit we had no idea what Bassett was. I leaned in toward Durai. "I'm sorry but we aren't from Bassett. We don't know Bassett. We came from Salem."

Durai and Geilis exchanged glances before he leaned toward us. "Look, I have lived in the Darklands for more winters than most people live, and age has taught me to say things as I see them. Many winters ago, the most important person in my life, Kluzahr . . ." His eyes filled with a sadness I recognized as he spoke. "She was a great woman. She asked me to guard and watch for a visitor from the mortal world. Geilis and I have lived here alone for a long time trying to honor her wishes, even after King Arthanius provided homes for the many refugees who used to live here."

My brain sputtered at the mention of King Arthanius, dragging back memories of my mother's tales of magical worlds and my father. The tales I had written off long ago as works of childish fiction. I battled to form the questions whirring around in my head into sentences.

"I don't know what the mortal world is or who King Arthanius is, but we mean no harm to anybody."

He looked at Iggy. "You're not from Bassett?"

"No. I'm from Canada, and I have no idea what you're talking about." Iggy's voice grew louder and I could hear the exasperation as he tried to understand what was going on.

Durai lowered his eyes, glancing at Geilis before looking back at us. "Do you know where you are?"

Iggy's brows furrowed, anger darkening his eyes. "We are somewhere called the Darklands, and I don't know how we got here. We were in Salem and then . . ." His voice trailed off.

I reached for his hand and squeezed it before I turned to face Durai. "Imagine we were from this mortal world you speak of; what would you tell us about your world," I asked.

He stood and walked toward the fire, prodding it with a stick, sending sparks dancing through the air. Without looking up, he spoke. "Your wonderful fiery hair is something to behold. Tell me, did you get that from your mother or your father?"

Confusion spread through me, my brain struggling to keep up with the conversation. "I don't see what that has to do with anything. My mother had the same red hair as I have, and my father—Well, I don't know him. I've never met him in my life. I imagine he is long dead." I knew I was beginning to shout, and as I walked toward Durai, his stooped figure stoking the fire caused me to stop. This man was older than anybody I had ever known, older than anybody that had survived the Orange.

He turned to me. "What was her name?"

As I said, "Jennifer. Jennifer Somerville," I saw tears run from his eyes and I stared at Iggy.

Durai stumbled backwards and lowered himself onto a log. "She knew. She was right. She knew." He turned to Geilis. "She was right. The Fire Flier has come." He turned to stare at me. He wiped his tears on the sleeve of his coat. "The Fire Flier. You came. Kluzahr was right."

There is a comforting peace in realizing you must have gone mad, in the moment you accept the futility of arguing against insanity and go with the flow of the raging torrent of absurdity.

"Who is Kluzahr?" I asked before the weight of my tired body dragged me to the ground. I landed on my knees. "I'm hungry, thirsty, and tired. Could we carry this on tomorrow?"

After that, I remember tiny fragments of the night. Iggy picking me up, and voices speaking as we moved. For seconds or minutes or hours, I lay safe in his arms. I remembered being placed and wrapped in a thick blanket and light appearing above my head and the gentle caress of Iggy, his stroke an anchor to reality. I drifted off to sleep, blind to the world, mine or the strange one I found myself in now.

I curled up, the blanket warming me, content with the knowledge Iggy was with me. I slept cocooned in safe oblivion.

The emptiness of my dreams recharged me and the magic of the ground I lay on filled me. I stretched my arm to feel the warmth of Iggy, tucking my hand under his arm and pulling myself close to him. The wind whistled a melodic tune, like a lullaby sent from Mother Nature for me.

A cold breeze, daring me to step from my blanket and face it, swept around me. I rolled over, wrapping the soft fabric around me as I snuggled closer to Iggy. To where he should be, where he was supposed to be.

I sat up, the chill biting my skin, to stare at the space that should have been Iggy. The dull light came from a small glass globe hanging from the ceiling flickering with impossible flames, casting warning shadows around the dome I was in. I pushed my hands against the ground to stand up, hitting my head on the rounded roof. Its rough texture catching the light sparkled with energy. Yet, to the eye, it was nothing more than mud. Sculpted for nothing more than sleeping, it hemmed me in, and I knelt on the bundle of blankets that had warmed me minutes earlier.

A scream escaped, and my hands flew to my mouth as if surprised by the sound that had come from it. I scrambled on my knees, the dim lighting and unknown environment adding to the surreal atmosphere of my domed tomb.

Light streamed in as a door, so dark and well concealed, opened. The blinding of the light and the fear I was already battling against sent panic shuddering through my brain. I had to get out, and the only exit was now being blocked by a large, shadowy figure.

Instinctively, I raised my hands, squeezing my eyes shut as I forced a wave of energy toward the shadowy shape.

The dome began to collapse around me and I heard Iggy. His voice awoke me from the waking nightmare. I scrambled toward the light, large sections of the mud roof falling on me and blocking my way. The silhouette no longer stood in the doorway, and I pulled myself through it to see Iggy, sprawled on the ground, staring at me.

"What was that?" he asked as I realized the shadow had been him. "That's a new trick, or have I just not had the pleasure of witnessing it before?"

I ran—more of a speedy crawl—to sit next to him. "Did I do that? I am so, so sorry. I woke up and didn't know where I was or where you were. I just panicked. I am sorry. Are you hurt?" My words shot out at lightning speed, a mash-up of incoherent words.

He pushed himself up, resting on his elbows. "I'll be fine. That was impressive, but I'd rather not be on the other end again." He sat up, rubbing his shoulder. "Are you okay?"

"I am so sorry. I just got scared," I said, kneeling next to him.

He pulled me into him, hugged me, and calmed me. "No, I'm sorry. I shouldn't have left you."

I sat back on the ground, gazing around the camp at the empty logs around the fire and the mud domes until my eyes reached the rubble of what had been the dome I was in. My shoulders sank.

"I feel really bad. They're going to hate me when they see what I've done," I said, looking back at Iggy. "Where are they? How long have I been asleep? The last thing I remember was that madman claiming I was the Fire Flier or something."

He stood up. "Come and sit down. I'll get you something to eat. You've missed a lot."

I followed him to sit in silence, watching him fill a bowl from a pot hanging over the fire. Hunger gripped my stomach and the smell tantalized my nose, tickling it. "That smells glorious. I had forgotten how hungry I was," I said, grasping the old clay bowl he handed to me.

He perched next to me. "I don't know but it tastes great."

I ate with greed and enjoyment. When the bowl emptied too soon, I gazed at the pot over the fire, old, battered, and stained black from goodness knows how many years hanging over the fire. "Do you think they'd mind if I had some more? I'm suddenly starving."

He laughed. "I'm sure they won't. You've been asleep for a day and a half; it's no wonder you're starving. Although, it's just Geilis at the moment. Durai had to go somewhere; and Geilis isn't the most sociable person. She seems to prefer her own company but that could just be me." He refilled my bowl and put his hand on my knee. "You've missed a lot and I need you to listen with an open mind. Much of it sounds seriously strange."

The spoon gave a hollow rattle as I dropped it in the bowl. "Do I want to hear this?" I asked.

"Yes. Trust me, you do." He sat astride the log, one leg on each side, staring straight at me.

"Go on," I said with a sigh.

"Okay, first things first, Durai claims to have met your mother a long time ago with the king. King Arthanius Chegasa. He says he is one of the few people who knew she came from the mortal world. I'm guessing that King Arthanius Chegasa is your father. Perhaps your mother's stories were more than childish fantasy."

I turned my body, mirroring his stance. With my feet planted on either side of the log, I stared at him. "You're trying to tell me my father is a king, and that he is the king of this country?"

He squirmed—whether for discomfort at the log or my words, I don't know—but he couldn't look me in the face. "Well, yes and no." He gazed into my eyes and I could see the words swimming through his, the strange little wrinkles forming around them when he didn't want to say something.

"Which is it? Yes or no." I could feel my throat tightening and my words crunching through my teeth.

"Yes, I do think your mother was telling the truth. I mean it would be too weird a coincidence that she just made up a King Arthanius Chegasa. However, and this is the no part . . . he isn't the king of this country. He is the king of this planet, apparently; it's called Chegasa. I know, it isn't very imaginative. He is also king of a collection of worlds. Another planet, Sinjin, and three moons called Bassett, Lyman, and Godytha."

"Wait, my mother told me about a Faeridae Godytha; that's where she got the book from." My hands flew to my back to check my waistband. The book was gone. "My book," I yelled, jumping up. "Where's my book?"

Iggy stood up, grabbing my shoulders. "It's alright. I've got it. I took it when you were asleep. It didn't look very comfortable. It's safe."

He reached behind his back, pulling the book from his waistband, and I squatted back on the log. "Okay, so let's say I believe there are all these moons and planets and—"

"No, it's true. Last night when you were sleeping I could see two moons. This world has two moons. It was something else to behold. You need to see it." Excitement painted his face, all worries disappearing from it, and his eyes, full of wonder, squeezed at my heart. His face, like that of a child, accepted the impossible wonders of the universe.

I bent forward to kiss his cheek, laying my hands on top of his. "So tell me, this king who might be my father, what about him?"

Iggy shuffled closer to sit directly in front of me. "Well, good news and bad news on that one," he said, the smile disappearing from his face, replaced by the tiny creases that appeared when he didn't want to say something. "Durai fought alongside him in the Battle of Unity. About the same time you were born, the kingdom had a massive problem with refugees and what they call hybrids, people who have parents from two different planets. He had not long been king when the battle happened and he fought to provide for everyone. He sounds honorable."

"Really? He left my mother to raise me alone. He left her to die and he left me to live among strangers on a dying planet. Honorable?" I replied, leaning back, moving out of reach of him. "So he fought for hybrids. I must qualify as a hybrid, eh? Half Chegasa and half what? Mortal? Human? Sounds to me like a hypocrite."

I swung my leg over the log, striding off toward the trees. I heard Iggy's footsteps behind me. "Wait. I get your point, but we don't know that he even knows you exist."

I spun around to face him. "So, let's go and knock on his door and introduce ourselves, shall we?" He grabbed my arm and I pulled away, stepping farther back. "So is that the good news or the bad news? If that's the good news we are sunk."

My body screamed inside, the warring emotions fighting in a struggle that I knew would have no victor. Pain scratched into his perfect face.

"Oh Iggy, that was the good news, wasn't it?" I mumbled, falling to my knees. "Why can't we just be happy? Can't we just stay here and hide from the world?"

Bending to kneel in front of me, he lifted my chin. "We will be happy. I promise. We will find a way. Please trust me." He leaned in to kiss my tears and my anger evaporated, floating off in the cold air.

"I do trust you, but why can't it be simple?" I said.

"We have a plan and a small problem. Please, come and sit down till I explain."

I gave a small nod, wiping my face with my hands, and followed him back to the logs. The warmth from the fire tingled my feet and I realized how cold I was. "Start with the problem, please. I just want to get it over with."

Back on the log, he straightened his back, sitting tall, and I prepared for whatever was to come. "Well, after the Battle of Unity, he created a Board of Representatives, a group of people from all planets, so the people could govern themselves. He is the head of this Board, but they rule Spirismus, and . . . well, this is where it gets complicated. The door thing we smashed to come here was one of many portals to our world closed hundreds of years ago, and, despite his request to open them, the Board said no. We have broken a massive rule. If they catch us, we are likely to be in trouble and there will be nothing he can do to help. We will be at the mercy of this Board of people."

I could feel my aura sucking back the anger that had dissipated earlier. "So what were we meant to do? Send a polite note asking to visit? That's nonsense. He fought for refugees but we don't count?"

The pain etched in his face sent pangs of guilt through me. None of this was his fault. "I'm sorry. I'm not angry with you." I pushed myself forward to kiss him. "Sorry."

He smiled. "You have every right to be angry. I was angry last night when Durai explained it to me. I mean, what choice did we have? Although, on the plus side, we—or rather *you*—managed to break the magic that closed them hundreds of years ago. Quite an achievement.

"Anyway, many will be with you if they believe you are the Fire Flier. For just now Durai suggests we hide on the Bassett Moon. I think they might be my ancestors and they have waited for the Fire Flier for generations. They will hide us. Durai has gone to find a friend who can help. We just need to hide here until he gets back."

"We'll be safe there?"

"Durai said we would be. We could just live there quietly."

"What about our friends? What about all those left behind? Who will look out for them?"

He bent to kiss me. "Just trust everything will work as it was meant to."

THIRTY-FIVE

ALEX

Darkness was taking hold, shrouding the sky in a blanket of invisibility, when we appeared from the new dome Geilis had been kind enough to move us to.

If she had minded the destruction I had inflicted on the previous dome, she gave no sign of it. She ate in silence and we followed her example.

The tiredness that draped over me like a heavy, itchy blanket weighing me down and clawing at my skin faded, and I sat enjoying the peace. The sound of the wind blowing through the leaves reminded me of the life that still existed in this world. Where there is life, there is still hope. Hope became me, filled me, and warmed me.

Footsteps, gentle but persistent, broke the silence. It was Geilis who first jumped. "Go and hide under the blankets. Don't come out until I say. No matter what happens," she whispered, grabbing a sword from behind the log she sat on.

My eyes fixed on the sword. I had never seen one outside of books. I found myself entranced until Iggy grabbed my arm and broke the spell. We ran, stumbling and landing in the dome. He pulled blankets over us as we peered out of the open door, watching Geilis brandish her sword.

"Put it down, Geilis. It's only me," came the voice of Durai. Although we couldn't see him, she relaxed, allowing the sword to hang at her side as a shadow moved toward her.

We watched from our blankets as Durai and a smaller man with long black hair plaited down his back entered the camp. The light from the fire cast on them, and the wrinkles of the smaller man created an image full of dark valleys. As they neared the fire, Geilis placed her sword on the ground.

I sat up, pushing the blankets off us. "Not yet," said Iggy.

We lay there watching but struggling to hear. The smaller man stood in front of the fire; he appeared older than anybody I had ever seen, older than Durai. With a blanket wrapped around his shoulders and trousers that barely reached his calves, he cast an intriguing silhouette. We watched as Geilis pointed to our dome.

"You can come out now," she shouted, but I waited for Iggy to move before I did.

The man headed toward us as we emerged from hiding. Nearing him, I noticed his feet were bare despite the cold and painted blue. He moved to hug us. "I am Caleb Dragonrider Thrumblar and it is an honor."

I looked at Iggy. "Welcome home," he said, tucking a feather behind Iggy's ear.

He turned to face me. "Welcome to Spirismus."

I looked at Iggy and then back at Caleb. "I think I know the answer, but what is Spirismus?"

He reached to hold my hand and I recoiled. He stared into my eyes. "Spirismus is the union of worlds we are in. You have much to learn and I am so excited to help you." He looked back at Iggy. "Both of you."

I watched as his aura glowed around him, with a multitude of colors pulsing, dancing, and reaching for the stars. I had never seen anything more beautiful and found myself smiling at him.

I held out my hand. "I am Alex Chegasa and it is a pleasure to meet you," I said, looking at Iggy, watching his face. An unreadable emotion filled it. I raised my eyebrows. "And this is . . .," I prompted him.

He held out his hand. "I am Ignathius Dragonrider Thrumblar, but everybody calls me Iggy."

Caleb ignored his hand, wrapping him in a hug. "A Thrumblar and . . . and . . . you broke the portal?"

Iggy turned to stare at me. "No, she did," he said, tilting his head toward me.

Caleb's face filled with his smile. "Wow. What a day. I am so privileged to meet you both."

Perhaps it was his aura or the fact he looked like a strange, shrunken version of Iggy, but intuitively I trusted the man. I placed my arm through his and we walked back to the fire, with Iggy following. I heard a small chuckle from behind me and turned to see him laughing. I could feel my eyebrows crease as I mouthed, 'what?' He shook his head and smiled.

I battled through tiredness for hours while Caleb described his Bassett Moon. A small mountainous moon with numerous small oases. He explained life for his people had changed little over the generations. They lived at peace with the universe, and it, in return, provided for them. It was a simple life, he said, and simple sounded attractive to me.

He began to explain their belief system based around spirit animals, but my body refused to stay awake. I found myself drifting off and didn't have the energy to question what the plan was.

I sat up as straight as I could, determined to sound coherent through the fog of my haze. "I need to sleep. I'm sorry but I am tired. No, I'm more than tired. I can hardly think, I'm so tired."

Everybody turned to look at me and their faces told me I looked as tired as I felt.

"I'm surprised you're awake at all," said Durai. "When I left to get Caleb, I didn't expect you to wake for days after using that much magic. I can't imagine how much connection passed through you to do something like breaking open a portal that's been locked for almost forever."

"Thank you."

I put my hands on the log to push myself up and walk to the dwelling, but my body wouldn't cooperate, and for the second time since we had arrived on Spirismus, I allowed Iggy to carry me to bed.

I slept, trusting everything would work out as it should.

Iggy shook me. "Wake up," he yelled, and I could tell from the tone of his voice this wasn't the first time he'd tried to wake me.

I pulled the blanket over my head. "I'm coming," I mumbled.

I felt him move away, and, hoping he was going to leave me in peace, I tucked my feet in the blanket, the furry texture tickling my toes. An abrupt blanket of cold wrapped my body and I sat up, gasping at it. Iggy stood in the doorway waving my blanket, laughter causing him to bend over.

"I'm sorry," he said, still giggling. "I am, but we need to move."

I crawled out of the doorway, the icy air biting at my skin. "At least give me my blanket back. I'm up now."

He threw the blanket at me as I knelt to put my shoes on.

"No point in doing that. You won't be wearing shoes." I looked up to see Caleb walking toward me. "A blessed morning to you both," he said.

He explained we were going to catch a train and I grew excited. I remembered going on a train as a child but such things were distant memories. He described the plan, which involved us looking like native Bassetts. Easy for Iggy. He already did. I would prove more of a problem.

Geilis tied my hair back, wrapping a black scarf around it, covering my hair. I was happy to go along with this until Caleb decided to paint our feet blue. The earth was freezing and walking without shoes did not appeal to me, but I agreed. I had to trust Caleb at this point.

He stood back, evaluating my appearance. "You look too dark. We'll have to hope everybody assumes you're a hybrid. Try to keep your blanket wrapped around you as much as possible."

I glanced at Iggy; his hair was pulled back from his face and plaited down his back with the feather Caleb had given him. He looked younger. He looked over at me, a smile filling his face. I got the feeling he was more enthusiastic about this plan than I was.

Durai appeared, holding three packages. "I made breakfast for you to eat on the way." He grabbed me, wrapping me in a hug. "I hope I see you again, Alex. I wish you good fortune for the future. Hopefully, someday I will meet you in happier times."

I kissed him on the cheek. "Thank you for everything. We were lucky to have met you."

"I was fulfilling a promise to a very dear friend. She knew you would come and she was never wrong. Kluzahr would be so happy to see you here in Spirismus." He turned away, hiding a tear in his eyes.

He hugged Iggy, whispering in his ear, before walking away without looking back.

We were about to leave the camp when Geilis ran to me. "This is for you," she said, holding out a small gold pin. "If ever you find yourself in trouble with the guards, give them this and say you demand to see King Arthanius. Tell them to say Geilis is here and asks for the return of the favor. I'm sure he will honor the promise. Trust me, he'll know what it means."

I stood stunned; she had said little more than two words the entire time we had stayed. "Thank you." She turned and walked away.

Caleb led the way through the trees, my feet burning with the cold gnawing at them. The forest hushed, reminding me of home. I struggled to keep up with Caleb. He had told us we would have a short window of time to get on the train. It didn't stop here. He had arranged to have it stop so we could climb on.

Before long the trees thinned and the rising sun warmed us. Caleb, when we were close enough to hear the train coming, sat down and unwrapped the fabric parcel. I laid my blanket on the ground and sat on it, tucking my feet in it, and Iggy sat next to me, placing his blanket over my shoulders. We opened our parcels and I stared at them. I knew what they were, but I'd only ever seen them in books.

I held an egg in the palm of my hand, staring at it. After the Orange, there were no animals left and those who survived were never eaten. The pollution poisoned them. I couldn't take my eyes off it and whispered to Iggy, "I don't think I can eat this. It was a living thing. It seems wrong."

I watched as he placed his back in the packaging. He looked at me. "I know what you mean. I remember eating meat as a small child, but back then life was cheap."

We glanced over at Caleb eating. He glanced back. "I know what you mean. On Bassett, we don't eat animals. They are sacred. Some of us do eat the bounty they provide us though. Eggs. Milk."

I could feel my face flush. I hadn't meant for him to hear me. "I'm sorry. I didn't mean to offend you. I just can't bring myself to eat it, knowing what it was. It makes my stomach turn just thinking about it."

His shoulders shook with a small laugh he chose to keep hidden inside. He rummaged in his bag, pulling out another package. "Here, try these," he said, throwing them to us.

Iggy caught it, unwrapping it to find small colored biscuits. The sweet smell drifting from them brought a grin to my face and I grabbed one. I let out a small groan. "These are the nicest thing I think I've ever tasted," I mumbled, stuffing more in my mouth.

"Margery, the king's head cook, makes them for me when I visit. I'll bring you some back next time I go to Peyton Palace."

"Is that where King Arthanius lives?"

"Yes. Peyton is where most of the population lives. The palace has been there for generations. It's quite magnificent. You should see it."

"I think I'd rather not," I said, continuing to eat the biscuits.

A sizzling sound hissed toward us and I noticed Caleb tying his package. He turned to us. "Stay out of sight until it stops. When I say go, you run. We need to be fast."

Pulling my blanket tight around me and burying my face in it, we waited. The train, unlike the trains I had seen before the Orange, pulled into sight. Glistening and reflecting the sunlight, it shone like a silver-and-gold flowing river, slithering toward us. It began to slow.

Sensing our desperation to move, Caleb held out his arm, blocking our path. "Wait until it stops. It'll pull up just past us. It's glass, so everybody can see out. Stay hidden until it passes us."

It slowed to a gentle stop, its energy casting light all around it. With a hesitant step, Caleb edged forward, and we prepared to run when the glass along the side of the train began to lower, revealing at least twenty men and women, all dressed in a black-and-purple uniform, swords hanging on their hips. Caleb turned, fear etching pain into the wrinkles of his face as the muscles stiffened.

"Quickly, up a tree. Hide."

We clambered upward, my feet catching and cutting on the gnarled bark. The sounds of their voices got closer. My hands slipped and I felt Iggy pushing me upward. The voices grew louder. No more than halfway up, we clung on and held our breath as they marched past us.

Pain coursed through my muscles. I glanced up through the branches, the indigo glow of the sunlight casting shapes and shadows on Caleb's face. His pained expression begged me to remain silent; the pain and urgency were painted in his wide eyes. His face twisted as he tried to smile, but it only served to highlight the pain in the creases growing around his eyes and mouth.

He held his hand down to me, and I reached, my fingertips grazing the rough skin of his hands when I heard the branch I knelt on creaking. The creak became a groan and, too late, I jumped as it cracked. The branch plummeted toward the ground, taking other branches and leaves with it. With an echoing smack, it landed on the grass, announcing our presence.

My fingers grasped for anything to hold onto. They scrambled, grabbing at the air. My body dropped, limbs wriggling in a vain attempt to stop myself. The thud of my landing forced the air from my lungs and pain engulfed me. For a moment I struggled to understand what had happened and rolled onto my front, laying my hands on the ground. I tried to push myself up but was met with a burning pain shooting up my left arm. An involuntary scream escaped my lips, and I heard a muted thump echo near me.

Throwing myself backwards to land on my buttocks with a groan, I shuffled to place my back against the rough bark of the tree trunk. Using my right arm, I tried to push myself up the tree. It was then I heard Iggy. He stood in front of me. The thud had been him.

Placing his hands under my arms, he pulled me upright and my legs rebelled, screaming in agony. He placed his hand over my mouth, and his wide-eyed stare in front of me spoke of his fear. "Shh."

I could hear the voices of the guards who had passed us. Their voices reverberated around the trees, making it impossible to determine the direction they were coming from, and we stood. There was nowhere to go. No escape. Iggy wrapped his arms around me, whispering in my ears, "If they catch us, don't fight back. We don't know what your magic will do here. It isn't worth the risk."

I nodded. The magic and connection, so much more powerful here than at home, was beyond my control. Every atom of my being pulsed with desperation to fight, to flee, to never give in, but I knew the wisdom of his words.

We waited. We knew the inevitability of what was coming.

Iggy lunged for the guard as I landed on the ground. So much for not fighting back, I thought.

The young guards, no taller or no older than me, had looked surprised when they spotted us between the trees. They pulled their swords, one of them releasing a glowing ball from his other hand.

I watched the ball as it grew and floated upward, disappearing in a flurry of explosions. The beauty of it grabbed my attention, and the rest of the events fell into unreal oblivion until a hand grabbed my arm. The pain dragged me, with fierce aggression, back to reality.

Then Iggy screamed, "She's hurt. You don't need to do that. We'll come with you. Just leave her alone." He pushed the guard who had grabbed for me and anger boiled behind his eyes. The other guard stepped forward with small reticent steps, pulling a glowing rope from his belt. He threw it toward Iggy, and it wrapped around his arms and legs, causing him to land on the ground with a whack.

I hobbled forward. "Stop. We aren't going to fight back. You don't need to do this," I said, trying to hold my arms up, but the pain stopped me.

"I arrest you in the name of the king for treason against Spirismus," he said, his voice wavering as he tiptoed toward me. I watched the shaking of his hands as he held out another glowing rope intended for me.

I held out my hands in front of me. "It's fine. We mean you no harm," I said, lowering my voice and staring into his eyes.

He placed the rope around my wrists and I winced in pain. The negative energy of the rope appeared to dampen my magic. He stepped forward, holding eye contact with me.

"You can put one of those around our ankles if you want, but do you really want to carry us? We will follow you." My words stopped him in his tracks, and he turned his head to look at the other guard, now standing over Iggy. I could see the effect of my words in the guards' stuttering movements. They nodded at each other, and with a sweep of a hand, Iggy's feet were released.

The sound of voices and hurried footsteps cracking the twigs strewn on the ground broke the tension, and Iggy walked toward me, holding out his arms for me to lean on.

More guards appeared between the trees, slowing as they spotted us, their eyes fixing on us with a sense of disbelief. Without any instruction they fanned out to form a semicircle, blocking our path should we decide to attempt to run into the forest. The deep purple and black of their uniforms caused them to blend with the indigo sunlight that barely entered the dark of the trees.

Unnatural ease and calmness filled me, as though something had taken possession of me, a connection with the trees, the ground, a something that I couldn't identify. I can only explain it as an alliance with the trees. I stared past the guards, no longer aware of what they were saying, convinced I could see a face in the shadows with strange orange, glow-like eyes, staring at me from the depths of the forest.

I knew I was in the right place. I couldn't define what I became aware of at that moment. I heard no words yet knew the trees were talking to me. I just couldn't tell what they said.

A rough push threatening to send me flying on the ground came from behind me, and I spun around to see a female guard. Taller than me, in fact, taller than anybody I had ever met, I found myself fixating on the whites of her eyes, and her face hardened. Her skin, an ebony black matched only by the darkness of her eyes, served to cast a statuesque presence. Unable to determine her age, I knew from her eyes she had seen and done things I could never imagine, and I knew I didn't want to argue.

"I don't know what you're on about, Terrivon. She doesn't seem that powerful to me. Her magic isn't doing her much good now. Is it?" she boomed at the young guard who had first found me.

His face fell and he gawked at his boots. "She has weird magic coming off her. I don't recognize it and I thought . . ." His voice trailed off as he fell in behind us.

"You're not at the University now, Terrivon. We don't deal in magic," she said.

"Maybe I'm just not trying. Maybe I'm exactly where I want to be," I muttered, speaking to myself but knowing I should have kept my thoughts to myself. The pain coursing through my legs was building a wave of anger inside me, deep in my chest, and I breathed, knowing I would react if she shoved me once more.

I glanced back over my shoulder to the tree I knew held Caleb. Had he set us up? I wanted to believe it was just bad luck. Where he should have been, there was nothing but space. He had escaped. I hoped he had. He didn't deserve to pay for trying to help us.

The walk to the train grew slower, the pain in my feet and legs grew unbearable, and I could sense the anger growing inside the female. She was now holding me by the elbow, both to support me and to keep me moving, and I could feel the bristling of her aura. I smiled, knowing I could merge my aura and she wouldn't notice.

This world may be full of magic but she showed me that, even here, not everybody was open to the connection.

I blinked in the light when we left the trees, realizing how dark the trees had been and how much of the light had been blocked. I fought to focus my eyes as my guard gave me one last shove. My patience broke as I landed on the ground and on my sore arm, unable to protect it.

I focused on the pain and the rope draining my magic. I imagined the rope falling off and pushed my magic. Iggy's words echoed through my head as they fell off. Ha! I could still control my magic. Now kneeling on the ground, I moved my hands and grabbed the rope on my good arm.

"Get up," yelled my guard.

With a smile, I looked up at her, my heart chuckling inside. "Why don't you give me a hand up then," I said, reaching my hand up to her. I saw her jaw clench. She took a step back and I knew from her unblinking eyes I wasn't supposed to be able to do that.

Her eyes began to cloud and the wide-eyed expression was replaced by narrow eyes, and I enjoyed a few seconds of watching her bite her cheek as her brain whirred. I sat upright, holding out my hand, and stared into her eyes.

"Can you tell me what is going on here?" a voice called from a distance, and I looked toward the train to see a man dressed in an exquisite white suit without a hair out of place. He pulled a silver handkerchief from a pocket inside the tight-fitting jacket and took a step toward us. His confident gait as he strode in our direction, compounded by a smile that, although only just visible, filled his face with polite entitlement.

I looked behind him to see two other men. One was a muscular man with his hair tied back in a bun, dressed in a pale beige tunic and matching pants tucked into gold boots that clung to his legs. I struggled to see the third man and then realized it was Caleb. He had escaped. He had beaten us to the train. I was about to smile when he took a step to the side, giving everybody a clear view of him, and he gave his head an almost imperceptible shake. His mouth went to form the word no but he didn't speak.

My guard straightened her shoulders and held her head high, and I could tell she was preparing to argue, to assert her authority. Oblivious to me, she stepped forward, placing her back to me, and I was tempted to shove her (or worse) but resisted the urge.

"Please return to the train, gentlemen; we are here on the king's business. We shall be returning to Peyton. I apologize for any inconvenience," she said, her body stiff and ready to prove her position.

The tanned gentleman in the beige outfit moved in our direction, his posture verging on arrogant but stopping just short of it, the embodiment of confidence. "I doubt the king would expect you to be treating a prisoner this way. The woman is injured and appears to be no risk to you or anybody else. It appears to me she requires care."

"Sir, please return to the train." Her voice grew louder, her fingers stiffening and fidgeting in a reflex action. "As I said, we are here on the king's business."

"Perhaps I wasn't clear. Excuse me, I'm just used to people knowing who we are. I am Fen Lyman-Sinjin, the King's Healer, and this is my husband, Representative Olan Sinjin-Lyman and our friend, Representative Caleb Bassett. We were escorting him home as he was feeling unwell. Perhaps, I could be of use." He continued walking toward us, and I enjoyed watching her squirm.

"No. It is quite alright, sir. I assure you we have it under control," she said, moving to stand in front of him.

He sidestepped around her and continued in my direction. She put out her hand to stop him but thought better of it when Representative Olan Sinjin-Lyman and Caleb began to move in our direction. He held out his manicured hand to me and I grabbed hold of it. He pulled me up in one move, whispering in my ear, "I am sorry we didn't get to you first, but we will help sort this." He squeezed my hand before sweeping me into his arms.

He looked at the guard, her face beginning to contort as she glared at us. Her eyes narrowed and the muscles of her jaw pulsed. The casual politeness of his tone disappeared as he stood in front of her. "I'm sorry, I don't believe I caught your name."

I watched as her chest expanded, imagining I could hear the deep breaths of her anger. "I am Captain Kecat Chegasa, and I assure you, we appreciate your help but we have it under control."

He turned a fraction to his right so I could see the train, Iggy, and Captain Kecat. I looked at Iggy, who shrugged at me, his relaxed posture belying the anger sparking in his aura. I could hear a sigh deep in Fen's chest, unsure whether only I could hear it because I was leaning against him.

"Well, Captain, I have no doubts you have it under control, but from where we are, it appears you have an injured prisoner, one who appears compliant judging by the lack of shackles, yet she is being forced to carry herself despite her injuries," he said, turning to walk away from the guards heading to the train, and I could tell she wanted to argue. "Anyway, since you appear to have failed to bring a Royal Train, I am curious where you intend to detain these hardened criminals?"

I couldn't resist a smirk as I heard her mumble under her breath. He stopped at the steps of the train and, without turning to see her or wait for an answer, he said, "I think the best plan might be to take these prisoners to our carriage, where I can heal these hardened criminals."

Captain Kecat's voice barked orders behind me, and I looked at Caleb, who now stood beside me.

"Iggy," I said. "Is he okay?"

He avoided eye contact. "Yes, he is coming and he's fine, if a little angry looking," he said, trying to sound more lighthearted than his face looked. "I am sorry. I promise we'll sort this, somehow."

I held out my hand to touch the glow of the train. "It's beautiful," I said, "like a silver glass snake. It's as though it has an aura, but it doesn't."

Fen carried me through the corridor of the train, its glass outer walls giving way to polished dark wood partitions and doors. Everything about the train was pristine. The metal trimmings gleamed, and the fabrics of the seats and long stretches of bench-like sofas were a glossy grey velvet. The lack of color, rather than being oppressive and dull, created a sense of calm and luxury. This didn't look anything like the trains I had read of before the Orange.

Fen lay me on the sofa stretched along one side of the carriage, and Iggy sat next to me. I tried to force my aching body to sit up and a moan escaped from my mouth.

"No. You lie there and I'll fix you up," said Fen.

"It's best not to argue with him. I don't. Trust me, it isn't worth it," joked Olan, moving to kneel in front of us. "I am Olan and it is an honor to meet you, Alex and Iggy. Caleb has told me much about you. I am so sorry we were unable to help you earlier. I promise we tried." Olan's voice filled with a sadness that touched me, and I stretched my hand, placing it on his.

"You tried, that's all we could ask for. We appreciate that," I said.

Iggy moved to sit near my head, lifting it to rest on his legs. He placed his hand on my shoulder and I lifted my arm to touch it.

"Your hand," I said. "You've cut yourself."

"Have you seen what you look like?" he replied. "Let's just say you've looked better and it isn't my blood. It's yours." He looked up at Fen and Olan. "Thank you for helping us."

Fen pulled open a small shiny metal case and his eyes drifted to Olan. They gazed at each other before both let out a low, pained sigh in unison.

"I'm afraid our problems have only just begun. You are going to be a problem in so many ways. We had hoped to hide you on Bassett while we figured out what to do, but that is no longer an option. Now, we need a solution," Caleb said, standing and pacing the length of the carriage. "I'm afraid we are in for quite a journey."

THIRTY-SIX

ALEX

The train traveled at such a speed that the scenery whizzing outside the glass walls of the carriage smudged into a head-spinning blur. The dark shadows of the Darklands's trees gave way to an expanse of blue, apparently the sea that separated the community of Chegasa from the largely deserted Darklands.

Fen explained to Iggy and me that Chegasa was the biggest of the planets in Spirismus; however, since it had two moons, Lyman and Bassett, the tides of the sea around the middle covered a large amount of the land. The south of the planet was either destroyed, ruinous wasteland, or the Darklands, none of which had many people living there.

We were headed for Peyton, the capital of Chegasa and the home of both the Board of Representatives and my father, King Arthanius. We had all avoided discussing him.

Fen rubbed herbs and spices on my legs, feet, and arm, muttering words in a language I didn't recognize. A warm burning flared through my body. Not painful, just weird. The pain vanished and a numbness replaced it.

"It'll take a day or two to properly heal, but I can stop the pain while the healing takes hold. You're lucky nothing was broken. If nothing else, it'll get us a couple of days to sort things before the Board interrogates you. They won't be able to talk to you until I say you are well enough."

I watched Iggy pacing the carpet, wandering back and forth, muttering to himself. He eventually sat next to me; and Olan, Fen, and Caleb sat opposite us.

"Tell me," Iggy said, "when we arrive in Peyton, what will happen? What do we need to prepare for?"

I pulled my legs up until my chin rested on my knees. My fingers shuffled across the soft velvet of the seat, stretching to find his hand, but it wouldn't stay still.

"If we know what we're faced with, we can at least try to formulate some sort of plan," he said, and I could feel him squirming in his seat, resisting the urge to pound the carpet.

Olan leaned forward, running his fingers through his hair. "Well, they'll take you to the cells in the basement of Peyton Palace. You'll stay there until you speak to the Board of Representatives. They'll decide on your innocence or guilt." He looked at Fen, who nodded.

"You need to be honest with the likely outcomes here," Fen said.

Olan took a deep breath. "It seems difficult to imagine a scene where they won't find you guilty. You did open a portal. Our only argument will be that you didn't know. Caleb and I are on the Board of Representatives, so we will obviously be on your side. There will be others who I think we can convince to be lenient. Constantine and Faeridae are the rulers of Godytha and very good friends of your father and will probably be on our side. Constantine and Art were raised as brothers. For years they were inseparable."

Fen threw himself back in his chair. "My father is one of the representatives of Lyman. I think he can convince the other Lyman Representative. That's six of the thirteen that we can call on. We just need to find one more." He paused for a moment, his mouth forming words, and I knew what he was thinking. "I'm sure your father would help if he knew who you were."

My body tensed at the prospect. When I was a child, I had longed for my father, but now I just felt anger consume me.

"Queen Lorica is my oldest friend and I'm sure she'd help, but I can't ask her without expecting her to lie to Art. I can't do that. Besides, we have a rather more pressing issue nobody seems to be addressing." Olan moved to perch on the edge of his seat, leaning toward me.

"Wait," I said, my voice louder than I intended. "My father is married? Do I have any brothers or sisters?" Why had I never thought of that?

Olan rocked slightly in his seat, his fingers drumming against the hard front of the sofa. "I'm sorry. Yes, he's married and no, there are no siblings. But, we have a more immediate problem. You have a Tundra Stone. We can feel it and it's almost impossible to hide from anybody with even the smallest grasp of magic. Most people won't know what it is. It'll just be a weird magic, which is bad enough, but some will recognize it and having it is a crime. Tundra Stones have been illegal for generations."

I moved my mouth to speak when a knock at the door disturbed us. Olan let out a deep, anguished moan, and Fen walked to the door, smoothing his hair and rubbing his hands over his clothes.

He pulled open the door to be faced with Terrivon and the other guard that had been placed outside the cabin to prevent us from escaping.

"Captain Kecat asked me to inform you that we will be arriving in Peyton soon, and the prisoners will need to be restrained and taken to the palace." He shuffled his feet and stared at his hands as he spoke.

Fen turned to look at us before speaking. "Thank you. Please tell Captain Kecat that we are well aware that we shall be arriving in Peyton soon. As my patient, I shall be accompanying the young woman. I am surprised the Captain feels the need to waste pointless restraints on them but that is her choice."

Terrivon nodded, not speaking. Fen closed the door, pausing for a second and then pulling the door open again.

"Terrivon, I know you, don't I?" he asked.

A smile creased at the corners of Terrivon's mouth as he fought to hide it. "Yes, Professor Fen. You taught a module at the University of Magic on the healing properties of everyday plants that I attended."

Fen visibly relaxed, his shoulders dropping and his face softening. "I remember you. Of course, I do. There aren't many Chegasa who take my class. Your mother is Lyman, right?"

Terrivon's face stiffened and his jaw clenched. "My mother recently rejoined, but yes, she was a Lyman." He stepped back, gazing into the carriage, his eyes stopping on me before looking back to Fen. "Anyway, we'll be arriving soon." He gave a nod and pulled the door closed, leaving Fen staring at the door.

He spun around to face the rest of us, all staring at him. He shrugged and walked back to sit opposite me. "The Tundra Stone?" he said, his eyes creasing in frustration.

I pulled my mother's Firestone from under my clothes. "Is this what you mean?" I asked, placing it in the palm of my hand. "I'm not giving it up. It was my mother's."

Caleb edged forward until he knelt in front of me. "I recognize that. I gave it to your father, and I guess he gave it to your mother." He held out his hand over the stone and closed his eyes. He looked up into my eyes. "Do you know how to use it?" he asked.

I curled my fingers around the Firestone and held it to my chest. I lowered my eyes to gaze at Iggy, his hand squeezing my other hand. He nodded and I sighed. "I created fire with it. I had to defend myself and I ..." My voice trailed off.

Caleb stood with a small chuckle. "I bet they were surprised," he said, shifting to sit on the floor and cross his legs. He looked over his shoulder at Olan and Fen, then said, "I only know one person who could help us hide this." They both nodded and stared at me.

Caleb held his hand, palm up, in front of me. "I think you need to give it to me. I promise I will look after it. But, you need to learn how to use it properly, to learn its full potential. There is only one person we know who can use it. I am afraid we keep going in circles and coming back to your father."

I pushed myself up, having completely forgotten I was supposed to be in pain, and Iggy stood to help me. I glared at him. "I am capable of standing." His face twisted and an uncomfortable combination of anger and frustration froze his face.

His eyebrows rose and arched. He stared at me. His mouth opened, just enough to indicate he was thinking about his words before he spoke.

My shoulders slumped and I rubbed my forehead. "I'm sorry," I said, looking into Iggy's eyes. A tiny flicker of a smile danced behind his eyes, and he reached out his hand. I held it and faced the others. "I'm sorry to everybody. I know you are all trying to help but I'm not your problem to solve. But—but, if you promise to return it, you can look after my mother's stone," I said, holding out the Firestone to Caleb. A lump caught in my throat and I placed it silently in his hand. I looked into his eyes.

I knelt on the sofa, my nose so close to the glass that I could feel the buzz of energy from the train. The land, so green and full of life, undulated gently. Monstrous, tall, and gnarled trees lumbered around in a casual pattern.

The train climbed a subtle slope, so understated as to be almost imperceptible until I tilted my head to face the direction we were traveling in. The vast green expanses gave way to houses and buildings. Initially, the large houses and buildings were spaced well apart gave an artificial, toy-like impression. The pretty colored and patterned houses, each competing to be brighter, more fanciful, and bigger than its neighbor, spoke of a joyful and blessed people.

As I watched the horizon come to meet me, the houses became smaller, thinner, taller, but no less colorful. They sparkled in the reflected glow from a large golden building with towers at the corners that appeared to reach for the sky at the center of them.

I was aware that Iggy had stood behind me, and his hand on my shoulder created a temporary bubble. Our auras merged and we spent a few seconds living in a state of oblivion, denying any knowledge of what we knew was coming.

A small rat-a-tat at the door burst the bubble and I turned to face Iggy. He wrapped his arms around my waist and pulled me toward him. He kissed my forehead and a tingle spread through me.

"Let's go and see what tomorrow holds for us. Every day with you is an adventure. Follow your heart and no regrets, right?"

I nodded. "No regrets." I gazed over his shoulder. Olan, Caleb, and Fen stared at us.

"Sorry, I need to answer that," said Fen, his hand brushing mine as he swept past me on his way to the door.

We let go of each other in a flash of unison, our eyes moving in time to see Captain Kecat at the door. I had forgotten how tall she was, towering over Fen, who in turn towered over me. Her head skimmed the doorframe as she walked toward us.

Terrivon and the other young guard from earlier stepped out from behind her. "Terrivon, restrain her. Granville, restrain him." Her voice lacked any warmth and I had the sense that she enjoyed watching me suffer.

Terrivon marched to stand in front of me. "I'm sorry," he mumbled, lowering his eyes and releasing the glowing rope. It wound around my wrists and the familiar negative energy from earlier battled within me.

"It's alright, Terrivon. I know you have no choice. Sometimes life is like that. I'm Alex, by the way," I said, staring into his face.

He edged his eyes up, just enough to look me in the eyes. "Thank you, Alex."

I twisted my neck to gaze at Iggy, who nodded and smiled a long smile that creased his entire face and sparkled in his eyes.

Olan stood behind me; I sensed him, although I didn't look. He whispered in my ear, "I'll be around and I'll see you soon. Keep your head held high, Alex Chegasa. You are amazing."

The light in the carriage darkened and I looked out the window, realizing we were now inside. The view of the houses and buildings had become a large empty building with frosted-glass windows blocking everything but light. Long, slender gold pillars reached up to the ceiling and gave the illusion of passing straight through it.

My attention was grasped by the guards now lining the walls of the building. Were they all here because of us?

I swallowed a deep gulp of air when Caleb hugged Iggy.

"You're a Bassett and a Thrumblar. That makes us family now."

I could feel the tears build up in my eyes. I refused to cry. My mother raised me to be many things, but weak was not one of them. I wouldn't give Captain Kecat the satisfaction.

I shuffled behind Iggy, Terrivon's hand never leaving my elbow, along the length of the corridor. The glass and wood no longer held my interest. My mind swirled and questions floated.

The warm, comforting air wrapped me, and I looked at the faces of the guards, all staring at us. Who did they think we were? What did they think we had done that was so terrible?

Olan and Caleb had agreed that the Board of Representatives would not want news of the breaking of the portal to be common knowledge. I wondered what these guards had been told.

Life was sleeping around us, and the streets of Peyton lay empty with only a few traders busy setting up stalls around the walls of the palace.

If my heart hadn't been attempting to pound through my ribs, I might have found the sight of such normal life exciting. The whole place had the appearance that it had been colored by a collapsing rainbow, or an infant, which gave everywhere a fun and warm attitude.

The roads we traveled, filled with shops, enticed me, and I wondered what it was like to not have to scavenge. Do the residents understand how lucky they are to be able to buy what they want?

The overpowering golden palace was, I had no doubt, visible throughout Peyton. It dominated the skyline, although, if the gaping windows, like nosey eyes desperate to see everything, were to be believed, there were no more than three floors. The towering viewing points stretched high above the building. My mind wandered and I remembered the stories my mother told me about the invisible top floor and the hidden garden.

Ornate golden gates with inlaid silver, wood, and crystals of some sort swung open as we approached, and I glanced at Iggy. His eyes soaked in the sights, wonder swelling his eyes and appearing to banish his fears.

My aches and pains began to creep through my body and I found my pace slowing. Terrivon's hand never moved, maintaining a constant, if increasingly damp, hold on me. I tilted my head to the side to edge closer to him. "Is it much farther?" I asked, desperate to get there on my own feet but becoming doubtful I could walk much farther.

He leaned in to whisper in my ear, "We're almost there, honestly. Can you manage?"

"Yes, I can manage. I'm not giving her the privilege of seeing me struggle." My heart rate increased, and the anger pulsing through me gave me a renewed energy. My anger blocked the pain but took with it the scenery and any awareness of what was happening. My focus was consumed by my need to not give in and to fight through the pain.

The soldiers ahead stopped next to a wooden door, plain and nearly hidden behind rambling hedges of dark-green leaves. I watched Captain Kecat gesturing as if her facial ticks and frowns were to be my guide; she barked orders, sending guards vanishing in all directions.

Olan walked from behind me and a wave of gratitude fluttered inside my chest. I assumed that he would go to wherever he was supposed to be once we reached Peyton. His face, filled with a stiff and contrived smile, glared in Captain Kecat's face, deliberately close to hers.

"How exciting. I didn't know there was a secret little door here. I've only ever visited the cells from inside the palace."

Her forehead crinkled, and her eyes narrowed. I watched the words squirming in her mouth contort her face.

Olan, rather than wait for her reply, turned to face away from her in a dramatic, sweeping gesture. "I'll see you two as soon as you're both settled," he said, his eyes drifting between Iggy and myself. He lowered his voice as he passed me. "If you change your mind about your father, just send a guard to find me." His voice lowered, and despite his bravado and confidence, I knew he was hoping I would just let him explain this to my father. Let my father sort out the mess my arrival would cause.

I watched Olan, Fen, and Caleb disappear back around the way we had come, and loneliness swamped me. It made no sense, given that I had only met them a few hours ago. Fen stopped before he rounded the corner and smiled at me. He mouthed something at me and I had no idea what. I glanced at Iggy, who shrugged his shoulders. I smiled and turned back to face Captain Kecat.

Darkness fluttered as we walked through the door. In contrast to the colorful and playful vision I had so far of Peyton, this place had no color and little light. The walls, floors, and ceiling appeared to be a dark brown stone. We traveled down a narrow set of steps, turning in a constant spiral. The only light came from dull metal cubes hanging on the walls. The pale-green light it emitted flickered like a candle, but I knew the cube was too small to house a candle.

Arriving at large glass double doors, I looked into a glass room. The walls, ceilings, and floors were still the rough brown stone of the entrance and the stairs, but now the glass formed a room within a room. Multiple rooms, or cells. Long thin glass crystals hung from the ceiling, flickering an unnatural glow along a corridor as wide as the open glass cells that lined the room.

No matter where I went, I would always be a prisoner of someone or something. The Orange, my magic, the school, Jericho, and now Spirismus.

My sigh filled the cell.

Home sweet home.

The
Light Of The
Crann

Beverley J. Hall

Prologue

Billey

The life of the forest met me, the trees sharing energy, the animals running, hunting, burrowing, and watching. The farther we ventured into the dense, dark greenery, the more I knew home was indeed a feeling and not just a place. The thing I missed in Nuadh Caled was life itself.

Energy so crammed and full of vibrancy was impossible to avoid. I connected my energy and shared in the love of life. This sensation was the thing I had searched for.

Storm allowed me to follow in silence, her relaxed personality shining through. The more time I spent in her company, the more I understood why we had always been friends. Her aura was open and freely shared with everything and everybody. She must have been full of questions, yet never sought to ask them. She waited, happy to be with me.

The uneven and heavily overgrown ground made for difficult passage, and my legs struggled with the terrain. My good leg strained to compensate for my wooden leg and my hobble became more pronounced.

A memory pinged into my head. My mother and her anger.

Being raised with a possibly infinite lifetime ahead of you gives time a very different perspective. Falling in love with Geilis changed everything. She would have a mortal life. She would die too soon.

The day I suggested taking her to the Crann to join us together had been the most monumental day of my life. More so than the death of my father. More so than breaking the portal open when she called from across the universe. More so than when I escaped to Nuadh Caled.

The Crann is as old as time itself and larger than any palace I had ever seen. Yet, its simplicity was in its knowledge. It held the answer to any problem. It held infinite insight.

My father, always happy to indulge me, brought Geilis to the Crann with the strict understanding that the Crann would unlikely allow her to enter.

It did.

It had an answer.

It also had a high price. Higher than it appeared on the surface. Everybody had been shocked we had been willing to give a part of ourselves, to physically share with each other and the Crann. When we had reappeared with one leg each, the other solid Crann wood, the Druids had claimed it a miracle. We became virtually gods. We were one with the tree in a way none before was.

However, the Crann required something more. Something only I knew.

It needed me to fulfill the unification of our universe. It showed me the prophecy of my future. I would work with a human, one whose blood was Chegasa and Druid. In exchange for my assistance, it would allow me to have Geilis until the peace was won. Her life, unlike mine, was not infinite. It had an end.

The end was coming too quickly.

My mother had guessed there was more to the deal with the Crann, and, when her magic couldn't restore my leg, she flew into a fit of rage.

From that day forward, she refused to speak to Geilis.

"You have betrayed your essence. You were perfect. Every Seelie is. You gave the Crann the one thing it never had. You gave it a connection to the Seelies," she had screamed at me. It was that day I realized my being her daughter didn't matter. She needed her power more than she needed peace, or me.

I was imperfect.

ONE

ALEX

Time lost all meaning. Without any windows to see the day and night leave and arrive, I no longer knew when night arrived or when morning replaced it but for the arrival of food from time to time. I imagined the light from the dangling crystals changing from brighter to duller, but I knew it was all in my head.

Iggy had been placed at the opposite end of the room and there was little chance of conversation. Instead of the fear and anxiety that should have filled me, I was bored by the mind-numbing, nail-biting tediousness.

When we were given separate cells, I shouted. I continued to yell and scream until I realized the sound of my yells served no purpose other than to give me a sore throat. Something blocked the noise.

Something blocked the connection to the magic. A part of my heart shivered.

Had this been what my world felt like before the Orange altered it? Had it echoed with the emptiness of disconnected solitude? Had they been as alone as I was?

I leaned back, the chill of the glass sending a shiver down my spine. I slid down the glass wall, my legs crumbling beneath me. My eyes scanned the room, taking in the guard perched on the back of a solid, squared metal chair, swaying back and forth as he watched me. His eyes, full of cold indifference, fed my self-pity, and I sat on the floor, wrapping my arms around my knees.

With no sight of Fen, Olan, or Caleb, the constant changing guards, and lack of daylight, my familiar friend, loneliness, returned.

***

I perched on the edge of the glass bed, which I knew was unbreakable. I had tried to smash it in a fit of rage when I first arrived. My fingers fidgeted, running over the pin that was hidden under my cloak. The air in the cells, so still and stale, clawed at my chest as my soul searched for a connection.

My inside echoed with the emptiness created by the lack of connection.

I pushed my cloak to the side and stood. I could see Iggy's eyes following me as I paced. I paused for a few seconds, the sound of my breathing filling the glass box that had become my new home, and removed the pin. I stared at it in the palm of my hand. It was a little bigger than my thumb, shining from the reflected light that the crystals cast on the cells. A small tree carved in it had gathered dirt and aged such that it was now almost black. I ran my fingernails in the grooves of the engraving as the gold beneath it appeared. My fingers closed around it, forming a fist, and I continued my pacing.

I knew Iggy was watching me, and when I glanced in the direction of his cell, I saw a smile directed at me. I sighed, a long groaning sound that came from deep in my stomach, before I placed my right hand on the glass wall of my cell, waiting for Terrivon to notice me.

He sat slumped in a chair at the end of the central corridor, his feet scuffing back and forth, the boredom making his face look darker and more forlorn. Over the past two days, he had been kind and talked to me like a person and not a prisoner, unlike the other guards that Captain Kecat had assigned to us. He squirmed in his seat, and I knew, from two days of watching, that he would stand and march up and down the space soon. I continued to stare in his direction.

Sure enough, he pushed himself up from the seat, rubbing his hands over his trouser's creases. His gaze met Iggy's first, and, with a nod of his head in my direction, Iggy directed Terrivon's attention to me. I tried to force a smile but managed little more than a pained grimace. A sense of guilt ate at my stomach for what I was about to ask of him. His casual smile when he opened the small opening in the glass wall of my cell door merely added to it, and I took a step back, my determination making a bid for freedom.

"You alright, Alex?" His voice seemed so incompatible with the uniform that didn't quite fit. I had often thought, over the past few days, of

Danny and Calesta and their lessons on appropriate clothing for survival and defense and questioned the wisdom of such a tight-fitting, tailored uniform. I had already established that few of the guards had any distinguishable magic—indeed, Terrivon seemed one of the few with any worth noting—and wondered about their physical ability in the uniform.

I glared at the inconspicuous pin, a dread pouring through me at the consequence of my next move. The pain must have been evident in my face as he asked, "Are you in pain? Do you want me to get Fen?"

I forced my eyes to meet his. "I need you to do me a favor. I know I have no right to ask and I don't want to get you into trouble. But . . ." My voice vanished and my mouth refused to comply. I found my gaze fixed on my hand, and when I looked up into his eyes, the look of pity swimming in them caused me to clench my hands into fists. I closed my eyes and sucked in a deep breath before opening them. "I need you to get this to King Arthanius," I said, holding out my hand.

His eyes followed mine to look at the pin. The confusion created small lines to form around his eyes, and when he raised his eyes to look at me, a frown formed across his forehead. "I can't . . . I mean, I can't just wander up to him." Confusion filled his eyes. "I'm sorry but I need this job. My fa-father," his words stuttered, and I was about to say not to worry about it when he carried on. "My father and mother died recently and I have to support my brother. I just can't."

I reached out my hand to touch the glass. "I'm sorry, Terrivon. I . . ." I tilted my face to gaze at Iggy. "We know what it feels like to lose family. Really. I'm sorry to ask, but he once said that this pin would be all it took to ask for a favor to be returned. I don't know your King Arthanius, but if his word is worth anything, he'll come to me when you give it to him. I wouldn't ask, but I don't know if I have time to wait for Fen. Could you find him then and ask him to do it?"

I could see Iggy out of the corner of my eye, pressed up against the glass of his cell, trying to establish what we were discussing.

Terrivon opened his mouth to speak but his mouth just hung open. No words came forth. His face contorted, twisting with the pain of his refusal. "I'm about to finish, and I promise I'll find Fen." He forced a half smile. "My friends call me Von. I'm sorry for everything that's happened to you." He turned to shuffle off back to his chair, still staring at the pin in his hand.

"You need to tell Fen that he can't say who I am. Just tell King Arthanius that Geilis demands to see him." He spun around and, realizing he had left the opening unlocked, returned to stand in front of me.

"I will. I promise." He began to close the opening when he hesitated. I could see a question forming behind his twisting lips. He chewed on his lips before finally staring at me. "Did you break the portal? I won't tell anybody. I just need to know. Is that kind of magic real?"

"Yes, Terrivon. Sorry, Von. I did break it. I came through it. We came through it."

"Are you . . . are you the Fire Flier?" His eyes sparkled like a child's. Excitement sparkled in the grey-blue that usually looked so sad.

"I don't know what you're talking about. I'm sorry." I sighed. "Sorry."

He smiled at me. "You must be. You just must be."

He had just closed the opening when the outer door opened, and I watched as Von pulled himself up straight and marched toward the new guard, putting his hand into his pocket.

***

With no concept of day and night since I had been forced into my cell, my eyes began to grow heavy. I had watched the door waiting for Fen or Von until my brain ceased to function. Doubt crept over me, sending shivers of fear racing over my skin. I climbed onto the bed, pulling my cloak over me, hiding me from the world and the world from me. I wanted to close my eyes but they refused; instead, they lingered in a state of heavy defiance.

Just as my eyes began to concede to the tiredness, the door opened and I saw Von. His smiling face chased away my weariness. I placed my hands on the bed and was about to stand up and take my cloak off when I spotted a man behind him. His confident stance needed no crown. I stared into his eyes. My eyes.

He stood in front of the glass door and looked at Von. "Well?" he barked and then, looking from Von to the other guard, continued, "You can both leave. I wish to talk in private."

He watched them until they had scurried out of the room, pulling the door closed. He approached my cell, and with a wave of his hand, the door flew open. In a moment of euphoric bliss, my body soaked up the return to the connection, and magic filled me. He stood staring down at me, and I found myself pulling the cloak tighter around me. My hands began to sweat and my heart raced as I stared at my father. I knew it was him. I could see myself in his face.

"You are not Geilis. It was a long time ago, but you don't even look old enough to have been born then. So, I suggest you start talking and explain why you have this," he said, holding the pin I had given to Von.

I opened my mouth to speak and it became unbearably dry. I coughed and swallowed. The child I had been all those years ago waiting for my father to come and rescue her suddenly took possession of me. I stood in front of him, trying to ignore the shaking in my legs. Despite the obvious invasion of personal space, neither of us stepped back. We glared at each other.

"Who are you and why do you have this?" he asked, his voice becoming deeper, and the anger caused his face to wrinkle. The lines around his mouth hardened.

"You'll need both of us for this story," I mumbled, twisting my head around to look at Iggy. I struggled to gain my composure.

"I'm not in the habit of being told what to do. Again, I ask, who are you?"

I pushed back my shoulders and swallowed against the lump blocking my throat. I dropped my cloak on the floor and watched his eyes move to my hair. "I am Alex Chegasa, daughter of Arthanius Chegasa and Jennifer Somerville. I have that," I said, pointing at the pin in his hand, "because, Geilis and the Darklands are far more hospitable than Peyton."

His face froze and his hand floated between us. "No. I . . . That can't be. I—"

"Honestly I don't care what you think. I don't care if you believe me or not, but right now I need your help. No"—I nodded my head at Iggy–"we need your help."

"How could I not have known? Surely, I mean, how?" He reached his hand out to touch my hair and I stepped back.

"You don't get to do that. I'm not your daughter in any sense other than biologically. I needed you when Mom died, but that has gone. Now, I just want to get out of here and leave all this behind."

I watched his face crumble and his regal confidence shatter into tiny pieces that float in the air. He stepped back to rest against the glass wall. "She died? How? I . . ."

Anger surged through my veins, forcing its way into every atom of my being, giving me a new steely determination. "Unlock Iggy. Now."

He stared at me, his eyes blank. His expression twisted his face, creating new signs of his age that hadn't been there when I first saw him. His eyes seemed to have sunk into his skull and now appeared hooded. His face, so strong and confident, now wrinkled and creased as the mass of emotions consuming his body took hold.

I walked past him and strode to stand outside Iggy's cell door. He placed his hand on the glass and I placed mine on the opposite side. I spun around to face my father. "Iggy!" I barked, surprised by my forthright attitude.

"She died? How?" His voice wavered and his eyes blinked, battling to hide the tears making them glisten in the light.

My heart hardened at the sight of his tears. Too late. The weight of my newly leadened heart weighed heavily against my stomach, sending a wave of nausea through me.

"No! You don't get to do that. Too late to care now. She and millions of other people in my world died after a war that wiped out most of the planet. Those of us who survived struggle to continue in a world that had lost everything, and you . . ." My voice croaked and a strange little squeak escaped my lips. My face set in stone-clad anger. "And you were nowhere. You left us to rot. NOW. OPEN. IGGY'S. DOOR." My hand slammed against the glass.

He spun to face me and took a step toward me. "I'm . . .," he mumbled and looked into my eyes.

"Iggy," I shouted, slamming my hand against the glass again, and he pulled himself upright, taking small steps toward me. "I've had enough of this," I spat through my teeth and waved my hand, forcing the door of Iggy's cell open. If he wouldn't use his magic, I'd use mine.

He stopped in his tracks as a smile spread across his face. "You got my magic?"

"No. I got nothing more than afro hair and a surname from you. I got magic from my mother, from the universe, from the source, but not from you."

Iggy stepped out of his cell to stand next to me.

"And you, I presume, are King Arthanius?" he said, placing his arm around me, and my body relaxed, my muscles releasing the tension that had held them firm.

The arrogance of his regal birth returned and King Arthanius, my father, glared at Iggy. "I am indeed, and you are?"

I could feel Iggy's body stiffen. "Ignathius Dragonrider Thrumblar. I'd like to say it's a pleasure but, considering you've had us locked in here, I won't lie."

"Dragonrider?" He glanced from Iggy to me. "And how did you end up with my daughter? How did a Thrumblar end up with the future Queen of Spirismus? This I'm keen to hear." His face aged before my eyes as every muscle of it stiffened, casting dark shadows that emanated from the creases.

As panic took hold of my body, sending electric shock waves through it, I took a step forward, moving from Iggy's grip to again stare into the eyes of my father. "No. You don't get to do that either. I am not a future queen of anywhere. I am Alex Chegasa of Danvers, Massachusetts. You made sure of that when you left me there."

He stared through me, his eyes reflecting the thoughts that had taken him elsewhere. "Wait. How did you get here? Can you travel across worlds?" His brow furrowed as thoughts rampaged through his mind. "Or" —he twisted his head to glance over my shoulder at Iggy—"or is it you that is the traveler?"

My body stiffened, my hands clenched, and I could feel the magic of my connection pulse through me. My anger battled an internal war, producing a pain that constricted my guts, and I could feel my aura expand. Iggy's fingers tightened around my arm when I struggled to breathe.

"I'm not sure what you mean by a traveler," said Iggy, his voice calm and reassuring. "If you mean, was I the one who broke the portal open, that would depend on whether you're liable to punish the person responsible."

"No. No, I just . . . Well, I'm trying to understand. I made a conscious decision to never inflict the throne on any children. Lorica and I had no children so the throne would die with me, but it appears the universe had a different opinion. Even if I accept that you"—he reached his arm out to stroke mine, and I recoiled—"Even if I accept that you are my daughter, it doesn't explain how you got here. I'm just trying to get my head around all of this."

"Accept me? I'm not asking you to accept anything, and I have no desire to be your daughter or anything else. I'm fed up with Spirismus and with you. I just want to go home. Now," I yelled at him. His eyes widened as the floor began to vibrate and rumble, and I felt Iggy's arms circle me. My eyes fixed on the floor as I watched cracks snake across it and begin to climb the glass. The sound of the splintering glass clashed with the low thundering noise of the stone floor.

I had made a mistake but my anger consumed me, and I could no longer control the sudden rush of magic.

The outer door opened and Fen's smiling face appeared. He froze to the spot, his mouth gaping as he took in the picture before him. He rushed to stand in front of me, placing his hand on top of my head. Staring into my eyes, he spoke with a calmness that didn't match the mood of the room. "Look at me, Alex. Let the anger go. I'm here to help. I understand you have had so much pain right now, finally facing your father. Trust me, please."

The words he muttered, so quiet as to be almost silent, became further and further away. I drifted from the room to a world inside my head, a new and unknown world that I somehow knew. I found myself a home among the trees that called me. The voiceless conversation with my new family consumed me, and I held only the love and life they shared with me. I curled up at the foot of a large gnarly tree that twisted and spiraled toward the orange sun of home.

A distant voice, one that I recognized, yet didn't, called me. "Welcome home, Alex."

Then other voices intruded. The harsh tones, the words I couldn't hear but understood. The words of me. I opened my mouth to speak and a strange, pitiful groan escaped.

"What . . .," I managed to mumble as I struggled to focus, trying to tune in to what was being said. Silence returned and a hand stroked my arm, the touch that spoke of comfort and reassurance. A touch I recognized. The hand that had been there before. I moved my arm with slow deliberation to place my hand over his. "Iggy," my voice whispered from deep inside.

The feel of him centered me and I became aware that I was curled up on the bed, still in the cell, and the trees vanished. They evaporated in the mist of my mind and yet I still sensed them.

I was connected to them.

I half opened my eyes to peer through them and saw Iggy's face, his forehead frowning so that his eyebrows almost met in the middle. He knelt on the floor next to me, his face aged with worry as he bit his lip, and guilt filled me. I had lost control, and as I stared at the faces of Fen and my father, I understood I could have hurt him. I could have hurt the only person in my life I knew was there for me. My heart sunk, colliding with my stomach, and any anger I had managed to cling onto evaporated.

My eyes refused to look at Iggy and closed as my mind drifted back to the trees. This time the voices in the room merged with the unheard voices of the trees.

"I had to," Fen muttered, and I could tell without seeing him that his words came through gritted teeth. "What were you doing to help her, eh? Why didn't you control her mood? What's the point in being so powerful if you can't control your daughter?" His voice grew louder and louder and I could hear the anger.

A pause pulsed around the room, and I squeezed my eyes closed, desperate to avoid the situation I knew I had caused, and focused on the trees in my head. I stretched my hand to touch a large, slender tree that seemed to know me, and my being filled with love and peace.

Laughter filled the room as Fen struggled to speak. "Ha, you couldn't control her, could you? Your magic couldn't penetrate hers. That's hysterical." His laughter echoed and rebounded off the glass and dragged me from my trees and my peace.

My eyes opened and Iggy clutched my hand. Fen stared back at me; his laughter had been replaced by a frown that more than expressed his concern. "Are you alright?"

My father, however, I struggled to read. His face twisted into a picture of angry sadness, his eyes hooded and glassy, and the gentle lines around his eyes now deepened. He chewed on his bottom lip, clearly biting back his words, but his body, standing straight and with more than a hint of anger, contradicted this. His body looked ready for battle, while his face looked ready for tears.

Darkness hung in the air that I had grown accustomed to, but now, after the light among my trees, it brought a dismal mood with it. I took in the light penetrating the many fractures in the glass, doubtlessly caused by my anger. The factitious light from the crystals hanging from the ceiling, with no natural light to compete, seeped through the snaking cracks in the glass that had previously dampened the cells from magic. The light reached the dark-brown stone of the walls and floor, highlighting the golden flecks in them. Alongside the magic's rainbow meeting the fractures, the effect was mesmerizing. If magic could be seen, this is what it would look like.

"I'm sorry. I am truly sorry. I know I lost it and I can't make any excuses." I sat up on the bed and stretched for Fen's hand. "Thank you. I don't know what you did but thank you."

A smile tried to force its way through his frown. "It's nothing. I just forced the anger out of you. I—Well." He twisted his head to look at my father. "I was surprised somebody hadn't already altered your mood. But, then again, I get the feeling your father had said and done more than enough."

My father didn't even move his head to acknowledge Fen's gaze or words; his eyes fixed on me. "We'll talk later about how you knew about

Alex and I didn't. And why you didn't tell me." He moved toward me, his anger bouncing in his aura and bristling against mine.

His shoulders relaxed and his body appeared to shrink as his posture lost its aggressions. His eyes still showed the thoughts that were flying around in his head, contradicting the smile. The light forcing its way through the glass surrounding us painted his face with rainbow lines of magic that caught in the fine wrinkles around his eyes. Stripping back the layers, I could see the young man my mother had seen eighteen years ago. His presence, an unmistakable alpha male, along with the magic that bristled out of every pore, was enough to make anybody swoon. I guessed. The majestic dreadlocks that crowned his head, more impressive than any golden crown, and the light in his piercing blue eyes, so prominent against his dark skin, pulled your focus toward him, and I imagined my mother all those years ago and what she had seen.

"She thought you would come for us. Right up till she died, you know. She never gave up. She said you could see across the worlds. Why didn't you come?" I asked, my voice low and full of sadness, not for me but for the wasted life of my mother. I stood up from the bed and walked toward him, stopping directly in front of him. Tall as I was, I still had to look up to stare into his eyes. "I'm not angry now, but understand, I don't care if you believe me or not. I am the daughter of Jennifer Somerville of Earth, and I have faced worse than you." I spoke with a slow deliberateness to control my emotions and voice. My voice remained quiet and without emotion.

He placed his hands on my arms, his fingers pushing against the tense muscles that wanted to tear away from him. "I would have. I didn't know. You need to believe me."

I became aware of Iggy's hand on my lower back, although the magic suffocating the room stifled his auric field and only the physical sensation told me that he was there.

"I don't need to believe anything, but then again, perhaps you aren't as powerful or magical as she told me." I pulled my arms away, stepping back into Iggy's arm. My gaze wandered just long enough to catch the amused expression of Fen. "Besides, from what I've heard of the great King Arthanius since I arrived here, you failed to achieve your goals, and now you are just a puppet to this Board of Representatives. Sorry to disappoint you, but democracy isn't all it's cracked up to be. It almost killed my world. Power always ends up in the hands of those at the top. You've wasted your time."

His eyes darkened, and I watched as his finger twitched, and I could tell

I had hit a nerve.

"I gave my people a voice. That's worth something, and I'm nobody's puppet," he said, his voice carrying the tension of his body.

"Really? Tell me, how many of this wonderful Board of yours are of noble or moneyed descent? How many of them are obvious rulers, well schooled, and from a long line of rulers? The rich rule. Go on, tell me I'm wrong!"

I took a few steps backwards until my calves caught the bed and I flung myself onto it. I tilted my head to peer around my father at Fen. A naughty smile filled his face.

"Fen, you can tell the Board of Representatives that I am fully healed and ready to meet with them. And, Your Majesty, I thank you for your time but I think my first instinct was right. I only regret that I can't untell you who I am. But, I assure you, I want nothing from you."

Fen bent over, silent laughter shaking his body. "Oh, she could be nobody else's daughter. I told Olan she was a feisty one. She has to meet her Uncle Constantine. That would be fabulous! I've never met anybody besides him that would talk to you like that."

My father spun around. "Olan. Olan knows about her as well? Who else knows?"

Fen chewed on his lip, trying to stifle the laugh, casting me a sideways glance with his twinkling eyes. "Just Olan and me. Oh, and Caleb, obviously. Then there's Geilis and Durai. But that's it."

"That's it! I'm sixth to know, and why is Caleb obvious?"

I let out a groan as the hunger and tiredness ate at my muscles. "Caleb asked you to hide my mother's Firestone."

Sleep was beginning to grip my body and I ached. Iggy stood and stretched, staring into my father's face. I almost laughed at the show of masculinity, but I knew it must have been difficult for him to stay silent while I had ranted. He stared at me and then at the others.

"Look, I appreciate your help, Fen. I appreciate you and Olan coming to help Caleb when Durai asked. You owed us nothing and didn't know us. I think a part of you did it for him," he said, nodding his head at my father, "but I know you risked everything to help us. I'm sorry Alex wasn't destined to be the Fire Flier like Durai's friend Kluzahr had told him. It's her life and her choice. But we're just fed up and, honestly, it doesn't feel like we should be here. We made a mistake and I'll happily tell the Board that. They can send us home to Earth and we'll leave you in peace."

My father walked away without saying a word and stretched his arms in front of him, laying his palms on the wall and leaning. We couldn't see his face but knew he was concentrating on his breathing. I fixed my vision on his aura and watched as it grew smaller. I had been taught to hide my emotions and mask them, but he managed it with such ease and speed I had to admit I was impressed.

Iggy and I stared at him and then at each other and shrugged. He whispered, "What have we done to him now?"

In a sudden whirl of movement, he turned, glanced at Fen, and, as he marched toward the door, said, "Come tell me how far you've come with sorting this. I know you have been doing something behind my back."

Fen smiled at us and followed him, pausing for a few seconds as he passed us to say, "I've almost sorted it. Trust me, and no more"—he waved his hand around the cracked walls of the cells—"no more of this." He wrapped one arm around my shoulders and the other around Iggy's, pulling us into a hug. "You two are just what we need to shake things up around here," he whispered in our ears.

Iggy and I looked at each other, and we both knew at that second that Fen had more going on than we understood, and a sneaking suspicion began to creep up my spine, refusing to be ignored, that the 'we' he spoke of were people we had never heard of or imagined.

My eyes peered over his shoulder to watch my father's back disappear through the door, unsure what I wanted from him but hoping for more than I got. His step lingered for a second or two as he reached the doorway, and I held my breath, expecting him to turn around, but he didn't. I watched his shoulders expand and straighten as he pulled himself up straight. King Arthanius left the room, not my father.

His voice resonated as he barked commands at Von and the other guard, whom I had forgotten about. They must have been standing outside the cells during the entire event.

"Terrivon, wasn't it? See Princess Alex Chegasa and her friend, Ignathius Thrumblar, to my quarters. My daughter does not belong in a cell. I would speak with your superior as soon as possible. And you, can you please find Queen Lorica and ask her to meet me in the library. Tell her it is a matter of urgency, please."

My stomach bubbled with confused emotions. He hadn't even acknowledged me, not a look, a hug, or a word. Yet, within seconds of leaving, he had acknowledged my existence to others. My fingers tightened their grip on Iggy as I realized my life as Princess Alex Chegasa might be something I regretted.

The Light of the Crann

Release Date:
October 18th 2022

ACKNOWLEDGMENTS

They say it takes a village to raise a child. Over the past few years, this book has become my baby, and it took a team to produce this book. My name may be the one on the front cover, but every person who contributed to making this book, and me, has been a vital support on this journey. It is the cumulative efforts and contributions of many that have brought me to this point.

First, the person to whom this book is dedicated: my mother. To have been raised by a strong woman who instilled such a positive attitude that gave so much more than lip service to the phrase, "You can do anything, and be anything, you set your mind to," was a unique and privileged blessing. She was the single most influential factor in the person I am today. She taught me to know my heart's desire and strive for it, no matter how unattainable it may at first seem.

However, like many of us, I strayed from the path she set me on and doubted myself many times on this journey.

Therefore, I can say with utmost conviction that, without the constant positivity from Marcus Alik, I would have continued to flit about and spend the next ten years getting to this point. He has been my biggest believer and the person who pushed me furthest. He inspired me to become the person I had been raised to be. He helped me remember my heart's desire, strive for it, and achieve it.

When my brain wanted to give up, he was there guiding me, helping with the hiccups, and enabling me to become the person he saw in me. Also, what is any book without a solid marketing plan? Having him on my side was not just good for me but my book.

Then there is my editor, Sarah Hawkins, who has the patience of a saint and has polished a very rough diamond. Her amazing diplomacy and tact as she saved my story while keeping my sanity intact was a godsend. It confounds me how she made sense of some parts of the story and assisted me with such ease to produce the book you all read. As the only living soul, besides me, to have read the unedited version, I am eternally grateful that she didn't jump ship. Instead, she found the gems and helped me perfect them.

We all judge a book by its cover, so thanks to Angelee van Allman for making sense of the chaos of ideas running wild in my head, and again (and there is definitely a trend happening) for her patience. Over the space of hundreds of emails in which I changed my mind, questioned, and quizzed the design, she stood by her phrase, "Pedantic is how we get perfect." Thank you for understanding what most wouldn't have.

Long before adult Beverley J. Hall sat down to write, the child version of me devoured reading, knowledge, and dreams inspired by so many. There are many great books that formed the starting point for my love of storytelling. Would I have become the person I am without Ursula K. Le Guin and my dreams of wizarding, magic, and alternate worlds? I doubt it.

So, thank you to every writer out there. You are somebody's favorite writer. You may never know the impact your words had on somebody, but your words mattered.

Alongside the great stories that I read were the great teachers who helped mold me. Most of them probably don't remember me and have no idea how they influenced my life. My secondary school history teacher Mr Gunnion taught me to think for myself, question everything, and form my own opinions. He may have created a monster, but I will forever be grateful. What greater gift can any teacher give a student? And, my English teacher, Mrs Bryden, who taught seventeen-year-old me. I was uninterested and shutting off from learning, and she gave me belief in my talent. Who knew someday I'd be here? I would never have guessed back then, but she saw something in me and helped me believe too.

Even once I had found my determination to pursue my dreams, a lecturer on my MA studies, Peggy Riley, with one sentence, changed the way I saw that dream. She told me that before I sat down to write, I must know what I wanted to say. She was right. Telling a story must have a purpose. All great stories share something. I have tried to keep that ideal in everything I have written since that day. She helped me find my voice that day.

However, I have kept the best until last. Without my son, Alex, life would have had no purpose. It has been the greatest privilege of my life being his mother, and now Lulu's granny. He made me determined to lead by example. The words of a parent are worth nothing without action. I couldn't expect him to value the moral code I wanted to instill in him unless I was that person. You inspired me to be the best version of myself.

Who would have thought, all those years ago when we were making up bedtime stories of portal-jumping-Alex, with elemental magic and dragons (and I'm sure back then there were robots as well), that the seed we planted would grow into this book? Thank you for allowing me to share our story with the world.

Thank you, of course, to all of you who have bought, read, and shared this book. Without you, I would have been shouting into the vast abyss of nothingness. Go and find your beauty in a world with too much ugliness. If you can't find it, be it. Stay beautiful inside.

ABOUT THE AUTHOR

Beverley J. Hall was born in Kent, England, and raised in Scotland. Most of her childhood was spent with her nose in a book, and her love of stories was born.

While studying Art and Design, she discovered her love of storytelling, whether with paint, sculpture, fabric, or words.

After completing an MA in Creative Writing, she is now living her best life, writing stories at the seaside with her son, her granddaughter, and her lazy cat Bertie.

To find out more about Beverley J. Hall head over to **www.beverleyjhall.com**, TikTok, Instagram, or Twitter to join her overthinking and daydreaming (where she's still hoping for a pet dragon).

@bevjhallauthor

www.beverleyjhall.com

Lightning Source UK Ltd.
Milton Keynes UK
UKHW031354010622
403836UK00002B/592